Further P

The Sult

"Ms. White's prose glints like the shores of the Bosphorus she brings to life with breathtaking detail. Unfolding in an exotic world of djinns, tube flowers, and belladonna, two mysterious crimes collide in a startling resolution. An astonishing debut novel that is impossible to put down."

—Dora Levy Mossanen, author of *Harem* and *Courtesan*

"[White's] evocative prose and plot twists pull the reader to a satisfying ending." —Blythe Copeland, *Boston Magazine*

"CSI goes Ottoman Empire. . . . Court life and customs . . . are thrillingly captured here, with readers easily transported back to those days when mystery and intrigue lurked around every corner."

—*Booklist*, starred review

"It is an unputdownable read. . . . In her debut novel Jenny White has produced a multilayered story in a skillful blend of fiction and real history. . . . It is a book you just want to immerse yourself in."

—Sally Roddom, *Murder and Mayhem*

"A page-turning history lesson and relevant allegory of today's East-West divide. . . . White is bold and imaginative, able to find an original thread in this enormous pastiche, in order to weave a delightful story." —Elmira Bayrasli, *Turkish Daily News*

"White's intelligent, sensuous writing marks a promising debut."

—*Kirkus Reviews*

"White has a thorough knowledge of the country and period she writes about, and depicts them with considerable skill. The novel should be a pleasure even for mystery readers who aren't particularly fond of historic settings. For anyone who is, this is the best of its kind." —John A. Broussard, www.ilovemysterynewsletter.com

"A terrific late nineteenth century police procedural that shines a deep light on Turkey at an interesting moment when the Ottoman Empire is starting to collapse. . . . Fans who enjoy a lot of history in their mystery will want to read Jenny White's fine tale."
—Harriet Klausner, *The Midwest Book Review*

"White skillfully evokes the turbulent zeitgeist of 1880s Turkey, and the atmosphere that she conjures is perfect. . . . A lavish enjoyable read." —Bethany Skaggs, *The Historical Novels Review*

"Excellent historical flavor and details permeate a fast-paced historical suspense novel." —*Bookwatch*

"White's prose is full of silky, sometimes ominous lyricism."
—Mopsy Strange Kennedy, *The Improper Bostonian*

"All the mystery, fantasy, romance and allure of the Ottoman Empire await in this historical fiction about the murder of an English governess." —BookWoman/BookMan

"White's prose is dramatic, a subtle mix of fiction and history."
—www.curledup.com

"An atmospheric experience. . . . She's given herself a pretty high standard with which to keep up." —*The Bohemian Aesthetic* e-zine

"Lyrical writing, bright characterizations, and a sympathetic evocation of an era packed with intrigue and conflict."
—www.poisonedpen.com

The Sultan's Seal

The Sultan's Seal

Jenny White

W. W. Norton & Company

NEW YORK   LONDON

"You are My Lord" by Seyh Galib and "Nedim to His Heart" by Nedim, translated by Bernard Lewis, and "You Have Shot Me So Full of Arrows" by Fuzuli,
translated by Walter G. Andrews. From *An Anthology of Turkish Literature,* edited
by Kemal Silay. Bloomington: Indiana University Turkish Studies, 1996. Used by
permission of Kemal Silay.

"The Purpose of the Wine" by Bâkî and "Men String Their Cords of Tears"
by Hayalî, translated by John R. Walsh. From *The Penguin Book of Turkish Verse,*
edited by Nermin Menemencioglu, in collaboration with Fahir Iz. New York: Penguin Books, 1978.

Every effort has been made to contact the copyright holders of these selections. Rights holders of selections not credited should contact W. W. Norton &
Company, Inc., 500 Fifth Avenue, New York, NY 10110 for a correction to be
made in the next reprinting of our work.

Map design by Paul Guthrie

For information about permission to reproduce selections from this book, write
to Permissions, W. W. Norton & Company, Inc.,
500 Fifth Avenue, New York, NY 10110

Manufacturing by The Courier Companies, Inc.
Book design by Brooke Koven
Production manager: Amanda Morrison

Library of Congress Cataloging-in-Publication Data

White, Jenny B. (Jenny Barbara), 1953–
The sultan's seal / Jenny White.—1st ed.
p. cm.
ISBN 0-393-06099-3
1. Governesses—Crimes against—Fiction. 2. Young women—Crimes against—
Fiction. 3. Police magistrates—Fiction. 4. British—Turkey—Fiction. 5. Istanbul
(Turkey)—Fiction. I. Title.
PS3623.H5763S85 2006
813'.6—dc22
2005023332

ISBN 978-0-393-32920-9 pbk.

W. W. Norton & Company, Inc.
500 Fifth Avenue, New York, N.Y. 10110
www.wwnorton.com

W. W. Norton & Company Ltd.
Castle House, 75/76 Wells Street, London W1T 3QT

1 2 3 4 5 6 7 8 9 0

"The purpose of the wine is that the cask be pure inside."
Our men of learning cannot plumb the sense these words
*   convey.*

—Bâkî

Men string their cords of tears to either end of postures bent
*   with care;*
From these they shoot the shafts of hope, unmindful of what
*   made the bows.*

—Hayalî

Contents

The Sultan's Seal

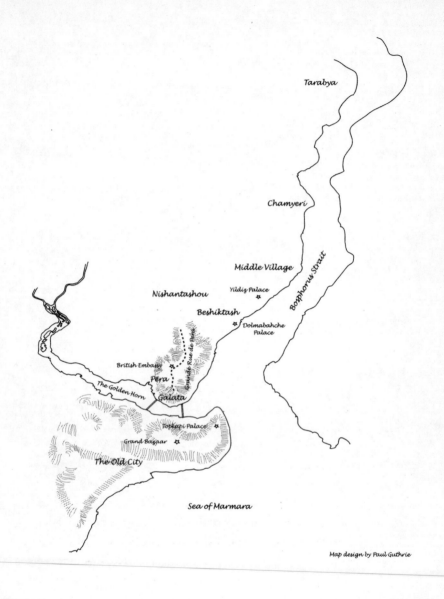

Tarabya

Chamyeri

Middle Village

Nishantashou

Yildiz Palace

Beshiktash

Bosphorus Strait

Dolmabahche Palace

British Embassy

Grande Rue de Pera

Pera

The Golden Horn

Galata

Topkapi Palace

Grand Bazaar

The Old City

Sea of Marmara

Dark Eyes

A dozen lamps flicker across the water, moving up the strait in silence, the oarsmen invisible. A dry scuffling noise drifts from shore, the breeze too indolent to carry it very far. Wild dogs bark and crash through the bushes. There are snarls, a short yelp, then silence again.

As the boats cross the light of the full moon spilled across the Bosphorus, the fishermen take their places, actors on a luminous stage. In the stern of each boat a man rows, the other stands, holding a conical net attached to a pole. Attracted to the light of the oil lamps hanging from the bows, zargana fish crowd the surface. In a single motion the fishermen slip their nets through the black liquid, then raise them high above their heads. The sound of nets breaking the skin of water is so soft that it cannot be heard from shore.

There is a splash. The closest fisherman to land turns his head and listens, but hears nothing more. He casts his eye over the rocks and trees bleached by moonlight, what is beneath or behind them lost in shadow. He notices a circle of ripples moving outward from the shore and frowns, then points and mutters something to his brother, who is rowing. The other man shrugs and applies himself to the oars. It is so quiet that the fisherman imagines he can hear the scrabble of crabs across the stone point at nearby Albanian Village, where the current is so fierce that the crabs cannot proceed up the strait through the water. Centuries of crabs taking this shortcut have worn a path through the stone. Just an animal, he thinks, and tries to banish from his mind the stories he has heard about djinns and demons abroad in the night.

KAMIL PASHA GROPES on the bedside table for a match to light the lamp. He is magistrate for Istanbul's Beyoglu Lower Court that includes Pera, where the Europeans have their embassies and business houses, and Galata, the crowded Jewish quarter below Pera, a warren of narrow streets that wind and coil down the steep hill to the waters of the Bosphorus and its inlet, the Golden Horn. The pounding on his door has given way to loud voices in the entry hall. Just then, his manservant Yakup enters with a lit lamp in hand. Enormous shadows sail across the high ceiling.

"My apologies for waking you, bey. The headman of Middle Village says he has come on an urgent matter. He insists on speaking directly to you."

Squinting against the light, Kamil pushes back the satin quilt and stands. His foot slides on the magazine that has slipped off his bed. Sleep finds Kamil only when he loses himself in reading, in this case in the *Gardener's Chronicle and Agricultural Gazette*, several years out of date. It is now June in the Rumi year 1302, or 1886 by the Christian calendar. He had fallen asleep over the German botanist H. G. Reichenbach's reclassification of *Acineta hrubyana*, a many-flowered orchid recently discovered in South America with stiff, unarticulated brown lips. Kamil has slept uneasily. In his dreams, an undertow of small, leather-skinned men, faceless, agile, pulled him down. Yakup, ever vigilant as are all residents of the wooden houses of Istanbul, must have come in and extinguished the oil lamp.

Kamil splashes water on his face from the basin on the marble washstand to dispel the numbing hollowness he always feels in those gray moments between waking and the first soothing intricacies of his daily routine—shaving, wrapping his fingers around the calm heat of a steaming glass of tea, turning the pages of the newspaper. The mirror shows a lean, tired face, thin lips pressed in a grim line beneath his mustache, eyes obscured by unruly black hair. A single bolt of gray arcs above his left brow. He quickly rubs pomade in his wet hands and slicks down his hair, which springs up again immediately. With an exasperated sigh, he turns to Yakup, who is holding out his trousers. Yakup is a thin, dour man in his thirties with high cheekbones and a long face. He waits with the preoccupied look of a lifelong servant no longer concerned with the formalities of rank, but simply intent on his task.

"I wonder what has happened," Kamil mutters. Believing himself to be a man of even temperament, he is wary of the surfeit of emotion that would cause someone to pound on his door in the middle of the night.

Yakup helps him into a white shirt, stambouline frock coat, and yellow kid boots, intricately tooled. Made by a master bootmaker in Aleppo according to a method passed only from father to son, they are as soft as the skin at a woman's wrist, but indestructible and impervious to both knife and water. Etched in the leather inside the shaft is a grid of tiny talismanic symbols that call on powers beyond those of the bootmaker to strengthen the wearer. Kamil is a tall man, slim and well muscled, but his slightly rounded shoulders and upward-tilting chin convey the impression that he is bending forward to inquire about something, a man lost in thought, bowed over old manuscripts. When he looks up, his moss green eyes contradict this otherworldliness with their force and clarity. He is a man who controls his environment by comprehending it. As a result, he is uninterested in things beyond his control and exasperated by that beyond his comprehension. Fate belongs in the first category. Family, friends, women inhabit the second. His hands are in constant motion, fingertips slipping over a short string of amber beads he keeps in his right-hand pocket. The amber feels warm, alive to his touch; he senses a pulse, his own, magnified. The fingers of his father and grandfather before him have worn tiny flat planes into the surface of the beads. When his fingers encounter these platforms, Kamil feels part of a mortal chain that settles him in his own time and place. It explains nothing, but it imparts a sense of peace.

He lives frugally, with a minimum of servants, in a small, ocher-colored wood-frame villa that he inherited from his mother. The house is set within a garden, shaded by old umbrella pines, cypress, and mulberry trees, on the Bosphorus shore above Beshiktash. The house had been part of his mother's dowry. She spent her last years there with her two children, preferring the quiet waterfront community, where everyone knew her and had known her parents and grandparents, to the palatial mansion on a hill overlooking the Golden Horn from which his father, Alp Pasha, minister of gendarmes, had governed the province of Istanbul.

Kamil kept the boatman who for years had ferried his father on weekends to his wife's villa. Every morning, Bedri the boatman's knotted arms row Kamil down the strait to the Tophane quay, where a phaeton waits to carry him up the steep hill to the courthouse on the Grande Rue de Pera. On days when his docket is light, Kamil walks from the quay instead, delighted to be outdoors. After his mother died, Kamil had a small winter garden added to the back of the house. As magistrate, he has less time now for botanical expeditions that require weeks of travel, so he tends and studies the orchids he has gathered at his home from many corners of the empire.

Taking a deep breath, Kamil strides down the wide staircase to the entry hall. Waiting impatiently inside the circle of lamps held by Kamil's servants is a short, red-faced man in traditional baggy trousers, his vest askew and one end of his cummerbund coming undone. His red felt cap is wound in a striped cloth. He shifts his weight restlessly from one sturdy leg to the other. Upon seeing Kamil, he bows deeply, touching the fingers of his right hand against his lips and then his forehead, in a sign of respect. Kamil wonders what has happened to agitate the headman to such an extent. A murder would have been brought to the attention of the district police first, not to the magistrate at his home in the middle of the night.

"Peace upon you. What brings you here at this early hour?"

"Upon you be peace, Pasha bey," the headman stutters, his round face reddening further. "I am Ibrahim, headman of Middle Village. Please excuse my intrusion, but a matter has come up in my district that I think you must be told about."

He pauses, his eyes darting into the shadows behind the lamps. Kamil signals to the servants to leave the lamps and withdraw.

"What is it?"

"Efendi, we found a body in the water by the Middle Village mosque."

"Who found it?"

"The garbage scavengers." These semiofficial collectors begin just before dawn to gather the refuse washed up overnight on the shores and streets of the city. After extracting useful items for themselves, they load the rest onto barges to be dumped into the Sea of Marmara, where the current disperses it.

Kamil turns his head toward the sitting room door and the window beyond. A thin wash of light silhouettes the trees in his garden. He sighs and turns back to the headman.

"Why not report this to the police chief of your district?"

Kamil shares jurisdiction with two other magistrates for the European side of the Bosphorus all the way from the grand mosques and covered markets in the south, where the strait loses itself in the Sea of Marmara, to the frieze of villages and stately summer villas extending along its wooded hills north to the Black Sea. Middle Village is little more than half an hour's ride north of Kamil's villa.

"Because it is a woman, bey," the headman stutters.

"A woman?"

"A foreign woman, bey. We believe Frankish."

A European woman. Kamil feels a chill of apprehension. "How do you know she is Frankish?"

"She has a gold cross on a chain around her neck."

Kamil snaps impatiently, "She could just as easily be one of our Christian subjects."

The headman looks at the marble-tiled floor. "She has yellow hair. And a heavy gold bracelet. And something else. . . ."

Kamil sighs. "Why do I have to drag everything out of you? Can't you simply tell me everything you saw?"

The headman looks up helplessly. "A pendant, bey, that opens like a walnut." He cups his hands together, then parts them. "Inside one shell is the tughra of the padishah, may Allah support and protect him." He reaches one cupped hand forward, then the other. "Inside the other are odd characters. We thought it might be Frankish writing."

Kamil frowns. He can't think of any explanation for the sultan's personal signature to be on a piece of jewelry around the neck of a woman outside the sultan's household, much less one with European writing. It makes no sense. The tughra, the sultan's seal, is affixed on special possessions of the imperial household and onto official documents by a special workshop on the palace grounds. The tughranüvis, royal scribes charged with creating the intricate and elegant calligraphic design of the royal name, and the royal engravers are never allowed to leave the palace for fear that they could be kidnapped and forced to affix the signature to counterfeit items. Since the empire is so large and such forgeries might go unnoticed, the only solution is to keep the sultan's "hands" close by his sleeves. Kamil has heard that these scribes carry a fast-acting poison on their person as a further precaution. Only three people hold the royal seal used for documents: the sultan himself, the grand vizier, and the head of the harem household, a trusted old woman who grew up in the palace. Royal objects made of gold, silver, and other valuable materials are engraved with the tughra only on their orders.

The headman's roughened fingers clasp and unclasp as he waits before Kamil, head bowed, eyes shifting anxiously across the marble floor. Noticing his increased agitation, Kamil realizes the headman thinks Kamil blames him for awakening him. He eases the frown from his face. Kamil remembers that even law-abiding citizens have reason to fear the power of the police and courts. The headman is also a craftsman responsible to his guild master for his behavior and afraid of bringing official wrath down on his fellows. He probably brought the matter to the magistrate's attention instead of the Middle Village police because of the gold found on the body. The local police might have stripped the body of valuables as efficiently as the garbage scavengers and he might be held responsible. But the sultan's seal and the fact that the woman might be European also indicated that the matter would fall under Kamil's jurisdiction of Pera. While the sultan had given foreigners and non-Muslim minorities of Pera the right to administer their own district and to judge cases related to personal matters, like inheritance and divorce, the population still relied on the palace for protection and the state courts for justice in other matters.

"You did well bringing this to my attention immediately."

The headman's face relaxes and he bows low. "Long life to the padishah. May Allah protect him."

Kamil signals to Yakup, standing just outside the hall door. "Ready a horse and send messengers to Michel Efendi and the police chief responsible for Middle Village district. Ask them to meet me at the mosque and to keep away idlers until I arrive, especially the garbage scavengers. They'll pick her clean. I want to see that pendant. The police are to make sure nothing is disturbed." He adds in a low voice so that the headman does not hear, "And the chief is to make sure the police disturb nothing."

"I sent a messenger to the local police, bey, and told my two sons to stay with the body until I returned."

This headman has healthy ears, Kamil notes.

"You are to be commended, Headman Ibrahim. I will make sure

the proper officials are notified of your diligence and desire to please the state." He will ask his assistant to send a commendation to the headman's guild boss.

"I rode here on a neighbor's horse, Pasha bey, so I can show you the way."

THE VILLAGERS HAVE pulled the body out of the water and onto the quay and covered it with a worn sheet. Kamil pulls back the cloth, looking at the face first, out of respect and a certain reluctance. In the year since he was appointed magistrate, most of his cases have involved theft or violence, few death. Her hair is short, an unusual style, pale and fine as undyed silk. Strands of it cradle her face. A cool breeze strokes his neck, but he can feel the heat crouching in the air. Already he is sweating. After a few moments, he pulls the sheet away slowly, exposing her naked skin to the sky and the burning eyes of the men around her. The sharp ammonia stench of human excrement from the rocks at the base of the quay makes him jerk his nose away and step sideways toward the corpse's legs.

He can no longer avoid looking at her body. She is short and slender, like a boy, with small breasts. Her skin is stark white, except for a dark triangle at her pubis. Crabs have begun their work on her fingers and toes. She wears no rings, but a heavy gold bracelet weighs down her left wrist. The currents have cooled her body, so it has not yet begun to change into a corpse; it is still a dead woman. Later, she will become a case, an intellectual puzzle. But now he feels only pity and the shapeless anxiety death always awakens in his body. She is not pretty in the accepted sense; her face is too long and narrow, her features too sharp, with wide, thick lips. Perhaps the face in motion might have been attractive, he muses. But now her face has the cool, dispassionate remove of death, the muscles neither relaxed nor engaged in emotion, her skin an empty tent stretched over her bones.

A gold cross hangs from a short chain around her neck. It is remarkable that the cross has not come off during the body's tumultuous ride through the currents, he thinks. Perhaps the body has not come far.

He bends closer to examine the necklace. The cross is wide and showy, of beaten gold, decorated with etched roses whose outlines have been filled in with red enamel, now cracked. The metal is twisted where the chain passes through, as if it had snagged on something or someone had tried to pull it off. He lifts the cross with the tip of his finger. Hidden beneath it, in the deep hollow of the woman's throat, is a round silver pendant, simple but beautifully designed. A thin line bisects it.

He leans closer to the dead woman's neck. A damp, mineral cold seems to rise from the body, or perhaps it is his own face that has become clammy. He looks up into the glare of the strait to steel himself. Drawing a deep breath, he returns his attention to the pendant. He inserts his thumbnail and pries the halves apart, angles them so that they catch the morning sun, and peers inside. A tiny recessed lock that had held the halves together is broken. The inner surface is engraved with a tughra on the top half and, on the bottom, strange markings—as if a child had tried to draw a picture using only short, straight lines—unlike any European language he has seen.

He lets the cross and pendant fall back onto the woman's neck and turns over her wrist to examine the bracelet. It too is unusual; as wide as his hand, it is woven of thin filaments of red and white gold in a checkerboard pattern. The bracelet fits tightly around her wrist, held in place by a slim metal post inserted into interlaced channels.

The crowd of locals jostling to see has increased; it is time to move. He gestures to one of the policemen.

"Cover the body and bring it to the hamam."

The policeman bows, pressing his fist solemnly against his forehead, then against his heart.

Kamil looks around for the headman, who is standing proudly in a knot of local men, answering questions. The two strapping young men flanking him must be his sons, he thinks with a twinge of regret.

Kamil has not married, despite his parents' and now his sister Feride's introductions to any number of suitable young women from good families. He would love to have a grown son or daughter, but the emotional messiness and demands on his time he imagines would be made by a wife and young children repel him.

"Where was the body found?"

The headman leads him down a short flight of steps to a narrow rocky cove behind the mosque. The rococo mosque stands on the tip of a spit of rock that stretches out into the Bosphorus like a hook, making a natural barrier. It looks like an ornate wedding cake of white marble on an outstretched hand. On its southern side is a small open square where men come to sit and drink tea under the plane trees, watching the fishermen make their boats ready and mend their nets.

Kamil picks his way, stepping carefully to avoid the night's effluvium. He squats at the water's edge. Opaque in the early light, it sloshes heavily against the rocks as if weary.

"This is where they found her. There's a whirlpool that washes things up. My sons are fishermen and were in the square cleaning their boat when they heard a commotion. They ran over and stopped the scavengers from taking the bracelet."

"Your sons are admirable young men, Ibrahim Efendi."

The headman bows his head, suppressing a smile. "Thank you. I'm proud of my sons."

"Did the scavengers take anything else?"

"Not that I know of."

"I'd like to speak with your sons."

Kamil questions them. The younger boy, his mustache still only a soft shadow above his lip, answers so earnestly that his words pile up one on another and the magistrate is forced to ask him to repeat. The body had been caught on a rocky protrusion and the young men happened upon the scavengers just as they finished pulling it onto the shore. They had called their fellow fishermen over and together they kept the scavengers from looting the body while the younger brother ran to fetch his father. The men had no idea who the woman was.

This did not surprise Kamil, since the only women whose faces these men were likely to have seen were their own relations or women of easy virtue. While the Christian and Jewish subjects of the sultan did not always veil their faces, they were nevertheless modest and did not display themselves to strangers in the streets unnecessarily. Kamil sends the eager young man to find the village midwife. He will need her help to examine the body. From his elder brother, Kamil learns that the fishermen had heard strange noises coming from shore the night before, the barking of wild dogs and a splash.

The men place the body on a board that only moments before had carried loaves bound for the bakery ovens, drape it with the sheet, and carry it up a narrow dirt alley between the overhanging roofs of wooden houses. Their feet stir up white puffs as they pass. Soon the householders will emerge for their morning chores and sprinkle water on the streets to lay the dust. Pigeons and doves murmur behind the high garden walls.

The hamam is a square stone building topped by a large round dome. Since it is early, the fires that heat the pipes under the floor have not yet been stoked, and water does not yet flow into the basins set into the wall around the room. The gray marble rooms are cool and dry. The men file through a series of small echoing antechambers until they reach the large central room beneath the dome. When the hamam is in use, bathers soak in this room in cascades of hot water brimming from marble basins in a haze of steam. Kamil directs the men to lay the body on the marble belly stone, the round, raised massage platform dominating the center of the room, and to light the lamps.

"Good morning." Michel Sevy, the police surgeon, appears behind Kamil, startling him.

"I didn't expect you so soon."

Kamil had requested the young Jewish surgeon's assistance on this case, as on others, not just for his medical knowledge, but for his skill in documenting the telling details of a crime scene in his notes and sketches. Still, Kamil finds Michel's habit of appearing at his elbow, seemingly out of nowhere, vaguely disquieting, as though it were not in his power to command Michel. Rather, the surgeon arrives as a djinn might, stealthily and unpredictably.

"You must have galloped the entire way from Galata," observes Kamil dryly. Michel's heavyset face and thick neck are red from exertion. His hair and mustache are the color of wet sand and his large, doleful eyes an indeterminate hazel. They roam the room slowly as he takes off his outer robe and hands it to the policeman by the door.

Kamil reflects that Michel reminds him of the brown spiders in the northeast mountains. The spiders were the size of a fist, but their coloring perfectly camouflaged them in the low, sere brush, so that travelers did not see them until they were underfoot. They were fast and, when they ran, let out high-pitched squeals, like babies. He had seen a man die after being surprised and bitten by such a spider. Usually, Michel's penchant for colorful dress draws attention to him that his person does not, but when pursuing criminals into their neighborhood dens, Kamil has seen Michel in dun-colored pants and robe that render him all but invisible.

Today Michel is wearing baggy blue shalwar trousers under a red-striped robe held in place by a wide belt of yellow cloth. His black leather shoes make no sound as he walks across the marble floor toward the belly stone. He moves with the careful deliberation of a wrestler.

"I was curious. The messenger gave me only half a story. Something about a drowned foreign princess."

His smile fades as he looks down at the dead woman.

"Besides," he continues, looking more serious, "this is partly a Jewish neighborhood, so I thought I could be of some assistance."

Despite Michel's abruptness, Kamil appreciates his direct answers, so different from the usual polite circumlocutions with which conversations are initiated. He finds that people often are afraid to tell him what they know, in case they are wrong. They also are afraid to say that they don't know something. His teachers at

Cambridge University, where he had studied law and criminal procedure for a year, assumed that when questioned, a person would answer with either truth or falsehood. They had no concept of Oriental politeness that avoids the shame of ignorance and shies away from the brutal directness of truth, and that encourages invention and circumlocution as the highest markers of ethical behavior.

Accuracy in a subordinate means sacrificing the buffer of respectful indirectness and obfuscation of problems that would have spared his superior from worry. But Kamil, laboring since his youth under the heavy mantle of his father's status, is only too happy to shrug it off.

"I HAVE the tools."

Michel pulls a leather-wrapped kit from his belt and places it on the belly stone, at the head of the corpse. He takes a folder of thick blank paper from a saddlebag, and a narrow lacquered box from which he extracts a pen and several sticks of fine charcoal.

"Ready."

"We'll wait for the midwife. In the meantime, go to the street and see what you can learn. Was anyone traveling last night or out on a boat and did they see or hear anything? The fishermen mentioned barking dogs. Did anyone notice an unknown woman in the vicinity? Also, send two policemen along the shore north of here. Her clothes are missing and there may be some signs of a struggle. Perhaps someone heard something in one of the other villages near the shore. Have them check in the coffeehouses. That's always the best way to learn anything. On your way out, clear the room of onlookers. Have them leave the lamps."

Michel does as he is told and then is gone, leaving the door ajar.

A few moments later a woman in a frayed cloak appears in the doorway just inside the circle of light. Her head and shoulders are draped in a brown shawl. Slipping off her outer shoes, she pads softly across the marble on leather socks. She removes her cloak and shawl with swift, practiced motions, folds them neatly, and drapes them over a nearby basin. Underneath, she wears a striped robe over wide trousers and a kerchief tied around her graying hair.

"Are you the midwife of Middle Village?"

"Yes, my name is Amalia." She averts her face modestly, but alert eyes sweep the room. Seeing the body on the marble slab, she comes forward.

"Poor woman." She smoothes the hair gently away from the dead woman's face.

"Is this as she was found?" She moves to the body and begins examining it. She is used to being in command of a situation and seems oblivious that she is sharing this activity with a magistrate.

"Yes. We need to know if she has been tampered with and anything else you can tell us. I will wait over here."

He withdraws to the outer shadows and waits at a discreet distance, but where he can still see what she is doing.

The midwife's practiced hands probe the body of the dead woman.

"A woman in her twenties, I would say. Not a virgin. She has not previously given birth; there are no signs of stretching."

Kamil frowns. "Perhaps she killed herself over the loss of her honor and threw herself into the Bosphorus. She wouldn't be the first girl to do so. Some of the Franks are as fastidious in their expectations of women as we are. If she is unmarried, it could ruin her."

"Possible, I suppose." Amalia moves her fingers over the dead woman's face and pulls up her eyelids.

"Dark eyes." She bends closer and then looks up abruptly. "Look at this, Magistrate bey. The eyes are blue, but the pupils are too large. There is only a small rim of blue visible. Perhaps she was drugged."

Kamil steps forward and looks down at the woman's eyes.

"What could cause the pupils to expand like that?"

"Apoplexy, but she's far too young for a disease like that." She thinks for a moment. "Many years ago, an old uncle in my family died of opium poisoning. He had such eyes. At the end, he was a bone with huge eyes, black like cups of coffee."

Kamil feels chilled and plunges his hands into his pockets.

"Opium poisoning?"

She looks at him curiously, alert to a change in the quality of his voice. "Yes, but I don't think that can be the case here." She points at the body. "She's too healthy. Opium addicts stop eating and taking care of themselves."

"But maybe she just started smoking opium. Maybe it's not that far advanced."

"Then her eyes wouldn't be dilated. That happens only at the end."

"At the end," Kamil repeats in a low voice. Abruptly, he walks over to one of the basins against the wall. He turns the spigot handle, releasing a gush of water. He quickly turns it back, but not before wetting his sleeve.

Amalia watches him carefully and reaches her own conclusions. "If there is anything—" she begins, but Kamil cuts her off.

"So if it's not apoplexy or opium, may Allah protect us, what else can it be?"

"There's one other possibility," she says slowly, thinking her way toward the answer. "Tube flower."

"Tube flower? Isn't that for colds?" Kamil has a vague childhood memory of inhaling steam from a cup of viscous yellow liquid to quell a cough.

"Yes, it's used as a cough medicine. The herbalists in the Egyptian Spice Bazaar sell it. But I've heard that drinking it makes people see and hear things that aren't there, and can even cause death if it's strong enough."

Kamil is surprised. "Why on earth would they sell something like that in the bazaar?"

The midwife shakes her head at the ignorance of men. "You're not supposed to drink it, just inhale or smoke it. You'd be surprised how many things in an ordinary household can cause death."

"That would make our job endless."

"It shows that people are not evil," she responds, "and can resist temptation. Believe me, every house in this village has a motive for murder. All you need is a mother-in-law and daughter-in-law under the same roof. It's a wonder tube flowers aren't more popular." She turns before Kamil can see the smile flit across her face.

Her face is serious again when she bends down and picks up the dead woman's hand. She examines the palms and fingers, looks at the intricate clasp of the gold bracelet. The limbs move reluctantly. Rigor mortis is finishing what the crabs left undone.

"A lady. These hands have never worked the fields, scrubbed laundry, or labored in a kitchen. The nails are perfectly shaped, not cut straight across like those of women who must work in their households. They're not torn, as they might be from a struggle. Indeed I see no marks on her that indicate she struggled. The skin is unmarked except for the effects of its passage through the strait."

She steps back and looks at the body.

"Her hair is short. I don't know the meaning of that. Among some minorities, women cut their braids when they marry. But there's no wedding ring and no mark on her finger where it would have been."

She turns her head toward him.

"She doesn't appear to have been dead very long. The water has done little. I've seen fishermen and young boys who drowned in the Bosphorus and washed up in Middle Village. This young woman didn't come very far."

Kamil shifts restlessly. He scans the room in vain for Michel's bundle, where he might find paper and ink to take notes. It was a mistake to send him out before the midwife's arrival.

"Please continue. So you believe she drowned."

She pulls at the dead woman's shoulders to turn the body. Kamil helps her. The cold, clammy texture and unnatural firmness of dead flesh shocks and disgusts him, as it always does.

What is life, he wonders, when death can claim so much of what we are for itself? Here is the woman, whole, yet where is she who had thought, eaten, and perhaps laughed or wept the day before?

At such moments, he wishes intensely that he could believe in the afterlife promised in Islam, the clear rivers and unending companionship. But he had not been able to believe in his youth, and now he believes in a future of science and progress, which is inevitable and eternal, but does not include him beyond his life span. A belief of little comfort to the weak in their flimsy barques, or to the strong when the unforeseen upsets the course upon which they have set their ships. Kamil has known both kinds of men and the immovable anchors of faith that give them the illusion of a steady harbor. They do not understand that they are still at sea and that the danger has not passed. Faith is an anchor in a bottomless sea.

The midwife instructs Kamil to prop the body on its side. When she pulls down on the jaw, a stream of dark water spills from the mouth. She pulls the head forward and pumps the body's arm. A pink froth bubbles at the lips.

"Drowned. If she were already dead when she entered the water, she would not have breathed water into her lungs."

They let the body slide back onto the marble. Kamil is grateful to let go. His hands are clammy and he resists the temptation to thrust them into his pockets to warm them.

The midwife points to a large mole on the dead woman's right shoulder. "That might help to identify her."

She stands back, waiting for further instructions.

"Thank you. You've been most helpful and highly observant."

She smiles thinly. He muses that this simple village midwife has more scientific acumen than many educated bureaucrats of his acquaintance. It's a simple matter of reading the given evidence for data, not conjecturing on the basis of possible hypotheses.

Popular fears can fatten fatally on the thinnest gruel, especially in times of insecurity. Like the present. The imperial treasury taken over by European powers as a result of the empire's debts, wars on many fronts, and factions battling over what kind of government the empire should have—a parliament or undiluted power in the hands of the sultan. In every direction, the empire's provinces are being clawed away by nationalists supported by Europe and Russia. The streets of Istanbul teem with refugees. Kamil doubts whether even a parliament could stem the bleeding of treasure, land, and people from the great, unwieldy body of the Ottoman state, the boundaries of which these days are as soft and indistinct as those of Fat Orhan at the Turkish bath.

Change creates anxiety, Kamil muses, in high places and low. An anxious populace is eager to be distracted by dark fairy tales. This midwife will keep her sense, though.

She sees the approval in his eyes and smiles again, genuinely this time.

"I would like you to do me one more favor," he adds. "Ask in the village whether anyone knows this woman, or has heard or seen anything unusual. If so, send a messenger to the magistrate's headquarters directly, and I will send my assistant to speak with you." He assumes that, like most of the population, she is unable to read or write.

"We will thank the messenger," he adds, politely skirting any open discussion of money. "One more thing. You will not mention"— he pauses and gestures toward the body—"the condition of the deceased."

She agrees and bows her head slightly. She pulls on her outer garments and leaves.

Kamil is alone with the corpse. The body has not yet begun to decompose. It gives off a wet, empty smell.

A sudden movement just outside the circle of light startles him.

"Michel! How long have you been there?"

"I came in right after she began her examination. I sent the police off to find out what they can. I'll talk to the residents myself later. I thought you might need me here instead."

Kamil is simultaneously aware that Michel had disobeyed him, but, as if he could read Kamil's mind, had instead done what Kamil had silently wished.

"Yes, of course," he agrees reluctantly, aware that somehow he has lost, but unsure in what game.

"I've been in the next room, taking notes. The rooms echo. I could hear her perfectly in there. What a perceptive crone, eh?" he says admiringly. "She saved us a lot of examination."

"Yes, she was very good. We should check with the merchants in the bazaar to see whether they remember who recently bought dried tube flowers."

"You know, the Istanbul Sephardim tell about drops used by their Spanish ancestors to make their eyes seem black and large; they call the substance belladonna, beautiful woman. I wonder if it's the same as our humble tube flower."

Michel walks over to the body, a small bowl in his hand. With a sudden movement, he turns the body onto its side and presses on its chest. A thin stream of liquid spurts from its mouth into the bowl.

Michel examines the liquid. "I'll be able to tell from this whether she drowned in salt water or fresh." He eyes the leather bag of tools still lying at the head of the corpse. "I could check the contents of her stomach."

"I think we can't afford to do anything before contacting the foreign embassies. If this is one of their nationals, they won't want us to return a carved-up body."

"Yes, you're quite right." Michel looks disappointed.

"Give me the cutters."

Kamil snaps the necklace chain. He works at the clasp of the bracelet and pulls it off. Opening the pendant, he hands it to Michel.

"There is a tughra inside."

Michel turns the pendant over in his hand and examines it from all sides. "And some other markings. Do you know what they are?"

"I don't."

"She has some connection to the palace, then?"

"Perhaps. I wonder. Eight years ago, an Englishwoman was found dead just north of here at Chamyeri. A governess at the palace, Hannah Simmons. They found her floating in a pond. She'd been strangled." He frowns. "I don't suppose there's a connection."

He doesn't mention that the victim's name stuck in his mind because the superintendent of police for Beyoglu was removed from office by the minister of gendarmes—the man who had replaced his father—because he had failed to find the murderer. Kamil had perused the file on the murder when new at his job, but decided not to reopen the case. Too many years had gone by and it was not politically expedient to try to solve an unsolvable crime, especially one that involved members of the powerful foreign community and the sultan's palace. Now here is another young foreign woman dead, this time on his watch. He stiffens his posture to hide his anxiety and his excitement.

"That was the body found on the scholar's property above Chamyeri. It made for a lot of gossip at the time," Michel remembers.

"That's right. Ismail Hodja's house." The lesser details in Hannah Simmons's file had been shouldered aside by the continual press of new cases.

He ponders the young woman on the platform. "Just a coincidence, probably. She could be Circassian or from the Balkans. They're often yellow-haired with light-colored eyes. Anyway, Chamyeri is quite a ways north of Middle Village."

"Not that far by water. The current is powerful there. A corpse thrown in at Chamyeri would end up at Middle Village in no time at all. If the killer is the same person, then either he lives in that area or is a frequent visitor. One has to know the Bosphorus to navigate it or to wander its shores at night. The wild dogs alone would keep people away."

"I can't imagine it has anything to do with Ismail Hodja," Kamil responds firmly, his eyes following the cones of light as they descend from the dome and pierce the body on the belly stone. He is distressed by how quickly the surgeon accepted a link between the two murders. "The hodja's reputation is impeccable."

And there was no one else at his house who would come into question. The details in Hannah Simmons's file were jostling at the gates of Kamil's memory. The hodja's sister was a recluse, his niece a mere child at the time. There were only a few servants; not a large household.

"Anyway, the body was found in the forest behind his house, near the road, I believe. So it could have been anyone. Still," he muses aloud, "I wonder whether it would be worthwhile to talk to the hodja or his niece."

Michel doesn't answer. Kamil turns to find him still holding the pendant and staring intently at the body.

Michel turns and asks in a carefully neutral voice, "Do you want me to wrap this up?" He indicates the pendant in his hand.

"The cross and bracelet too. I'll take them with me." Pointing his chin at the body, "We don't even know who the woman is. She appears to be foreign, so I'll begin with the embassies."

Michel hands him the small bundle. He lays his cloak over the cold belly stone, sits on it, and takes out his sketching materials.

"But first I'll go home to change," Kamil adds companiably.

Michel doesn't look up, but begins drawing the body.

Kamil watches Michel's head bowed over the paper, fascinated by the creation emerging from beneath his stick of charcoal. He reflects about how little he knows of Michel's personal life, other than that he is unmarried and lives with his widowed mother in the Jewish quarter of Galata, and the story of their shared history. They spend time together in coffeehouses and clubs discussing everything under the sun, but Michel never opens to Kamil the private book of his life.

He and Michel attended the same school and knew each other by sight, but belonged to different circles. Michel, whose father had been a dealer in semiprecious stones, won a scholarship to attend the prestigious imperial school at Galata Saray. Children of wealthy Muslims, Jews, Armenians, Greeks, and other sons of the far-flung empire bowed their heads together over texts in history, logic, science, economy, international law, Greek, Latin, and, of course, Ottoman, that convolution of Persian, Arabic, and Turkish. It was not social class, religion, or language that separated Michel and Kamil in school, but the nature of their interests.

Soon after becoming magistrate, while Kamil was walking up the narrow streets toward his office, a man got up from a stool outside a coffeehouse and approached him. Kamil recognized the flamboyant colors of his old schoolmate's clothing and his wrestler's glide. That evening, they sat together in the coffeehouse and, over narghiles of apple-cured tobacco, exchanged news of their activities since graduation. Michel was finishing his training in surgery at the Imperial School of Medicine. Kamil was among the young men chosen for training in France and England as magistrates and judges in the newly introduced European-style secular courts that had shouldered aside the religious courts of the kadi judges. Michel had volunteered his services to Kamil, who eventually sponsored his appointment as police surgeon. Michel's intimate knowledge of the neighborhood had helped Kamil solve several cases. Michel also introduced him to the Grand Bazaar, a city of tiny shops all under one roof, surrounded by a warren of workshops—hundreds of establishments, some no bigger than a man's reach, owned by men of all the empire's faiths. Michel's father and two generations before him had been merchants there.

Kamil pauses under the arched doorway leading out of the hamam, the polite formula of parting dying on his lips, unwilling to intrude on Michel's concentration.

Kamil turns and makes his way through the echoing antechambers. He stops at a basin, turns the metal cock all the way open, and rubs his hands together under the cold water. There is no soap, but he feels less polluted. He shakes the excess water off his hands and strides out of the gloom. At the threshold, he is momentarily felled by the brightness of the world.

His hands still chilled, he mounts his horse and winds his way up past the village and into the forest. Here, the morning sun filters softly through the trees. Birds chirrup madly; the shrill calls of young children fall through the air like knives.

When he reaches the road beyond the forest, he spurs his horse to a gallop.

2

When the Lodos Blows

Every morning, my dayi, Ismail Hodja, put a soft-boiled egg in his mouth and sat without chewing, eyes lowered, until the egg was gone. It was not until I was in my twenties that I understood. Anticipation is the brilliant goad to pleasure. But at the time, I was only a child of nine, transfixed at the breakfast table. Ismail Dayi always ate the same breakfast: black tea in a tulip-shaped glass, one slice of white franjala bread, a handful of black, brine-soaked olives, a chunk of goat's cheese, a small bowl of yoghurt, and a glass of whey. In that order. Then the egg, which lay peeled and shivering in a cobalt blue saucer, blue-white and glinting with moisture. Its broad end was slightly raised, the yolk casting a sickle-moon shadow. My uncle ate his breakfast slowly and methodically, without speaking. Then he reached for the egg with two long, slim fingers. His fingers indented the pudgy waistline of the egg as he lifted it, quivering, to his mouth. He deposited it carefully on his tongue, taking care not to brush it with his teeth. Then he closed his lips around the egg and, eyes lowered, sat until it had magically disappeared. I saw him neither chew nor swallow.

During this time, Mama was in the kitchen, rinsing the plates and topping up the double boiler in which the tea brewed. We did not have live-in servants in Ismail Dayi's house and Mama herself prepared our breakfast before the cook and her assistant arrived for the day. When I would ask Mama, "Why does Ismail Dayi keep the egg in his mouth?" she would look away and busy herself.

"I don't know what you mean. Don't ask silly questions, Jaanan. Drink your tea."

Ismail was my mother's brother. We lived in his house because Papa had taken a second wife, and Mama had moved out of our big house in Nishantashou, where Papa lived now with Aunt Hüsnü.

Ismail Dayi's house was two stories high, its smooth wooden flanks painted rust red. It was set in a garden on the shore of the Bosphorus just outside the village of Chamyeri. Behind the house, a forest of plane trees, cypresses, and oaks painted the steep hills. The house was set on the narrow stage of the shore in front of this towering green backdrop. Before us, the broad band of the Bosphorus glittered with light, its currents twining and coiling like a living creature. Sometimes the water threw up arcs of dolphins trailing aquatic rainbows. The colors of the water changed constantly in response to forces I still do not understand, from oily black to bottle green and, on rare magical days, to a translucent pastel green so clear that I felt if I looked long enough, I would see the bottom. On days of such clarity, I lay on the warm stones of the shore wall and let my head hang over the edge, looking for quicksilver sprays of anchovies. Below them I imagined the cool, heavy bodies of bigger fish turning and slipping through the liquid light. The shifting sands beneath uncovered the pale moon faces of dead princesses, eyes closed, lips slightly parted in fruitless protests against their fate. The gold thread of their brocaded gowns weighed them down. Their delicate hands lay, palms up, pinned to the sand by enormous emerald and diamond rings. Their black hair streamed in the current.

On cold days, I lay reading on the cushioned divan in the garden pavilion. It was a one-room structure with tall windows looking out over the water. Stacks of mattresses and quilts were kept ready for visitors who preferred to sleep there on hot nights. In winter, wooden shutters protected it against the wind and a brazier provided warmth and heated water for tea, although hardly anyone went there once the weather turned chill.

Mama complained about being isolated from her friends and the social life of the city. It was a long way to come from Istanbul by bullock cart or boat just to share a cup of coffee. The ferry from Istanbul took almost two hours and docked north of here at Emirgan. It took a carriage another hour to come the rest of the distance. Not many ladies had their husbands' permission to stay the night. Only in summer, when the ladies moved to their summer houses on the Bosphorus, did we socialize. But I loved Ismail Dayi's house. I was allowed to roam the garden in the benign care of Halil, our old gardener, and, later, under the watchful eyes of Madam Élise, my French governess and teacher.

Those first years in Chamyeri, Papa came once every week to try to convince Mama to return. I heard them arguing behind the carved wooden doors of the receiving room. He told her he would buy a separate house for her, that there was no need for her to live with her brother. But no matter how much I flattened my ear against the door, I never heard my mother's response. In retrospect, I can see that her refusal to return to Papa's protection must have shamed him before his family and peers, and this small protest gave my mother strength. By moving into my father's house, even into a house apart from the one in Nishantashou where he lived with Aunt Hüsnü, Mama would have signaled her acceptance of Aunt Hüsnü as his kuma.

I don't know whether Papa sent my mother's financial due to Ismail Dayi, or, if he did, whether Ismail Dayi accepted it. Despite his eccentricities, Ismail Dayi was a respected hodja, a jurist and poet who had inherited his parents' house and considerable wealth.

Mama's inheritance had gone with her into her marriage dowry, but remained hers to claim. Between Papa's visits, Mama sat at her needlework in the receiving room, waiting for visitors who rarely arrived, her fingers dancing over the silk thread.

This was our life at Chamyeri until I was thirteen, in the Rumi year 1294, or 1878 by your reckoning, when I found the body of a woman in the pond behind our house. The pond, fed by an invisible spring, is shallow at one end and unfathomably deep at the other. It is so wide that a stone hurled by a young girl will not reach the other side. It is hidden behind a ruined stone wall in the forest. The woman Hannah was floating in knee-deep water, face down, her arms outstretched in an embrace. I did not realize she was dead, having no experience in such things. I stroked her hair. She looked peaceful, like a water princess, and I tried not to disturb her too much as I took her hand and turned her face to the sky. Her blue eyes were open. I told her that I lived here with my mother and my dayi. She looked surprised. I combed her hair with my fingers, arranged her dress, and placed a wildflower against her throat before going back to the house. When I told Madam Élise that a woman was asleep in the water and I could not wake her, I did not yet know the water there was deep enough to drown in.

The Bosphorus is a powerful sinew of water that flexes and pushes and roils down its long, wide chute to the Sea of Marmara, impatient to find the warm Mediterranean and dissolve into the salty womb of the ocean. Young boys from the village jump in and disappear, moments later emerging hundreds of yards downstream, where they must use all the force of their thin brown arms to reach shore again. Despite vigorous rowing, a boat headed upstream seems held in place by an unseen hand. When one next looks out, magically the boat has progressed.

Boats headed south, toward Istanbul, shoot along, passengers holding firmly to the creaking shell as the boatmen battle with their rudders. Halil, who had been a fisherman before he lost two fingers to a runaway net and became our gardener, told me that the Bosphorus has two currents. One runs north to south along the surface, carrying cold fresh water from the Black Sea to the Mediterranean; the other, a slippery rope of warm saline liquid, slithers south to north forty meters beneath the hard-muscled surface. The fishermen know that if you drop a line a certain length, you will catch palamut, lufer, and istavrit that in spring dangle like silver coins from the fishermen's lines. If you lower your hook farther, there abide mezgit and kalkan. A net caught up by the lower current will pull a boat inescapably northward. When the lodos blows from the southwest, the currents tangle and shift. The wrong fish are caught. Village boys do not reemerge. Young women drown in knee-deep water.

When Madam Élise saw the dead girl in the pond, she left us that same afternoon, crying and flailing her arms if anyone came near her.

After Madam Élise's abrupt departure, I was happy. With no lessons, I spent hours perched on the stone wall dangling my legs toward the water below, watching large pleasure kayaks go by like creatures with many legs moving up and down in unison. I could make out the conical red felt hats of the teams of rowers. Veiled ladies sat on cushions and carpets on the foredeck, their heads nodding to one another in conversation like doves. Maidservants shaded them with fringed parasols. If they were women of high officials or the royal family, between the women and the rowers, under a particularly large parasol, would sit a fat eunuch, his dark skin melting into the shade. Sometimes I lay on my back on the warm stones, watching the sky careen about me. The scent of jasmine trailed across me like a cloak worn by the breeze.

When I went to the long, gold-framed mirror in the receiving room, the only mirror Mama allowed in the house, I saw a girl-child with black curls that hung to her waist, eyes a pure azure blue, as if they had absorbed the summer sky. My eyes, mother told me, were inherited from a Circassian ancestor, a slave who had become the wife of a high official.

I LEARNED TO swim. I owe that skill to Violet. Violet is the daughter of Mama's distant relation, a fisherman in Cheshme on the Aegean coast. As a child, I had never been to the coast, but Violet brought it to me—the warm sand, the smell of pine, and above all the kinship with the sea that flows in the veins of all its residents. Violet grew up a dolphin. When she came to us as my companion and servant, I was fourteen and she fifteen.

Violet had been sent to us by her father because he was in need of a new fishing boat. It was not uncommon for a wealthy family to adopt a poorer relative as a servant. The girl was expected to obey and serve her new family and to behave in a manner that brought credit to them. In return, the wealthier family gave her room and board, perhaps a simple education, eventually found her a suitable husband and paid the considerable wedding expenses. Through intermediaries, Ismail Dayi had sent out word that his niece needed a companion and had sent Violet's father the price of a new boat in return for a chance at a better life for his daughter. As was traditional for servants entering a household, Mama gave her a flower name. Violet, because she was small and shy.

Halil brought her in the cart from the boat landing in Chamyeri. A small brown figure in a rough cloak, she slid from the cart, clutching her bundle. She refused to surrender it to Halil to carry. In the first months, she kept her eyes lowered and spoke only when spoken to. Mama gave her a room at the back of the house that looked toward the road and into the forest. The green of the forest colored the air in Violet's room, unlike our own bright bedrooms floating between the blues of water and sky. At night, I crept down the corridor and set my ear to her door, listening to the faraway sound of her weeping.

Violet's body was slim, taut, and brown as a nut. It gleamed with the energy of the sea. She boasted of her ability to swim and I begged her to teach me. We shed our cloaks and hovered like water fairies in the silk gauze smocks I had assumed would be appropriate swimwear.

In Cheshme, Violet confided, she had entered the sea—the sea, she stressed, not a small pond—wearing, scandalously, nothing. When no one was about, she hastened to assure me.

"How can you swim in this sack?" she asked scathingly, bunching the gauze in her small brown fists.

That afternoon, Halil had walked to the coffeehouse in the village, and I knew he would be gone for hours. There were no visitors expected. I pulled off the chemise, the white silk pooling at my feet. My skin had a blue cast to it, and I was immediately covered in goose bumps. Violet was like an animal of a different species. She glowed with a mineral health. I could not then differentiate between earthy enjoyment of the common brown nut and the delicate flavor of the peeled unripe almond newly released from its green veil. At the time, I envied Violet the unconcerned windmilling of her arms and her broad-legged stance, unmindful of the cut of her sex, that place that Madam Élise had impressed upon me was to be guarded against intrusion, never to be revealed.

Violet slid into the deep end of the pond and bobbed up, looking at me expectantly. Keeping my legs together, I sat at the edge of the water, the cold, slick stone unfamiliar and thrilling to my naked flesh. I do not recall thinking long about things. That is the advantage and disadvantage of youth. In one motion, I let myself fall into this new world. I remember the thrill of swift silk drawn over my body. I fell and fell into a world of dumb cries, huge shadows, and a lethargy of limbs. I remember noticing the sunlight cutting the water like a gem. And opened my mouth. Panic. Flailing. A grip on my waist, and I was hauled up into a blinding world, the light inside my head too bright to bear. Pulled onto the stones. Beached. Exposed. Violet was heaving beside me, dripping everywhere. When I could breathe again, I squinted at her and we began to laugh.

3

The Ambassador's Daughter

amil stands in a reception room at the British Embassy while a servant carries his calling card on a silver tray to the ambassador of Her Majesty's government to the Ottoman Empire. Someone has tried to offset the heavy, dark furniture with rich, warm fabrics and a bright carpet. Kamil steps over to a small fireplace behind an ornate ironwork grate and is disappointed to see it is not lit. He can't shake off the chill of the old building, despite the early summer heat gathering outside the windows. His eye is drawn to a large oil painting above the mantel depicting what he assumes to be a scene from classical mythology: a pale, naked youth reaching for a nubile and equally bare young woman fleeing his embrace. Discreet billows of white cloth snake across their loins. The woman's limbs are round and solid as pillars so that, incongruously, she appears stronger than the delicate young man pursuing her. Her small, plump lips are parted in a half smile, her nipples bright pink and erect, and a wash of red over areas of her pearly skin hints at arousal. Kamil wonders what the outcome of this chase would be.

He thinks sadly of his own limited experience: the French actress who played for a season at the Mezkur Theatre; the young Circassian slave to whom, after a time, he had given enough money for a dowry so that she could be freed and married to a young man of her station. He thinks of her now, her long, white limbs blending with those in the painting. He wonders if she ever thinks of him. Dust motes dance in the weak sunlight filtering from behind the heavy plum-colored drapes.

The door opens behind him. Kamil is startled and does not turn right away. Suddenly he has a deeper understanding of the Muslim prohibition of depictions of the body. How odd to hang such a provocative artwork in a room where guests are to be formally received. He notices that the light has changed. How long has he been left to wait in this room?

The elderly servant stands just inside the door, staring at a spot beyond Kamil's left shoulder. Kamil wonders whether the man sees the angel sitting on the shoulder of every Muslim, one on the left, one on the right, or is looking at the naked woman on the wall behind him. Is that a smirk in the corner of the butler's mouth? Perhaps he finds it amusing to trap Muslims in a room with a naked woman. Kamil presumes there are other, more sedately decorated reception rooms. Surely women visitors are not brought here. He struggles to hide his annoyance. He remembers other butlers from his stay in England, all the warmth and personality bred out of them. While Kamil respects and admires European knowledge and technology, there are many areas in which they have much to learn from the Ottomans.

Kamil does not acknowledge the butler, but stands unsmiling, his hands clasped behind his back.

"The ambassador will see you now, sir." Kamil is certain there was an infinitesimal pause before the "sir."

The butler leads the way across the white marble tiles, through the echoing, arched hall and up a magnificent curved stairway. As he follows, Kamil admires the frescoes and peers into the dark lacquered depths of the paintings that line the hall. A frowning Queen Victoria, her neck sheathed in a painful ruff, stares at a point above his head. A race of butlers, he thinks again, bloodless butlers. How have they managed to make such inroads into his lovely, vibrant society, so rich with color and emotion? He remembers the clean logic of his college texts and sighs. Perhaps this is the future, he thinks gloomily. Chaos vanquished by cleanliness, nuance lost to order.

The butler knocks on a heavy white door embossed with gold. At a sound from within, he pushes the door open and stands aside. Kamil enters. The door closes behind him with a click.

THE AMBASSADOR'S OFFICE seems even colder than the reception room, despite the heat Kamil can see shimmering beyond the heavy velvet curtains. Kamil suppresses a shiver and crosses the expanse of gold and blue carpet toward an enormous desk that dwarfs the man sitting behind it. The room has an unwashed smell, as if it has not been aired in a long time. As Kamil approaches, the man stands and moves to greet him, placing one lanky leg before the other in slow motion as if to mime a stride across a larger space. The ambassador is taller than he appears when folded behind his ship of a desk. Almost painfully thin beneath his dark, tailored suit, he has a long, elegant face devoid of expression. Thick whiskers swallow his cheeks, making his face appear even narrower. Kamil remembers that the English call these "muttonchops." The reason escapes him. As he approaches, Kamil sees that the ambassador's cheeks and nose are dusky red, his skin a lace of broken capillaries. His small eyes are a watery blue. The ambassador blinks rapidly, then reaches out a bony hand to Kamil. Kamil, pleased at the courtesy, smiles as he shakes his hand. It is dry as paper and exerts almost no pressure. The ambassador's smile is thin. His breath has the same damp odor as the room.

"What can I do for you, Magistrate?" He motions toward a padded leather armchair and retreats behind his desk.

"I have come on a grave matter, sir," Kamil begins in his accented English, the careful formality of the Orient burnished by a British lilt. "This morning we discovered a woman, deceased. We think she may be one of your subjects."

"A deceased woman, you say?" He shifts nervously in his chair.

"We need to know whether someone has been reported missing, sir. A short, blond woman, about twenty years of age."

"Why are the Turks involved in this?" the ambassador mumbles, as if to himself. He squints quizzically at Kamil, drawing up one side of his lip, exposing a yellowed tooth. "What did she die of?"

"She was murdered, sir."

"What?" The ambassador is surprised. "Well, that is a different matter. Awful. Awful."

"We don't know whether she is English or not, and we don't know the circumstances of her death. I had hoped for your assistance in that."

"Why do you think she's one of our subjects?"

"We don't know that she is. She was Christian. A cross was found around her neck. Judging from her jewelry, she was well off."

"What was she wearing? That should give it away, shouldn't it?"

"She was not wearing clothing."

"By God." The ambassador reddens. "A crime of the most heinous kind, then."

"It may not be . . . such a crime. There was no evidence of a struggle. She was wearing a pendant with an inscription. I have it here."

Kamil reaches into his jacket and withdraws a small bundle wrapped in a linen handkerchief. He unties the cloth and places it on the desk.

"The cross and gold bracelet were hers too."

The ambassador cranes his neck and with the tips of his fingers slides the handkerchief nearer. He picks up the gold bracelet to test its weight.

"Nice piece of workmanship." He replaces the bracelet carefully on the cloth and touches the bent enameled cross with the tip of one bony finger.

"Where is the inscription?"

"Inside the silver pendant."

The ambassador picks up the small round ball of silver, opens it, and peers into the two halves.

"Can't see a thing." He returns the pendant to the handkerchief. "What does it say?

"Sultan Abdulaziz's tughra is on one side and a design or an ideogram of some kind is on the other."

"Interesting. Any idea what it all means?"

"No, sir. Do you recognize these?"

"What? No. What do I know about ladies' jewelry? I'll tell you who will know. My daughter. Not much for jewelry herself. Like her mother that way." The ambassador stops for a moment, his face still except for the nervous fluttering of his eyelids. "Just like her mother."

Kamil is embarrassed. One never speaks openly to a stranger of one's family. It is almost as if the ambassador has pulled his wife into the room naked.

"She's all that's left to me now." The ambassador shakes his head slowly, his hand toying absently with the pendant.

Kamil searches for the correct words of condolence, but English is so frustratingly devoid of formulaic responses. In Turkish, he would know exactly what to say. In Persian. In Arabic. What does it say about the Franks, that the language for every important event in life has to be invented anew each time?

"I'm terribly sorry, Mr. Ambassador." It seems a feather-light phrase to Kamil. The Turkish formula, "Health to your head," seems more caring and immediate, but he isn't sure how to translate it.

The ambassador waves his fingers in Kamil's direction, then reaches for the brocade bellpull on the wall behind his chair. A moment later, the butler steps in. Kamil wonders whether he has been listening at the door.

"Sir?"

"Please ask Miss Sybil to join us."

SOME MINUTES LATER, with the sound of silk rubbing against silk, a plump young woman enters and stands by the door. She is wearing a lace-edged indigo gown. A single teardrop pearl, suspended on a gold chain, rests at the base of her throat, matching the pearls at her ears. Her light brown hair is caught in a halo around her head. Her face is round, with small features, a plain face given grace by a dreaminess that animates her mouth and wide-set violet eyes. She reminds Kamil of the sturdy but perfectly proportioned *Gymnadenia* orchid common in forests around the city. Its sepals curve downward and with the petals form a shy pink hood that releases an intense perfume.

The young woman's brightness is shaded by sadness, perhaps resignation. She moves with the comfortable efficiency of a treasured servant.

"Yes, Father. You asked for me?"

Kamil stands hurriedly and bows. Her father waves her over.

"Sybil, my dear. This is Magistrate Kamil Pasha. He says someone was found. Well, it's rather awkward. I'll let the magistrate explain." His eyes drift to the papers on his desk.

Sybil turns to Kamil with a questioning look. She reaches only to his shoulder. Her curious violet eyes regard him earnestly.

"Madam." He bows deeply. "Please sit."

She sets herself down primly onto the chair opposite him. The ambassador has begun to read his dispatches.

"What is it that you wish to know?" Her voice is soft but lilting, like water in a stream.

Kamil feels awkward. He is not used to speaking of such things to ladies. He hesitates. What should he say to cushion the effect?

She tilts her head and says encouragingly, "Please, just tell me what the problem is. Who was found?"

"We found a woman, dead." He looks up quickly to see the effect of this on the ambassador's daughter. She is pale but composed. He continues, "We think she may be a foreign subject. I have been given charge of the matter because it is possible that she was murdered. At the moment we are trying to identify her."

"What makes you think she was murdered?"

"She drowned, which, in itself, is not unusual, given the powerful undertow in the Bosphorus. But she was drugged."

"Drugged? With what, may I ask?"

"We believe she ingested belladonna. I think you call it deadly nightshade."

"I see. Belladonna," she muses. "Does that not make one drowsy?"

"Not drowsy, but, in sufficient quantity, paralyzed. In such a state, a person could drown even in a puddle."

"How awful. The poor woman. What else can you tell me about her? What was she wearing?"

"She was found without . . ." Kamil pauses, wondering how to continue.

"Without clothing?" The young woman's face flushes pink.

"She was found in the Bosphorus within hours of her death. It's possible that the currents are responsible for her state, but it's unlikely."

"Why would that be outside the realm of possibility? You said yourself there are powerful currents."

Kamil considers how to put this. "European women's clothing is not easily disarranged."

The ambassador's startled face rises momentarily from his papers.

Sybil's eyes flash with amusement. Then she says softly, "How terribly sad. You say she was young?"

"Yes, in her twenties. Small, slim, blonde hair. Some jewelry was found with her." He reaches for the handkerchief still on the ambassador's desk. "Would you permit me?"

"Yes, I'll look at them." Her skin has gone the color of parchment, revealing a scattering of tiny freckles across the bridge of her nose.

She leans over to take the bundle from Kamil. Her hands are plump, dimpled at the knuckles. Her fingers taper to tiny oval fingernails translucent as seashells. She places the bundle in her lap and unwraps it.

"Poor woman," she murmurs as she strokes each item in turn. She picks up the cross, her face creasing into a frown.

"What is it?" Kamil asks eagerly.

"I've seen this, but I can't remember where. At an evening function of some sort, probably at one of the embassies." She looks up. "Can you tell me anything more about her?"

"Only that her hair was cut rather short and that she had a large mole on her right shoulder."

"Yes, of course!" Her face crumples. "Oh, how simply awful."

Kamil feels a thrill. She knows who it is.

The ambassador looks up at her, then over at Kamil, his face disapproving. He sighs heavily, "I say, Sybil, dear." He remains in his chair, his fingers compulsively smoothing the paper before him.

Kamil stands and walks to her chair.

"Sybil Hanoum." He gently takes the bundle from her hands and replaces it with another clean handkerchief drawn from his pocket. Her slim, tapered fingers twine themselves in the fine linen and she dabs her eyes. Kamil never uses handkerchiefs for their intended purpose, a disgusting Frankish practice, but has found many other uses for a handy square of clean cloth.

"I'm sorry, Kamil Pasha."

Kamil sits again and looks at her expectantly.

"It must be Mary Dixon."

"Who is that, my dear?" the ambassador asks.

"You remember her, don't you, Father? Mary is governess for Sultan Abdulaziz's granddaughter, Perihan."

"Abdulaziz, yes. Neurotic fellow. Committed suicide. Couldn't take it when those reformists deposed him. Pushed him right over the edge. Must be hard when you've been all-powerful for fifteen years, and then, suddenly, nothing. Asked his mother for a pair of scissors to trim his beard. Used them to open his veins instead." He regards the palm of his hand, then turns it over and stares at the back. "Nothing left. Just a suite of rooms in some hand-me-down palace."

He looks up at Kamil, showing a row of crooked yellow teeth. "Been a decade now. 1876, wasn't it? June, I remember. Seemed an odd thing to do on such a warm day. Nice chap, dash it all." He moves the piece of paper before him to the corner of the desk, then looks puzzled, as if he has lost something.

"Didn't go much better for his replacement, eh?" he continues. "That Murad fellow, a tippler, from what I hear. Wasn't sultan long enough for me to meet him. Had a nervous breakdown after only three months. Seems to be an occupational hazard." He whinnies a laugh. "Can't imagine why these reformists keep trying to put him back on the throne. Congenial fellow, I hear. Maybe that's why."

Kamil avoids meeting the blue eyes that are seeking his. Critical as he is of his own government, he feels offended by the ambassador's disrespectful commentary.

He is startled by Sybil's cheerful voice. "Wouldn't you like some tea, Kamil Pasha?"

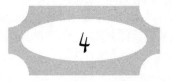

4

June 15, 1886

My Dearest Maitlin,

I hope that this letter finds you well and in good health and spirits. I have received no letters from you for several weeks. Much as I am aware of the vagaries that beset a missive on the long journey between Essex and Stamboul, nevertheless the lack of news from you, dearest sister, has worried me. I hope and pray that you, Richard, and my darling nephews Dickie and Nate are well. I picture you all sitting in the garden over tea and cakes, or sprinting across the lawn in one of those lively and contentious games of badminton we played as children. As always, the indomitable Maitlin wins.

The heat has been oppressive, with not the slightest breeze to relieve us. The hot days have unleashed a series of calamitous events that have kept us all alert. The most grievous is that Mary Dixon has been murdered. Mary was a governess in the imperial household. I'm sure I mentioned her in one of my earlier letters.

She arrived here a year or so ago. I didn't know her well—she kept mostly to herself—but it is still a shock. It appears that she drowned, an awful tragedy, and so like the drowning death of that other governess, Hannah Simmons, eight years ago. Hannah's murderer was never found and the police superintendent's head rolled over it (given that this is the Orient, I need add that I am speaking figuratively).

His replacement is a keenly intelligent man named Kamil Pasha. His father also is a pasha, a kind of lord, who used to be governor of Istanbul. Kamil Pasha isn't a policeman, but a magistrate in the new judicial system the Turks set up a few years ago, inspired by our European model. He trained at Cambridge University, if you can imagine. In any case, I think we are in much better hands this time with regard to finding Mary's murderer. The old superintendent was quite a curmudgeon. He came by to see Mother once after I had arrived. An unpleasant man with a misshapen fez, as if it had been crushed in a fight and he couldn't afford to replace it. By contrast, Kamil Pasha is quite personable.

Poor Mary. Just over a month ago, she joined us for the first garden party of the year. It was a lovely night with one of those full moons that fills the horizon. I remember seeing her in the garden, chatting with the other guests. She was one of those brittle little blondes whose bones seem always about to snap. I gather that some men find that sort of fragility attractive, even though she wore her hair short in a rather shocking and unfeminine style. She was laughing so gaily, it breaks my heart to think of it. I thought at the time that I should sit with her and gently explain the mores of Ottoman society so that she wasn't tempted to transgress them.

Madam Rossini, the Italian ambassador's wasp-tongued wife, came over and informed me quite tartly that Mary and one of the Turkish journalists, Hamza Efendi, appeared to be quarreling, as if I could do anything about it. I told her my impression was that they were simply having a lively conversation, probably about politics. Mary had quite definite opinions and seemed to take great pleasure in being provocative. Is it not remarkable that anger and joy should be so alike as to be indistinguishable? Whichever it was, I would have recommended moderation. At least then one knows what is what. But that advice is too late for poor Mary. I am not, of course, suggesting that she provoked her own murder, my dear. Only that she was of immoderate temperament.

Cousin Bernie sends fond greetings. I'm so happy to have had his company these few months, though I selfishly wish for more. He comes often to dine with us and his witty conversation is a blessing, as it draws father out. But with the exception of the opera, I rarely can persuade Bernie to accompany me anywhere. He spends all his time researching his new book on Ottoman relations with the Far East. Pera is a hive of social activity and it would be nice to have an escort, but it seems I will have to content myself with Madam Rossini and her brood. In any case, Bernie said to let you and Richard know that, despite some setbacks, he is pushing ahead with his project and hopes to have it done before the year is out.

Has your work at the clinic found more acceptance among the doctors, now that you have demonstrated your skill during the last epidemic? I suppose their reluctance to give you more challenging cases can be attributed as much to their suspicion of the French, in whose hospitals you trained, as to their conviction that our sex has limited talents. Still, my dear, you must persevere. Doctoring has always been your goal, and you have suffered much to attain the skills, even if denied the formal acknowledgement of a title. You must set an example so that other women see it can be done. I do so admire you. Would that my talents and courage were a fraction of yours.

I do what is within with my humble abilities to help Father. When I think what a child I was when I came to Stamboul! You should know that Father has requested again that his duty here be extended. He expresses absolutely no interest in going home to England. He is to be ambassador for at least another year. I admit to being saddened that neither he nor I have had the opportunity to get to know Dickie and Nate. By the time we return, they'll be grown men! But I see no alternative. I must remain by his side until he is strong enough to return. At the moment, he rarely leaves his library except to attend to his official duties. When these include traveling to another part of the empire, he becomes particularly anxious, driving the servants mad by having them check and recheck his baggage and papers. So you see, he is still unwell. I take it as an indication of the depth of his love for Mother that he has taken her death so badly for so long. Here, at least, his duties keep his mind occupied, for there is much going on that requires the attention of the British ambassador.

Sultan Abdulhamid has taken offense at our government's steadying hand on the reins of his rebellious Egyptian province. He calls it an occupation and, out of spite, has invited German advisors to his court, thinking to push us out, as if that were possible. The Ottomans need British support. If we hadn't stepped in after they lost their war with Russia eight years ago and insisted that the San Stefano peace treaty be renegotiated, the sultan would have lost a great deal more to the Russians than a few dusty Anatolian provinces. Father has been trying to convince them for years that we have only their best interests at heart. We want the Ottoman Empire intact as a buffer against Russia, always fattening on its neighbors. You remember that Queen Victoria even sent bandages to the Turkish troops when they were fighting the Russians. What more proof of friendship can the sultan need?

Bernie's presence here has brought back memories of those lovely summers together in England, when Uncle Albert and Aunt Grace brought him to meet his British cousins. Remembering again the sights and sounds of those summers brings me closer to you as well, my dear sister. Pray keep well and give my love and all the good wishes in the world to your husband and my precious nephews. My congratulations to Richard on his promotion at the Ministry.

I shall end here. The Judas trees are in bloom outside my window in Pera. The Bosphorus glitters like the scales of a sleeping dragon. As you can see, the quiet summer has given way to great, if distressing, excitement. Our paths in life are so complex, dearest Maitlin, and cross at so many unexpected intersections. Who would have expected, when we were children playing catch-me on the lawns, that someday I would be writing to you from what the Ottomans call The Abode of Bliss? Or that Mary should find her end here? Perhaps the Orientals are right when they point out, as they continually do, that we are all in the hands of a fate written on our foreheads before we are born.

I wish you, dear sister, and your family, which is my family, a straight path through life to your own abodes of bliss.

> Your loving sister,
> Sybil

5

The Sea Hamam

ichel stands inside the door to Kamil's office, his feet slightly apart, hands loose at his sides, as if ready to take on an opposing wrestler. Kamil looks up and lays aside the file he has been frowning over. He waves Michel over to a comfortable chair.

"Two herbalists in the Egyptian Spice Bazaar sell dried tube flowers," he reports, hunched forward in the chair, arms on his knees. "It's not belladonna, but a related plant, *Datura stramonium*. The symptoms are almost the same. There's quite a lively trade in tube flowers, unfortunately." Michel grimaces. "In the past month, at least four people bought them, three women and an old man. There are other sources. It's fairly common. It even grows wild outside the city walls."

Kamil sits behind his desk, its dark, polished mahogany visible in neat avenues between stacks of letters and files. He drums his fingers on the wood.

"I had them track down two of the women," Michel continues. "Both are midwives who use the herbs to cure bronchial troubles. The man too had a cough."

"So this leads us nowhere."

"There's more. One of the midwives bought a large quantity. She sold them to several households around Chamyeri the week before the murder."

"Anyone suspicious?"

Michel frowns. "Unfortunately not. The men checked every household and asked the neighbors. They verified that someone in each of the homes had been ill that week. That doesn't mean someone couldn't have taken some of the herb and used it for another purpose, but it seems unlikely. These are common village families. What contact would they have had with a British woman?"

"How was it administered?"

"We have to assume she drank it. The only other way to ingest the dried flowers is to smoke them, but that has only a mild effect and doesn't dilate the eyes. The seeds are poisonous, but there was no sign that she died of something else before falling into the water. Perhaps it was given to her in a glass of tea. Too bad we couldn't take a look at her stomach fluids," he mutters.

"Where would such a woman drink tea? And with whom?"

"Not in a village. They wouldn't even be able to communicate."

"Chamyeri again. Both women were English governesses." Kamil draws his fingertip along the edge of sunlight on his desk. "I wonder if anyone in Ismail Hodja's family speaks English." He looks up. "What about his niece?"

"Jaanan Hanoum?"

"She must have been there when Hannah Simmons's body was found. She was a child then, of course." Kamil's lips tighten. "It must have been difficult for her. The young woman has had a rough time of it." He shakes his head sympathetically.

Michel ignores Kamil's evaluation. "Probably educated by tutors at home, like all women of that class. She had a French governess, but it's possible she also learned English. Her father is one of those modernist social climbers."

"He's an official at the Foreign Ministry, I believe."

"Yes."

"But she lives with her uncle at Chamyeri, rather than at her father's house."

"Her mother went to live with her brother, the hodja, when her husband took a kuma. A modernist," Michel adds sourly, "and a hypocrite. The more things change, the more they stay the same."

"The man is insane. Two wives." Kamil shakes his head in disbelief. "He might as well hurl himself in front of a tram."

They share an uneasy burst of laughter.

"When Jaanan Hanoum came of age, she moved back to the city, to her father's house. It's pretty isolated up there, no place for a girl looking to be married. But since her troubles this past year, she's been staying at Chamyeri again."

"Istanbul society can be unforgiving. Poor girl. I wonder how she's doing."

"She's gone. I asked around the village yesterday. They said that three days ago Jaanan Hanoum's maid had an accident. She slipped and fell into that pond behind the house, and almost drowned."

"Women should learn to swim," Kamil snaps irritably. "Just last week I heard of two seventeen-year-old girls that drowned in a shallow stream. One fell in and the other tried to save her. They panicked and pulled each other under. It's absurd that women are kept ignorant of even the most basic survival skills."

"Jaanan Hanoum pulled the maid out," Michel continues, "but she lost her sight. She must have hit her head on a rock. Jaanan Hanoum is on her way to relatives in Paris, left early yesterday morning. Planning to study, apparently."

Kamil thinks about this, flipping his beads around his hand. "I wonder if either of them knew Mary Dixon."

"Coincidence?" suggests Michel.

"I have no faith in coincidences," Kamil mutters.

"If they heard the news in Chamyeri about the Englishwoman's death, maybe it was just one tragedy too many for the young woman."

"Maybe. But I still would have liked to speak with her. Who is left up there at Chamyeri now?"

"Just her uncle Ismail Hodja, his chauffeur, the gardener, and some daily staff."

"I can't imagine any of them having tea with an English governess, much less drugging and killing her." Kamil shakes his head. "What else is near Chamyeri?"

Michel stands and paces the room, thinking. The folds of his robe tangle his muscular legs like tethers on a horse. He stops suddenly.

"I wonder."

"What?"

"The sea hamam. It's below Emirgan, just north of Chamyeri."

"Ah, yes, I've heard of it," Kamil muses. "It's built on a jetty over the water so people can swim in private."

"More like wading in a cage rather than swimming. The Emirgan one is for women."

"I misjudged our women's progressiveness. What made you think of the sea hamam, of all things?"

"It's a perfect place to meet if you want complete privacy. It's closed at night, but it wouldn't be hard to get in. In fact, it probably hasn't been used since last year. It usually doesn't open until midsummer. Other than a few villas and fishing settlements, there aren't a lot of other possibilities. No one in the villas claims to remember an Englishwoman."

Michel opens the door to the judicial antechamber, letting in a din of voices. He and Kamil push through the tide of plaintiffs, petitioners, clerks, and their assistants and emerge from the squat stone courthouse onto the busy Grande Rue de Pera. A horse-drawn tram clangs along the boulevard, carrying matrons from the new northern suburbs into town for shopping. As they wait for their driver to bring the carriage, Kamil surveys the early morning bustle of Istanbul's most modern quarter. Apprentices balance nested copper tins of hot food and trays of steaming tea, hurrying toward customers waiting in shops and hotels. Carts rattle as vendors pull their wares along the cobbled street. Advertisements for their services, or for mulberries, green plums, carpets, or scrap metal, issue from practiced throats. Shop windows display the latest products.

This tumult, Kamil knows, is surrounded by the tranquillity of old Constantinople, the name many residents still use for their city, its Byzantine roots as capital of the eastern Roman Empire still everywhere in evidence. At one end of Pera is a pleasant cemetery beneath a vast canopy of cypresses where people stroll and picnic on the raised tombs. Embassies set in lush gardens line the boulevard. To the west, Pera overlooks the waters of the Golden Horn, which takes its name from the reflected fires of the setting sun. To the east, the land falls off precipitously to reveal the Bosphorus and the wide triangle of water where the strait and inlet merge to push into the Sea of Marmara. Cascading down the hillsides are canyons of stone apartment buildings and old wooden houses strung together by alleys meandering around the remains of Byzantine and Genoese walls, towers, and archways. Where the inclines are too steep, roads become wide stairways.

Kamil and Michel head north in an open phaeton, bundled against the wind. It is a long, dusty trip winding through the hills above the Bosphorus, but their driver knows the road well and keeps a steady pace. Kamil's eyes graze the edge of the forest as they pass, alert for telltale colors and shapes of flowering plants, challenging himself to remember their botanical names. His fingers worry the warm amber in his pocket.

If he fails to solve this case, he will have the unpleasant task of reporting his failure to Minister of Justice Nizam Pasha. On the first Thursday of every month, Kamil must stand, hands folded before him, eyes lowered, in the drafty reception hall and wait for permission to speak. Nizam Pasha, seated cross-legged on a raised divan, listens in grim silence, regarding him with flat, unreadable eyes. When Kamil has finished, Nizam Pasha whispers to his subordinate, then dismisses Kamil with a careless wave of his fingers and a moue of the mouth, as if he has tasted something foul.

Only once has the minister spoken directly to Kamil, this during his first audience.

"Do not presume here on the cloak of your ancestors. You are naked in the sight of the padishah. Do not disappoint him."

Nizam Pasha reports directly to the sultan, but his is only one vein among many pumping information into the heart of the empire. The secret police are the insomniac sultan's eyes, watching, suspicious, invisible to all but a few in the palace. They spy on the police and the judges, as they do on all the other servants of the state.

Kamil reflects that his position as pasha and son of a pasha affords little protection from the secret police, who will punish not only those who displease them, but their entire families. The images of his unhappy but determined sister Feride and her young daughters flashes though his mind. And his silent father, captive to an inner world populated only by his dead wife. Kamil knows he must steer a delicate path between politically astute silence and the demands posed by proper judicial procedure and scientific investigation. This was never more important than in these uncertain days.

While the sultan wraps himself ever more closely in the cloak of religion by catering to the powerful sheikhs and leaders of Islamic brotherhoods, it is rumored that even among the sultan's inner circle there are those who would like to see a representative government and an Islam compatible with modern notions of progress and reason. These are the men who pushed through the new legal system that has effectively taken away the power of religiously trained kadi judges and given it to magistrates, young men like Kamil with secular training and a preference for science and logic. In the new courts, magistrates argue cases before a state judge and supervise investigations. The formerly all-powerful kadis are restricted to handling local divorces and inheritance disputes, although a kadi still has a place on the bench in the Majlis-i Tahkikat, the Court of Inquiry, the highest court in the province of Istanbul. It is not surprising, Kamil thinks, that men like Nizam Pasha, whose education has been in religious medreses and who speak no European languages, should feel threatened by the magistrates under their jurisdiction.

He glances fondly at his companion in the phaeton. Michel has been his ally in puzzling through the logical complexities of many cases. His mood lifts as he remembers the pleasant hours spent listening to Ladino songs and Italian cantos in tiny clubs hidden in the alleys of Galata, Michel as his guide to the richly textured but insular world of the Jewish community. Jews and Christians had been the merchants, bankers, surgeons, and artists, the beating international heart of the empire for hundreds of years. Their presence here predates that of the Ottomans. Jewish migrants and refugees not only were gladly sheltered, but sought after by the sultans, who valued their education and acumen. The Sephardic Jews expelled in 1492 by Queen Isabella and King Ferdinand of Spain were invited by Sultan Bayezid II to settle in the empire under his protection, with the following comment: "How can one call this king wise and sensible, when he beggars his own country and enriches mine?" Their descendants in Istanbul, like Michel, still speak Ladino, the Spanish of the expulsion.

On their free afternoons, Kamil and Michel meet in the café where they had become reacquainted, discussing the latest medical advances and scientific techniques in the books and journals with which the book dealers in the courtyard behind the Grand Bazaar keep them well supplied. Sadly, the young surgeon does not share his interest in botany, but is more interested in the volatile properties of plants, the secrets they are forced to release under duress.

After a while, Kamil leans his head against the padded leather headrest and allows himself to drift. He finds himself dwelling on a memory of Sybil lifting the bundle of the dead woman's jewelry from her lap. Her hands were plump and dimpled as a baby's. The tender feeling evoked by the memory surprises him. Then he realizes, they are his mother's hands.

AMID A RACKET of gulls, they make their way along the creaking jetty to the small square structure at its end. The Bosphorus here has thrown up a long scallop of rough brown sand and rocks. The sea hamam is built on stilts over shallow water, reached by a long pier. Its bleached boards are bearded with sea moss. The door is latched but not locked. There would be nothing inside to protect. Kamil opens the door and enters a windowless room. There is a musty smell of swollen wood and unwashed laundry. The Bosphorus has no odor. It is too swift. It tears the briny air with it like a flag in a gale. But there is a sense of the sea inside the dark room, a feeling of motion, as if the room is tilting.

Kamil stops a moment to let his eyes adjust, then looks around. The entryway is blind, designed so that no one standing outside can see into the inner quarters. There is a rack for shoes, empty now. He moves to the door at the end of the hidden leg of the room. He does not hear Michel enter behind him, but knows he is there. This door leads to a platform around a square expanse of water. The sea sucks noisily at the flimsy pillars that hold the structure above the level of the water.

He clicks his tongue in disapproval. "I doubt this will be standing by midsummer."

"They'll repair it before they open. They can't afford to have naked society ladies swept away by the current."

Ringing the platform are wooden cubicles with low wide shelves that, in season, would be cushioned so that bathers could lounge on them and drink tea. Each cubicle is faced with a slatted double door that can be closed for privacy or flung open so that the occupant can face the captured sea and chat with other bathers.

They begin methodically to search each cubicle, Kamil moving clockwise and Michel counterclockwise around the hamam.

"There's a mattress here," Michel calls. Kamil comes over to look. It is an expensive one, stuffed with wool and covered in flowered cotton. On a high shelf, he finds two tea glasses, of cheap quality but showy, decorated with crudely painted gold flowers. Michel gets his leather bag.

"What do you have in there?"

"Things we might need." He pulls out a squirming sack and extracts a black and white kitten. "A quick test. I dilute any residue, then put a drop of the liquid in his eyes; if they dilate, we know we have datura." He pushes the kitten back into the sack and cinches it.

Kamil is amused by the surgeon's innovation. He hands the glasses to Michel, who examines them thoroughly.

"Too bad," a disappointed Michel comments. "No residue."

Kamil is looking over the lip of the bathing platform.

"This isn't very deep. I wonder if there's anything down there."

"If I wanted to get rid of something quickly, what better way than to drop it into the water? The current would take it away."

Kamil lies on his stomach and looks under the floorboards.

"Yes, but look."

Michel kneels and looks under the floor as well. Backsplash wets their faces. A fishing net, attached to the bottom of the hamam, extends around the entire perimeter.

"I suppose that's to keep undesirable creatures—human and otherwise—out of the pool," comments Michel, grinning. "Let's see what we've caught."

Michel strips to his undergarments and lowers himself into the chilly water. He seems not to notice the cold, but goes about his work slowly and methodically, his powerful legs cutting effortlessly through the chest-high water. He ducks under the floor and pulls the net toward the center, then hands it to Kamil squatting on the platform above. Slowly, hand over hand as he saw the fishermen do in his youth, Kamil hauls it in. Michel pulls it up from below so that nothing is lost. When the entire sodden net has been dragged onto the wooden floor, Michel climbs out of the water and dons his clothing. The two men untangle the net and check their catch. Before long, Kamil points to a white gleam amid the slippery brown sea grass, pieces of clothing, and other debris. It is a teapot.

Its lid is missing but the contents are still inside. Michel reaches in and extracts a wad of faded yellow-green matter, bloated and slimy from long immersion in the water. The shape is no longer recognizable, but it is not the short black bristles of ordinary tea. Michel folds the leaves into a piece of oiled cloth.

They place several other items from their catch into a small bag: a broken tortoise-shell comb, a small copper-backed mirror, a woman's slipper—items owned by a thousand women. Kamil examines a small knife, its horn handle swollen and separated into layers, but its blade clean of rust and still sharp.

"Odd thing to find in a woman's bathhouse." He wraps it up and places it in the bag. "Let's look outside."

Stooped low, hands clasped behind his back, Kamil paces the rocky sand surrounding the structure. He stops for a moment to listen, sniffs the air, then strides over and pulls aside the low-growing branches of a pine tree. He averts his face to avoid an explosion of flies and calls Michel over. At his feet is the carcass of a dog.

THE FOLLOWING DAY, Kamil watches as Michel cuts up the tea leaves, soaks them in alcohol mixed with sulfuric acid, and heats the mixture slowly.

"This will take a while. It has to heat for half an hour, then cool." Michel sits at a desk in the cluttered room that serves as his laboratory and office in the Police Directorate, a large stone building on a side street off the Grande Rue de Pera. Tethered by a string to the base of a cabinet, the kitten is lapping at a saucer of milk.

"Call me when you're done." Kamil returns to a divan in the

entrance hall and props a writing desk on his lap. He extracts from his coat a file on the case he is prosecuting the following morning, a Greek man accused of stabbing his wife's brother to death when he tried to intervene in a family argument about property. The other family members refuse to testify, but several neighbors heard the altercation.

Murder is always about property, thinks Kamil, not passion in the way poets define it. Passion about something or someone simply means demanding ownership or at least control. Parents want to own their children, husbands their wives, employers their apprentices, supplicants their God. The most passionate of all destroy what they own, thereby making it forever theirs. Much of the world, from politics to commerce, is driven by fear of losing control over people, land, things. Fear that fate is stronger than will. Kamil places his trust in will.

What do I fear? he muses. Is there anything I love so passionately that I would kill to retain it? He can think of nothing and this makes him sad. A memory stirs in him of the moment he found the rare black orchid now in his greenhouse, of breathing its perfume for the first time. This evokes an image of Sybil's violet eyes. He feels his senses, the surface of his skin, expand to an almost painful brilliance; his breath quickens. He smiles and thinks, I am not as desiccated as all that. As if passion were a virtue.

A young clerk bows, startling him. "The Doctor Efendi is waiting for you." Abashed, Kamil hides his face from the young man before him, busying himself by gathering his writing utensils and placing them in a narrow box that he slips into his sash. By the time the clerk leaves him at the door of Michel's office, Kamil has pushed all thoughts of Sybil from his mind and his body is once again the clean-swept temple of will and reason.

Michel has already strained the mash of leaves and is passing the liquid through a moistened filter. He transfers the strained liquid to a test tube and adds ether, then shakes and strains it again. He then adds potash and chloroform, which cause the liquid to separate. The room reeks of chemicals, but neither man notices. Michel pours the remaining liquid onto a watch glass and waits for the chloroform to evaporate. He scrapes the residue into a test tube and dilutes it with water and a drop of sulfuric acid.

"Now we can examine it."

He takes a drop of this solution and places it on a glass. He stirs in a drop of bromine and waits. The liquid doesn't change color.

"There should be a precipitate," Michel mutters.

He tries various other reagents, but the liquid does not crystallize. The workbench is littered with watch glasses and test tubes. He turns to the sodden mass of cut-up leaves.

"This is not datura. Sorry. An unusual type of leaf, a tea of some kind, but not tube flower."

Kamil sighs. "Too bad." As he turns toward the door, he pauses. The saucer lies overturned on the floor near a white slick of milk. He bends his knees to look under the chair. The kitten is gone.

"What happened to your cat?" he asks.

Michel turns suddenly and looks at the saucer. At that moment, before Michel can compose his face and offer a bland reply, Kamil sees in it a mixture of guilt and fear.

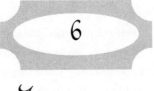

June 18, 1886

Dearest Maitlin,

I am unsure how much news reaches you in Essex. As if the murder of Mary Dixon were not enough, there has been a wave of arrests. Sultan Abdulhamid has taken it into his head that the group calling itself the Young Ottomans is plotting against him, with the help of foreign powers, and has decided to stamp it out. They have been publishing literary magazines in which they write about ideas like liberty and democracy that, understandably, cause some anxiety at the palace. For the most part, they are French-educated Ottomans from good families. Not a few are translators in the Foreign Ministry at the Sublime Porte, where they have access to foreign publications. This makes them even more dangerous, of course, as they are situated within the administration itself. I find their company most stimulating and have invited several to soirees at the Residence. The conversations on those evenings are so lively and interesting that even Father relaxes, even though, given the disfavor in which many of these young men are held by the sultan, our invitations might be taken amiss. Nevertheless, for Father's sake, I would gladly brave palace disapproval. It is one of the few activities that he seems truly to enjoy.

It seems to me that the sultan has less to fear from these bright young men, most of whom simply wish to keep the sultan to his promise to revive the constitution and reopen the short-lived parliament he shut down seven years ago, than from those who have twice attempted a coup intending to replace him with his elder brother Murad. Murad is first in line of succession, but was replaced after only a few months as sultan due to a nervous condition. The radicals think Murad is now cured and more receptive to a constitutional government—or perhaps simply more tractable. In any case, Sultan Abdulhamid has decreed a hunt on all equally, loyal and disloyal. He shifts members of his staff continually and reportedly trusts no one. Several of our regular dinner guests were recently sent into exile. I find it frightening to think of the consequences.

To make matters worse, the city is full of refugees. Now that some of the Ottoman provinces in the Balkans have become autonomous, terrible reports have reached our ears of Muslims killed by Christian neighbors in revenge for the sultan's brutal repression of their earlier rebellions. They are all fleeing to Istanbul, the center of the Muslim world, where they believe themselves to be safe. The streets are a Babel of languages and colorful regional dress, even more so than usual.

There have been more riots in the streets of Stamboul—not to worry, my dear, not in Pera—about the banned parliament, although food shortages and high prices contribute to the instability. We are safely fortified here amid the other foreign residences. I suppose it is not surprising that the sultan has tightened his grip on the reins, although it is hard to imagine what might topple a sultanate that has reigned for half a millennium. Pax Brittanica surely would benefit the people here, as it has done the peoples of India and Asia. Father tells me that this is a possibility. I dearly hope so, for the sake of peace. At any rate, the sultan is no enemy of Europe. I've heard he is a devotee of theater and opera and of detective stories and police thrillers, if you can imagine. I'm told his chief of wardrobe sits behind a screen and reads to him every night, sometimes an entire book, as he is an insomniac. He is particularly fond of detective mysteries and has new books immediately translated and read to him. He also engages in wood carving and cabinetmaking, rather unusual hobbies for a regent. I can't help but think that a man who loves to read and who crafts his own furniture will bring progress and discipline to his empire. Mother thought him quite charming, but he rarely receives visitors anymore simply for the pleasure of it, so I shan't have a chance of making up my own mind.

As for my own entertainment, you needn't worry, dear sister. There is much to do here. Thursday evening, I am going to the theater with Madam Rossini and her family to see a new French play, and a few weeks hence the Italians are holding their annual saint's day fair in the garden of their Residence. There is a charity ball soon at one of the new hotels. Tonight, in fact, we're having a ball here at the Residence. There's no shortage of entertainment in Stamboul. You needn't worry that I have withered on the vine. And I have Father. His work keeps him occupied, but I share in this, to his great satisfaction, I believe. I must run now and consult with the chefs and the musicians.

Be well and give my love to all our family. Perhaps I can convince you yet to come on a visit. You will be well surprised at our comforts and the color and excitement of living in the Orient.

Affectionately,
Sybil

7

Your Rolling Pearl

I never did learn to ride the water like Violet. Our pond was a different kind of classroom than the sea. Eventually I learned to move freely in this different medium. Tired of the confines of the pond, Violet wanted to swim in the Bosphorus. I told her about the boys who had not reemerged. She wanted to ask Halil about the currents, but I was anxious about questioning him. I had the sense that he knew about our swims at the pond and disapproved, but his loyalty to me, I think, kept him from reporting our indiscretions to my mother. After all, Violet, as my servant, was responsible for looking after me. But I doubt he would have kept a dip in the Bosphorus from my mother, since, apart from the danger, it was likely we would be seen and bring disgrace on the family.

Violet stamped her foot. "Well, I'll go to the village, then, and ask the fishermen. You're afraid," she taunted me.

I was scandalized. A young woman did not venture outside the home except to go, accompanied, along a circumspect route to the home of a relative or female friend. She wore a feradje and covered her face. Under no circumstances would she speak with a male stranger. That had been my life up till then, and I had no reason to believe anyone else's life was any different.

I accompanied my mother on her visits to Istanbuli women of our standing during their weekly at-home days. During the hot months, the women, children, and their entourages moved from the city to their summer houses along the forested northern banks of the Bosphorus, where it was cooler. This proximity made visiting easier and my mother seemed to regain her spirit during those short months. But for me, summer meant perching on cushioned divans in cool, tiled harem sitting rooms and shady courtyards, sipping black tea from gold-rimmed glasses and listening politely to the women discuss the coming and going of relations and debate the qualities of prospective grooms and brides for their children. They dissected upcoming marriages, the amount of bride wealth paid by the grooms' families, and the dowries the brides would bring with them. Colorful silk thread slipped through the delicate fingers of the younger girls as they negotiated the tight choreography of embroidering their trousseaux. In those years, I paid little attention to the conversations, but instead lay on the divan, elbow propped on my cushion, examining the details of other people's rooms, letting the timbre of their voices draw across me like a musical instrument in reverse.

The women wore white chemises of the softest silk, their breasts braced in low brocaded vests. Over this, they wore flowered or striped silk robes in all the colors of the garden and the jewel box: apple green, cherry red, heliotrope, peacock blue, the yellow of songbirds, pink, ruby and garnet, eau de nil. The robe was wrapped about with a silk girdle, and a bright, contrasting tunic with long, slit sleeves and trailing, divided skirts. Their hair was plaited into many braids, entwined with ropes of pearls and strings of jewels, or twisted up in colorful scarves dripping with embroidery and beaded fringes that framed their faces and swayed softly against their cheeks when they moved. They looked gay, like the colorful parrots and sweet-singing canaries some kept in fanciful cages in their courtyards. Their chirp-ing lulled me into the languorous restfulness when nothing is expected of you and everything is given. The short bliss of childhood.

In ensuing years, the mesh of information and conjecture became tighter and caught up young girls like myself, ladies in training who were expected to be of serious mien, although pleasant and polite. Giggly girls who ran about and smiled too easily were spoiled and inevitably would come to a bad end. I tried my best not to smile out of place or too often, and I believe I succeeded all too well, given my increasing boredom at such functions.

My secluded life at Chamyeri gave me no practice in the skill of light conversation. I knew next to nothing about our family, except what news my cousin and tutor, Hamza, brought when he visited, and what Violet, who had her own mysterious sources, shared with me, much of which was unrepeatable. Nor did I know the stories of other prominent families and the characters peopling them. Our secluded lifestyle left me ignorant of changes in fashion. Mama and I were always at least a season behind. Once a year, in the fall, Mama sent for a Greek woman from Istanbul who came to the villa with samples of cloth and took orders for new clothing. But by the following sum-mer, these were again outdated.

The fact that our household did not include live-in servants caused great consternation among the other women. Every house-hold had to have servants, they chided my mother. It was a necessary sign of social stature, the more the better. Some middle-class homes had dozens of slaves and servants, society households many more. It was a duty to support as many poorer people as possible, a pious act that brings sevap, Allah's reward. Besides, they asked my mother, how did she manage at night? It was unimaginable that she would make her own tea and undress herself. They would look at me and say to my mother, "A young girl needs to know how to run a household." I never knew how Mama felt about the lack of servants. Papa's house at Nishantashou had many servants, but Mama never complained about Ismail Dayi's odd aversion to them. After Violet came, she helped Mama and me in the evenings after the servants had left. For my part, I did not even know how to make tea.

I did, however, know quite a bit about literature and international politics, thanks to afternoons under my cousin Hamza's tutelage, and about Islamic jurisprudence and Persian poetry learned on long winter evenings in Ismail Dayi's study. I could recite the Quran and, moreover, knew enough Arabic to understand it. I also knew the tides of the Bosphorus and how to move through water. I did not know fine needlework or how to embroider linens and prayer mats for my trousseau. I did not know how people died, but I was to learn that soon enough.

I much preferred spring with its blossoming cherry trees and chilly squalls of rain and the marmalade colors of autumn when the summer houses stood empty, and I began again my love affair with water. A year older, Violet knew more of the world, and I was her willing pupil. On warm days, she spread a carpet along the mossy edge of the pond. When we tired of swimming, we stretched out in our shifts and unpacked the basket she brought along. With her knife she disrobed red peaches flush as babies' cheeks. When their juices flowed across my wrists, Violet bent over and licked them clean. She wedged open black mussels and taught me to suck their brine and take the pearl of flesh between my teeth. In the season of artichokes, we took turns plucking the leathery outer leaves one by one. Then, with her sharp knife, she cut the inner leaves down to the heart, exposing the fur, which she scraped until the choke was smooth and bare. She handed me a lemon and a twist of salt to rub into the flesh of the chokes. It stung my hands, but I did as she asked. With her thin fingers, she took the chokes from my slippery palms and immersed them in water infused with lemon, heating it slowly to a boil on a portable charcoal stove. When it was done, she fed me morsels of the delicate, fragrant flesh.

Violet did not accompany us on the summer trips; she was not of our class and would have had to stay in the servant quarters, something my mother found unacceptable, since she was, after all, a blood relative. I envied Violet the privacy of our house in summer. I imagined her slipping through the black pond like an eel, while I rested, a stone in a kaleidoscope, in the colorful rooms of the summer families. Violet, I was sure, delighted in her freedom and gave no thought to me, confined in a gilded cage like the nervous songbirds. My boredom was tinged with jealousy.

Until Violet, I had no real friends except Hamza, who accompanied my father during his weekly visits. When my father stopped coming to Chamyeri as often, Hamza still rode up from Nishantashou regularly and brought me books. He would tutor me in the garden pavilion, going over my lessons for the week, then sit for a while with my mother. He spent the night in the men's reception room, and left after breakfast the following day. As a child, I moved freely through the house and crept at night under Hamza's quilt for an hour or so. Holding me in the crook of his arm, he read to me from books he had hidden in his satchel, colorful tales of Frankish fairies and Arab djinns, French love poems and fantastic stories quite different from the earnest literature we read and discussed by day. When his eyes began to close, he put his hand below my chin and turned my face to him. He kissed my forehead and whispered, in French,

"Who is your prince?"

"You are, dear Hamza."

"Am I your only prince?"

"Of course, my only one."

"Forever?"

"Forever."

His breath was hot on my ear.

"Sleep now, princess. Dream of your prince."

It was our secret signal that I should return to my room. I disentangled myself from his arms regretfully. He did not tell me to walk softly and make certain no one saw. Somehow I knew that this cherished ritual would vanish if exposed to the gaze of others.

My uncle was my other tutor. On evenings when he did not have company, Ismail Dayi was happy to discuss what I had read and guide me to other readings he considered appropriate for my age. During the cold months, dressed in quilted robes, we put cushions on the thick wool carpet and tucked our legs under an enormous cotton-filled comforter that had been stretched over a box-like brazier to trap the heat. My eccentric dayi had no sense, of course, of what was considered appropriate for a girl, so he trained me as he would a young apprentice, a relationship both familiar and comfortable to him. Snug under our comforter, we sat opposite each other, read Ottoman jurisprudence, and took turns reciting mystical poetry.

> *One who sees my aimless turning might take me for the*
> *desert whirlwind*
> *I am nothing within nothing, if I have any being, it comes*
> *from you.*

> *While I was your rolling pearl, why did you let me go astray?*
> *If my dust is on the mirror of life, it comes from you.*

"Look to your own heart for knowledge of the divine," my dayi instructed me, "not the interpretations of scribes and clerics. Nature is a sage; hear it with your heart. Be humble in your knowledge, but glorify Allah with what you have learned. Sheykh Galib was educated at home, like you, and was composing poetry when he was little older than you are now. Nothing in life is aimless or out of place. All is inspired."

Ismail Dayi urged Mama to join us, but she preferred to stay in her rooms, wrapped in the ermine robe Papa had given her the first winter of their marriage. She had developed a taste for reading French novels and, although he disapproved of what he said was the frivolity and dangerous foreign pollution of novels in general (and French novels in particular), Ismail Dayi kept Mama supplied with them from the booksellers in the city. A steady stream of apprentices brought him parcels of new books. Indeed, I saw scattered about the library a great number of books and journals in French and other languages I did not recognize. Those I could read tended to be difficult treatises that I attempted but soon laid back on the shelf.

Some evenings, I did not find Ismail Dayi, though I had heard the carriage arrive and the groom Jemal sing a soulful folk song as he walked the horses past the kitchen door toward the orchard. Jemal was slender and boyish, but very strong. Unlike most men, he did not have a mustache, although he wore a felt cap and the long, baggy shalwar pants of country men. He loved pomegranates. When they were in season, he would keep one of the leathery red orbs in his hand for hours, carrying it about with him and kneading it with his fingers. One late summer day, I was watching the silver-bristled kangal dogs that slouched around his yard. I was afraid of these large dogs, so I crouched behind the jacaranda bush. Jemal was sitting on a chair just outside his blue-painted front door, sleeves rolled above his elbows, concentrating his full attention on the pomegranate he was rotating rhythmically in the palm of his right hand. His back was tense and the muscle in his arm rippled. Suddenly he stopped and, raising the fruit to his nose, sniffed it, then stroked it gently across his cheek. He put the red skin to his mouth and slowly nipped it with his teeth. Examining the opening he had made, he raised the pomegranate to his mouth and sucked at the opening until all that remained was a leathery sack. Afterwards he sat, staring into space, his face flushed, his lips slightly pursed. Ruby drops glistened on his chin. The husk lay on the grass at his feet.

Late one night in the lonely period after Madam Élise's departure, I was roaming the house and was startled to see Jemal moving stealthily in leather house socks through the dark kitchen toward the rear door, his outdoor overshoes and turban in his hands. His black hair was long as a girl's. His face had the same expression as when he had finished with the pomegranate.

8

Rules of Engagement

*L*ight floods through the open doors onto the lawn of the British Residence. Orange paper lampions have been strung along the paths. Servants circulate with trays of savories and fruit and bottles of chilled French wine. Kamil is here in search of someone who knew Mary Dixon. He finds this the most difficult part of his work, interacting socially with strangers. As a young man during his father's reign as governor, he had endured long hours of empty pleasantries at endless functions, each word inflicting a dull pain until he had to pull away. From a vantage point in the garden or a quiet room, he would watch as figures met and merged, then withdrew and rejoined others in a complicated board game. He could see patterns in these interactions: the wealthy, the powerful, and the beautiful, and those who vied to be in their presence; respect shown or withheld; the sheep cut from the fold by a predator; the individual of wit or erudition and an admiring but unstable crowd of consumers; too obviously averted glances; the interplay of men and women when the rules of engagement were unclear. It was endlessly fascinating. He still prefers to watch, unless he finds an engaging partner for conversation. Good conversation is becoming rarer, he muses, since the sultan increased the number of his spies and people no longer dare venture opinions on even the most mundane subjects in their own drawing rooms.

Stepping indoors, he sees the ambassador stoop to listen to a dignified man in a uniform with red piping and gold epaulets. Women in low-cut evening dresses stand in groups like bouquets of gaudy, overblown roses. None are veiled. It startles Kamil to see such expanses of gleaming hair and pale skin exposed to view. The orchestra plays a waltz. Women lean backward into men's arms, their opposing forces channeled into a vortex of movement. The women's wide skirts swing like bells, their jewels blaze in the lamplight. Men in dark suits and uniforms, their shadows. Kamil thinks of bright autumn leaves captured by the current.

He wanders back into the garden. Sybil came to him briefly after his arrival, a swirl of skirts and color, to take his hand and welcome him before she was swept away by newer guests. The pressure of her hand remains in his.

A middle-aged man with irregular features and carrot-colored hair corners him against the patio railing.

"So, you're the pasha. Sybil said she had managed to browbeat you into coming to this shindig. It's a rough game, ain't it?" he says, shaking his head and sweeping a hand toward the buzzing crowd. "Nobody wants to talk about the really interesting stuff anymore." He squints his small blue eyes at Kamil. "Glad you could make it, though. I've been looking forward to meeting you. I'm Sybil's cousin, Bernie Wilcott. From the U. S. of A., as I'm sure you've guessed." His breath smells of mint. Serious eyes trapped in a taffy-pull face.

"Kamil. A pleasure to meet you." Kamil extends his hand.

Bernie grasps it and pumps it, once. "Forgot. Sybil told me you learned your English in the Old Country."

"Cambridge University. I studied there for a year. Before that, I learned English here, with tutors. How is it that Sybil Hanoum has an American cousin?"

"Sybil Hanoum? Has a nice ring to it." Bernie chuckles. "Well, her uncle, that's my father, was the younger brother. You know what that means. Eldest takes all, the whole farm. Or, in this case, the manor house. So he did what younger brothers have done since time immemorial, left the kingdom to seek his fortune. Found it in railroads, but his kids inherited a gawd-awful accent." He bends over, chortling at his own wit.

Kamil can't help but laugh along with him.

"You are visiting Istanbul?"

"Well, actually, I'm here for the year. Teaching at Robert College."

"Ah, you're a teacher." Kamil thinks this unlikely, given the man's eccentric nature, but he hasn't met many Americans.

"Bernie Wilcott, itinerant scholar." Bernie bows low and touches his hand to his brow and chest in a mock Ottoman greeting.

Kamil, disbelieving, asks, "What is your area of study?"

"Politics. East Asia, China, but I have a weakness for the Ottomans, and am mighty curious to know more." He takes Kamil's arm and steers him into the garden. "Maybe you could be my guide."

It doesn't take long for Kamil to feel at ease with Bernie and to recognize that what he had perceived as buffoonery was simply a lack of the formality that usually encases people like lacquer. Moving in society, people rub and clack their carapaces against one another like mating beetles. In contrast, Bernie seems immediately available. They sit on a bench, facing away from the crowd and chatting. Kamil is relieved and pleased to find an intelligent observer of the world. The embers of their cigarettes pulse alternately in the dark.

Later that evening, Bernie brings Sybil to the garden. She is breathless and appears tired, but her eyes are bright as they meet Kamil's. Wisps of hair have come loose and are plastered to her forehead.

Kamil lowers his eyes and bows. "Madame Sybil." It is rude to look at someone so directly, especially a woman. Nevertheless, he is smiling.

"I'm so glad you were able to come."

Before long, Bernie excuses himself and disappears into the Residence. Kamil and Sybil sit on the bench facing the garden, their faces in shadow. Kamil is uncomfortably aware of the revealed expanse of neck and the plump mounds of Sybil's breasts pushed upward by her décolleté gown. He imagines he feels the heat of her body radiating into his, even though they are sitting a discreet distance apart. It both pleases and disturbs him. He keeps his eyes focused on the shadowy blooms of a nearby oleander, the tree that the Quran says grows even in hell.

"Your cousin is an interesting man."

"He's always been like that, even as a child. Irrepressible, I think is the word."

"I find him quite refreshing. Is the rest of your family like him?"

"No. He's one of a kind. I do have a sister, though, Maitlin, whom I admire tremendously. She's irrepressible in a different way—she never gives up pursuing what she truly believes in. So she's led quite an adventuresome life." She tells Kamil about Maitlin's travels, and her long and ultimately unsuccessful struggle to become a physician.

"So now she volunteers at a clinic for the poor where they take advantage of her medical skills, but without giving her any formal recognition. She doesn't seem to mind, although I mind for her." Sybil's voice becomes wistful. "Maitlin just takes the next step. She never lingers over setbacks."

"And you, madame, if it isn't impertinent to ask? Is this not an adventure?" He gestures with his hand toward the ancient city slumbering behind the garden wall.

Sybil doesn't answer right away. She is strangely off guard with this man. She feels innocent, like a child, willing to confess, penitent.

"Yes, yes, it is. But it always seems out of reach, on the other side of that wall."

Kamil looks at her curiously. He knows that she sometimes goes out escorted only by her driver. The police are aware of the movements of all embassy foreigners.

"Do you not go out?" he asks.

"Oh, of course I do. I'm quite active. I go on visits. Father has a busy schedule and I help him whenever I can." Her voice is defensive.

"You are far from your family," he suggests gently. "That is always difficult."

It is too much for Sybil. She blinks angrily.

"Yes, I do miss my sister. I've never even met my nephews. I have no other family, except for my aunt and uncle in America and cousin Bernie. My mother, you see, passed away." She pauses, balancing her head so the tear that has formed in the corner of her eye will not spill and betray her.

"Health to your head," he says softly in Turkish.

The light from the party behind them reflects on her wet cheek.

"Thank you, teshekkur ederim," she replies in kind, her tongue tripping over the many consonants.

Not wishing to draw attention to her distress, he waits silently for her to continue.

Frightened by her sudden weakness, Sybil straightens her back and continues in English. "That was five years ago. Father keeps her memory alive by staying on here, where she was by his side."

"A mother's memory is precious."

"I think he simply finds it easier to bear Mother's absence if he doesn't break the rhythm of their life together. He keeps up an endless round of functions and formal visits. I think Father finds the routine soothing. It helps him forget. And this is where he was happy," she explains.

"You are to be commended. Our society values a child that looks after his mother and father."

"It isn't difficult to direct the household, and Father doesn't impose too many other duties on me."

"Does this make you happy as well?" he ventures.

"Of course!" She turns to him indignantly. She sees mild green eyes, full of concern.

She turns her face from the light. Several moments pass before she speaks again.

Kamil feels an urge to take her hand, to confide his own father's seemingly inconsolable grief, his unraveling ties first to work, now to his family, and, Kamil fears, eventually to life. He would like her advice on how to help his father. The death of his wife had catapulted Kamil's father into training for his own oblivion. After her body was taken to the mosque, washed, wrapped in white linen, and consigned to the tomb under a hail of prayer, Alp Pasha never again stepped foot in a mosque or in the house where she had lived. Instead, he devoted more and more time to smoking opium in a darkened room, eventually giving up any pretense of governing.

When the grand vizier reluctantly took the office from him, Alp Pasha moved into his daughter Feride's home. He refuses to visit Kamil in the villa where his mother had lived, preferring the opium-induced vision to the real thing. When he prepares himself with a pipe, Alp Pasha told Kamil once, he can smell the roses in the garden and feel the breeze in his hair. Kamil worries that he hasn't done enough, that he is not a dutiful son, leaving the entire burden to his sister. He ponders how to bring up such a personal subject, then wonders if it is appropriate. The opportunity passes.

"I've never thought about it, to be honest. I suppose keeping Father happy keeps me happy as well," Sybil answers finally. She sounds unsure. "I do have other interests," she continues in a stronger voice, "that keep me amused." She tells Kamil about the tutor who comes twice a week to teach her Turkish.

"It's infuriating when someone speaks at length and then the ter-juman translates it with only three words, so I determined to learn it myself."

She admits to Kamil that she occasionally slips out on her own, concealed under a feradje cloak and dark yashmak veil, and walks around the city, wanting to try out her Turkish without a retinue of servants, guards, and official translators.

"They're probably spies! So how much will anyone really tell me in their presence?"

Animated now, she shares with Kamil her interest in religion. They discuss Islam, not simply as a revealed book, but as a way of life. He finds that she knows a great deal about the present political debates and intrigues. After all, she has hosted many of the participants in her own home.

Sybil suggests that she practice her Turkish, and they end the evening laughing over mistranslated witticisms and slips of the tongue. Nevertheless, Kamil thinks her command of the language remarkable. She has none of the finesse of those raised at court or schooled in the byzantine labyrinths of bureaucratic politesse, but can converse quite freely and understand much of what she hears. He compliments her sincerely and, for the first time in a long while, is sorry to see a social evening end. On his way to the door, Bernie catches up with him, pats him on the back, and winks.

"Fancy a game of billiards sometime?"

As his horse negotiates the steep paths on the way home, Kamil wonders at the sudden flashes of companionship and trust that sometimes kindle between total strangers. Can he trust his new friendship with Bernie or is real friendship something that emerges only over years of shared history and challenges faced together, like the bond that has developed between him and Michel? In his experience, the initial bridge of trust and comradeship too easily splinters under the pressure of personal ambition or rots through as proximity leads to a greater understanding of the other's flaws. Before long, a promotion or a move to a different province sends the last planks sweeping down the river.

He realizes there had been no opportune moment to ask Sybil about Mary Dixon.

9

Memory

his is Kamil's third visit to the British Embassy and he is still not inured to the paintings on the reception room wall. He has elected not to bother the ambassador with any further questions; it is Sybil who generally answers them in any case. He wishes to ask her about women's activities, he tells himself. The door opens and he rises, expecting the butler to lead him to another area of the cavernous embassy.

Instead, it is Sybil herself, in a gown embroidered with blue flowers. Emerging from the lace collar, her throat has the same round solidity of the woman in the painting behind him.

"Hello, Kamil Pasha. What a pleasure to see you again so soon."

"It was a lovely evening, Sybil Hanoum. Thank you." Kamil tries but fails to stop himself from looking into her eyes. "It's good of you to see me again."

Sybil lowers her lashes, although Kamil can still feel the weight of her gaze. She holds out her hand toward a comfortable chair near the fire. "Please sit."

Kamil realizes with some distaste that they are to remain in this most inappropriate room.

He sits, his back to the painting, but remains distracted by the thought that Sybil, who has settled herself in the chair opposite him, will have to look directly at it while they speak.

She doesn't seem to notice the painting, but sits smiling, her eyes on his face. Her face is slightly flushed. "Can I offer you some tea?"

"Yes, that would be most agreeable. Thank you."

Neither looks directly at the other.

She stands and tugs at the bellpull on the wall behind the settee. Above the lace collar, the back of her neck rises white and smooth until it is lost in a widening arrow of brown hair. Her hips swell beneath the gown. Kamil looks at his hands and forces himself to think of Mary Dixon, dead, a body, a cipher. That is what he has come for—an answer.

Sybil settles herself back into her chair.

"To what do I owe the pleasure of your call, Kamil Pasha? I imagine it must be something quite urgent."

"I wanted to speak with you about my investigation into Mary Dixon's death. Perhaps you have some insight where I have none."

Pleased, Sybil leans imperceptibly forward. "Whatever I can do to help."

The lack of demurral and false modesty pleases Kamil. The maid pushes in a trolley of tea and ginger cakes. She pours the tea and leaves.

It soon emerges that Sybil has little to add to what is already known about Mary Dixon. She had been in Istanbul for just over a year. Her position had been arranged by a member of the board of trustees of Robert College in response to a letter from her minister attesting to her good character. She traveled to Paris and was given instructions and papers by someone attached to the Ottoman Embassy there. A week later, she took a coach to Venice and a steamer from there to Stamboul. She had complained to Sybil about having to share a compartment with three other women for the four-day trip. She was met at the landing by a closed coach that took her directly to the women's quarters in Dolmabahche Palace.

"She came here several times to deal with visa matters. At first she was quite mocking of her new environment and so put out about her accommodations, one would think she was coming as a guest rather than as a governess. She said the girl who showed her to her room . . ." Sybil hesitates, but decides that in a murder investigation, she has no right to let modesty censor her account. "She said the girl was dressed in nothing more than, as she put it, knickers and a wrap." Kamil swallows a laugh. Sybil blushes, then hurries on. "And she complained that her room was completely unfurnished. She was horrified when she realized they expected her to sleep on a mattress that they brought out of the cupboards at night and to eat, as she put it, on the floor."

"It must be a great change for someone used to beds and tables and chairs."

"I thought it a bit unreasonable in someone coming out here to work. Surely she should have expected the experience to be different. Or else, why would she have come?"

"I'm sure she was paid well."

"I suppose she must have been, although, of course, we never spoke of that sort of thing."

"How did she get on with her employer?"

"Perihan Hanoum? Mary didn't seem to like her. She said she was haughty and unreasonable."

"You know Perihan Hanoum?"

"No, but I met her mother, Asma Sultan, many years ago."

"The wife of Ali Arslan Pasha, the grand vizier?"

Sybil nods. "It was the winter of 1878. I remember because it was snowing. A young Englishwoman, Hannah Simmons, had been killed that summer. She was employed as a governess and Mother was visiting the royal harems to see if she could find out anything. The police seemed to have thrown up their hands." She looks up at Kamil, smiling sadly. "You didn't know my mother. She was very determined."

She pauses. "It's such a sad story, but, you know, what I remember best is that we rode there on a sleigh. Isn't that awful of me?"

"You were very young then."

"Fifteen." Sybil smiles shyly.

An image of Sybil in the snow comes unbidden to Kamil's mind. "It's commendable of you and your mother to do so much."

Brushing off the praise, Sybil responds, "It's not right to be nostalgic when another young woman has been killed.

Kamil ponders a moment. "Do you know anything specific that Mary Dixon disliked about her employer? Did they ever argue?"

"She never mentioned anything specific. I wonder, in retrospect, whether Mary liked anyone. It's improper to speak ill of the dead, I know, but she seemed so disaffected. The only time I saw her happy— although I suppose animated is a better word—was at the soirees she attended at the Residence. She attracted quite a bit of attention with her short hair and bold manner."

"What kind of attention?"

"Men. Men seemed to be drawn to her."

Kamil smiles. "Anyone in particular?"

"Not that I know of. Well, she did have a rather lively discussion with a young Turkish journalist, Hamza Efendi, not long before she . . . passed away. But I don't think it meant anything," she added briskly. "Just a conversation. I only mention it because other people noticed."

"She seems to have taken you into her confidence."

"Oh, no. Not at all. I think she needed someone to complain to, but we never had a real conversation. We spoke only a handful of times and I remember feeling quite put off by her reticence. That is, well, I shouldn't think such black thoughts, but it did occur to me at the time that perhaps she sought me out simply to gain invitations to the Residence."

"Do you know if she had any friends?"

"I didn't see her very often." Sybil pauses. "But I do remember that one evening last autumn she spent quite some time chatting with a young Turkish woman. I wondered about it at the time. It seemed as if they knew each other well."

"Do you remember the young lady's name?"

"I think it was Jaanan Hanoum, the daughter of an official, I believe, at the Foreign Ministry."

"The niece of the scholar Ismail Hodja?"

"Yes, that sounds right. I believe someone mentioned that he was a relation. I suppose it's possible that Mary met her before at one of our soirees. Jaanan Hanoum sometimes came with her father. I just never noticed them together before."

Kamil leans forward, pondering this further link to Chamyeri.

Sybil looks down, her fingers entwined in her lap. "Oh, dear, you must think me quite wicked for being so critical, when the poor woman is no longer here to defend herself."

"Not at all, Sybil Hanoum. You've been extremely helpful."

She doesn't look up.

"Please don't worry yourself. You're mistaken to think you are somehow unjust to Miss Dixon's memory by telling me what you know of her. On the contrary, you are helping me sort out what I believe you English call a 'fine kettle of fish.'"

Sybil laughs. "Your English really is remarkable." Then, turning serious violet eyes on Kamil, still sitting with his back to the offending paintings, she ventures, "Could I entice you to stay for lunch?"

"I would be honored."

Sybil calls the maid to give instructions, then, to Kamil's great relief, leads the way out of the reception room.

"FROM WHOM DID you inherit your discerning palate, then?"

A servant in a pressed black suit stands just inside the French doors, far enough away that he cannot hear their conversation, although Kamil sees the young man's head straining their way. They sit on the patio, cooled by breezes from the Golden Horn.

"From my grandmother. Since my parents were abroad so much, my sister, Maitlin, and I lived with my grandmother in Essex. Nana was quite a bon vivant. She had the most fabulous dinner parties with coq au vin, flans, these delicate almond fingers . . . I can almost taste them now. You know, she hired a French cook for her kitchen. It was quite a radical thing to do, since the French were—and still are— quite unpopular. In fact, some of her kitchen staff quit because they refused to work under a "Frenchie." But the cook, Monsieur Menard, was such an unassuming person that the staff eventually accepted him. His passion was cooking and he produced the most remarkable meals. Other people served stodgy English fare, but Nana's dinners were always interesting. Not all of her guests approved, of course." She laughs, exposing tiny round teeth. "I remember one particular lamb chop that was so tender that I can still, to this day, taste the bubble of flavor that burst in my mouth when I took the first bite."

Sybil stops abruptly and leans forward, embarrassed. "You must think me trivial to be obsessing over a lamb chop when you are here on a matter of murder."

"One's past is never trivial. Your description made me think of the house I grew up in, my mother's house in Bahchekoy. I still live there." Sybil's vivid account of her grandmother's house has pulled him into a conspiracy of memories from which he doesn't have the will or the desire to disentangle himself.

"My father was governor of Istanbul, and he was also responsible for the police and the gendarmes, so he was busy much of the time. Even when he was at home, we rarely saw him. The governor's palace was enormous, with so many rooms always crowded with servants and guests and people coming to petition my father or pay social visits to my mother as the governor's wife. I think it was all a bit too much for her. So when we were still quite young, she moved my sister and me to her childhood home. It's a lovely villa, surrounded by gardens. You can see the Bosphorus from the gardens. And instead of your Monsieur Menard, we have Fatma and Karanfil," he adds with a smile.

"Are they your relations?"

"No, they're local women who cook for the household. Fatma lived in the cook's quarters that were behind the house then, at the back of the yard. She never married. Her sister Karanfil came in the morning and then returned to her own home. Her husband was a water carrier."

He remembers them as they appeared in his childhood, two short, round women, their baggy, brightly flowered shalwar trousers expanding upward to meet layers of brightly patterned sweaters and cardigans. Their faces are full moons, but set with disconcertingly delicate features, as if the women have different, slender selves that somehow have been mistakenly absorbed by their heavy bodies.

A powerful, sensual memory of the kitchen of his childhood floods him as he waits for Sybil to refill his water glass. He toys with the fried mullet on his plate.

The women were in continual motion, cooking and cleaning. In summer they brought their work into the yard. He has an image of Fatma, squatting beside a basin of soapy water, her powerful arms twisting a rope of wet laundry. In winter the blue-washed kitchen walls were festooned with ears of corn and strings of red peppers, pulsating with color. A ceramic water urn stood just inside the door, a tinned copper plate across the top to keep out dust. A copper mug rested on the plate. Kamil remembers lifting the plate and looking into the urn, which stood almost to his chest, the hollow quality of the air and the loamy smell of wet clay, the resistance of metal against the skin of water and the satisfying whirlpool entering his mug. Water directly from this urn always tasted like an entirely different substance than water drunk from a glass. To this day, he keeps a clay jar of water and a tinned mug on the dressing table in his bedroom. He drinks from it to clear his mind and calm his senses.

He sips from his glass. Sybil waits expectantly for him to continue, unwilling to break his reverie by prompting him.

He tries to describe the garden, the kitchen, the fresh, lightly spiced cuisine: roasted aubergines, chicken pounded with walnuts and sesame oil, tart grape leaves stuffed with savory rice mixed with currants. Fatma and Karanfil called him their little lamb and plied him with flaky cheese-filled pastries and sweet cakes, washed down with glasses of diluted sugary black tea. Through the crackle of fire and the slap of dough against wood, Fatma's husky voice wove Turkish fables and legends and cautionary tales of djinns and demons.

"What happened to them?"

"Karanfil's husband died in a fire and now she, her son Yakup, and Fatma live in an extension I had built onto the kitchen house after my mother died. With the help of a few other servants, they keep house. They cook for me and tend the garden and my plants."

"You live there alone, then, with your servants." A statement.

"Yes."

This time, the silence is awkward. One word carries an insupportable burden, where an hour-long conversation has flown by with unguarded wings.

Sybil's face and neck flush red. She motions brusquely to the servant waiting by the door and asks for tea to be served in the garden. She stands and leads Kamil to a table set beneath an incongruous palm tree.

"Tell me about your plants," Sybil suggests in a voice too charged with interest.

"I have a small winter garden, I believe you call it. I collect orchids."

"Orchids? How delightful! But how do you get them here? Aren't they from South America? I've heard they're quite delicate."

"Not just from South America, Sybil Hanoum. There are many varieties of orchids all around us."

"Here? In Turkey?"

"There is a lovely orchid with sprays of violet blooms that grows in the forests around Istanbul, *Cephalanthera rubra*." He smiles at her. "It is our connection to Europe, where this variety is also found."

Sybil is flustered. "How lovely. Imagine my ignorance. But, but I would so like to see your collection," she blurts out. She looks down to rearrange her skirts with exaggerated care. "I'm sorry. That would be inappropriate, of course."

"It would be a great pleasure"—he pauses briefly—"but perhaps it would be better if your father accompanied you." The sight of her crestfallen face dismays him, but he is unwilling to risk her reputation —or, he admits to himself, his privacy. Still, the image of Sybil bending appreciatively over his scented orchids has taken root in his mind.

Regarding Sybil over the rim of his cup, Kamil lets the warm, eggshell-thin china rest for a moment against his lower lip before he sips from it.

THAT EVENING, KAMIL blots the ink on the letter he is trying to write. The words he has written seem to have taken on too much color, lost the dry rustle of truth and factualness that makes them scientific and, thus, to be believed by the recipient, H. G. Reichenbach.

Since the garden party, his thoughts have slipped their accustomed tether and he finds himself dwelling on Sybil's tapered fingers twined around the stem of the wineglass; the plump mound at the inside of her wrist; the hollow at the base of her neck. He thinks with disquiet, but also a little more sympathy, of his father, who, in his opium dreams, has surrendered to blissful communication with his dead wife. He takes up his pen and continues writing.

Dear Professor Reichenbach,

I write as an amateur botanist, but one with scientific observations that I hope to bring to your esteemed attention. I am in possession of a glorious and most unusual orchidae that to my knowledge has not been described elsewhere. It is a small plant with two roundish, semi-attached tubers and basal leaves with one spike culminating in a single showy flower. The flower is velvety black, with an arched labellum and densely hairy petals. The speculum is divided into two symmetrical halves and is a bright, shining blue, almost phosphorescent. I observed the plant in its habitat over several weeks. The arched labellum attracts male insects that cross-pollinate the flowers, perhaps lured by some volatile chemical compound released from its surface.

I collected this orchid in marshland at the edge of a forest in northwest Anatolia near the Black Sea. I have never seen another, nor does it fit the description of any of the orchidacae in your famous Glossary.

It is but one of many wondrous orchidacae in the Ottoman Empire, some of which I have described in previous letters to you. Many are found only here in Turkish lands; others join us to Europe in a continuous ecology. The tulip, the carnation, the lily, these are everywhere depicted, yet the true treasure of the empire, the orchid, is inexplicably absent.

I most respectfully await your response. If you desire it, I can arrange to have a sketch of the orchid sent to you so that you may inspect it further.

> Yours most sincerely,
> Kamil Pasha
> Magistrate and Fellow Lover of Orchids

This is not his first letter to Professor Reichenbach, but he has not yet received a response.

10

Hill of Stars

amza had been my friend almost as long as I could remember. When Mama and I still lived with Papa on the hill in Nishantashou, he engaged Hamza, his sister's son, as my tutor. Hamza had graduated from L'École Supérieure in Paris and, thanks to Papa's influence, was awarded a position as translator at the Foreign Ministry in Istanbul. His family lived in Aleppo, where, Papa told me, his father had been a kadi. Since his father was retired and unable to set Hamza up in his own household, Hamza lived with us as part of our extended family. Every morning, he set off for work dressed in Frankish trousers and the long, slim stambouline jacket fashionable among modern Ottomans. Papa too had long since discarded the traditional long robe and turban for trousers and a dashing red fez.

I watched from behind the wooden lattice that screened the women's quarters from the street as Papa and Hamza got into the carriage for their trip to the Sublime Porte. I caressed the words "Sublime Porte" in my mouth. I imagined it to be the entrance to the palace, an enormous carved wooden door studded with jewels and guarded by Nubian eunuchs, through which Papa and Hamza entered every day to go to their offices. When I was little, driving by in a carriage, my governess had pointed out the palace gates. They were enormous, of white stone, and set into an endlessly high wall the color of dried blood that rose on both sides of the narrow road. That first time, driving past the gates, I panicked and screamed, imagining that, with so little of the sky visible, the walls had begun to move together and would crush us. I learned that this was the Dolmabahche Palace, the home of Sultan Abdulaziz, not the Old Palace of many gates and pavilions that sat like a jewel box on a promontory at the confluence of the Bosphorus and the Sea of Marmara.

Some years later, when Sultan Abdulhamid had replaced Abdulaziz and I was living with Mama at Chamyeri, Hamza pointed these palaces out to me as we slid past them on the bright water in a caïque. Hamza was escorting Mama and me on a summer picnic trip to the islands at the mouth of the Marmara, our caique propelled by six strong rowers. Even though mother and I were invisible under our feradje cloaks and yashmak veils, the rowers studiously avoided looking toward the stern of the boat where we sat on cushioned benches. Hamza sat beside me, not touching, but so close I felt the heat of his body. The Russians had invaded the empire two months earlier and were slowly making their way toward Istanbul, but on this peerless summer day, the horizon was that of a young girl in love.

The first palaces we passed were ornate white confections, first the smaller Chiraghan Palace, crumbling around Sultan Abdulhamid's elder brother Murad and his family, who Hamza told me were imprisoned there, then the endless expanse of Dolmabahche right along the water's edge, wing after wing of ornamented white stone behind enormous white marble archways. I realized it must have been the landward walls of Dolmabahche that had so frightened me, but I did not tell him that, so he would not think me a baby. I was, after all, eleven.

"Sultan Abdulhamid's family and retainers live and work in Dolmabahche," Hamza told me, "but the sultan wants privacy and security. He trusts no one, not even members of his own family and staff." He pointed toward the top of the hill. "So he has built himself a new palace on the hill above the old one."

I looked up and saw a yellow wall snake through the trees. Looking higher, I caught glimpses of pitch-roofed buildings within the forest. From Nishantashou, I could see the lighted Yildiz Palace fill up the night like a hill of stars. I had always wondered who lived there, but since no one in the household ever looked in its direction, I hadn't wanted to reveal my ignorance by asking.

Finally, as the boat slipped from the narrow Bosphorus into the open sea, Hamza pointed to the breast of land riding the confluence of the Bosphorus, the Golden Horn, and the Sea of Marmara. The Old Palace on the hill was like the magic land from Hamza's tales, its turrets and pavilions set like jewels among trees and gardens.

"This is Topkapi Palace, where servants and slaves are sent to live out their days when they are old. And the harems and households of former sultans, and their widows." He pointed to a door in the enormous red wall that stretched along the entire expanse of the waterfront.

"That's the only door through which the women can leave again. It's where the dead are taken out for burial."

Irritated at Hamza for spoiling my vision with his depressing observations, I responded in a determinedly sprightly voice, "Still, I think it's a lovely place. I should like to live there."

Hamza looked at me thoughtfully.

"You shouldn't wish that, princess. They are not allowed to leave, nor are their children. Sultans fear their brothers and their children. If they're in line for the throne, they might try to depose the ruler. If they're not, they'll scheme to eliminate those in line before them. Even the daughters, should they marry, might be used by their in-laws to meddle in palace affairs. Connections and family links between the royal House of Osman and the rest of the empire are always kept to a minimum. One way to do that is to isolate members of your family. Another way is to kill them."

I averted my eyes from the Old Palace then. A leaden chill made me pull my feradje more tightly about my shoulders. I felt vaguely resentful at Hamza for telling me this. In a small gesture of punishment, I let my yashmak fall forward so it hid my eyes and mouth and didn't speak again until we landed on Prinkipo Island.

The Sublime Porte, I learned later, was nothing more than a heavy stone building crouching by the side of the Golden Horn.

WHEN I WAS a child at Nishantashou, only Papa moved freely between the harem, where Papa's mother and Mama presided, and the rest of the house. As a child I had a certain freedom to explore, as long as I did not interrupt the gatherings of men that my father held many evenings in the salon. That was easy enough to do, as the rumble of their voices could be heard at quite a distance.

Hamza and a succession of other tutors taught me to read and write Ottoman and Persian and introduced me to French and English, all of which my forward-looking father considered necessary skills for a modern Ottoman woman in order for her to be a suitable wife, entertaining and speaking intelligently with her husband's guests. I overheard Papa explain this to Hamza and wondered at the time why Mama refused to help Papa entertain. Later, I understood that Aunt Hüsnü was willing to dress in a Frankish gown, her face uncovered, and mingle with Papa's male guests and their modern wives, while my mother was unable to bring herself to drop her veil and stand naked, as it would seem to her, before strangers. Servants used to stretch a tunnel of silk between the front door and the carriage so that Mama could leave the house without being seen.

Of all my lessons, I looked forward to Hamza's the most. I practiced intensely in order to impress him, to gain the reward of his broad smile and words of praise when he realized what I had accomplished—and to avoid the thin drumming of his fingers on the table when I struggled. I strove to tether his eyes and was anguished when his gaze floated free, perhaps mesmerized by the brilliant reflections on the distant water or drawn through the vivid sky to thoughts that precluded me. I was jealous even of the sea. I was infatuated with Hamza and in love with Papa and, at least in that, I did my duty as a young girl. I learned in order to please them. It was my luck (although some might think it misfortune) that just then I moved into the orbit of Ismail Dayi, who had no such preconceptions about what and why young women were to learn.

But when we moved to Chamyeri, I was heartbroken at leaving Papa and Hamza. I missed the familiar rooms and servants and the view from my window of the minarets of the grand imperial mosques. In Nishantashou, we had countless servants. I was surrounded by the babble of their many languages: Turkish, Greek, Italian, Armenian, Arabic.

Chamyeri, by contrast, was frightening in its silence. The servants came during the day, as needed. For the most part, they did their work silently, sliding sideways looks at Mama and me when they thought our attention elsewhere. I wondered what they gossiped in the village about this unusual household—my uncle, his dreaming sister, and the lonely girlchild no one was raising. But eventually I came to appreciate the silence, the unlimited time to read and explore, the riches of my young life—a library, a wide sky, mine for as long as I cared to hold it, the flexing waters of the strait, a fragrant garden, and, in the forest, the pond with its ebony depths that made me just fearful enough to be satisfied.

I realize now that Hamza's visits to Chamyeri were possible only because of my mother's and Ismail Dayi's loose supervision. We would meet in the pavilion in the darkening afternoon. Sitting cross-legged on the divan, we discussed books and poetry. Hamza described Europe, the boulevards and cafés of Paris. If, on occasion, he seemed distracted, I attributed it to the insignificance of my experiences. After the cook left the kitchen at night, I stole lemons and brought them with me to bed, inhaling their scent under the quilt, imagining it to be Hamza's citrusy cologne, the roughness of the peel against my nose the sting of stubble on his cheek.

Not long after our boat trip to Prinkipo Island, Madam Élise came to live at Chamyeri. Before long, Ismail Dayi forbade Hamza to visit. I heard him tell mother that it was improper for a young man in the crazy blood of youth to spend the night in a house with unmarried women. Mama protested, but Ismail Dayi would not relent. He even forbade visits during the day. Hamza disobeyed him, arriving after Ismail Dayi's carriage had disappeared down the road. But he came less often and never stayed very long. He told me not to let Mama know he was there. I was sad for Mama because I knew how much she enjoyed his company, but flattered that he had braved the danger of my dayi's wrath to see me. Still, I missed our ritual and, for a long time, was unable to sleep until the early hours of the morning. I wandered through the dark rooms, listening for the clear chime of his voice, and huddled on the divan in the room where he had slept, the mattresses and quilts now stored away in a cabinet. Though Madam Élise's French was more fluent than Hamza's, in her mouth the language was a pale, sticky gum of sounds. Sometimes, sitting in the fragrant garden watching the night fishermen, I imagined I heard his voice.

11

Your Brush Is the Bowstring

iko's smile wavers only a moment as he opens the heavy, brass-studded door to find Kamil Pasha next to a skinny man with a face the color of yoghurt and hair like the setting sun.

"Your arrival pleases me," Niko booms, a gap-toothed grin beneath his luxuriant black mustache. At first glance, the hamambashou appears fat, but his chest is deep and well muscled from kneading the bodies of his charges. It is thatched with wet black hair. A red-checked peshtemal towel covers him from waist to knees.

"I am pleased to see you." Kamil turns to Bernie and is disconcerted to see his teeth in a wide grin. "Decorum," he can't help himself from saying. "Decorum is important."

"Yeah, right. Sorry, buddy." Bernie composes his face into a caricature of seriousness.

Kamil is apprehensive. It is the first time he has allowed anyone to accompany him to the hamam. He is no longer sure how it came about that Bernie is standing here now. Had he suggested it yesterday evening, or had Bernie? Either way, a bottle of potent raki had played a part. He has undertaken to bring Bernie to the baths, and he must make sure the experiment does not go awry. He follows Niko into the cooling-off room, trailed by Bernie, whose eyes are everywhere at once. The other men in the room look shocked, then quickly hide their expressions.

There are whispers. "A giavour, a heathen."

Kamil sees Fat Orhan propped on his side on a divan, a sheet wrapped about his middle. His red face is immobile, but his eyes follow their progress across the room.

Niko gives Bernie the cubicle next to Kamil's.

"Hang your clothing in there." Kamil indicates the wardrobe with the palm of his hand. "Then wrap yourself in this towel."

"What towel? Oh, you mean this cloth." Bernie picks up the peshtemal. "You could make a suit out of this amount of material. Or maybe a kilt." He whinnies a laugh, then catches himself.

"Sorry, sorry. Decorum. I know." He pats Kamil on the back. "Don't worry. I won't embarrass you."

Kamil cringes at the unaccustomed intimacy. He forces a smile. "I'm not in the least worried." He goes to his own cubicle and, with relief, closes the door. He hears knocking and rustling sounds from next door, as if Bernie is examining everything. Which he probably is, decides Kamil. Perhaps I would do the same. The thought cheers him, with its intimation of scientific inquiry and exploration of new things. But with decorum, he decides. Truth and decorum. The stamen and pistil of civilization, by which it reproduces itself. Either alone is sterile.

He removes his clothing and opens the armoire. Suddenly he hears the door behind him open. He swings around and grabs the peshtemal to cover himself. Bernie is standing in the doorway, the thatch of hair around his organ glowing brilliant red against his lean white thighs. Kamil grabs him and pulls him into the cubicle, his face pulsing with shame at what the men outside must be thinking. He snatches the peshtemal from Bernie's hands and orders him roughly, "Put this on." In that first moment of looking against his will, Kamil has seen something even worse—Bernie is uncircumcised.

Bernie wraps the peshtemal awkwardly around his waist so that it trails on the floor.

"Like this." Kamil indicates his own neatly tucked towel.

"Right." Bernie reties his. "You looked like you'd seen a ghost when I walked in." He flushes slightly. "You know, I've never been to one of these shindigs before. It's a bath, right? So, people do take their clothes off."

"It isn't proper to show oneself between the waist and knees."

"Oh." Bernie looks puzzled. "You know, there are all these engravings and paintings of the Turkish bath that show women in their birthday suits lounging around."

"Birthday suits?"

"Naked as the day is long."

"Men have different responsibilities." Kamil is displeased with his answer. He really doesn't know why the rules differ for men. He finds the usual answers unscientific: that it's traditional; that women are like children, irresponsible. He decides for honesty. "I simply don't know, Bernie. That's the way it is in the men's baths. Keep your towel on at all times."

"Will do, partner."

Kamil braces himself to leave the cubicle. He imagines what the audience in the cooling-off room will think when two men emerge from the same cubicle. Such a thing isn't uncommon, nor is it frowned upon, but Kamil doesn't want it associated with him. Not because of any principle against male intimacy, but because it rends Kamil's precious privacy. He prefers to be the watcher, not the watched.

SITTING IN THE bar of the Hotel Luxembourg, Kamil wonders at the rapidity with which one's attitude toward life can alter. Instead of poring over his books and orchids, here he is meeting a friend. After their inauspicious beginning in the hamam, Bernie had followed Kamil's lead assiduously. The giavour's red hair occasioned curious, if veiled looks, but nothing else had gone awry. Bernie quailed under the forceful blows of Niko's massive palms and bone-cracking massage. After only an hour in the steam-filled inner room, ladling hot water over his head with his hamam bowl, Bernie complained of shortness of breath and they retired, each to his own cubicle, in the cooling-off room. Refreshed by cool sherbet and a nap, they parted amicably at the door and summoned separate carriages to take them home. A few days later, Bernie sent a message challenging Kamil to a game of billiards.

Bernie is lifting his raki glass to him.

"Lousy game, friend. To your health, though."

Kamil lowers the lip of his glass so that it meets Bernie's below the rim. Bernie counters by lowering his. Laughing, they finally clink their glasses near the carpet, with Bernie winning the contest of showing respect.

"I should never teach you our customs. You then use your knowledge to shame me. You are the guest here and should be honored more."

"I'll only accept that if you swear you'll come to the States, so I can reciprocate and teach you American customs."

"And how do Americans honor a guest?"

"Well," says Bernie, rolling the words on his tongue in a thick American brogue, "I reckon we give 'em the last swig outta tha whiskey bottle. We sure as hell don't strip 'em naked, pour hot water on their heads, and beat the crap out of 'em."

Kamil laughs. "You survived just fine. That makes you an honorary Ottoman." Bernie takes out a cigarette and offers one to Kamil, who tamps it into the end of his ebony and silver cigarette holder. He lights Bernie's cigarette, then his own.

"Any luck on your case?"

"Eleven days, and all we have is a fisherman who heard noises from shore that night, a dog barking, and something being dropped into the water. My associate Michel Sevy and I went up there and looked around. There's a sea bath, a kind of enclosed bathing pool. We found a dead dog nearby, with its head smashed in. But nothing else."

"Your associate's name is Michel Sevy?"

"Yes, why? He's the police surgeon."

"Nothing. Just curious. Where was this?"

"Between Chamyeri and Emirgan. There's a fairly large village there. The body was found halfway down the Bosphorus, but the things I've learned all point north to Chamyeri. That's the place where another British governess, Hannah Simmons, was found murdered eight years ago. Her name keeps coming up. I can't help but wonder whether the two deaths are related somehow."

"Chamyeri. It means 'Place of the Pines,' doesn't it?" Bernie asks pensively.

"Yes. I didn't realize you speak Turkish so well."

"I need to read some Ottoman for my work, but can't speak it to shake a stick at."

Kamil repeats slowly, "Shake a stick at."

Bernie laughs. "Don't bother learning that one, old buddy. I can't explain how to use it. You'll be shooting blanks."

"Shooting blanks. Now, that makes more sense."

Kamil suddenly remembers Sybil mentioning that she had just missed Bernie when she first arrived in Istanbul. Thinking Bernie might have crossed paths with the murdered woman at the embassy, he asks, "Did you know her?"

Bernie looks startled. "Who?"

"Hannah Simmons."

Bernie looks at the raki glass between his fingers as if he hopes to find an answer there. His boyish face looks older when he frowns, Kamil observes. His skin is thick, like that of an animal. It bends rather than creases. His face will have few wrinkles in old age, he thinks, but deep lines.

"No." Bernie says finally, avoiding Kamil's eyes.

Kamil lifts the cigarette holder to his lips, draws deeply, and waits.

After a moment, Bernie asks with what Kamil judges a shade too much enthusiasm, "So what do you make of it?"

Kamil ponders how much to reveal. "I don't know. The dead woman, Mary Dixon, apparently was friendly with a Muslim girl that lives in the same house at Chamyeri where the other body was found eight years ago. The house belongs to a well-known scholar. The girl is his niece. Odd, isn't it? Both murdered women were English governesses in the imperial harem." He shrugs. "It's probably a coincidence."

Kamil frowns at his own admission. He doesn't believe in coincidences.

"The girl, Jaanan Hanoum," he adds, "was a child at the time of the first murder. She's in France now."

"What about the scholar?"

"It's impossible. He's one of the most respected religious men in the empire. I simply can't imagine him having anything to do with an Englishwoman, much less with killing her. He has no connection with the foreign community and he's not involved with any particular faction in the palace. He keeps his distance from the power struggles. He doesn't have anything to gain by them. He is head of a powerful Sufi order. His position is unassailable because it's based on his reputation and on an influential circle of relations and friends. His family consists of famous poets, jurists, philosophers, and teachers. He's also independently wealthy. Why would he kill young Englishwomen? No, my friend, I think we must look elsewhere."

Bernie takes another sip of raki followed by a water chaser, then leans back and folds his hands across his stomach.

"I brought the pendant along," Kamil says. He takes the handkerchief with the jewelry from his jacket pocket and spreads it out on the table. "I thought since you know so many languages, you might have have some idea what these lines mean." He opens the pendant and holds it out to Bernie. "Is it some kind of writing?"

Bernie takes the small silver globe. It rests on his palm, lobes open, like a fat insect.

"Jesus, Mary, and Joseph," he exclaims under his breath. Freckles stand out on his blanched face like liver spots.

"What is it?" Kamil's senses become alert for nuance.

Bernie doesn't answer. He tilts the open silver shell toward the light and peers into it with great concentration. Kamil becomes aware of the clink of glasses and low murmur of male voices around them, the musk of tobacco smoke. The cigarettes burn down in the ashtray. Finally, Bernie closes the pendant and strokes it with his finger gently as a lover. When he looks up, he seems startled to see Kamil sitting opposite him. The surprise in his eyes is replaced by a look of consternation. He seems to be struggling with something.

He turns the pendant, examining the surface, then holds it to the light and squints to see inside again. Finally, he places it gently on the table between them. He takes a deep breath.

"It's Chinese."

"Chinese?" Kamil is taken aback. "Are you certain?"

"Of course. I read it fluently."

Kamil looks at him curiously. "It's an amazing coincidence that you should be here to decipher it for me."

He studies the markings for a moment as if he can decipher them himself. He is thinking, however, about Bernie's reaction.

"What does it say?"

"The two characters on the pendant stand for 'brush' and 'bowstring.'"

"What?" Kamil is flabbergasted. "What does it mean? Does it mean anything at all?"

"It refers to a Chinese poem, 'On Seeing an Early Frost.'" He recites:

In autumn wind the road is hard,
Streams fill with red leaves.
For crows what is left but stony soil and barren hills?

I can endure, a withered pine
clinging to a cliff edge,
Or set out on the road brocaded by frost.
Your brush is the bowstring that brings the wild goose down.

"You know it by heart."

Bernie attempts to look modest. "I know a few of them. This is a poem by Chao-lin Ch'un, a concubine to a Manchu prince about a hundred years ago. Apparently, she and the prince shared a love of poetry and calligraphy. It's said she was his political advisor, which didn't endear her to the rest of the family. She collected art objects too, a fantastic collection, apparently. Some European travelers wrote about it. She must have been some lady."

"What happened to her?"

"When the prince died, his son by an earlier marriage inherited his title and he kicked her out."

"Would she have returned to her family?"

"No, women like that usually choose to become nuns—Buddhist or Taoist nuns. It gives them a lot more freedom and respect than chasing back to their parents, assuming they'd even take them back. It's a life of contemplation, not very comfortable, but a lot of people find it rewarding. I sometimes wonder whether I wouldn't like to try it myself."

"I can see why it would be attractive."

"You? Really?" He regards Kamil curiously. "I never figured you for the introspective sort. Somehow I can't see you spending hours reflecting on the transience of plum blossoms."

Kamil laughs. "You'd be surprised."

"Well, friend. I respect that."

"What about the poem?"

"The poem. Well, it's a bitter poem. Probably written after the prince died." Bernie takes a long swig of raki and washes it down with water. "But the last couple of lines always struck me as more of a call to action than contemplation. And I've always wondered about the 'you' in the last line, 'your brush.' Who was she referring to?"

"So this is what scholars of literature do," Kamil comments with a sly smile. "Like cows eating grass. It gets chewed, digested, regurgitated, and chewed again before it becomes the cow's food."

Bernie lets out a guffaw that threatens to spill the drink in his hand. "And we all know what comes out at the end!" Wiping the tears from his eyes, he adds, "You should be a book critic."

When their laughter subsides, Bernie muses, "She had a lover, a scholar named Kung, who published some fiery articles urging reform of the Manchu government. He left Peking in a big hurry the year after Chao-lin Ch'un disappeared. Reportedly went to Hangchow. Makes you wonder, though, doesn't it? Maybe he's the one with the aggressive brush." He holds up his glass. "Here's to love and revolution."

Kamil hesitates, then touches the rim of his glass to Bernie's. He puts it down without sipping.

"Why revolution?"

"A few years after the two of them left Peking, there was an attempt to overthrow the Manchus. Unsuccessful. Might have nothing to do with these two, but it makes a good romantic yarn."

"Is this poem well known?"

"Not at all. I'm not sure whether it was even published. I got hold of it as a privately circulated manuscript. Looks like someone at Dolmabahche Palace has the same manuscript, although I don't know of any sinologists who would have been around here to translate it."

"Why do you think the pendant came from Dolmabahche? Why not Yildiz Palace?"

Bernie appears nonplussed. "Well, that's where most of the women are, right? They'd be the ones wearing a pendant."

"And reading Chinese poetry?"

"Probably not. I know some of them have really good tutors, but learning Chinese is a lifetime project. Unless the sultan has a concubine from China or from the tribal peoples that border it."

"The palace prefers Circassians, but it is possible. There's no way to know; there are hundreds of women in the imperial household."

Kamil reflects on the coffered ceiling. "I guess it was too much to hope that the necklace would offer some kind of clue. Perhaps some-one simply had unusual taste in jewelry and it wasn't made here at all." He turns it over with his thumbnail. "But what about the tughra?"

Bernie's smile does not reach his eyes, which seem fixed on a deep memory, as if the present moment were no more than thin ice. He shakes his head and faces Kamil.

"It's an odd thing. Can't help you there. Maybe the pendant was made somewhere else and inscribed with the Chinese characters, then found its way here and was monogrammed with the tughra. Or maybe someone at the palace was interested in Chinese poetry and had it made, then gave it to Mary as a gift."

The tone is in the wrong key, too lighthearted. Kamil is sure Bernie is hiding something.

"It's possible. Mary was here for almost a year. But who would know Chinese?"

Besides Bernie. Kamil frowns. He will have to find out more about his friend. The thought saddens him. Kamil rises to go, plead-ing an engagement.

12

The Old Superintendent

he young boy tamps a golden wad of fragrant tobacco into the bowl of the old man's narghile. As he kneels, head lowered, to attend to their water pipes, Kamil can see the whorls of his short hair, like the grain in wood, and the flanges of his ears.

Ferhat Bey waits until the boy leaves and he has taken a deep draught of fresh smoke before turning to Kamil and continuing.

"There isn't much I can tell you. We searched the area thoroughly. There were no clues."

They are sitting in a coffeehouse in the Beyazit quarter, not far from the entrance to the Grand Bazaar. The coffeehouse is part of a large complex of buildings attached to a venerable old mosque. It is late afternoon, a hiss of rain on the flagstones. They sit on a bench, feet tucked under their robes against the wet chill. An old man reclines on the bench in the far corner of the room, his eyes closed, a gnarled hand curled around the mouthpiece of his narghile. The air is redolent of scented tobacco and drying wool.

Kamil takes the amber mouthpiece from his lips and exhales slowly. The light from the window shudders and is gone. Kamil adjusts his woolen mantle around his shoulders.

The former superintendent of police is a wiry, gray-haired man with a deeply seamed face but hands incongruously unmarked by time, as fair and supple as a girl's.

"We thought immediately of Ismail Hodja's household, of course. The body was found right behind his property, after all, and there are no other residences in the area."

"Yes," Kamil murmurs his assent. "That would be the first place to look. Did you find anything?"

Ferhat Bey does not answer for a moment, his eyes fixed on the coals, then returns his attention to Kamil. He is painfully aware that Kamil has neglected to defer to him and assumes this is because Kamil is the son of a pasha and used to taking on airs. Still, in deference to his age, Kamil should speak less directly. One shows respect through formality, through indirection; there are necessary locutions within which questions and responses should be couched, muffled, like winter padding on a horse's hooves, so that the ring of fact on stone remains the prerogative of the elder, the teacher. What has he got to teach this upstart? thinks Ferhat Bey bitterly. He had failed and this brash young man will fail too.

"Who made up the household at that time?" Kamil asks.

The old man sighs and answers slowly, showing his displeasure at being interrogated. The young upstart should read the file; he had noted at least this much before he stopped writing.

"Household? Ismail Hodja, of course. His sister and niece. The niece's governess, a Frenchwoman. She found the body. A gardener and a groom that live on the property. Daily maids and a cook that live in the village."

He stops and draws on his pipe. Kamil waits until Ferhat Bey has expelled the smoke into the room, but when the old superintendent does not continue, he presses him eagerly.

"Can you tell me what they said, where they were that day and the night before? Did they see anything?"

Ferhat Bey wishes he had not agreed to this meeting. Stubbornly, he draws out the silence.

Kamil understands that he has been too forward. This man is too old to be converted to a modern approach to solving crime, Kamil thinks. To him, the important thing is that he is an elder who was once a man of rank. The puzzle of a crime is worth nothing when measured against your place in society. The fact that Kamil resists this himself does not mean that others agree. He adjusts his manner accordingly.

"Superintendent Efendi," he says, using the man's title out of politeness, "I would much appreciate any help you could give me in solving this crime. I wonder whether your experience with the other investigation could help me shed light on this one. There seem to be some similarities, although I could be wrong. I defer to your judgment in this."

Mollified, Ferhat Bey's interest is piqued.

"What similarities?"

"Both young women were English and had positions as governesses with members of the imperial family. Both bodies were found in water. The second woman probably was thrown into the Bosphorus between Emirgan and Chamyeri." He tells Ferhat Bey what the night fisherman saw. He does not mention the pendant, or the dilated pupils.

The superintendent looks up at Kamil craftily, his eyes scanning Kamil's face for a reaction to what he says next.

"Do you think there's a connection to the palace?"

If there is, Ferhat Bey is thinking with satisfaction, it will ruin this man like it ruined him—left with a pension that barely covers his tobacco. The scorpion, he knows, has made its nest in the magistrate's woodpile. Feigning disinterest in the answer, with a barely discernible smile, he brings the tea glass to his lips, then sets the empty glass down.

Kamil doesn't answer right away. He signals to the boy, who

rushes over to refill their glasses from the enormous brass samovar huffing on a corner table. The men silently go about the ritual of preparing their tea. Each balances the saucer and glass on the palm of his hand, measures sugar from a jar, and stirs up a small whirlpool that skirts the lip of the glass but remains confined within it as if by a mysterious force. Kamil holds his glass up to the light, admiring the amber red of the liquid.

"Excellent tea!"

Ferhat Bey doesn't care about the color of his tea. He is waiting for an answer. He wonders if Kamil is being insolent or whether he truly doesn't know. Well, if he doesn't know, I won't tell him, thinks the old man. Let him find out the hard way that crimes linked to the palace are crimes best left unsolved.

Still, he is curious about the new case.

"It may be a coincidence," he offers slyly, hoping to get Kamil to lower his guard and tell him about the present case. He isn't interested in discussing history.

Kamil sets his glass down carefully.

"Perhaps." He sits quietly, eyes caught by the motes of dust jostling in the beam of light from the window. Such chaos, he muses, yet the world is by its nature orderly. There is always a pattern.

The loud click of glass meeting saucer brings his attention back to the superintendent. He is impatient, Kamil thinks. Good. Perhaps he is willing to share some of his memories of the case. He turns to the old man.

"I can't tell whether there is a link because I know so little about the first murder." He does not add that Ferhat Bey's case notes were so incomplete and poorly organized that it had been impossible to gain insight from them.

Ferhat Bey sighs. It seems he will have to pay for his entertainment with memories after all, but he will not reveal everything. Let him figure it out for himself. And by then it will be too late. He can't help smiling at the thought, but it appears on his face as a smirk.

"What do you want to know?"

"Whatever is most important to know. Where the body was found, who you spoke with, what they said. The condition of the body," he adds carefully.

"The body? She was dead, that's all. Face up in the pond. We thought she had drowned, but the surgeon pressed on her chest and found there was no water in her lungs. She had been strangled. You could see the mark on her neck. Knife-sharp, but not a knife. A very thin, strong cord."

"Silk?"

Ferhat Bey grins. "Yes, a silk cord. No other cord would leave that kind of mark." Everyone knows that is the method preferred by the royals. He is no better match for them than I was, despite his fancy new title.

"Was she a virgin?"

Ferhat Bey is somewhat taken aback by Kamil's straightforward way of bringing up a most delicate subject, even among men. It would be quite different if they were drinking buddies or school friends, then they could discuss such obscene things freely. But they are colleagues and he is an elder. He deliberates briefly whether this is disrespectful or not, but concludes that Kamil is simply socially inept. Not uncommon among spoiled children of the elite, he thinks. That will make him all the more susceptible to the rot at the palace, he thinks with satisfaction.

"No."

"Another similarity." Kamil pauses. "Was anything else remarkable about the body, other than this and the cord line at her neck?"

"Well, I'm not sure one could call the fact that she wasn't a virgin remarkable," Ferhat Bey chortles. "After all, she was a Frank, and you know how their women are." He settles himself back and puffs with satisfaction on his water pipe.

Kamil smiles wanly, refusing to be drawn in.

"Anything else?" he repeats.

The superintendent stirs restlessly. He doesn't know what this young upstart is after.

"Nothing else. Unless you're interested in rumors."

"What rumors?"

"There was some talk that she was having an affair with a Turk, a journalist."

"Was she?"

"How would I know? No one had any real information, and there are hundreds of journalists these days, far too many, if you ask me."

"How did you make the connection to the palace?"

Ferhat Bey winces.

"There was a witness," he admits grudgingly.

Kamil is surprised. He hadn't heard there was a witness.

"To the murder?"

"No, to the abduction. Except that apparently she went willingly. One of the eunuchs said a carriage picked her up by the back gate. And it wasn't the first time. She always went alone, always with the same disreputable-looking driver. The eunuch planned to tell her employer to fire her for lack of—what did he call it?—moral fitness. That was before she turned up dead." He squeezes out a wheezing laugh.

"Whose eunuch?"

Ferhat Bey is agitated. He has let himself slip. He hadn't meant to let Kamil know about the eunuch.

"He belonged to Asma Sultan's household in the harem," he admits reluctantly.

"Asma Sultan?" Kamil tries to remember where else he has heard the name recently.

"Sultan Abdulaziz's daughter, may he rest in peace. She's married to Ali Arslan Pasha."

The grand vizier's wife. Sybil in the snow. He sees her, cheeks red, traveling in the sleigh with her mother to Ali Arslan Pasha's harem.

"But there were a lot of other women in that harem," Ferhat Bey continues.

"Other high-status women?"

"The pasha didn't have the same appetite as his father-in-law. Or else his wife made sure he kept his sword in his scabbard." Ferhat Bey wheezes a laugh. "So no concubines, just Asma Sultan and his daughter, Perihan Hanoum. The rest were servants, like the Englishwoman. Although Asma Sultan's relations came and went so often they might as well have been living there. They all knew the governess," he adds.

"Who else visited?"

"Her nieces Leyla and Shukriye were there a lot. Shukriye Hanoum was engaged to that sot Prince Ziya, who was killed with his pants down in Paris."

Kamil tries to keep his irritation in check. He had never met Prince Ziya, but knew enough of his reputation as a thoughtful man and supporter of just causes to have a great deal of respect for him. He had never believed the rumor that Ziya died in a brothel.

"So what is the link between the palace and the murder?" Kamil asks. The old superintendent had implied there was a link. He is certain he hadn't misheard.

"That's the link. Asma Sultan's hawk-eyed eunuch. Go ask him yourself. Be sure to bring a large gift." He sniggers. Asma Sultan, her eunuch, and the woman Hannah were pawns in a game played by giants. He has just put this young upstart on the game board. Still, he shouldn't have brought Asma Sultan's name into it. He doesn't want any more trouble than he already has.

"You never found the carriage or the driver?"

"No."

The superintendent knows his reputation as a failure. He could explain that he was forced to take early retirement and leave this case unsolved. But trading his reputation for the truth might very well lose him more than his position. His notes on the case had been incomplete for this very reason.

Kamil asks, "What about the household at Chamyeri? What did they tell you?"

"Nothing. No one claimed to have seen anything. Other than that hysterical goose of a Frenchwoman. She found the body, ran to the house, packed her things, and was ready to go even before we arrived. She didn't even speak our language, so we had the young girl, Ismail Hodja's niece, translate for us."

"What was the Frenchwoman doing back by the pond?"

Ferhat Bey thinks a few moments. "Well, she said she had been taking a walk. I suppose that's reasonable."

"Was she in the habit of walking there? If I remember correctly, the pond is quite secluded, in the forest."

"Who knows the minds of women?" Ferhat Bey answers in an exasperated tone. "They walk in the woods. Maybe she had a lovers' tiff and wanted some privacy to lick her wounds."

"Did she have a lover?"

The superintendent has reached the end of his patience. Clearly, the man has no imagination, he decides.

"How should I know? I can't very well ask a young girl to ask the woman if she has a lover, can I? And she'd never admit to it if she did. What difference does it make anyway? We had a witness. It had nothing to do with that household." He decides to stop before his tongue slips further along the path he has already negligently directed the young man toward.

The light filtering in the window has become tepid and wan. Outside, the rain has stopped and a chill night wind has begun to blow. The room has begun to fill with men who have closed their shop doors and look forward to their moment of comfort before they walk through the dark streets to their homes. Their breaths have condensed on the windows in a ragged tongue of moisture.

Ferhat Bey mutters that it is time for him to leave and rises shakily to his feet. Kamil thanks him for his kindness and assistance and offers to help him home. The old man growls and waves him off.

"I don't live far. I'll walk."

He hobbles into the courtyard. Kamil stays behind to pay the owner. When he emerges, the superintendent is gone. Kamil shrugs, wraps his cloak closer about him, and passes through the great stone gate into the street beyond.

As soon as Kamil is out of sight, Ferhat Bey emerges from the shadows at the back of the courtyard. He stands for a while, squinting against the wind, as if waiting to see if Kamil will return, then goes back into the coffeehouse.

13

A Perfect Fit

amil and Sybil sit opposite each other in the reception room. He is eager to talk and has refused the inevitable offer of tea. He avoids looking at Sybil and keeps his mind resolutely on the purpose of his visit. To his relief, Sybil is dressed demurely in a china-blue gown.

"Sybil Hanoum, you said you were here when Hannah Simmons was killed."

"I thought you were looking into Mary's death. Is there some connection?"

"I don't know. There may not be, but I'd like to be sure. I spoke yesterday with the police superintendent that handled the case. Perhaps you might remember something more."

Sybil looks thoughtful, then says slowly, apologetically, "Perhaps I wrongly disparaged the police. Mother couldn't find out very much either. Hannah was last seen in the harem nursery, reading to the children."

"Did you know her?"

"She must have come 'round the embassy, but I don't remember ever meeting her."

"Who was her employer?"

"Mother said she was hired by Asma Sultan. But there are usually other women in the harem too."

"Do you know who else?"

"No, but I can try to find out. I'll send a note to Asma Sultan and ask to call on her."

"There's no need for you to do that," Kamil says quickly. "I'd rather you didn't. I mean, I don't know what is involved, or who. It could be dangerous."

"You can't talk to the women, so maybe I can find out something useful. I'll only go for tea, not to put my head on the block," she jokes.

Kamil doesn't smile.

They sit silently for a few moments, each lost in thought.

"Poor Hannah," Sybil says finally. "Mother wrote a letter to Hannah's parents in Bournemouth, explaining as delicately as she could what had happened to their daughter, but never received an answer. We buried her in the English cemetery in Haidar Pasha."

"It is terribly sad," he says awkwardly. "So you know nothing about Hannah Hanoum's family?"

"We were able to learn nothing at all. Except for a few people's memory of her, it's as if she never existed." Sybil turns her face away.

Kamil dismisses an impulse to take Sybil's hand and comfort her.

"She must have family somewhere that remembers her," he reassures her. "And she did have a memorable life, at least while she was among us. After all, it's not every day that a young Englishwoman comes to Istanbul to work for the royal family. Surely there were good things in her life that made it worth living. That served her better than someone's memory of her after she was gone."

"I suppose you're right. I wonder what happened to her belongings. I remember they were sent here to the embassy. I doubt Father would know. He doesn't concern himself with that sort of thing. Mother would have dealt with it. There's a room off the kitchen where she stored odd things. Why don't we look there?" Sybil straightens in her chair and gives him a small smile, cheered by the prospect of a common task.

THE KITCHEN MAID stands by the door, mouth open, as Kamil and Sybil pull out endless jars of preserved peaches and jams that had been stacked at the front of the shelves in the storage room, obscuring a variety of neatly arranged objects: an old marble mantel clock surmounted by a gold eagle; three dented copper bowls with worn tinning; a box of silver spoons; and, at the back of the lowest shelf, a suitcase tied shut with string. Attached to the handle is a neat label addressed in a spidery hand: "Hannah Simmons, d. 1878. Belongings. Unable to forward."

Kamil carries the suitcase to the kitchen table. Sybil gestures for the maid to leave.

"Let's see what's in it." Sybil pulls the case toward her and begins to worry the string. Kamil takes a short, horn-handled knife from his jacket pocket. He slices the string, opens the suitcase, and gently lifts its contents onto the table: two plain dresses, a pair of lace-up shoes, a chased-silver brush set, a pair of embroidered Turkish slippers, and some documents.

"The remnants of a life," Sybil muses sadly. "So little."

Kamil runs his fingers around the edge of the suitcase's lining. He finds an opening and tugs at it, revealing a small velvet box inside a hollow space behind the lock. Kamil pulls the box out and lays it on the table. He stands abruptly and goes to a large clay jar in the corner of the room, removes the lid, and dips in the tinned copper cup attached by a chain. When he has drunk his fill, he replaces the lid and returns to the table.

Kamil pries the latch back with his thumbnail and swings the lid open. Inside is a padded nest of blue silk, a round indentation in its center. Kamil reaches into his pocket and brings out the pendant found around Mary Dixon's neck. He settles it gently into the impression. It is a perfect fit, as he knew it would be.

14

Blood

At the entrance to the grand vizier's villa waits a eunuch. He is wearing a spotless white robe that makes a startling contrast to his blue-black skin. His face is smooth and rounded as an aubergine, but his limbs seem stretched, longer than one might expect for his size. Into the broad sash that binds his substantial middle is tucked a flywhisk at a rakish angle, like an ornament or egret feathers on a turban. As Sybil climbs from the carriage, he bows deeply, sweeping his hand against his mouth, then his forehead, in a grand gesture of obeisance. There is a haughtiness about him too. His eyes always rest on a spot above Sybil's head. He takes no notice of the British regimental lieutenant in scarlet coat saluting Sybil with a white-gloved hand, then leading the remainder of her armed escort toward the guardhouse. The eunuch never speaks. When he guides Sybil through the massive marble doors, the palms of his hand flash yellow, like fish turning.

Sybil trails the eunuch through rooms of rich furnishings and enormous fine carpets. Oil paintings and framed Quranic inscriptions are hung high up near the ceiling. She can see her reflection in the mirrored walls—a white wraith gliding behind a black eunuch, two ghosts in the halls of empire.

At a door carved with gilded swags of roses, the eunuch gives her yellow slippers embroidered with flowers made of tiny colorful crystals. But the women who receive her beyond the door are dressed in European fashion, Oriental only in the surfeit of gold and silver thread and embroidery covering every surface. They are encased from top to bottom in jewels, like Fabergé eggs. They sit stiffly in upholstered armchairs, held upright by their corsets. Some have silk scarves draped rakishly over their hair, pinned by diamond brooches.

What, oh, what have we wrought, Sybil thinks dejectedly, if this is what the world has learned from us?

Asma Sultan rises and walks toward Sybil, hands spread in greeting. Her face is round and pleasant, with a button nose and small eyes. An undistinguished face, the kind one sees but doesn't remember seeing, sipping afternoon tea in a hotel lobby or handing tuppence to a grandchild. Delicate white skin hangs loose along her cheeks and below her chin. The eyes that look her guest over, however, are sharp as flint.

"My family is honored by your presence at my grandson's circumcision."

"I'm happy to be here, Your Highness." Sybil can't remember whether she should bow or curtsy, does both, and stumbles in the unaccustomed slippers.

Large windows frame the blue expanse of the Bosphorus. A French door stands open. The scent of jasmine drifts in from the terrace. The room is flooded with light.

"May I introduce Sybil Hanoum, daughter of our illustrious English ambassador," the hostess announces in slightly accented French.

The women smile and greet her in their high-pitched voices.

Sybil responds in Turkish, causing murmurs of approval. She moves around the room, stopping before each woman and waiting while the hostess introduces the guest and mentions, in flowery Turkish praise, the positions of each woman's husband or father. The women are introduced in order of their prestige.

"Your coming is welcome."

"I am happy to find myself here."

"How are you?"

"Fine, thank you. And you, how are you?"

"I am fine, thanks be to Allah."

"How are your father and mother? Your family?"

"They are well. And your father, is he well?"

Of course, the hostess will have told the women all she knew about Sybil before her arrival. They would not ask about a mother who was dead, or a child, when Sybil is unmarried at what most would consider the advanced age of twenty-three. Clearly, after the death of her mother, Sybil has devoted her life to caring for her father, forgoing a family herself. A good, dutiful daughter.

All the chairs are pushed against the walls, as if the women are still reclining on a long divan. This makes conversation impossible with anyone other than Sybil's immediate neighbors, so she has trouble following the conversations. One of the women switches to French, but Sybil's French is poor, so they return to Turkish.

The seven-year-old boy who will shortly be lifted into manhood at the point of a knife is dressed in yellow and blue silken robes and struts about among the women like a peacock, trailed by his governess.

Later in the afternoon, the women move through the French doors and across the patio toward a shaded grove beyond sprays of jasmine and stands of roses for refreshments. Sybil finds herself walking beside Asma Sultan. Her hair is bound up in a turban of silk gauze edged in pearls and held in place by a diamond and ruby ornament made to resemble a bouquet of flowers. One side of the turban hangs free. The silk slips across her face when she moves.

"Tell me," she asks Sybil as they walk through the garden, "what is life like for a woman in Europe?"

Having had little experience, Sybil tells her about Maitlin's struggle to become a doctor.

Asma Sultan interrupts. "What about Paris?"

"I've never been to Paris, Your Highness," Sybil admits reluctantly, stung by her lack of interest in Maitlin's accomplishments. "But London is a fascinating place," she ventures, launching into a somewhat imaginative account of life in London, where she has been only briefly, but has read about in Dickens and Trollope. She throws in the new underground railway she heard was recently completed.

Before long, Asma Sultan interrupts again. "My nephew went to Paris many years ago." Then she falls unaccountably silent.

Sybil now realizes that Asma Sultan's previous questions were mere preludes to this, the important matter. She also has the impression that Asma Sultan herself is surprised and disconcerted by her admission but, at the same time, compelled to speak it.

She inquires tentatively, "Did he enjoy his stay?"

"He died there."

This, Sybil thinks, is the key to the matter.

"May your head remain healthy."

They walk in the garden apart from the others.

"Ziya was a good man. I wished him to marry my daughter, Perihan, but as the sultan's granddaughter, her hand was too valuable to waste on a relative. My husband thought it more useful to buy the loyalty of a minister. My husband is clever, a ship with sails that catch the slightest wind. He did well under my father until he helped depose him. Now my husband serves the present sultan."

Sybil tries to hide her surprise at Asma Sultan's admission. "But that's normal, isn't it? When there's a change in government, people serve whoever is in charge of their country."

"You do not understand, Sybil Hanoum. We are all slaves of Allah. But we are also slaves of the sultan. His will determines all our fates. The palace is not a place or a government, but a body that reaches every corner of the empire. My nephew could not escape it even in Paris. I am less than the tip of a small finger. Even though I myself am the daughter of a sultan."

At the palace, Sybil has heard, loyalty counts for everything, kinship and friendship not at all, unless one is born of the same mother. Those closest to the sultan are in the most danger, as they are directly in the compass of his critical eye. She wonders whether this is true also for the relations of former sultans. Perhaps more so, she decides, since they might be competitors for the throne. The eldest male of the family inherits.

"I was there when my father was deposed by his own trusted ministers," Asma Sultan continues softly. "They shamed him until he took his own life. The most powerful man in the world and he wasn't allowed to see anyone except his women. Ordinary guards watched his every move, can you imagine? It was unspeakable."

Shocked, Sybil can offer little comfort. "How dreadful, Your Highness."

In a melancholy voice, Asma Sultan continues. "He loved my mother and he loved me because I was her daughter. He loved us most of all. We wiped the blood from his arms with our own veils."

Sybil doesn't know what to say. She had arrived in Istanbul just before the coup and remembers the frightening riots in the streets, the talk of troops and warships surrounding the palace.

"It destroyed my mother," Asma Sultan whispers.

"My mother told me about her, Your Highness. She met her once," Sybil says in a sympathetic voice.

Asma Sultan turns sharply. "When?"

"It must have been 1876, just before . . ." She leaves the thought unfinished. "Mother visited the harem in Dolmabahche Palace while my father had an audience with your father. I remember she said he had brought a pair of pheasants as a gift for the sultan."

"My father had a passion for colorful animals," Asma Sultan recalls fondly. "Parrots, white hens with black heads. He even had a collection of cows of many colors, beautiful animals."

"My mother told me she thought your mother very beautiful."

"She was a highborn Russian lady, educated in France. Her ship was captured on the high seas and she was sold to the palace. Her given name was Jacqueline, but in the harem, they called her Serché, "the Sparrow," because she was so small. The other women were jealous of my father's love for her."

Sybil waits for Asma Sultan to continue the story of her mother, but she turns and walks on without another word. Still curious, Sybil follows her.

After a few moments, Asma Sultan turns to Sybil and says, "There is no loyalty except blood, Sybil Hanoum. One's duty to one's parents is paramount. You have done the right thing by staying at home with your father. The world is in your hands. When one marries, the flame extinguishes."

Sybil is taken aback by this admonition. "But Your Highness, a woman's duty to her parents doesn't have to take the place of having a family and a home of her own."

Asma Sultan turns her sharp eyes on Sybil.

"How is your father, Sybil Hanoum? Is he well?"

Sybil is startled by the sudden change in her tone. She is briefly tempted to say the truth, but instead responds diplomatically, "He is well, thanks be to Allah."

"You use the name of Allah, yet you are Christian."

Sybil has not expected a theological argument. "It is the same God, Your Highness."

Asma Sultan sighs as if vexed with herself. "Don't mind me. I'm only concerned for your health and that of your family."

She leans toward Sybil, her veil falling across her mouth, and lowers her voice. "Perhaps you could deliver this message to your father."

"A message?"

"Yes, that we are concerned for his health, which is so vital to the health of our empire. It's hard for us to know what is happening outside these walls, and it is really not the concern of women. But I would like your father to know that I rely on him, as the representative of your mighty empire. You have helped us in the past, and you will help us again. Our road is hard, but we endure. Will you tell him this, in these words?"

Puzzled, Sybil responds, "Of course, Your Highness. I will tell him. And we thank you for your trust. We do what we can for freedom in the world." Sybil winces at her own grandiose statements, but reminds herself that this is the way diplomats speak.

"There is no freedom, Sybil Hanoum," Asma Sultan responds dryly, "only duty. We go where our betters command. Equally we do not go where they forbid us. Please deliver the message just as I have spoken it."

Some of the other women are looking at them.

"May Allah protect you." Asma Sultan turns and walks down the path.

Asma Sultan's daughter, Perihan, appears beside Sybil and, giving her a long look, compliments her on her Turkish.

15

July 1, 1886

Dearest Maitlin,

My life has taken quite an exciting turn. Please do not scold me for taking this initiative, dear sister, you who have always known your own mind. I know that you would disapprove of my interest in these murders for fear that I might stir up a hornet's nest and be myself stung. But, dear sister, those fears, while demonstrating sisterly love, are misplaced. After all, I am not a governess and I have a protector, which Hannah and Mary did not. And it is to help Kamil in his inquiries that I am pursuing this matter. I can't imagine that you would behave any differently, given the opportunity to help solve not one murder, but perhaps two. Your life has been filled with such excitement. Do not begrudge me my own small portion. But, as you know, I am nothing if not careful and deliberate in my actions, so there is no need for you to fret.

I have made some interesting discoveries. I hasten to assure you that I was not pushing myself forward, but that the information fell

into my hands much like a ripe apple falls from the tree into the
apron of someone standing, quite by chance, beneath it.

Yesterday I visited the grand vizier's wife, Asma Sultan. Her
father was Sultan Abdulaziz, who was deposed in 1876 and then
committed suicide. The sultan's ministers forced him to abdicate
because they wanted a constitution and because he was bankrupting
the empire with his extravagances. Mother told me he kept a thousand women in his harems and had over five thousand courtiers and
servants. He built two new palaces just to house them. Asma Sultan's mother was one of his concubines. Mother met her once,
before the coup. She said she was tiny, with a pale cameo of a face.
She thought her beautiful and romantic.

At that time, Asma Sultan was already married, so she escaped
the fate of her mother and the other women in the sultan's harem
after he killed himself—banishment to the old, crumbling Topkapi
Palace. Asma Sultan's husband was made grand vizier in the new
sultan's government, so she is now very powerful. I don't know what
became of her mother. I hesitated to ask in case the answer was
unwelcome. Understandably, she is quite bitter about the coup
against her father. Apparently, her husband was involved, and she
witnessed her father's suicide. Isn't that dreadful? I feel very sorry
for her. Despite all her wealth and power, she is a sad woman.

She seemed quite concerned to wish Father well, as if she knew
about his condition. For obvious reasons, we've tried hard to keep it
from becoming public knowledge. Still, she did ask me to tell him
that she—I think she meant the empire—continues to rely on him,
so perhaps I misinterpreted her words and she was not referring to
Father's illness at all. I didn't tell Father. If he thinks word has gotten about, it would just make him more anxious.

I did learn something that might be of interest to Kamil. Asma
Sultan implied that her nephew, Ziya, was killed on a trip to Paris by
someone from the palace. This happened right around the time that
Hannah also was killed. I've since learned that Ziya's fiancée,
Shukriye, was in and out of the harem where Hannah worked, and

that Shukriye too disappeared from the city soon after. She was married to someone in Erzurum, on the other side of the country. So
many simultaneous disappearances and deaths of people who knew
one another surely can't be coincidence? In any case, Shukriye is
returning soon to visit her ill father. Being a man, Kamil won't be
able to approach her, so I'll pay her a visit and see what I can learn
about Hannah.

Bernie sends his best. He requested that I add a note to Richard.
Bernie wants to know whether he remembers the Chinese poem
about a brush and a bowstring (I hope I've remembered that correctly), and to tell Richard that he has recently come across the
poem again in a surprising place.

Well, with that mysterious flourish, I will end this missive. As
always, I send my love to Richard and the boys. Don't let them forget me.

> Your loving sister,
> Sybil

The Clean Soil
of Reason

On a September day in the Rumi year 1294, or 1878 by
your reckoning, I accompanied Hamza as he led his
horse toward the main road. Slick yellow leaves plastered the ground. The forest exhaled a dusty, pungent
odor of rain. It was one month since I had found the woman in the
pond. Madam Élise was gone and Ismail Dayi was away, so Hamza
had come to visit openly. He wanted to see Mama. She served us tea
in the reception room, pleased at seeing him after all this time.

"Mama so enjoyed your visit, Hamza. I haven't seen her this lively
in a long time. It makes me happy to see her smile; she doesn't very
often. I wish you would come more often."

"Your mother has always been very good to me."

We reached the gate.

"It has always surprised me that your father took a kuma," he said
without looking at me, "given his views."

"His views?"

"He's a modernist, Jaanan. A man who believes, as many of us do, that the empire will survive only if we learn the secrets of Europe's strength. Some think it's enough to copy their technology. But there's more to it than that. If we are ever to be respected as a great power again, we have to join the civilized world. That means we must change the way we think and live."

He turned to face me. "Polygamy has no place in this new world."

"Who will decide what's allowed in this new world of yours?" I asked with an asperity that surprised me.

"Scientists, statesmen, writers. There are more of us than you might imagine, Jaanan. Some of us have gone to Paris, but we have many supporters here as well." His voice was low and rapid. "We publish a journal, *Hurriyet*. Perhaps you've seen it in your uncle's library. I know he collects reformist journals, although I don't know whether he reads them. You should read the journals, Jaanan. We are going to rip the empire up by its rotten roots and plant it in the clean soil of science and rational thinking."

I felt rather alarmed at the extent of what he was proposing. There was nothing rotten here that needed fixing. Science and rational thinking rattled dry as bones in a cup.

But I did not say any of these things. To please him, I would look at the journals later.

Hamza smiled down at me, and tugged gently at a curl that rested on my shoulder beneath the loose drape of gauze.

"I won't be able to come see you for a while, princess." The soft, stretched vowels and sibilant tail of the French word wound themselves about me and muffled his unwelcome news in a haze of pleasure. "I'll be traveling."

"For how long? Where are you going?" I asked plaintively.

He shook his head. "I can't say. I have to be careful. The sultan has suspended parliament. He's gambled away a third of the empire to the Russians. If not for the British, we would have lost Istanbul and much more. And just when we need Europe most, he's threatening it with a worldwide Muslim revolt that he claims as caliph he could lead. It's time for us to act. We're Turks, Jaanan. Your ancestors and mine rode the steppes of Asia, women and men together. There's no need for religion in a Turkish empire. Religion is the enemy of civilization." He cupped my chin in his hand and added softly, "But not everyone wants change. I don't want to get you or your family into trouble, so I can't come here anymore."

"It's also your family."

I felt angry at Hamza and his politics that took him away from me. I didn't think my evenings studying Islamic texts with Ismail dayi were uncivilized. I took a step backward in protest. Hamza reached out his hand and gripped my arm so tightly that it hurt.

"Hamza!" I yelped in protest, and pulled away, but he drew me over so that his head was next to mine.

He slid an object into the shawl tied around my waist, his hands leaving a burning trail, and whispered, "Your eyes are as luminous as this sea glass."

Then he dropped my arm and, without another word, mounted his horse and rode away.

I reached into the folds of silk and extracted a smooth green stone that seemed to glow from within. It was encased in gold filigree, hanging from a slender chain.

Could this beautiful object really be the mundane shard of a medicine bottle after years of being battered by the sea and scoured by sand? I felt then that there was a meaning to be grasped, a parable of some kind, but it eluded me.

July 3, 1886

Dearest Maitlin,

Father has had one of his spells again. I think Mary Dixon's murder has upset him. He cannot bear to be reminded of Mother's death, of any death. He sleeps in the library and takes all his meals there. I will see to it that his mind remains untroubled by such things in the future. Otherwise, he is as dutiful as ever, seeing to the interminable paperwork himself. He recently let go of his secretary because he said he wasn't to be trusted. Perhaps Father is right, since after his dismissal, the man remained in Stamboul and has set himself up as an agent of trade instead of booking return passage to England. That may sound melodramatic in Essex, but it is true that, here, one must always be on guard against spies in the pay of the sultan or other foreign interests, even British ones. I still worry about Asma Sultan's concern for Father's welfare. How many people know about his decline?

I find myself wondering what it would be like to remain here,

especially as Father shows no interest in leaving. There is much to
be admired in the life of an Ottoman lady, although there is something childlike and seductive about it, quite unsuitable for the civilized mind. They seem never to use their heads for more than
interminable intrigues, like squabbling children, although with
rather more severe consequences. Still, these women are not as soft
and passive as they appear. They can move from languorous and
childlike to regal and commanding in moments. Their nature is not
fixed, like ours.

As you can see, I have retained my objectivity and have not, as
you suggested in your last letter, "gone native." These days, though,
the families of officials I visit with Father live much as we do. The
women's gowns are the latest Paris fashion, likely more up-to-date
than those of Essex ladies. The men too dress in European style.
Men and women dine at table together, then retire to separate
rooms, as we do at home. It is true that their taste in European furnishings is untutored. The coat rack might be placed right next to
the piano. They have a love of ostentation that renders even the best
gown hideous when topped by a jewel-encrusted kerchief. And the
men wear that tasseled, round felt flowerpot on their heads. But this
is simply inexperience with the medium of civilization, as natural as
children learning to walk. If ever I have my own household here, I
will entice you and Richard and the boys to come visit, and perhaps
the Orient will seduce you, as you claim it has seduced me.

I'm sitting in the shade of the pines on the patio and can hear
the cheerful toots of the steam ferries that ply the Bosphorus
beyond the Residence wall. I do so wish I could share my thoughts
with you here by my side. I have been trying to rein in my imagination, as you have so often advised me to do. Shukriye is arriving in a
few days. I think I will visit her first and see whether there is anything to learn before mentioning it to Kamil.

You know, when Kamil comes by, we sometimes sit in the
kitchen, quite companionably, like an old couple over a cuppa'. I've
invited him to dine with Father and me this evening. Our old chef,

Monsieur Menard, has come to mind quite a bit lately. A sign of
impending age, perhaps—reminiscing about the past, though I have
precious little past to occupy me. However, as you are fond of saying, there is always the future.

I've rambled on much too long again, my dear. You write that you
avidly read these digressions of mine and that they are a welcome
respite from your duties. Nevertheless, I feel I impose myself far too
much with these long missives. In my own defense, I have never felt
so alive. And who better to share this with than my devoted sister
with whom I have ever enjoyed a rare friendship and commonality of
mind and sentiment? In the name of that friendship, forgive my
imposition on your busy day with these fanciful accounts of mine.

As always, my love to you and the men of your family, for that is
what I will find when at last I see my dear nephews.

> Your loving sister,
> Sybil

Kismet

fter dinner, Sybil and Kamil stand on the balcony off
the second-floor reception hall and look out at the
dimly lit city beyond the high stone wall surrounding
the compound. Dusk has taken them by surprise. The
Bosphorus is an emptiness beyond the city, sensed rather than seen.
In the middle distance, a garland of lamps swings between the
minarets of a mosque marking the holiday that celebrates the breaking of the month-long fast. The moon, slim as a fingernail paring,
hangs above the dome.

"Do you really believe in kismet, that our fate is written on our
foreheads?" asks Sybil.

"There's no such thing as kismet. It's just an expression, a super-
stitious belief, the resource of those too lazy to struggle to make
something of themselves."

"That's rather uncharitable, isn't it? Think of all the people out
there"—she waves a hand toward the dark city—"who try their best,
but still lead miserable lives."

"Yes, that's true. But I think many people don't try as hard as they might. I mean, the thought of being completely responsible for one's own future is exhausting to contemplate. It's an enormous responsibility, some might say a burden, to place on the ordinary man."

Sybil turns to him in surprise.

"So you think people are simply too lazy to better their lives, or incapable of taking the responsibility?"

"I suppose it does sound rather mean-spirited, when you put it that way."

"I think that people can be relied upon to do their best with what they're given. A poor man, with only a shilling in his pocket, will nonetheless spend it to clothe and feed his children."

"Or buy rounds for his friends."

"That's terribly cynical." Sybil's voice has risen.

"I suppose it's true," he agrees, attempting to smooth the tension between them, "that I've been blessed with a wealthy, well-placed family, a house, an education, so it's easier for me to be progressive." He spits out the final word, surprising even himself. When did I become so cynical? he wonders.

"Do you think it's Islam that is holding people back?"

"Kismet has nothing to do with Islam. It's simply a superstition, like the evil eye."

"People need religion, don't they?" Sybil asks thoughtfully. "How else could they bear up under all the misery and hardship?"

"Religion is the scaffolding within which we build our lives. It falls away when we no longer need its support."

"What a curious definition of religion. What is religion without belief, without faith? Isn't faith necessary?"

"I wouldn't know," he answers wearily. "Religion seems to me nothing more than a set of empty rituals and linguistic niceties that mean nothing more than what they say."

"Everything means more," Sybil counters adamantly. "What you describe isn't a life, it's a shell of a life. What is progress, then, when nothing means anything?"

"Progress means to act rationally, on the basis of known facts, not according to one's kismet or the mumblings of a hodja."

"Surely it also means to lead a morally correct life. To give your shilling to your children, instead of drinking it away, as you yourself said."

"Yes, of course. Civilization doesn't mean everything is acceptable. On the contrary. There are standards that everyone can learn."

"And where do they learn moral standards? In church, in the mosque."

"From parents. And in schools that can correct for the parents' shortcomings. Proper schools that teach science and the arts, the truly great moral triumphs of the modern age, not the niggling do's and don't's of the prayer books."

"Niggling? My God, those do's and don't's *are* civilization. They're a moral compass. Without them, people are empty vessels, no matter how clever and rational they might envision themselves to be."

Kamil does not like heated arguments, but respects Sybil for holding her ground. He is tired, his investigation finding no foothold.

"I should go, Sybil Hanoum." He sees the sadness in her face and feels ashamed that he was the cause of it. He doesn't move.

"Yes." She seems at a loss for words. They remain on the balcony, leaning on the wrought-iron railing. Looking out at the dark shapes of trees and buildings, Kamil reflects on how many colors there actually are in what is carelessly called black.

Finally, she says, "I do agree that religion isn't the only way to learn moral behavior. And it is true that religion is often used unscrupulously to manipulate people and to encourage and justify uncivilized behavior. We've had enough of that in England, with our various kings and wars and injustices. But it would be so sad to lose"—she tilts her chin and looks up at him—"those 'little niceties.'"

"Yes, perhaps you're right." He is intrigued by the discussion and finds himself oddly at peace. She is standing by his left elbow, turned to face him. Their hands on the rail are almost touching. I could stand here forever, he thinks. He looks at her closely in the light spilling from the room behind them. Large, guileless eyes in an earnest face, plump neck, the pearl nestling in the indentation at its base, a faint lilac scent. Her hair is coiled loosely at the back of her head, tendrils escaping around her forehead and ears. He senses pressure behind the cloth stretched across her bosom, a will to expand toward him. As he looks, he sees Sybil's cheeks warm. The pearl stands out like a full moon against her flushed skin. Gerdanlouk, he thinks. An evocative Turkish word, with Arabic roots. It means jewelry, but only jewelry adorning a woman between her lower neck and the top of her breasts. Gerdanlouk. He looks away.

Kamil lingers on the balcony, looking out toward the darker space beyond the trees, hoping the chill, bracing air will cleanse his mind of distractions. The distant pinpoint lights above the mosques waver and wink in the wind, marking the end of Ramadan. A new season, he thinks, a new moon. People cleansed by a month of fasting. Maybe that's a good thing, to be able to start over every year, fresh as a newborn. Free of sin and vices, the Christians would say. For Muslims, who have no concept of sin, reform means to readjust one's behavior so that it is impeccable in the eyes of others. It's never too late for that. What others don't see, well, that's another story.

He turns abruptly and enters the room. A moment later, Sybil follows him. Neither looks at the other's face in the appalling light.

EARLY THE FOLLOWING morning, Kamil rides to his sister Feride's house. One morning every week, he visits his sister and her twin daughters, Alev and Yasemin—aptly named Flame and Jasmine, the one restless and inquisitive, the other amiably tranquil. They breakfast together. Sometimes they are joined by Kamil's father, Alp Pasha, who lives in a separate wing of Feride's mansion. Kamil avoids coming at times when he would encounter his brother-in-law at home. He does not like Huseyin Bey, a distant cousin and a minor member of the imperial family. To Kamil's mind, his brother-in-law is a palace loyalist, but more crucially, an opinionated and self-centered man.

Kamil senses that, despite her large house filled with servants and children and a constant round of visiting, his sister is lonely. For Feride, social life is a desperate, well-oiled mechanism.

Commotion alienates the heart, he muses. It's easier to be at peace when the world has retreated to an observable distance. But he knows Feride doesn't understand this and wouldn't believe him if he tried to explain it to her. As a girl, she desperately wanted to go on social outings and visits, yet when she returned, he remembers her face as wistful and bewildered. She rarely brought friends to the villa. He thought at the time that she was ashamed of living in such an unfashionable house, but now thinks she was lonely even then. The difference between them is that he relishes his solitude, while Feride fights it with continual activity. He spears a piece of melon from his plate and chews slowly, watching Alev try to squirm out of her mother's grip as Feride reties the satin bow at the back of her dress and then tells her to sit at the table next to her sister.

His father sits at the head of the table, gaunt and bowed over his untouched food. His lips and fingers are stained brown. Kamil can see the naked scalp through his father's thinning hair, a sight that pierces him with regret. Kamil tries to get his father to look up, so that he can see his eyes. Regret gives way to anger. Alp Pasha does not look up or respond to his son's attempts to draw him out. Alev and Yasemin also are unusually silent, their eyes drawn inexorably to the shadowy figure hunched beside them. Feride continues chatting amiably, as if she were in full command of her audience.

"When are we going to find you a bride?" she asks with a teasing smile. "The other day, I visited Jelaleddin Bey's household. His daughter is lovely, educated, and of the right age. She is as beautiful as a rose. Don't wait too long or another family will pluck her from under your nose."

Kamil circles his palm in the air to signal exasperation, but he is smiling. This is an old game between them.

"A well-run marriage will bring you back to us." She looks at her silent daughters and gaunt father. "If you were married, we would all go on outings together with our new sister-in-law. Wouldn't that be fun, girls?" Feride has two sisters-in-law, her husband Huseyin's formidable sisters, but they are not the friends she seeks. The two women jealously guard their brother's interests against any encroachment by his wife.

"Yes, Mama," Kamil's nieces answer in unison.

His father heaves himself to his feet and, with unseeing eyes, moves toward the door. A servant shadows him, in case he should fall.

Feride looks meaningfully at Kamil, but he doesn't meet her eye. He fights down the anger his father's rejection always evokes in him. It is an unworthy feeling that he tries to hide from Feride.

Kamil uses his bread to capture a piece of goat cheese from his plate and glances surreptitiously at his sister, who is helping the girls finish their breakfast. He wonders how, despite all her duties and worries, she always manages to look so calm, her hair sleeked back under an intricate cloth cap festooned with ropes of tiny pearls, her gown pressed, her hands resting quietly in her lap or working efficiently at some task. Her long, pale face, with its straight nose and thin lips, is not conventionally pretty, but has a seriousness about it, a peaceful radiance that is attractive. Has this life made her content?

It is a contentment that can kill, he thinks. Always forgiving the gentle violence done to one's time and aspirations. Making minutes into hours and days into years, when there is so much to be done. He does not want to pour his life into a leaky hourglass.

There is no concept of time in the Orient, he thinks grimly. Time is when you marry and have children, then your children marry and have children of their own. That is how lives are reckoned. Between those markers, people sit in the shade, drink tea with their fellows, and make their neighbors' hills into mountains or cause mischief.

He prefers to measure his time and calculate what can be done with it minute by minute. His hand automatically finds the pocket watch his mother had given him before he went away for his year at Cambridge. He strokes it absentmindedly.

When the girls have finished eating, they run off. Feride and Kamil move to the sitting room. Feride closes the door.

"I don't know what to do," she whispers anxiously. "You saw Baba just now. It has become unbearable. He rarely speaks and never leaves the house. All he does is sit in his quarters smoking his pipe. Not only does he refuse to speak with Alev and Yasemin, now he avoids them in the house. When I asked him about it, he claimed that they're of an age where it's inappropriate for them to be in the same room with an older man. He wants them to cover their hair!"

"But they're only children."

"I know. It's ridiculous," Feride says crossly. Two vertical lines between her eyebrows spoil her otherwise smooth face. "He's their grandfather, after all. No rules forbid him seeing them. The girls love their grandfather. He used to play with them when they were younger. Now they think they've displeased him somehow."

Kamil has a sudden insight. "You know, Feride, the girls are beginning to look just like their grandmother, with that reddish hair and freckles. And their voices, especially Alev. Do you remember how you once described Mama's voice, like doves cooing? Maybe Baba can't bear to be reminded," he suggests.

"Nonsense. He's simply allowing himself to be old and unpleasant."

"Have you told him that they're upset and miss his company?"

"Of course. But he says, 'It's Allah's will.' Since when has he cared a kurush about Allah's will? The only will he ever cared about was his own," she adds bitterly.

Kamil suddenly perceives that Feride has a very different experience of their family. Certainly he has never thought of his father as strong-willed—just the opposite. What else has he been blind to?

"I can't figure out what's happening to Baba. And he's not eating anything," she adds in a pained voice. "You see what he looks like."

Kamil takes her hand. "It's the opium, Feride. After a while, it weakens the appetite. Have you noticed anything unusual about his eyes?"

"His eyes?"

"Are they darker?"

"I haven't noticed. Is that a symptom?"

"I believe so."

She stares at him, then pulls her hand away. "Why didn't you tell me this before?"

"I only just learned it myself. I read it in a book," he lies. "It happens in the later stages of addiction."

"You and your books. Well, what should I do? Should I try to stop his opium? I can order the servants not to get it for him, but he might have other sources, and it would only make him angry. What should I do?" she asks again, exasperated.

Kamil is reminded of Sybil and her father. He wishes he could talk to her about his father. Perhaps he will. Why not? He looks again at his sister and wishes he could smooth the frown from her face as he had done as a boy. How would she and Sybil get along? Like fire and fire, he thinks. Or ice and ice. He leans over and brushes his index finger along her brow as if wiping away her frown. For a moment, Feride is stiff and silent, then she begins to cry.

"Don't cry, my soul." Kamil sits next to her and holds her until she is quiet. Then he pulls out a handkerchief and hands it to her.

Kamil sits back, frowning, and reaches for his beads. "It might be possible to take Baba's opium from him, but it will make things worse for a time, much worse. And it'll be you who bears the brunt of his wrath."

"But what else can we do? Things can't go on like this. He'll starve to death."

They sit silently for a while, side by side.

"Maybe we can arrange for the opium to be diluted slowly until he's weaned." Feride sits up straight, her eyes still blurred by tears, but excited by her idea. "Yes, yes. That's what we must do. Do you think he'll notice? If we do it very, very slowly? The servants will help me."

"I don't know, Feridejim." Kamil pats her hand. "The paste is very distinctive. He's sure to notice any change. I'm not even sure it can be diluted. I'll do some more reading about it. For now, try to cut down the quantity and make sure the servants don't smuggle in more. In the meantime, you should prepare the little ones for a difficult period. Baba might lash out at them. That will be even worse than neglect."

"Maybe I should send them to Huseyin's mother for a while." Her voice is unsteady and she begins to cry again.

"You know you don't get along with your mother-in-law, Feride. Let the girls stay here for now. Just keep them away from Baba if he begins to act differently. It's a big house."

"Yes, my little brother. Yes, that's what I'll do," she says with more confidence than she feels. "Thank you. You always know what to do."

You will face the consequences if I'm wrong, he thinks, but does not say to her.

19

The Crimson Thread

hen I was seventeen, Papa decreed that I move from Chamyeri back to Nishantashou to live with him and Aunt Hüsnü. He was claiming me, as he put it to Mama, for civilization.

"Enough of this indolence, sitting on cushions and eating honey lokum. You and your brother are filling her head with nonsense. Poetry is well and good, but what does she know of running a household or moving in society? What husband wants a wife who has been raised by wolves?"

Violet and I looked at each other. We were squatting behind the rhododendron bush beneath the latticed windows of the harem sitting room. I quaked with anger at my father's harshness. How could he know what went on in this house when he was never here? He had not visited for over a year. The angry words spilling from the window weighed down my limbs. I tried to rise and run away, but Violet took my arm and pulled me back. She shook her head impatiently and pressed herself more tightly against the house wall. I could hear my mother weeping quietly. I willed her to speak, but she didn't argue, she didn't fight for me. I knelt, shaking, under the bright blossoms until we heard the rumble of Papa's coach. I could not be distracted that night by Violet's petting, so she stilled me in the vise of her arms. The following day, I discovered five round plum-colored bruises on my arm where Violet had anchored me.

On the day of my departure, Mama did not look at me, although I knelt for some time on the carpet at her feet, holding in my hand the corner of her robe. She was hunched under her sable on the divan. I knelt before her and kissed the back of her hand, then pressed it respectfully against my forehead. Her hand was as light and insubstantial as a moth. My mind was racing to find the right words, the magic ones that would break her trance and bind her to me, a bright crimson thread wrapped once around her wrist and again around my waist, a thread that would extend between the farthest corners of the empire and this room in Chamyeri. Whenever I touched the thread, I would feel her pulse beat the lullabies of my childhood in Nishantashou, before Aunt Hüsnü came.

I assured her that I would be safe, that I would write and visit, but I could not be sure that she heard me.

"Goodbye, Mama. May Allah hold you safe."

She turned her head toward the golden light that flowed into the room from the garden beyond. I saw shadows move across her face, but no tears.

I pressed the corner of her robe to my lips and lowered it onto the divan, the material almost black against the bright cushions. My fingers slipped across the satin as I stood. I moved backward toward the door. I could still feel the cool slick of her robe like water on my fingertips.

Violet was ready with our few bundles and our wooden chests. We did not have much in the way of clothing. My chest was heavy with books. Ismail Dayi had called me to his study the night before and pressed upon me all my favorite volumes. The lamplight accentuated the sharp planes and hollows of his face. I thought he looked tired.

"I can always replace them, my daughter. They are yours—these and anything else you wish to take. This house will be yours upon my death. No, don't interrupt. And it is yours while I live, as well. I have no children of my own. You are my only child. This is and always will be your home. I tell you this now so that you will feel secure in your future and—well, perhaps I shouldn't meddle."

He took my hands in his slim fingers, pursed his lips, and examined my face in the candlelight while he considered.

"Do not think, my dear, that you need to marry in order to be secure. You have the wealth to make your own decisions. Take your time in everything, until you feel the pull within yourself. Do not let yourself be guided by fear, or even by desire. And certainly not by the will of others, although"—and here he smiled fondly at my upturned face—"I cannot imagine a will strong enough to pull you off your path, my little lion."

We walked over to the open window and watched the moonlight dance on the Bosphorus.

"Like the moon and the tides, the human heart has many phases. Wait for them. They will not be rushed."

I was not sure what Ismail Dayi meant, but in his gentle shadow, I was able to cry.

THE FORTUNE-TELLER behind the Spice Bazaar was almost blind. He had a long white beard and wore a tattered brown robe and a striped cap. Violet gave him a kurush and he opened the wooden cage. A fat white rabbit with black markings emerged timidly onto the fortune board. After a moment, he nudged the board with his quivering pink nose and the old man worried free the tiny piece of paper pegged to the board at the place the rabbit had indicated. Violet reached out to take it. I nudged her and she gave the man another kurush. The rabbit emerged again and nuzzled another piece of paper. Violet and I took our fortunes to the adjoining park and sat beneath a tree to read them. On my paper was written: "Always an abundant day. A life of movement and novelty." On Violet's paper: "Loyalty at the right place and the right time will rescue you from a difficult situation." The fortunes were written in an elegant script and we conjectured about the identity of such a fine hand. The fortune-teller's son, perhaps. Surely the old man did not earn enough money to hire a scribe to write out his fortunes.

My fortune, I mused, appeared to be marriage and I didn't see what that had to do with abundance. Movement and novelty, certainly. Abundance of wealth, too, perhaps. But not the abundance of cheerful, fat-cheeked women in their songbird-filled rooms. I would always be the sparrow pecking at the bars.

Papa had decided that I was to marry his colleague at the Sublime Porte, Amin Efendi. A man fifteen years my senior, with a bristling mustache that extended beyond his cheeks on either side. The first time I saw him was when he came with a group of men to visit Papa. I had thought it odd that Papa asked me, and not the servant, to bring the men coffee. I couldn't help but notice the man I later learned was Amin Efendi. His knees made sharp points in his trouser legs. He rested his right elbow on the arm of the chair and trailed his long, white fingers in a slow, indolent circle across his shirtfront. His eyes followed me around the room as I served small cups of coffee from a silver tray. When I leaned over to bring the tray closer, I smelled boiled wool and a faint odor of roses, which I find repellent on a man. I could feel his eyes follow the movement of my breasts under the cloth. He took the cup and, for a brief moment, we were touching through the tray. I jerked away, spilling coffee from the other cups.

Papa insisted that I dress in Western gowns when he entertained guests. He allowed a trailing scarf over my hair when strangers were present, but insisted that my face be uncovered. I did not mind wearing such dress, but I resisted the corset. What kind of civilization, I wondered, tortured the body by compressing it so that it was a challenge to breathe and move and even made it difficult to sit on the already uncomfortable Frankish chairs? As a servant, Violet had been spared my father's civilizing efforts. She laced my corset, but did not put much effort into drawing it tight. Aunt Hüsnü, whose maid laced hers so tightly that her body took on the shape of a wasp, looked askance at me when I emerged from my room. But she said nothing. My loose curves and easy movement set off to good advantage her own disciplined torso. My gowns slipped messily over my hips and along my shoulders, while hers looked perfectly proportioned, like the drawings of fashionable Frenchwomen in magazines.

A FEW WEEKS after I had served coffee to Papa's guests, he called me into his study. I stood on the blue Persian carpet in front of his desk. He sat behind his desk, hands folded on his lap, his lips curved upward at each corner. He had a wide, kind face, a face that promised that he would listen patiently and understand what you had to say. The only hint that you might be wrong in your presumption was that his eyes remained cool and appraising. The smooth outlines of his jaw and features made his face unreadable. I was wrong often enough then, but only now have come to realize that his face encouraged you to project the response you needed and desired onto it.

Papa told me that his colleague, Amin Efendi, wanted to marry me.

"Don't you think it's time for you to start a family of your own? You're twenty years old. He's a good, steady man, reliable. He can provide you with a fine household. His wife died two years ago. He wants to remarry, and he wants to marry you."

When I didn't say anything, Papa added, "You needn't be concerned. There are no children from the first marriage."

I looked at him and tried to smile. "But I'm not planning to marry, Papa. At least not at the moment. And I don't wish to marry Amin Efendi. He's much too old for me."

He opened his mouth as if to speak, but said nothing. During the long silence that followed, he sat back in his chair and regarded me with an unreadable expression. In order not to think, I counted the objects on his desk—two inkwells, a letter opener, a stack of white linen paper, four pens. One of the pens was leaking ink onto the blotter.

"Your pen is leaking, Papa," I blurted out nervously, pointing to the stain.

Papa stood abruptly and stalked out of the room. Later, at dinner, he didn't look at me but said matter-of-factly into his stewed lamb, "You will be engaged to Amin Efendi in three months. That will give you enough time to prepare. Allah knows where we'll be able to procure a trousseau for you. Your mother taught you nothing. We'll have to buy it." He looked at Aunt Hüsnü, who nodded.

"I will not marry him, Papa. It is forbidden by the Holy Quran to force your child into marriage." I set myself against my father. My mother's approving presence seemed to regard the scene from afar.

"What rot is that? Is this what that ignorant Ismail Hodja taught you?" Papa shouted. "Filled you with religion like a stuffed dolma. This is a modern household and I expect you to obey me, not a musty old book muttered over by a lot of dirty old men with one foot in the darkness of history and one foot in the grave."

Aunt Hüsnü continued chewing throughout this exchange, as if nothing at all could suppress her enjoyment of stewed lamb with apricots.

Violet came through the serving door behind Papa and Aunt Hüsnü carrying a tureen. I saw her spit into the soup.

20

Avi

The high, clear notes of the boy's voice rise above the clamor of Kamil's outer office.

"I can't tell you. I'm only supposed to tell the bey."

Suddenly the boy begins to cry. There is the sound of a scuffle.

Irritated, Kamil calls his assistant and asks him what is going on.

"A boy claims to have a message for you and refuses to divulge it to the head secretary."

"All right," Kamil sighs, "send him in here."

The boy is about eight years old, slim and wary as a street cat, his hair cut close to his head. He is dressed in lovingly patched trousers and a colorful knit sweater. Upon seeing Kamil, he falls to his knees and prostrates himself on the floor, his nose pressed against the blue arabesques on the carpet. Kamil sees that he is shaking. He walks over and puts his hand on the boy's bowed back.

"Stand up," he says gently. "Stand up, my boy."

The boy cautiously lifts himself from the floor, but stands with his head lowered. Kamil sees, however, that the boy's eyes dart around the room, noting everything.

"What is your name?" he asks, trying to put him at ease.

"Avi, bey."

"Well, then, Avi, why did you need to see me?"

Avi looks up at Kamil. His brown eyes are enormous in his fine-boned face. Kamil thinks to himself that these are eyes that see everything, ravenous eyes. He feels a pang of longing for the omnivorous freedom of a child's appetite for life, not yet disciplined to distinguish raw from cooked, feasting without caring whether life is served at a table or from a tray on the floor. He smiles at Avi.

"Amalia Teyze sent me. From Middle Village. She said to tell you that she has some important information for you." Kamil notes with approval that the boy's words are unhurried and that he has regained his self-confidence.

"What is the information?"

Hands clasped behind his back, Avi continues in a singsong voice, as if he were reciting, "She said to tell you that some weeks ago the gardener for a konak at Chamyeri found a bundle of clothing by a pond in the forest. She said you would know which house. The gardener burned the clothing, but one of the maids saw him. The maid has relatives in our village. When she came to visit, she learned that Aunt Amalia was interested in such things and came and told her."

The boy stops, still standing ramrod straight. His eyes, however, stray curiously to the silver inkwell, pens, and open books scattered on Kamil's desk.

"That is, indeed, important information," Kamil says, reaching in his waistcoat for a silver kurush. "We thank you for bringing it."

"I can't take payment," he replies. "I was doing my duty."

Kamil reaches over and plucks a quill pen from its holder. He holds it out to the boy.

"For your service, please accept this pen. If you learn to use it, come back and see me."

The radiance of the boy's face as he solemnly accepts the pen shoots Kamil through with a delicious pain, a mixture of regret, longing, and pleasure.

"Thank you, Avi. You may go. Please thank your aunt."

He turns his back to the boy so that he should not see the emotion on his face, he—the rational administrator, representative of the all-powerful government.

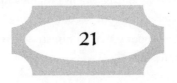

21

The Bedestan

"We're lost," I said querulously.

Violet claimed to know her way around the Grand Bazaar, but we had twice passed the same marble fountain on the Street of Caps.

"I know where I'm going," Violet repeated for the fifth time.

I stopped in the narrow street and took my bearings. Violet looked over her shoulder and, seeing that I was no longer following her, returned and waited impatiently beside me, her eyes roaming over the shop displays. She had assured Aunt Hüsnü that she knew her way through the maze of covered streets, even though Aunt Hüsnü knew as well as I did that this was untrue. As my companion, she went where I went, and I had never been to the Grand Bazaar. Aunt Hüsnü seemed as relieved as we were that she would not be required to accompany us on our expedition to purchase items for my trousseau. I had no intention of purchasing anything of the sort, but adventure beckoned. The glittering bazaar cast its spell over me as soon as I passed through its massive gates.

We were to go to the shop of a friend of Papa's, a goldsmith on the Avenue of Jewelers, to look at bracelets. At first we dawdled at every shop, overwhelmed by the sheer numbers of slippers, bolts of cloth, carpets, hamam supplies, and precious stones, each with its own street of shops selling the same items in almost unthinkable profusion. When a shop owner spoke to us, we shied away, only to stop again at a different shop a few steps on.

Finally, I said, "Let's find the goldsmith's shop. Otherwise Papa will be angry."

And that is when we became lost on the Street of Caps.

"Look," Violet pointed. "An entire street of clothing."

She drew me toward a shop selling brocaded vests. I purchased a vest for Violet and a bolt of cloth for myself and arranged to have them delivered to Nishantashou. Then I asked the shopkeeper for directions to the goldsmith's shop.

"Follow this street," he instructed us, pointing deeper into the bazaar, "until you come to a gate. That's the entrance to the Bedestan. Pass though it. Outside the gate on the other side," he assured us, "you'll find the Avenue of Jewelers."

Violet was already pulling me away.

Before long, we came to a set of thick, iron-studded gates. They led inside a room as large as a building embedded right in the heart of the bazaar. I craned my neck at the high, vaulted ceiling above the narrow lanes of shops. A wooden catwalk stretched around the periphery just beneath the ceiling. Violet nudged me and pointed at a tiny shop crammed with antique silver ornaments and vases. A slim woman in Frankish dress was bowed over a tray of necklaces. The shop next door sold gold jewelry, but of a design and quality I had never seen. Similar shops stretched before us down narrow lanes beneath the dome of this strange room like a stage set in a theater. My father's goldsmith was forgotten.

"What is this place?" I asked the old Armenian shopkeeper wonderingly as he placed another tray of gold bracelets on the counter before me.

"This is the oldest part of the bazaar, chère hanoum," he explained proudly. "It's where all the most valuable things in the bazaar are kept. It's fireproof and at night, after the gates are locked, it's patrolled by guards." He pointed at the catwalk high up under the roof. "This is as safe as any bank in Europe."

Next door, the Frankish woman was trying to bargain with the shopkeeper, who suddenly no longer understood English. Leaving Violet to pay for the gold bracelet I had chosen, I entered the silver shop.

"Can I help you?" I asked her.

She turned and I was caught up in the startled gaze of her blue eyes. She seemed to see directly into my own, as if through a window. We smiled at the same time and, without another word, turned to the shopkeeper. I did not have much worldly experience, but I had good nerves, and soon the Frankish woman had her silver necklace at less than half the price the shopkeeper had at first demanded.

"Thank you," she said when we had stepped back into the lane. "My name is Mary Dixon."

22

Crevice

Kamil finds Halil cleaning his tools inside a shed at the back of the garden. By the flickering light of an oil lamp, Kamil sees a single low room. Halil looks up from the bench. His eyebrows are so dense and wiry that his eyes are almost invisible. The front of the room is stacked with neatly organized garden implements and tools.

To Kamil's question, he answers, "Yes, bey. I found some clothes. It's true. And I burned them."

"Why did you do that?"

"They were women's clothes, bey."

"What difference does that make?"

"Who knows what went on with those clothes? In the woods. It wasn't fit for anyone else to wear them. So I burned them."

As an afterthought, Halil adds, "Why? Did someone complain they were missing?"

"No, but it's possible that they belonged to someone who was killed recently."

"Killed." It is a statement, not a question. With his good hand, he absentmindedly strokes the stumps of his missing fingers.

Kamil wonders how much he knows about Mary Dixon's murder. Surely the villagers all know.

"Where did you find them?"

"By the pond."

"Show me, please."

Without a word, Halil merges into the afternoon shadows outside the door and leads the way through the garden. The air is heavy with bees. They pass the pavilion and climb over the ruined wall into the loamy gloom of the forest. The pond lies behind a screen of rhododendrons.

"There." He points behind a group of moss-covered boulders.

Climbing carefully over the slippery stones, Halil points to a narrow cleft. "Pushed inside."

Kamil slips on a patch of wet moss and catches himself on a bush, swinging nearly to his knees as the branches give way under his weight and others flail at him. He hangs there for a moment, breathing heavily, before pulling himself upright.

He goes over the ground carefully, sweeping aside the leaves, but too much time has passed for there to be any sign of a struggle. Beneath a top layer of crisp brown leaves is a slick wet mulch of debris from previous years. He kneels beside the boulders and peers into the crevice. Deep inside the rock there is something light. He reaches in gingerly, but emerges only with scraped, muddy fingers. He takes off his jacket and rolls up his sleeve. This time, he forces his entire arm into the cleft. His fingers touch cloth. He snags it with the tips of his fingers and carefully pulls it out. It is a woman's blouse. He scours the area systematically and discovers inside a hole, at shoulder height in the trunk of a tree, a pair of women's lace-up shoes. Put there by someone who knows this forest well, he thinks. If the clothing is Mary Dixon's, it would be a concrete link between her death and Chamyeri. Another link is Mary's pendant. It fits into Hannah's box, and Hannah was killed here. Mary and Hannah, linked by the sultan's seal and a scrap of verse.

The shores of the pond are preternaturally still, except for a clearly etched ripple at the far end of the metallic water where it is fed by a spring. Kamil imagines Hannah Simmons floating in the black water, her clothes billowing about her. He looks at the slippery moss and layers of dank leaves with distaste.

His arms and face scraped and his trousers covered in mud, he returns to the city with the blouse and shoes wrapped in an oilcloth.

MICHEL CAREFULLY CLEANS the mud from the shoes and places them on the shelf in Kamil's office next to the folded blouse and the items found in the sea hamam. Kamil stands for a few moments before the neatly displayed items as before a shrine. He is reminded that most things we choose to care about are fleeting. To dispel the melancholy that had begun to settle on him, he turns to Michel and suggests, "Shall we go to the coffeehouse? I think we've earned a rest."

"I have a better idea," Michel counters. "Let me take you to a very special eating house I know. Their Albanian liver is delicious. And the owner's daughter is too," he adds, laughing.

23

The Modernists

Some days after Papa and I fought over Amin Efendi's marriage proposal, he invited his political friends to a soiree at our house. Aunt Hüsnü and I were to appear in Western dress and greet the guests, entertain them at dinner, and then withdraw, leaving them to discuss politics. I had listened to them before. On the evenings when Papa had guests, I moved quietly through the dark corridors and took up a position in a chair in the next room where I could hear their discussions. Servants are invisible even in the light, so Violet found reason to hover in the halls and warned me if anyone approached my hiding place. This rarely happened, though, since the men did not feel free to move through my father's house, lest they trespass into the private realm in which women dwelled. We were only appropriate when on display. Otherwise, we were dangerous and forbidden fruit.

The men arrived, along with their wives. The women, stiff and uncomfortable in their unaccustomed corsets, adjusted the pearl-seeded and embroidered veils that framed their open faces. They were dressed in the latest Paris fashion. The women's eyes were lowered, whether from modesty or embarrassment was hard to gauge. They flocked toward Aunt Hüsnü and me, away from the men, and greeted us effusively, as if we had rescued them from a shipwreck.

Amin Efendi politely greeted all the women together, but his eyes locked onto mine. I was embarrassed and looked away, hoping no one had noticed. I could not imagine him as my husband. I could not imagine a husband in any case. I thought of my cousin Hamza. I thought of Papa's exasperated voice behind closed doors. That was all I knew of men and husbands.

We walked in two flocks, men and women, to the parlor. The women clustered together on one side of the room. The men broke into twos and threes and thus took up more space, but did not move beyond the sofas, an unacknowledged boundary.

I heard the doors to the room creak on their hinges, and I heard the men's voices in the room falter, then increase in volume. I turned to see Hamza standing inside the door. At first I didn't recognize him. It had been seven years since the day he gave me the sea glass and went away, leaving me alone at Chamyeri. I had heard he was in Europe. His features were sharper, as if drawn by a knife. The thick curls I remembered were slicked back against the sides of his head. Permanent lines creased the space between his eyebrows, giving him a seriousness that I found intimidating. He looked leaner and more vital, like a spirited horse whose every small movement is a barely contained shorthand of great power.

He was looking at me, then turned his face to greet my father, who had walked up to him. Hamza leaned down to kiss Papa's hand in the traditional manner of honoring one's elders, but Papa pulled his hand away and reached it out to be shaken. I assumed Papa did not allow Hamza to kiss his hand because he had accepted him as an equal. But I caught sight of Papa's face as he snatched his hand away, and afterward I was not so sure. There are many reasons not to allow someone to honor you.

Papa pulled him briskly to the men's side of the room. Hamza shook hands all around, although I noticed a distinct lack of enthusiasm in the men's brief nods of acknowledgment. Then Hamza turned and strode behind the couches and extended his arms to me. We leaned toward one another and kissed on both cheeks. We were, after all, cousins and childhood friends. His touch sent my pulse racing. The room was entirely still.

"How are you, Jaanan Hanoum?"

I was flustered by all the attention and curtsied as I had been taught. Aunt Hüsnü moved between us and directed Hamza toward the men waiting on the other side of the room. Heads began to move toward one another, a flutter of sound like birds taking wing. Defeating my effort to focus elsewhere, my eyes fled again and again to his face across the room.

PAPA WAS A modernist, but he was also a loyalist and the men expended great heat excoriating the Young Ottomans that they believed were undermining the empire with their talk of a parliament.

"The empire is being threatened and all men should speak with one voice. Otherwise our enemies will perceive our division as weakness and take advantage of it."

The men clustered near the French doors open to the twilight garden. I could hear their conversation clearly through the chime and tinkle of women's voices around me. Hamza sat nearest the garden, his face in darkness.

"It's one thing to be modern," my father expounded, "but it's quite another to be a traitor to your sultan." Several men cast pointed looks at Hamza.

"These journals spread vicious propaganda. All this talk of liberty and democracy promotes the separatist movements in the provinces and plays into the hands of the Europeans. The journals must be closed down and the radicals arrested."

There was a general mutter of assent. Several men shifted uncomfortably in their chairs.

A distinguished, gray-bearded man turned toward my father. His broad chest was spanned by loops of gold braid and a sash gleaming with medals. Although he spoke slowly, weighting each phrase with the gravity of silence, no one interrupted.

"I agree. It's quite possible to be civilized without aping the Europeans in everything they do. We don't need a parliament. We have mechanisms that have worked perfectly well for five hundred years. Our experienced officials can do a much better job of running the government than a group of hotheaded young men uneducated in the principles of just rule. Who is to ensure that they promote the interests of the government and don't misuse their power to support this group or that, undermining the unity of our glorious empire? Do we not already have an enlightened system that allows everyone in the empire, whether Muslim or minority, to thrive?" He extended his hand expansively. "Look around you. The sultan's banker is an Armenian and his advisor on foreign affairs is a Greek. His physician is a Jew. Indeed, there is almost no work for us poor Muslims except in the army and behind a desk!"

This occasioned laughter among the men and even some titters from the women.

"Anyway, there is no such thing as a European civilization." My father picked up the thread. "Europe is nothing more than a region, home to a lot of squabbling nations that can't even agree among themselves. European civilization is a myth foisted upon us by those seeking to destroy our way of life and undermine our government. These radicals are working at the behest of the European powers, who would like nothing more than to divide us among ourselves and see the empire carved up into pieces that they can easily swallow."

Hamza spoke up. "The empire is weak because we've allowed the Europeans to buy us. We're in debt and whatever taxes we can flay from the backs of our poor peasants goes only to pay the interest. It's not ideas that threaten the empire. Only ideas can save it."

"There's nothing civilized about your ideas," a man countered heatedly. "They're a threat to public morality."

"Yes, that is so." A murmur of approval rose from the company. "You are absolutely correct."

Amin Efendi added, with a sly glance at Hamza, "The other day, a woman of my extended family attended, if you can believe it, a political lecture."

There was a ripple of laughter.

"A lecture by a man," he added.

The men turned to each other in consternation. Several women stopped speaking. Without turning their heads, they continued to smile politely at their neighbors, but their ears clearly were on the debate across the room.

"I put a stop to that, of course." A few of the men nodded appreciatively. "It is unbecoming for a man to lecture before women. It doesn't matter what the subject is, or even whether it's a lecture for women only. It's immoral."

Another man chimed in from an armchair across the room. His voice seemed too loud and more women stopped to listen.

"A woman's calling in life is to marry and be a mother, to be a support to her husband, and to run the household. She doesn't need to learn about science or politics. We don't need women technicians or, Allah forbid, women politicians. A woman should learn the things she needs to know to run her home and be satisfied with that."

The man with medals across his chest disagreed. "But you must admit, Fehmi Bey, that an educated woman makes a better mother."

"No doubt, but after she marries and becomes a mother, all her energies should be focused on her duty, guarding the well-being of her family. These modern women are selfish and egotistical. They think only about themselves. If we all thought like that, it would lead to the destruction of our society. We need mothers and wives, women who can train the next generation."

My voice, once launched, carried across the room like a bell chiming in an empty chamber. "The rights a modern society gives women are no different from the rights women enjoyed in the earliest periods of Islam. The rules laid down by the Prophet, peace be upon him, protect the rights of women. But over time, these rules have been diverted from their true purpose. By giving women rights and freedoms, we're not aping Europe. We're reaffirming our own tradition of respecting women. After all, Europe is far from being such an enviable paragon. It has long restricted the rights of its own women. Women have an important place in a modern, civilized Muslim society. They have a duty to society, as well as a duty to their families."

I found I had risen from my chair. There was a hush, a heartbeat of silence, before Papa coughed and turned to speak to the man at his side.

"Proper women have always fulfilled their duty to society by being good mothers and wives," he said. "There's no need to change the family just to be modern. The traditional family is wide open to modern ideals, whether that family is in Europe or here. There's no difference. What some consider Eastern manners are nothing more than the manners of the civilized world everywhere—solidarity, attachment to family, respect for elders, and concern for those who are weaker and dependent on you. The modern European family doesn't reject these traditional values; there's no contradiction there at all. Modern etiquette is an indicator of civilization everywhere. We must be open to this. I see no reason to fear the disintegration of society. Our family system is resilient, like a tree."

Taking Papa's cue, the men continued to converse, although the rumble of their voices had risen in intensity, as though their words had been driven to greater speed by embarrassment.

The women had begun whispering, the direction of their eyes indicating the destination of their tongues. I sat heavily, my entire body throbbing in time to my heart.

I could not see Hamza's face, once I dared turn my eyes to him. His posture was guarded. I simply assumed he agreed and approved. I could think no other way. When I looked next, he was gone.

24

The Kangal Dog

hey turn into a narrow alley, Kamil leading the way. It is dark, but a faded moon sheds some light. The day has been rainy and unseasonably cold. Yellow mud has congealed into viscous waves and troughs. Bernie slips and Kamil catches his arm. A faint tendril of music snakes through the alleys. They follow it like the lost children in one of Karanfil's tales. Kamil ducks through a low doorway into a smoky room lit by oil lamps. The proprietor hurries over and welcomes him effusively. He motions a young man to take their coats, then leads them to a table at the front of the room. Kamil whispers in his ear and the man bows his head and leads them instead to a small alcove at the back where they can converse undisturbed, but which still affords a view of the performance. A young male soprano is singing an Italian canto, accompanied by a mixture of European and Oriental instruments that add an air of lamentation to the song.

Two glasses of raki and small dishes of hummus, stuffed vegetables, yoghurt sauces, spiced fried liver, and bread appear magically on the table before them. As the evening wears on, empty dishes disappear, to be replaced by new and different delicacies. Empty glasses are refilled. Kamil and Bernie engage in spirited discussions on Italian opera and the role of folk songs in classical music.

"I must say," Bernie comments, stretching his legs contentedly, "people here certainly know how to have a good time." He nods at the plates spread across the table before them.

"We call it keyif. A feeling of well-being." Kamil tilts his chin toward the sweating musicians and the tables buzzing with conversation and laughter. "In the presence of friends, fine food, and a pleasant setting."

Very late, they stumble out of the low doorway, this time Bernie supporting Kamil. They head toward the Grande Rue de Pera, where carriages await customers until late into the night. Behind them, the compact shape of a man glides through the darkness, moving from one doorway to another. Suddenly an enormous black object hurtles forward and jumps on Bernie's chest, its weight throwing him backward. Kamil reaches for his dagger. The kangal dog's massive jaws struggle toward Bernie's throat, kept only centimeters away by Kamil's grip on the dog's neck. A sharp blast, then a high-pitched scream, and the kangal falls heavily to the ground.

Kamil shields Bernie, who is doubled over and gasping for breath, a small silver pistol dangling from his left hand. A tavern door opens for a moment as a patron peers curiously into the street. The light spilling from inside illuminates the face of a man pressed against the wall, watching intently. His eyes meet Bernie's before he slips around the corner into the alley.

"What in damnation was that?" Bernie coughs out.

"A kangal dog. They're bred to guard villages. One rarely sees them in the city."

Kamil puts his arm around Bernie, feels a sticky wetness on his shirt.

"Where are you hurt?" he asks anxiously.

Bernie stands up straight and pats himself, then brings his hands closer to his face.

"I think that's from the dog, but my hands are pretty darned banged up. Jesus," he whistles. "That was a close call." He looks down at the dog and nudges it with his foot. "It's good and dead."

"Come on." Kamil puts his arm around his friend, completely sober now. "Let's get you cleaned up. Do all Americans carry a firearm?"

Bernie attempts a weak grin. "Even in the bath, buddy. Even in the bath."

Deep Sea

In April, the slick currents teemed with fish struggling north to spawn in the Black Sea. Lufer, palamut, istavrit, kolyos, kefal, tekir. Large, heavy-bodied fish moved more slowly with the bottom currents, long-lived fish with histories and personalities, unlike the extroverted, superficial crowd above, dripping silver as they leapt and foolishly displayed themselves to the larger creatures haunting the shore. Kalkan, iskorpit, trakonya, kaya. Fishermen called these "deep fish." Their bodies had the meat and heft of an animal. They were hoisted by the tail to hang in the poisonous air. Their wounds bled where the rope cut their flesh. People wandered over and marveled at the animals that lived in the deep. Each was as big as a child.

Violet never minded these fish, hung from a wooden beam in the thatched café where the fishermen and other men gathered, but I felt wounded by their deaths. I laid my hand once against the belly of such a fish, almost as tall as me. Although the fish was dead, its brown eye fixed on a single, last point, its flesh felt muscular and vibrant, and I almost expected it to breathe. This was more startling to me than if the fish had been slippery cold and slack, as my inexperienced hand had expected, and I was torn between recoiling and continuing to stroke the dead body.

Despite my refusal, the date of the engagement ceremony had been set for two months hence, the next step after Papa's acceptance of Amin Efendi's suit. I waited for Hamza to call on me, but he sent no word. I felt if only I could speak with him, the path before me would become clear. Papa said he didn't know where Hamza was, but I didn't believe him. I thought of confiding in Mary Dixon, but when we met for our weekly lunch at the Palais des Fleurs and she made me laugh with her stories of the palace women, I realized I simply wanted to enjoy the bright company of my new friend without burdening it with earnestness.

Amin Efendi brought me a gold watch to seal the pledge, but I refused to open the box. Papa may have promised me, but I had promised nothing. Nevertheless, Aunt Hüsnü had allowed Amin Efendi to sit with me in our parlor attended only by the ever-present servants, while she disappeared.

I tried to make the best of things, but found little in common with him. He was a man whose eyes looked to himself and who saw the world only peripherally. Perhaps it was simply shyness. Violet did not like him.

As for me, I could not imagine spending all the evenings of my life sitting with such a man. I tried to engage him in political discussions, but he was a loyalist and understood as treachery all criticism of the sultan or talk on the merits and demerits of political alternatives. I knew that such things were discussed openly in my father's house and that Amin Efendi was present at these conversations, but I suspected he was concerned that as his future wife my ideas flew too wide. Perhaps Papa was right. Perhaps I had been raised by wolves and it was their spoor that set Amin Efendi's nostrils alert above the sharp line of his mustache. I sometimes thought that he did not see me, but sensed a disturbing presence that both attracted and repelled him.

I had given him no reason to think I was in agreement with plans for our engagement and, indeed, had tried to hint that I did not wish it. I considered the possible effect of stating this to him outright—perhaps he would agree to drop his suit. I would happily return the watch. But I feared not. He had the tenacity of a hungry street dog. I was uncomfortable when he looked at me. His eyes owned me. I consistently refused to meet with him, but Aunt Hüsnü ambushed me with his presence. I was too polite to walk away, as I wished to do. A guest is sacred, and I dared not breach the custom of welcoming one, even one that is unwelcome.

One day, Aunt Hüsnü announced that Amin Efendi and I would make our first public excursion, walking together in the pleasure garden of his patron, Tevfik Pasha. The pasha had agreed, all the preparations had been made, and the guests invited, she told me. Not to go would shame my father in the high circles to which he owed his position. I decided to go, but planned to use the occasion of a stroll, away from the ears of the household and Aunt Hüsnü, to tell Amin Efendi that I did not wish to marry him. I would give him the chance to save face by being the one to break it off.

I arrived in a closed carriage. He was waiting at a marble archway at the entrance to the park. I saw no servants to help me climb down from the carriage and, after a moment's hesitation, accepted his hand. His long fingers curved around mine. They were cool and dry as parchment. In deference to the unseasonably hot weather, I wore a white silk feradje. A yashmak of delicate silk gauze covered my head and lower face. As I descended from the carriage, the heel of my shoe caught on the step. I stumbled slightly and his hands flew up to hold me. The palms of his hands pressed against my feradje and seared my breasts. I was flustered and confused. Should I have expressed gratitude for his assistance or outrage? I looked at Amin Efendi closely but saw only solicitous politeness. Where were the pasha's servants?

Amin Efendi told the carriage driver to leave. He then led me through the gate into the park, where I expected at last to see our company and the other carriages. But we were alone. It was utterly quiet; even the birds were waiting.

"Where are the servants and the guests?" I asked, willing away the quaver in my voice.

Amin Efendi smiled. I saw his teeth under his mustache, stained brown with tobacco. "They're waiting for us at the lake with the refreshments. I thought it would be good for us to have some time together away from the others."

"I am not comfortable with this arrangement," I stated, trying on the haughty voice Aunt Hüsnü used to put errant servants and tradesmen in their place.

"Well"—Amin Efendi smiled tightly, pointing to the empty road behind and the red path ahead—"there's nothing to be done now."

He held out his arm. "Surely you can put up with your fiancé for a short walk along the sea."

"You are not yet my fiancé." I ignored his arm and strode ahead.

His steps were longer, and he easily kept pace with me. I opened my parasol and kept it between us. I knew we should not be alone before we were married, or at least formally engaged. It was very hot and my linen dress had many layers. The veil clung to my sweating face, making it hard to breathe. I slowed my pace. The hem of my feradje turned red from the dust of the path.

"Papa will not be pleased that we are unchaperoned. What is it you wish to speak with me about that requires such a breach of honor?"

He did not look startled by my words. Instead, his smile widened. "Your father doesn't mind."

I turned to look at him. "He agreed to this?" I asked incredulously. "Your father will do what is in his best interest."

"His best interest," I repeated blankly. "What do you mean?"

"I've watched you since you came back to live at your father's house and I've decided that you are exactly what I want, beautiful, smart, but with spirit. You don't want me. That much is clear. But that will keep things interesting. I'll make you into the perfect wife. It will be my great pleasure to instruct and form you, and you will eventually be grateful that I did so."

I backed up until stopped by the trunk of a pine tree. I was so angry, I could only repeat his words. "Instruct me? Form me?" He made it easy to speak my intentions. "I will not marry you."

One step brought him in front of me. "Yes, you will." He gripped my wrists and pushed me against the tree. The scent of roses was overpowering.

"You're hurting me. Stop it! Now!"

I could feel the entire length of his body pushing against me through the layers of my skirts. He placed a thick, hard object into my hand, like an eel, but warmly alive and with the silkiness of skin. I recoiled and tried to throw the object from my hand. Amin Efendi uttered an epithet that was as shocking to me as if he had slapped me. Using my wrists, he pushed me down onto the red earth. I struggled against his grip but my wrists were as delicate in his grasp as the pine needles on the ground around my head.

With sudden clarity, I remembered stories told by the women in their summer villas about young women compromised who were unable to marry or whose families or husbands rejected them. Stories spun in the minds of little listening girls who later weave lives from them. Or deaths.

He lifted my skirts over my face and trapped my arms in them. His sharp knees dug into my thighs, pressing them apart. Then my body was cut by a knife of pain that pierced even my brain. I was certain that I screamed, but I heard nothing except the grunting of an animal nearby. The sounds took on the same rhythm as my pain and I realized it was Amin Efendi. I could not see what he was doing. I saw only the red inside my head.

He shouted a blessing, a sacrilege, and my thighs were flooded with hot liquid. Suddenly the knife-edge dulled, and I could hear myself moaning. I opened my eyes and saw light through the cotton gauze. My arms and legs ached and something had opened a wound in my very center. The sky was a hostile witness.

The light blinded me as he pulled the skirts away from my head and disentangled my arms.

"Here." He pushed a towel into my hands. I realized with a start that he had planned this. I had not opened my eyes. They were still innocent.

I could feel his presence astride me, the toe of his boot pressing my knee outward. His gaze seared my wound, and I struggled to cover myself. I heard him chuckling.

"Now you will have to marry me, my lady. No one else will."

I opened my eyes. He looked exactly the same. His suit was immaculate. His fez rode his head like a demon.

"I will never marry you," I spit. "You can kill me first."

He chuckled. "I won't have to. Your father will insist, if he doesn't wish his honor to be stained. A daughter who gives herself like a common woman of the street. Imagine what that would do to his career."

"You did this to me against my will. He will believe me."

"If word gets out, that will make no difference. And whether anyone finds out . . . well, my silence will be my bride payment."

I thought of Hamza and Ismail Dayi. They would not accept this as a stain on me. They would avenge me. I was certain of it. Society's demands that a woman remain innocent of such cruelty clearly could not always be met. Nor should society's angry expectations always be honored that a wronged woman cleanse her sins—*her* sins?—by death or exile. I realized this in a momentous rush of clarity that was to change my life forever.

I sat up and gasped at the pain and the sight of blood on my dress.

"I'll take you somewhere nearby where you can clean yourself up. Then you can get back in the coach and go to the picnic or you can plead illness and the driver will take you home. No one will know what happened except your father, and he'll want to keep it that way. Come. The coach is waiting by the gate."

He reached his hand down for me, but I struggled to my feet

unaided. My stomach heaved at the thought of his touch. My parasol was covered with pine needles. When I lifted it, the needles showered my hand in a caress. The forest forgives me, I thought.

I straightened myself to face Amin Efendi. His hands were clasped behind his back, eyes unfocused, lips parted slightly, as if reliving a pleasurable moment. I cast the tip of my parasol deep into his right eye.

26

Salt, Not Sweet

"Yes, this might belong . . . have belonged to Mary. I think I saw her wear one like it." Sybil holds up the soiled blouse. They are sitting at the broad kitchen table, its rough wood worn concave by decades of scrubbing. Sybil led him here without thinking when he said he had something to show her, then asked the servants to leave and close the door. It seemed somehow appropriate that the kitchen be the scene of revelations.

Her voice cracks just enough for Kamil to see that, beneath her calm manner, she is aware that it is death she is touching, the last moments of Mary Dixon. He fights his desire to hold her in his arms as he has done Feride. She has much in common with her, he thinks. A kind, dutiful daughter dealing alone with a difficult father absent in mind and feeling. Spirited and intelligent. A modern woman with Ottoman virtues. A good wife for the right man. It is permissible for a Muslim man to marry a giavour woman, but he does not care about such rules anyway. He will marry or not as he pleases, and marry whom he pleases. He takes a deep breath, pushing his hands into his jacket pockets, and leans back in his chair. The fingers of his right hand tangle in the chain of amber beads, while his other hand closes around the cool metal of his pocket watch. In any case, he thinks with guilty relief, her family would never approve. He is aware that Europeans distrust a Muslim man, no matter whether he wears a fez or a top hat.

Sybil lets the blouse drop to the table. It is not ripped or soiled, but badly crumpled, as if it had been wadded up wet and dried inside the rocky niche. Its pearl buttons are intact. Life, Kamil thinks, clings desperately to everything, against all odds. He lets go of the watch and reaches for Sybil's hand. Sybil's eyes meet his. They sit unmoving, each unwilling to risk losing the other's touch by changing anything. Every word, every movement constitutes a risk.

A knock on the door startles them and their hands fly apart.

"Miss Sybil, should I make the tea now?"

"Not now, Maisie." She struggles to put a cheery tone in her voice, but it comes out hoarse with nervousness. "Later. I'll ring for you."

"Yes, Miss Sybil." The maid's footsteps recede down the hall.

Sybil smiles shyly, no longer willing to meet Kamil's eyes. Kamil too is smiling, his cup sunk deep in the jar of well-being. One sip, he thinks. Is that enough?

Suddenly aware of what might now be expected of him, Kamil rises abruptly to his feet.

"I apologize, Sybil Hanoum. I should go." He begins gathering up the objects on the table and wraps them in the oiled cloth.

"No, please don't go yet." His abruptness has soured her pleasure. Exasperated that suddenly it is she who is pleading, Sybil points to the table. "We haven't finished looking at these things." There is an edge to her voice that halts Kamil's hands in their frenzied activity.

He leans forward, props both hands on the table, and takes a deep breath. He doesn't know what to say.

"Please sit, Kamil Bey." Sybil regally indicates the chair at his side. "I know you're very busy, but since you came all this way"—she smiles brightly at him—"I would like to be of help."

Kamil sits and, for a brief moment, regards the objects on the table without seeing them, then looks at her. "Thank you, Sybil Hanoum." He relies on her to know what he means.

Sybil pulls the cloth bundle nearer, unwraps it again, playing her fingers lightly across the objects assembled there.

"I don't know about the shoes, but it seems the type she would wear. She wasn't terribly fashionable, and this is a common enough shoe in Europe. Turkish ladies, you know, prefer leather slippers, like this one here." She points to a torn and badly soiled slipper. "Wherever did you find these things?"

"We found the shoes and the blouse in the forest behind Ismail Hodja's house in Chamyeri."

"These," she adds, pointing to the hair comb and mirror, "are quite common. They could belong to anyone." She touches her thumb to the blade of the knife. "Sharp. Was this found with the other things?"

"These things are from a place north of there."

"Do you suspect Ismail Hodja, then?"

Kamil pauses, then draws a deep breath. "No."

Sybil brushes her hand across his sleeve. "Does this help you at all?"

"It confuses matters. She drowned in salt, not sweet water. But what was she doing at the pond?"

"Maybe she fell into the Bosphorus and someone hid her clothes at the pond later," Sybil suggests.

"We thought we had found the place where she drowned, a sea hamam. It's closed for the season, but someone used it recently. There was no evidence, though, that anyone was killed there, just a dead dog we found nearby." He shrugs. "Dogs are everywhere. Who is to say that this particular dog has anything to do with the murder?"

"Why a dog?"

"The fishermen heard a dog bark that night." He smiles wryly. "I know. Not much to go on."

"So she could have been pushed into the strait anywhere."

"What we really need to know is where she drank the tea that paralyzed her before she was pushed. A young woman like that might have been able to save herself otherwise."

"Does datura paralyze you?"

"It makes it difficult to move your limbs and to breathe. It depends on the dose. People don't die right away. It can take hours. First their throat becomes dry and they have difficulty swallowing. Their pupils dilate and don't respond to light. They can become blind. There's a slow paralysis of the limbs, vertigo, hallucinations. But she didn't die from that. She drowned."

Sybil feels her throat constricting. She does not move, but Kamil notices her pale face and the beads of sweat on her upper lip. He lays his hand on her shoulder.

"Sybil Hanoum, are you all right? I'm so sorry. That was needlessly graphic. I do apologize."

"No, no need to apologize. I want to know." Sybil's eyes meet his. "I need to know."

The space between them seems to shrink by some formula of physics as yet undiscovered. Their lips meet. Suspended in a universe that begins and ends at the intersection of their skin—until Maisie's footfalls outside the door repeal the wonder.

27

The Smell of Roses

I felt numb and somehow relieved. After I had stumbled out of the forest onto the grounds, the women who had gathered for the picnic led me to the pasha's garden house and laid me on a chaise. They crouched around me, their whispering voices lilting with concern, hissing with curiosity. I remember Violet's brown face leaning over me. One of the women sprinkled my hands and face with rosewater. The smell of roses made me feel ill and the rosewater, as it fell, burned my skin. I remember twisting violently to get away from it and the silver ewer crashing to the ground. The smell became overpowering and I vomited. Then I finally slid into the blackness that had been waiting invitingly at the edge of my vision.

I woke to a man's face by my chest and started back with fear. The man drew away, but continued to sit in the chair by my side. Violet sat grimly on my other side, clutching my hand. I turned and smiled at her. The world was only as deep as the people standing beside me.

The man was clean-shaven, making his face look like that of a child, but his voice was low and assured. He spoke with a pronounced French accent.

"I am the pasha's physician. You need not be concerned. You are safe now."

I stared at him. I was safe? I began to remember. Had they found him? Would I be arrested?

"Can you tell us what happened?"

Would anyone believe me?

"Amin Efendi."

"He has been taken to hospital. He was unable to tell us anything. Were you attacked by thieves?" His face betrayed anxiety that brigands were nearby and had penetrated the pasha's pleasure gardens.

The pain spread outward from my loins until I glowed with it. It made me feel strangely powerful. I told him everything.

I WAS BROUGHT home, put directly to bed, and sedated with a tincture of opium. Violet lingered downstairs. The pasha himself came, she told me, along with his doctor. Papa stood frozen by the door. Aunt Hüsnü leaned against the mantelpiece. The pasha apologized that such a terrible thing had happened while Papa's family had been under his protection. Violet said that when they finished, Papa tried to say something in response, but was unable to speak. The two men helped him to a chair and brought him a glass of brandy. Aunt Hüsnü's expression, however, did not change, Violet noted. When the men had settled Papa into his chair and had managed to calm him somewhat, Aunt Hüsnü offered them refreshments. They declined and, embarrassed and confused as to what else to do, took their leave.

WHEN I WOKE, I found Papa sitting on the divan, looking out my window, smoking with a soldier's intensity. The glass tray beside him was full of cigarette stubs. When he heard the bedcovers rustle as I attempted to sit up, he turned his face to me, but it was shadowed and I could not read his expression. Did he believe me? Blame me? What would he do now? I was too inexperienced to know what repercussions this would have on Papa, but knew well enough that the honorable standing of a man's family always affected his career.

"I'm sorry, Papa."

He did not seem to hear me, so I repeated it more loudly.

"I'm very sorry, Papa. Please forgive me."

Papa stood and walked slowly toward me. He settled himself with a sigh onto the chair next to my bed. His big body in its uniform of dark blue worsted looked too large and out of place in this room of delicate pastel embroideries and doilies. Lace fringe from my bedsheet clung incongruously to his woolen trousers.

"Jaanan." He stopped, embarrassed. He took a cigarette from his pocket, lit it, and inhaled deeply.

"Jaanan, I haven't been able to provide you with a good upbringing," he said into the smoke. "You've grown up wild. I blame myself for that."

"But Papa—"

"You must listen." His voice had regained the familiar clipped tones of authority, but I could hear the urgency in it. "This family has acquired a formidable enemy. Amin Efendi." He choked at the title. Efendi is not only a title of honor, but implies an exemplary lifestyle, a man of honor. "He has lost his position at the palace and the support of his patron, but he still has other powerful friends. And he has lost an eye." Here Papa looked at me curiously. The cigarette dangling between his fingers released arabesques into the air.

I did not respond, but waited for him to continue.

"He is not a man to forgive these things. He will work to destroy us."

I could not imagine what it meant to be destroyed. I thought of the fish hung by a rope. I began to cry.

His eyes swept the room as if an object there might rescue him, but saw only the delicate, fragile weavings of a girl's life, nothing to hold on to. When he turned back to me, I thought the corners of his eyes were moist.

"It's not your fault, my daughter. I shouldn't have forced this marriage on you. I had no idea of this man's low character. He was highly recommended by all who knew him professionally. Hüsnü Hanoum made inquiries into his character among the women. She assured me they all said he was a kind and generous man."

He paused as if something had just occurred to him.

Frowning, he continued, "I think it best if you went to your mother's side. You can rest there, while we decide how to proceed."

He patted my hand without looking at my face, then got up and strode quickly out of the room.

28

July 9, 1886

Dearest sister,

If it is not too much of an imposition on the bond between you and your husband, I would ask that this letter remain between us. I am in need of advice from you. There is no one here I can ask or trust. How I miss Mother. I'm sure she would have been able to guide me. No, there is nothing seriously amiss, although I am feeling quite dislocated these past few days. I find myself spending altogether too much time thinking about Kamil Pasha, the magistrate I mentioned before. After all, despite his civilized demeanor, he is an infidel and I have no right to imagine a life that would cast any aspersions on Father's career. Kamil Pasha has not stated his case for me in so many words—he is not given to rambling protestations—but his meaning is clear. What shall I do, dearest Maitlin? It is impossible to say I will not see him again—he comes here on official business regarding the murder of Mary Dixon. I have never before felt such attraction. It is quite as if I were astride an uncontrollable horse where my only choice is to follow his lead or to fall off at great pain to myself. Is this what happened between you and Richard?

But my real fear is that I might shame Father. I am filled with self-loathing that such thoughts should even enter my mind. I am speaking of marriage, of course, Maitlin. I would not countenance anything else, regardless of the attraction. We all have seen what happens to young women who are too eager to give up their only asset and find themselves devalued before society. I am less concerned with society for my sake, but much more for Father's sake. He could not do his work here if there were any taint of scandal. And there is the question of religion—the scandal of his daughter marrying a heathen would do almost as much damage.

Lately, Bernie has been spending the night. He says he has put his writing project on hold for the moment, that he needs time to rethink his approach. I'm so glad he has decided to stay here. I do so enjoy his company and welcome the diversion during the long evenings. I have for some time suffered from loneliness, particularly at night, something I never shared with you because I didn't want you to worry about me. That loneliness is now accentuated by the absence of someone whose figure does not even fit into the composition of my life, at least as it has been painted by British and Ottoman society. There is a stubborn strain in the women of our family, a deep need to alter the frame into which we have been placed. But I cannot sacrifice Father to that temptation. You know of what I speak.

I look to you, my wise and dear sister, for advice.

Ever yours,
Sybil

SYBIL PUTS DOWN her pen and, taking the sheer white veil from the bed, sits before a mirror and pins it to her hair, snugging it against her forehead. She flings the veil over her head so that it hangs like flowing hair down her back and laughs. The laughter bubbles from deep inside, from a place Sybil has not realized was hers. The veil is nothing, a bagatelle, if by wearing it she will be able to move in society by Kamil's side.

But she doesn't believe he will require her to wear it. She pictures a house, one of those lovely Ottoman confections overlooking the Bosphorus. She will decorate its rooms in Oriental style—flowered carpets, damask cushions, velvet drapes—with enough chairs and couches to host the receptions she is sure will be part of her role as wife of a high Ottoman government official. One could say, she thinks, that she has been training for this role all her life. She will also help Kamil with his work, as she has helped her father. She could be his eyes and ears among the women. Finding Shukriye, a witness to the circumstances surrounding Hannah's death, will prove her worth.

In her mind, Sybil populates her new house with children, a son and a daughter, and her dear nephews. Perhaps they would choose to stay. The boys could attend Robert College, in its forested eyrie high above the Bosphorus. Surely once they had seen it, they would want to stay. Maitlin could start a hospital for women. Richard would agree, as he always has. Perhaps he could hold an embassy post, finally take the reins from her exhausted father. And Bernie would be here, a familiar face.

A pleasant thought suddenly strikes her. They could all live on adjoining properties as Turkish families do. When Turks marry, they move into houses next to those of their parents and siblings. Their children grow up slipping through hedges that divide one garden from the next.

As she thinks of children, Sybil blushes. She pulls the veil across her face and sits heavily on the bed. Kamil's physical presence, the memory of his lips heavy and demanding on her own, overwhelms her senses like a tidal wave. The timbre of his voice thrums in her a desire to submit that, in her capable persona, she would never reveal. Beneath the veil, within that narrow, lush chamber of solitude, she feels unfettered. Nana would say, running with sap.

29

Visions

Kamil sits on a cushioned bench under a trellis of jasmine in the garden of his mother's house, reading Reese's *Manual of Toxicology*, which he has borrowed from Michel with the excuse that it would help him with his investigations. Kamil has always taken satisfaction from knowing exactly how things work. But his reading today is in the service of a more uncertain project, his father. Opium poisoning, he reads, leaves few consistent clues in the body after death. The pupils are often contracted, but may also be dilated. Death may be sudden, or staved off altogether, depending on whether the stomach was full or empty, how many grains of opium were administered, and whether the poison was in liquid form or solid, as tincture of laudanum or crystals of morphia. But a drop of starch diluted by iodic acid will identify a residue of only one ten-thousandth of a grain of morphia by turning blue. There is nothing in the book about weaning a man from the habit of opium.

Sparks of light from the strait give the garden an air of motion and exuberance that intensifies its tranquillity. One of Kamil's most vivid childhood memories is of the delicate, colorful crocheted butterflies edging the cotton scarf draped loosely over his mother's hair. When she leaned over his father to serve him tea, the butterflies vibrated in the breeze and seemed to be trying to lift the scarf away from her face.

Why had his mother chosen to live here on her own? he wonders again. Her presence in the garden is strong. He can almost believe he sees her, stitching her tapestry on the bench beside the roses. Maybe he is seeing visions like Baba, he muses. He supposes his mother tired of the immense staff, the constant surveillance, the wives and families of officials and other visitors she was required to entertain at the official residence. During this time, Kamil remembers watching his parents carefully when they were together. One day, from behind a door, Kamil saw his father embrace his mother, swiftly, almost furtively, in a passageway. This embrace, though brief, relieved Kamil's fear that his parents would part from one another, that he would lose them. At that moment he became aware of this possibility, lodged like a splinter in his heart.

After this, the family moved permanently to his mother's house. Kamil's father came twice a week, bringing his documents and a small retinue of assistants. He settled himself to work at a table under the short, sturdy pine tree overlooking the roses and, beyond them, the strait. Kamil's mother refused to let the servants pour her husband's tea, but took the empty glass herself to the samovar steaming on a nearby table. She spilled the remnants in a copper bowl, washed the glass with hot water from the spigot at the samovar's base, emptying this water too into the bowl. Then she carefully poured two fingers of the rust-black concentrate from a small china pot atop the steaming brass urn, topping it up with hot water. Holding the glass against the light, she carefully inspected the color of the tea, adjusting it with more tea concentrate or more water until the color was just right—a brilliant brownish red that she called rabbit's blood. She brought the glass to her husband balanced on her smooth palm and bent to place it on the table before him.

Enraptured by this peaceful memory, Kamil drowses. His grasp on the book weakens and it slips from his hand. He is awakened by the clink of glass against glass. For a brief moment, in the late afternoon shadows on the patio, he thinks he sees his mother standing by the door. Her face hidden behind a wing of cloth, she is wearing Sybil's dress. When she moves into the slanted sunlight, he sees it is Karanfil, the cook, bringing him tea.

30

Feet Like Milk

"$\mathcal{I}$'m like the cook on a Black Sea grain ship. The cook is set afloat in a small dinghy attached to the ship by a long rope, so that when he cooks over a fire, he doesn't endanger the ship with its combustible cargo."

Violet and I were walking in the garden. Over my shoulder, the sky smoldered orange behind the hill. Our leather slippers made delicate scuffing sounds on the paving stones as we approached the pavilion. The sky over the strait had been leached to ash.

"How do they get the food from him?"

"They wait until he has put out the fire, then pull him back in. But it's dangerous. If there's a storm or a fire, he is lost."

"How do you know this?"

"Hamza told me."

Violet said nothing, but I sensed her disapproval. She never liked Hamza and spied on us when he visited until I scolded her for it.

I had not heard from Hamza since the dinner at our house in

Nishantashou, even in the weeks since Amin Efendi's attack. This weighed on me. If he had sent a message, Aunt Hüsnü might not have bothered to pass it on to me here. Nevertheless, I was hurt by his silence. He must have heard what Amin Efendi had done. The city vibrated with the news.

My feelings had not been steady since the attack. Self-pity overtook me during sleepless nights. I disowned it and wished to cut it from me like a useless limb. The bitter rage I relished, as it made the pain recede. But my anger flooded over. I snapped at Violet, and raged silently at mother, Ismail Dayi, and Hamza for not protecting me, even though I knew they could have done nothing. Most of all, I was angry at myself for having gone along with the charade of visits. But beneath the anger was a calm lucidity, a new confidence that I was closer now to understanding death. That it was really rather simple, after all.

THE GARDEN PATH wound around the base of the small hill on which perched the glass-walled pavilion. Violet wandered a few steps ahead of me, but my eyes were drawn to a motion inside. At first I reached out to alert Violet, but then withdrew my hand at the thought it might be Hamza. Her dark profile turned back toward me. Behind her, the sky was ash gray.

"Go inside," I told her. She looked surprised, then displeased. Without a word, she swung around and marched toward the house, the tail of her head scarf swinging hard with every step.

I waited, gazing toward the water, until she had closed the door. My ears strained for Hamza's nightingale call, but found only the commotion of common birds. The ashes in the sky bled and infected the air, now dense with dusk. An owl mourned in the forest.

I turned and climbed the path to the pavilion. The door was ajar. I pushed it open and slipped inside. No one was there. I sat heavily on a cushion. Most of the shutters were closed and the room was

dark and chilly, but I no longer cared enough to rise. I heard a moan
and realized it had come from my own chest.

I remember clearly the small, cool hand that settled on my arm
out of the darkness. I looked around at a bright shimmer suspended
in the dark, like a white veil. Startled, I said nothing.

The apparition settled beside me. Its hand moved to my cheeks
and stroked them dry, first one, then the other. A small kindling.

"You mustn't cry," the face said in English.

"Mary? Is it you?"

"I came 'round to see you, but your maid said you weren't at
home. So I decided to rest here for a bit before driving back. It's such
a long way. I left the driver snoring in his carriage outside the gate. I
guess he's used to long-winded women's visits."

"I didn't know you were here."

"You weren't at the Palais des Fleurs at the usual time, so I sent
you a message at your father's house. I was worried you might be ill.
Then I heard about what happened to you and that you were staying
up here, so I had to come see you. I didn't realize it was so far. I sent
you a message to let you know I'd be visiting today, but you never
responded." She shrugged. "I came anyway."

"I never received any messages from you, Mary, either at Nishantashou or here."

Mary sat back, frowning. "But I sent them. The messenger said he
gave them to your maid."

For a few moments we gazed at the ink-washed sky outside the
unshuttered pavilion window, each lost in our own thoughts. What
else had Violet kept from me?

"So you had no idea I was coming," Mary said incredulously.

"No," I responded, smiling at her, "but I'm very pleased you're
here. I too wanted to see you, but life became too, how shall I put it,
different. Else I should have sent you a message too—or responded
to yours. You are so kind to come all this way."

"I'm sorry about what happened, Jaanan." She moved closer, link-
ing her arm through mine. We looked for a while at our reflections in
the black dusk of the window.

"You know," she whispered finally, "something like that happened to me too."

Her hand remained hot through the cloth of my sleeve.

I didn't know what to say, so I kept my eye on her reflection. Her hair looked like it was made of light.

"Your fiancé?" I asked finally, to help her.

"No. Punishment." Her voice was bitter.

"For what?"

"For not wanting them."

I didn't understand the meaning of her words, but saw she was sad and angry. She withdrew her hand and sat, head bowed, in the shadow.

"There were three of them. A lodger and his cronies. They saw me kissing a woman friend. They spied on me in my room while we were together."

"What evil is there in a kiss among women?"

Mary looked at me wonderingly.

"When my friend left, they forced their way in and said they'd hurt me if I didn't do the same to them."

"How awful," I exclaimed, remembering the stories of young women who flung themselves to their deaths rather than be touched by a man before their wedding day. I supposed that included a kiss, although now that seemed harmless enough to me.

"What did you do?"

She said softly, "I did what they wanted. What else could I do? They threatened me. They said they'd tell the landlady. I worked there, in the kitchen. I would have lost my position. I had no place else to go."

"What about your friend?"

Mary stared at the dark window for a long moment before answering. "She's the one who told them where to look. She sold me for a few pence."

I didn't see why men would pay to see women kiss. Perhaps in England women were kept hidden as they are among the Ottomans, and unscrupulous men paid to look at them.

"People heard about what happened anyway. They went around bragging about what they had done. No one would hire me. I lost everything." I could hear Mary quietly crying, her face in shadow. "The wife of the minister of our church took pity on me and gave me a good reference, but only if I promised to reform. So I came out here."

I leaned over and caressed the silken filaments of her hair. She let me stroke her hair, as she had my cheeks. She was lovely, taut, confused. I thought to gentle her in the way among women.

When after a while she touched her lips to mine, I misunderstood and she fell back.

"You startled me," I said.

"It's only a kiss," she said breathlessly. "Won't you let me?"

"You are right," I admitted, ashamed of having repulsed her. "There is no shame among women, only comfort."

We smiled bashfully at one another, our faces close enough to see in the gloom. I allowed her to kiss my mouth, then my neck. It reminded me of the balm that ran through me when Violet calmed my fears as a child and, after Hamza no longer visited, eased my sorrow. I had not desired Violet's pity since Amin Efendi's shameful attack, but this pale woman's touch brought me back to my body. It is a blessing of womanhood that we may gather strength and pleasure from one another.

Like a mariner in uncharted seas, her hand traced the pulse in my throat to the top of my breasts, sheathing them in flames. Our lips lay together as twins. I felt myself arching back against the cushions as her hands pulled away the layers of cloth between us.

"Never strangers," she breathed into my ear. "Not from the very beginning."

She did not speak again, not even when I lay shuddering in her arms, my body her supplicant.

This was not the bread and water of Violet's caress, but a veneration.

AFTER THAT WE resumed our weekly meetings. As the months passed, I thought less and less about Hamza, who did not come again. Instead, I savored the unfamiliar sensations of my first real friendship with a woman. Mary rented a carriage and we went for drives through the autumn countryside. When we discovered the abandoned sea hamam, we began to go there for our picnics. The driver returned at a given time or waited, snoring, by the road.

I unstacked the copper warming pots and laid them in a circle on the table. We threw a fringed cotton blanket on the mattress to cover the damp boards. Our bare feet hung in pairs, hers pale as milk, mine the color of fine china. As always, Mary had brought coal and kindled a small fire in the brazier. The jewelry I had given her winked from the shadows as she heated water for tea. From a corner nook, I extracted two tea glasses, the cheap kind bought in the market.

Perched on the mattress under a quilt, we fed each other pockets of flaky dough stuffed with cheese and parsley, tart fingertips of grape leaves rolled around rice and currants, fragrant bread kept hot in the tinned copper pans. After we ate, we smoked cigarettes and threw the remnants from the shady portico into the bright captive square of water. In another season these walls would hold the racket of children's calls, shrill volleys of sound amid the placid murmur of their mothers' voices telling and retelling. Their legs shyly entering the sea up to the ribbon at the knee. Bathing costumes worn like daring fashion gowns. The vulnerable body quickly pressed between plush towels so it did not sicken from a draft.

But not yet. It was still our sun and sea, our banging shutters, our sighing under the weathered boards. We lay still like split mussels, gathering a crust of salt. Her yellow hair was cut short, like a boy's, and when she slicked it back wet, her face became naked.

31

The Girl Wife

To Sybil's surprise, it is not difficult to arrange to see Shukriye. The women's gatherings buzz with the news that she is staying with her sister, Leyla. The women prepare to visit the house in droves to offer sympathy to the sisters, whose father lies dying, and to assuage their curiosity about this member of their society so long gone. On the family's first receiving day, Sybil joins the assault of the concerned and curious. Sybil hears the woman beside her whisper to a neighbor that Shukriye has borne three children, but that only one survives, a boy, just two years old.

"Mashallah, by the will of Allah," the other woman answers in surprise, turning her head and looking appraisingly at Shukriye. "The poor woman. But at least she has a son."

Shukriye, a plump woman in a caftan of exquisite brocade, sits on the divan, her face half hidden behind the wings of a gauze scarf that hangs to her breast. Sybil can see that her eyes are red from weeping. Shukriye's sister, Leyla, keeps up the formal greetings and directs the servants to offer the guests tea, cakes, and savories from large silver trays. Another servant stands in the corner with a small stove and implements, ready to make coffee for anyone desiring it.

Sybil notices Asma Sultan's daughter, Perihan, sitting next to Shukriye, her hand occasionally reaching to smooth Shukriye's robe. She remembers that Shukriye had been engaged to the man Perihan wanted to marry. Perhaps, she thinks, they are united as friends in sorrow at his death.

An old woman in a corner of the divan by the window moves her head rhythmically side to side, intoning a litany of prayer, interspersed with loud sighs and appeals to Allah.

"That is Shukriye's grandmother."

"May Allah protect her. She is praying for her son."

There is a commotion among the women, a rising whisper and flurry of silk as they make way for a tall eunuch that Sybil recognizes as the one that had ushered her into Asma Sultan's house. The women fall silent. Behind him, Asma Sultan enters the room. She looks tired and older than Sybil remembers from the circumcision party two weeks before. She is dressed in a tight-waisted European gown and walks stiffly past the row of women in loose Turkish robes propped comfortably on the divan.

Leyla hurries toward her, arms extended in welcome. Signaling to Shukriye and Perihan to follow her, she leads Asma Sultan into an adjoining private room. As Asma Sultan passes Sybil, she stops and, with an amused smile, gestures that she should come with them. This occasions a flurry of whispers among the other visitors. The eunuch waits beside the door, arms folded, and when the five women have passed through, closes it behind them.

Sybil finds herself in a sitting room furnished only with a low cushioned divan around three sides of the room. In the middle is a carpet of cheerful colors on which are scattered small low tables of wood inlaid with ivory and mother-of-pearl. The windows behind the divan open onto the Bosphorus, quaking with light. She hears the sad query of a dove from the garden.

Asma Sultan is given the seat of honor in the corner of the divan, Perihan beside her. With a curious look, Leyla seats Sybil to Asma Sultan's left.

This is followed by the formalities of introduction and inquiries about health. Servant girls bring refreshments, then withdraw. Shukriye slumps on the divan. She does not eat or speak beyond the required formulaic responses.

Finally, Asma Sultan asks, "What is the matter with her?" To Shukriye she says encouragingly, "Pull yourself together, dear girl, and tell us what has befallen you in these eight years since we last saw you."

Leyla, beside her, adjusts the cushions at her back and gently draws the veil back from her face. She speaks to her in a low, soothing voice, as to a child.

"My rose, remember, I've petitioned the palace to bring you back to the city. Everything will be all right."

Shukriye stops crying and sits up straighter. She squeezes her sister's hand. Her eyes are red-rimmed, but her face is white and round as a full moon, with even features and a small red mouth. A headdress of tiny gold coins sweeps across her forehead.

Asma Sultan continues in a kind voice, "That's better. Now we can see you. What is it that is troubling you, my dear? I know. Your poor father, of course. May his illness pass." Sybil knows this is simply a formula of comfort. She has heard that the man is near death.

Leyla holds her sister's hand and strokes her cheek, murmuring, "Shukriye, my dearest, my rose. You're home at last. We've missed you very much."

Shukriye sighs deeply, as if reaching for all the air in the room. When she finishes, she says to no one in particular, "What is to be done? It is in Allah's hands."

She notices Sybil for the first time.

"Who is that?" she asks.

Leyla introduces Sybil again, emphasizing the fact that her father is the British ambassador.

Sybil begins repeating the ritual formula of greeting. Leyla interrupts, waving her hand exhaustedly and says, "Sybil Hanoum, you are welcome. We consider you a member of our house. Please sit."

Leyla calls to the servant waiting by the door and tells her to bring coffee and then to leave and make sure they are not disturbed.

When the girl has served the coffee and gone, Leyla says, "When you're ready, my rose, tell us everything."

"I have a large house," Shukriye begins slowly, "with enough servants that I cannot say I'm not comfortable. And people say that my husband is a good man." She pauses and loses her eyes in the play of light beyond the window. "Perhaps he is," she whispers, "but he's also a weak man. I feel as if I'm married not to him, but to his mother." Her face winds into a grimace and she begins to cry again, an ugly outraged crying.

"She is responsible for the death of my children," she chokes out.

The other women sit tense and rapt. Sybil is startled to see a smile of satisfaction flash across Perihan's face, but then decides she must have been mistaken.

Finally, Shukriye calms down and continues in a hoarse voice. "My daughters fell ill after eating her food. I think she poisoned them out of spite because I hadn't borne a son. She didn't allow me to take the children to the doctor in town. Instead, she called her faith healer. All he did," she says disgustedly, "was write some Quranic verses on a piece of paper and throw it in water, then had the girls drink the water. Can you imagine?"

Perihan says softly, "Imbibing the word of Allah is a blessed remedy, Shukriye dear. Perhaps they were not meant to live. It is Allah's will."

Shukriye closes her eyes. "Surely treating illness with medicine also finds favor in Allah's eyes."

Asma Sultan asks, "Are you not worried about your son during your absence?"

"Of course I am, but he has a guardian now."

"Your husband?"

"No, he's still his mother's slave. After my children died, my husband took a kuma. His mother suggested it, of course. Then she handed him the stick for our backs," she adds angrily.

A second wife, thinks Sybil, appalled.

Seeing the women's stricken faces, Shukriye tells them, "It's not so bad. She became like my daughter. I tried to protect her, but every month laid a year on her face. She became pregnant and miscarried in midwinter, with no midwife able to reach her through the snow in time. She can have no more children, the poor girl."

Shukriye's hand traces the flowers on a cushion.

"Since her misfortune, her spirit has hardened. Even our husband fears her temper. And she has the support of three brothers who live nearby. My son is safe in her hands."

The room falls silent.

Finally, Sybil ventures, "You must miss your family terribly. I haven't seen my sister in England in more than seven years, and I've never met my nephews at all. Sometimes it's hard to bear. Tell me, why did you marry so far away?" Flustered, she adds, "I mean, if it's not impertinent of me to ask."

"I don't know, chère hanoum. I was engaged to marry my cousin, Prince Ziya." She struggles to control her voice. "He was killed and then my life was taken from me. Whoever killed him, killed me too. I refuse to believe that my life in Erzurum was kismet. Someone besides Allah had a hand in it." She adjusts her veil so that it covers the lower part of her face, then looks up at the women and adds softly, "Those who take fate from the hands of Allah are guilty of pride and will surely be punished."

"Allah knows our fates," Perihan counters. "They are written on our foreheads at birth. No earthly being can alter them." Her voice has a sharp edge that can easily be confused with sorrow. She pulls her veil across the bottom of her face, but Sybil sees the deep crease between her eyes.

"Perhaps you're right. But what was the point of his death? I don't believe for a moment that he was killed by thieves in a house of ill repute, as they told me. I'm sure the palace had him killed. They think all the Turks in Paris are plotting against the sultan. But they're wrong. Ziya was there to oversee the signing of a trade agreement, nothing more."

Leyla tries to hush her sister. "My dear sister, please don't excite yourself. Allah is the only witness." Trying to change the subject, she turns to Sybil.

"You remind me of a governess we had in the palace long ago, may Allah rest her soul. You have the same pale eyes."

"Hannah Simmons?" Sybil feels her skin prickling with excitement.

"Yes, that was her name. Did you know her?" Leyla leans closer to Sybil. "You seem too young."

"My mother did. Please tell me about Hannah."

"A calm girl, sweet as honey lokum." Leyla looks around the room. "What else is there to tell? Asma Sultan, you must remember her."

Asma Sultan thinks a moment, then answers, "No, regrettably I do not. Though, of course, we all know what happened to her."

Perihan looks at her mother in surprise and seems about to speak, then thinks better of it.

Leyla also appears surprised. "But she was a governess in your house."

"We have many servants," Asma Sultan snaps irritably.

Perihan adds in a conciliatory tone, "She wasn't very memorable. I'm sure her death is the only reason we can remember her at all."

"I thought her quite pleasant," Shukriye chimes in. "I often saw her at the women's gatherings and at the hamam. She had charge of the young girls. I once tried to give her some satin cloth, but she seemed content to dress like a colorless sparrow. Poor woman. She seemed uninterested in even the simplest embroidery or jewelry."

"Just that silver necklace she always wore," Leyla adds. "Do you remember it, Shukriye? The only time she ever took it off was to sleep and at the baths. I was surprised that she took it off even then, since she insisted on wearing a chemise. Perhaps she had a disability?" She looks at Sybil inquiringly. "I never understood why she hid her body in the bath. It's ridiculous. We're all women. What is there to hide?"

Sybil can think of no response that wouldn't offend her hosts. On the lowest physical surface, what Leyla says makes logical sense, but it takes no account of higher, more civilized notions of modesty. She smiles nervously.

"Why didn't she take the necklace off? Was it something special?" asks Shukriye.

"I don't think so. Just a round silver bauble," Leyla says dismissively.

Sybil speaks up. She wants to defend Hannah from these women's disparaging judgment. "I think it was probably quite a valuable piece. At least, it seems to have been made at the palace."

"Why do you think that? I don't remember anything particular about it," asks Leyla curiously. "Of course, it was all such a long time ago."

"It has a tughra inside," Sybil says brightly, relieved at not having to defend British modesty and proud that she has something to contribute to the conversation.

Leyla draws her breath in sharply. "What? Where would a foreign girl get such a thing? You must be mistaken."

"No, really. I saw it myself."

Leyla looks at Asma Sultan. "It must have been a gift from someone in the harem."

"I'm not in the habit of giving valuable gifts to servants," Asma Sultan answers with mild reproach.

"Sybil Hanoum," Perihan asks, "did you say you saw it? I thought the police would have taken it."

The women's heads all turn to Sybil.

"The young Englishwoman—Mary Dixon—who was killed last

month had it around her neck. You've heard of her death, surely."
Turning to Perihan, she adds, "She was your governess, I believe."

"Mary Hanoum," Perihan mutters. "An odd woman, but I wished
her no ill. May Allah have mercy on her soul." To Sybil, "I never saw
her wear such a necklace."

"How do you know it's the same one Hannah had?" Leyla asks.

Sybil explains about the box. "It's also special because it has Chinese writing in it."

"Chinese?" the women exclaim.

"Then it must be something from outside the country," Perihan
suggests. "Maybe the sultan's seal was added later."

Leyla agrees. "Our food in the palace is served on porcelain
brought from China."

"And aren't those enormous vases in the reception rooms from
China?" Shukriye adds. "I remember almost knocking one over as a
child."

"Didn't your mother have a collection of Chinese art?" Leyla asks
Asma Sultan.

Asma Sultan doesn't answer the question. Instead, she asks Sybil,
"How do you know it's Chinese?"

"My cousin Bernie is visiting here. He's a scholar of Asia. That is,
he's writing a book on relations between your empire and the East.
Anyway, he was able to read it. It's part of a poem."

"A poem," Asma Sultan repeats knowingly. "Of course. It was
probably a gift to Hannah from her lover. But how did this woman
Mary come to have it?"

"Hannah had a lover?" Sybil tries to hide her excitement.

"Someone she met on her day off. She was allowed to leave the
palace once a week, but Arif Agha kept an eye on her."

"Arif Agha?"

"One of the eunuchs. Every week, Hannah got into a carriage
with the same driver and didn't come back until early the next
morning. Arif Agha asked her where she went, but all he could get
out of her was, 'To visit a friend.' He tried to have her followed, but

that incompetent fellow couldn't manage it. And then it was too late."

"Did Arif Agha describe the driver?" Sybil asks.

Asma Sultan thinks about this. "He said the driver was scruffily dressed, not in livery as one might expect if she were visiting a home in good society. But such families would have sent an escort. Anyway, Arif Agha told all this to the police." Then she mutters to herself, "That fox-tongued fool always talked too much."

"Is Arif Agha here?" Sybil thinks Kamil might wish to speak with him.

"He retired. His incompetence lost him our trust."

"And his venality," adds Perihan.

"It was stupid of the girl to get into a carriage unaccompanied," Asma Sultan observes. "Anything could happen."

"And clearly did." Perihan completes her mother's sentence in a satisfied voice.

"Was the driver a Turk?" Sybil asks.

Asma Sultan sighs deeply, unable to hide her annoyance at the continued questioning. "I don't think so. According to Arif Agha, the man had Arab hair the color of sand. Perhaps a Kurd. Their hair is curly like that, but they are usually darker. One of the minorities? But which one?" She throws up her hands in mock despair. "How is one to tell?" After a moment, she adds darkly, "If you toy with a snake, it will bite you."

Perihan asks Sybil, a bit sharply, "Why do you want to know this?"

Leyla intercedes. "Of course, she was one of your people," she tells Sybil kindly. "It's natural that you should want to know as much as possible about her."

"Her killer was never found," Sybil adds.

"Under a rock, no doubt, among others of his kind." Asma Sultan shrugs.

"Do you think it's of any importance now?" Shukriye asks.

"I don't know. I'm helping Kamil Pasha, the magistrate investigating Mary Dixon's murder. He seems to think there's some connection between the two deaths." She turns to Asma Sultan. "Did you say your mother had a collection of Chinese art? My cousin would be most interested to take a look at it, I mean, if that's permitted. And I'll be sure to tell Kamil Pasha about it." She says his title proudly, as if it already belongs to her, relishing the heft of it on her tongue. "He's coming to dine with us the day after tomorrow."

"My mother has passed away," Asma Sultan replies stiffly.

Sybil is mortified. "I'm so sorry, Your Highness. I didn't know. Health to your head."

"It was a long time ago." Asma Sultan rises to her feet. "Now it is time for us to leave."

Shamed by her gaffe, Sybil watches as Asma Sultan, ignoring Leyla's protestations, walks to the door and raps on it. It is opened immediately by her eunuch. She waits while Perihan kisses her hostess on both cheeks in farewell. Sybil feels Asma Sultan's eyes on her, but when she turns, Asma Sultan is gone.

32

With Wine-Red Necks

It was early in the day. The lane leading to Chamyeri Village was still cool beneath the pines and I shivered in my light feradje. The air was lush with the smell of pine. I tasted salt on my tongue.

"It's been nearly a year. Why should I be banished any longer? There's no one to talk to here and nothing to do," I added petulantly.

I did not mention Mary. Violet did not like her, as she had not liked Hamza, my only two friends. I had scolded her for withholding Mary's messages. If Violet had not been a servant, I would have suspected her of jealousy. It was true that I no longer enjoyed her company as much as in the past when I had no friends of my own. It was true that I had outgrown her touch. The last time she came in the night wanting to share my quilt, I told her we were no longer children who could tumble about unconcerned like the kangal dog's new puppies. She sat on the edge of the quilt, sullen, her mouth downturned. I noticed the deepening lines beside her mouth and between her eyes. I reached, out of habit and concern, to smooth them away. She caught my hand and nestled her cheek in my palm. When I tried to withdraw it, she caught the edge of my hand between her teeth and shook it, for all the world like a kangal, before releasing me and slipping out of the room. I stared at the indentations left by her teeth in my flesh, wanting to laugh, but also curiously afraid, as if a violent current had disarranged the air.

She was dear to me nonetheless, as she ought to have known. We were always together, except when Mary fetched me for our excursions. During the coldest months, snow-blocked roads had ended our meetings. The boat that delivered our coal also brought letters from Mary early that winter. But I had not seen or heard from her in months, even though the roads were now open. She had written that she had some business to see to and would come to me as soon as she could. But I no longer wished to circle the shallows waiting, and decided to throw myself back into the current of life.

"Ismail Dayi is hardly ever here and Mama refuses to listen to anything. It's as if I'm a child again." I thought of poor Mama lying on her divan, coughing, wrapped in her fur cloak despite the warm balm of spring, and felt my complaint stick in my stomach. "I hope Mama gets well soon," I whispered by way of apology. What is written will come to be, but what is spoken also provokes fate.

Violet walked silently by my side. I had become accustomed to her new silences. I remembered her crying in her room when she first arrived at Chamyeri. She must be lonely, I decided. I looked at her out of the corner of my eye. Her mouth was tight and a frown had settled onto her forehead. Perhaps it was time I asked Ismail Dayi or Papa to find her a husband.

We passed orchards behind crumbling brick walls. Fig leaves draped the walls like dark green hands moving in the slight breeze, guarding the small, prim sacs of fruit. Pairs of doves with wine-red necks called softly to one another. We entered the shade of a narrow lane beneath overhanging second stories.

Violet looked about nervously.

"What is it?" I whispered.

"Nothing. Nothing at all."

Violet was lying. Something was worrying her.

At the open square in the center of the village, the small grocery stall was still closed. Two bony dogs slunk grudgingly around the back of the stall at our approach. Another dog lay on his side in the dust, his back leg twitching. Several old men were sitting on low, straw-thatched wooden stools under a tatty awning, drinking tea. Their eyes shifted to watch us pass.

We crossed the square quickly and plunged into the darkness of a narrow street leading to the shore. The overhanging upper stories of the wooden houses almost met overhead. We were here to rent a boat that would take us down the strait to Beshiktash, the nearest pier to Nishantashou. I knew Mama would not allow us to go. Without her authority, I could not send a servant to hire a boat, so I convinced an unwilling Violet to come along. I left a note for Mama and Ismail Dayi, telling them I had gone back to Papa's house. My uncle's house would always be home, but I felt the need to resume my life. Now that I was no longer to be married, I had to think about what to do. I had never much desired the company of society, but I was lonely too. In the city, I hoped at least to resume my education.

As we passed beneath the Muslim houses, I heard women calling to one another behind the wooden lattices covering the windows. Suddenly a bucketful of foul water landed beside us and exploded over our cloaks. Appalled, I stopped and looked up at the woman still leaning from her window, bucket in hand, smiling. Voices and muffled laughter came from behind the lattices along the street. Violet took my hand and rushed me forward, almost knocking over the man ahead of us.

We ran to the open area by the shore. Young men sat on the stones and mended nets. The fishing boats had left long before dawn. The men stopped their work and looked at us curiously. Our feradjes were spattered with yellow stains. We adjusted our veils more tightly. My hand was still in the vise of Violet's grip. I had understood what Violet already knew. We had to leave here. Surely the matrons of Nishantashou would not throw slop on us. I felt certain they had more sophisticated means of cutting the rope that tethered me to society's ship.

I was suddenly very angry. I loosed my hand from Violet's, straightened my shoulders, and walked to the man tending the samovar.

"I would like to rent a boat and a boatman to take us to Beshiktash pier. You will be well compensated."

VIOLET'S SMALL FACE was dark and strong, almost muscular, made up of planes and angles. She was attractive in a masculine way, the only hint of softness rich, liquid brown eyes that tilted up at the outer corners like almonds. Impatient, she continually shifted and readjusted her position, her thin fingers pulling at her clothing, so unlike when she was naked in the water, where she became tranquil and sleek.

I remember how disgusted she was at the exorbitant price of ten kurush the boatman demanded. Then he had the temerity to require another two kurush for the tea seller.

"They can smell desperation, these lowlifes," she whispered through our yashmaks. "They'd take advantage of their mothers."

The trip down the Bosphorus was uneventful. The boatman hardly had to move the oars; the current did all the work. He spent his time leering at us. When we landed at Beshiktash, however, he handed us onto the pier without incident.

Violet had charge of the purse. She was much better at keeping an eye on it in a crowd. The quay was crowded—boatmen, passengers, fishermen unloading their catches, buyers for the fish, and the usual street vendors, porters, and beggars. Violet kept hold of my arm as we pushed through the crowd, looking to hire a carriage to take us to Nishantashou. We were not on a main street. She pointed to a large carriage—really, much too large to have any business on that street—stopped right by the pier. We noticed it right away because the horses had such colorful traces—red and blue. The driver was short and powerfully built, with light-colored hair in tight curls, like the spring lamb Halil once bought to be slaughtered for our feastday meal. Dressed in ordinary working garments, he wore the black shoes of a Jew. Violet haggled briefly and then helped me into the box, while the driver climbed up front. I remember she was puzzled by the low price. "He wasn't at all interested in bargaining," she told me. "He looked rather like he was in a hurry."

The carriage was very dark when I climbed in. When I turned to look for Violet a smell suddenly caught at my throat. The coach jerked harshly forward. Dark wings gripped me in the small space. I saw a flash and Violet flung into the light. Then only the light remained, then nothing.

THE LOW, PLAINTIVE call of the itinerant scrap merchant. It was so familiar; the drawn-out first letter, a rapid stutter of consonants, then the tail of the word, laid like a peacock's fan over the street behind his cart. I was in my room at Nishantashou, waiting for Violet to draw the curtains and wake me. I began blissfully to stretch my limbs, but the dimensions of the bed were wrong, the covers too heavy.

I opened my eyes and saw an unfamiliar ceiling high above me, consisting of parallel rows of shallow arches. The tall windows were blocked with white-painted iron shutters, held shut by a heavy crossbar. I was in a narrow bed, covered by a heavy blue comforter. I was fully dressed, except for my shoes, feradje, and veil. I walked to a window, but the bar was locked in place. Street sounds penetrated faintly through the shutters—the rattle of a cart, vendors calling their wares, the sudden shriek of a child. I put on my shoes. My cloak hung from a hook on the wall. It had been cleaned and pressed. The yellow stains were gone. I moved quietly to the door. To my surprise, it was unlocked. I pulled down the handle slowly, opening the door only a fraction, then pressed my eye to the crack.

An old woman was sitting on a carpet on the floor, a copper bowl of aubergines between her legs. She took a vegetable in her hand, carefully cut off the stem, then skillfully cored it. Replacing the end, she laid the now-hollow eggplant into another bowl beside her.

"Come," she said, without looking in my direction. I opened the door another fraction. Where was Violet?

"Come, come."

I opened the door wide. There was no one else in the room. It was furnished with a divan covered not with silk and velvet cushions, but with colorful flowered cotton. The carpet was threadbare, but the broad wooden boards beneath it gleamed. The windows were open and a soft breeze carried into the room the sounds I had heard before. From one window, I saw the façade of another building through the lace curtains; from the other, the leaf-laden branches of a linden tree, wagging in the sunlight. The room was cool.

The woman looked at me and smiled. I could see that she was missing several teeth. "Welcome."

I squatted on the carpet. She continued disemboweling the aubergines.

"Please, can you tell me where I am? How did I come to be here? There was another young woman with me. Where is she? Do you know?"

The old woman laid aside her knife, wiped her hands on a cloth, and stood. She adjusted the wide white apron attached to the front of her dress. I recognized the style. She was Jewish.

"Come, sit over here," she said, pointing to the divan. Her Turkish was lightly accented. I climbed onto the flowered cushions, tucked my legs under me, and waited in the dappled light. I felt unaccountably peaceful, given the situation. What was the situation? Had I been kidnapped?

The woman returned with two glasses of tea on a gleaming silver tray with ornate handles, the only item of luxury I had seen. I thought: from her dowry.

We sat in silence for a few moments. Her face was serious, but her rheumy blue eyes regarded me kindly.

"I cannot tell you my name and I do not know yours," she began, in her lilting accent. "It is safer that way."

"Am I in danger, then?"

"I understand you are in very grave danger. That is why you were brought here."

I was stunned. "What danger am I in? And who brought me here?"

"It is better for you not to know right now. My son understands these matters. I don't interfere." She regarded her tea glass. "Although I am not in agreement. It's much too dangerous." She looked at me so that our eyes met. "He is my only son."

"It's generous of your son to help me. What is his name?"

She examined me cautiously, then looked away.

I was suddenly anxious. "Violet? The young woman who was with me at the pier?"

The old woman frowned. "Your maid ran away. This creates a dangerous situation for us. She will raise the alarm and they will try to find you in Beshiktash."

She looked at me questioningly. I nodded in agreement. She added thoughtfully, "But they should have no reason to widen the search to Galata."

I'M CERTAIN ISMAIL DAYI went for help as soon as he realized we were missing. I suppose, after reading my note, he would go directly to Papa's house, but find we had never arrived there. He would send Jemal to Chamyeri Village to ask whether anyone had seen us. The fishermen might report that two girls rented a boat and that the boatman dropped them at the Beshiktash pier. But the trail would disappear there. Was my uncle angry at me for leaving? I suppose he would seek advice from his old friend, the white-bearded kadi of Galata. What could a kadi do? He was a judge. The situation was still incomplete, like a cooked egg not yet peeled. Too early for judgment. The kadi would set the police on our trail.

The police would suspect the fishermen, of course. The lower orders are always looked at first, since, having so little, they have the most to gain or reason to envy. But if the police only thought about it, they would realize that the fishermen would never harm two girls from a well-known and important household. The police would disagree, arguing that someone might have paid the fishermen to abduct me. They would have learned from Papa—or, really, from anyone—that Amin Efendi was out for revenge.

Or perhaps Ismail Dayi told no one I was missing for fear of destroying what little remained of my reputation.

I felt no tug on the crimson thread around my waist that tied me to Mama. Did she think I was safe?

Violet would be awake, I knew, black eyes gleaming like fireflies in the dark, as I had often found her in my childhood when I couldn't sleep and asked to spread out my quilt next to hers.

THE JEWISH WOMAN sat on a cushion against the far wall, hands tatting furiously. Beside her squatted the broad-chested young man with the tight cap of blonde curls, the carriage driver, whom I assumed to be her son. Her agitated whispers refused to be calmed by his low, measured responses. They spoke what I recognized as Ladino, the archaic Spanish of Istanbul Jews who fled to the benign reign of the Ottomans after Queen Isabella expelled them from Spain. They kept their eyes averted from the divan where I sat. An untouched glass of tea rested on the divan between my knee and Hamza's.

"I've been here for days with no idea why and no way to tell Ismail Dayi that I'm safe. Allah only knows what he is thinking."

Hamza was dressed as a simple workman in baggy brown trousers and white shirt, a striped shawl wrapped around his waist. His cotton turban was gray from many washings. He had grown a beard.

"Forgive me, Jaanan. This was the only way I could think of to keep you safe."

"Safe? Safe from what?"

"I tried to reach you at Chamyeri but your Violet has set up an impenetrable cordon around you. Did you get any of my letters?"

"Letters? No, I haven't heard from you since that evening at Papa's house." A note of bitterness crept into my voice. "That was nearly a year ago. I assumed you had gone abroad again." Suddenly I remembered Mary's undelivered messages. Had she intercepted Hamza's letters too?

Hamza shook his head in frustration. "I was in Paris until recently. I wrote to you."

When I shook my head, he continued. "So that's why you never answered. Anyway, when I couldn't get in touch with you, I hired someone in the village to keep an eye on you. He learned where you were going, then overtook your boat to send me word that you were heading for the Beshiktash pier."

"You had me watched? Why?"

"You're in danger. I was worried about you."

"You keep saying that, but I don't understand what danger. Why didn't you just come to see me at Chamyeri and warn me against whatever it is that so worries you?"

"I wasn't sure Ismail Hodja would have approved. He never liked me."

"That's not true," I exclaimed.

"Anyway, I came by twice when your uncle wasn't home, but Violet wouldn't let me in."

"What? Violet is my servant. She has no control over what I do or whom I see."

"She told me you were unwilling to see anyone. I waited in the pavilion and called to you." He pursed his lips and fluted a nightingale call. "But you didn't come. I suppose Violet kept you occupied indoors when she suspected I was nearby. I don't know what her motivations were. Maybe she's in on the plot."

Exasperated, I raised my voice. "What plot? If you were so concerned about me, why didn't you meet me yourself at the pier instead of hiding inside the carriage like a thief? Or simply reveal yourself to me once we got in?"

I became agitated as I remembered the details of what I had experienced as yet another assault. "And why the chloroform? I presume that's what you used."

Hamza looked down, his long fingers toying with his tea glass.

"I can't show myself. I'm wanted by the sultan's spies for sedition," he added hastily, glancing at me. "I was in Paris when I heard about what happened last year."

I looked puzzled and he averted his eyes, turning toward the yellow light filtering through the leaves outside the window.

"With that pimp, Amin." He realized with a jolt his unseemly language and looked at me, finally. His face was red. "Sorry. I'm very sorry."

When I didn't answer, he stumbled rapidly on.

"I heard about Amin's plans for revenge and as soon as the roads were open, I started back. There's nothing I can do to change what happened, but at least I can make sure you're safe."

"You shouldn't have put yourself in danger by coming back."

"I know Amin," he responded fiercely. "You have no idea what he is capable of."

"What is this plot from which you're saving me?" I asked, gritting my teeth. "You should have told Papa or Ismail Dayi. What is the point of bringing me here? Everyone will be worried about me and think the worst. Have you considered the consequences?"

"I'm not worried. It's worth the risk to see you are safe."

"The consequences for *me*," I almost shouted.

Grim-faced, Hamza explained, "Amin is a scoundrel who will stop at nothing."

"Why didn't you tell me that last year when my father first spoke of an engagement? Why didn't you tell Papa then?"

Hamza gulped the tea from his glass in one draught and put it down on the saucer with such force that I jumped. I saw the old woman's eyes skim nervously in our direction.

"I had to spend years in Paris because someone turned me in to the palace as a traitor. When I came back two years ago, it didn't take long before I was being followed and harassed again. Do you think your father would listen to me? He despises me. He despises my ideas. He has befriended reactionaries in order to advance his own position. And I'm certain he is the one who reported me to the secret police, then and now."

"I don't believe that," I countered with some heat. "Papa would never do that to his own nephew. You lived in our house, ate our bread."

Hamza barked a short, bitter laugh and shrugged. "There's a lot you don't understand, princess."

"That does me an injustice, Hamza. I know my father and I'm not entirely ignorant of what goes on at the palace. I know there are factions and intrigues. Perhaps Papa doesn't share your views, but I'm certain that blood also counts. Papa is not always right in his actions, but at heart he is a good man. Who told you it was Papa who betrayed you?"

"I know it was him."

"Fine," I snapped. "Make your accusations, but if you care at all about the precious justice you are always going on about, then let me hear the evidence."

"Your father was promoted to the position of counsellor in the Foreign Ministry just days before treason charges against me were sent from that office to the minister of justice. His friend Amin sponsored him for that position. Now that Amin has been disgraced and transferred, your father's position is in danger too. Never take a criminal as your patron," he spit out.

"Well, then we wouldn't have many people left in government, would we? Papa was your patron," I shot back.

Hamza looked disconcerted. This conversation clearly was not what he had expected.

"Your father doesn't respect me," he mumbled.

"Nonsense. You have no evidence that Papa did this. It could just as well have been Amin. He has no liking for you." It occurred to me that Amin might have seen Hamza as a rival for my hand, but I didn't mention this. I remembered the look on his face the evening Hamza greeted me at the soiree at our house. It would have been typical of Amin simply to have the hurdle forcibly removed, rather than attempt the more complex and time-consuming task of winning my affections.

"Possibly," Hamza agreed reluctantly. "Someone turned me in after that evening at your house. I had to return to Paris or risk arrest."

I wondered why Hamza was so angry with my father. Was it because Papa had wanted me to marry Amin? Then why had Hamza not stepped forward and offered marriage himself? I had not been formally engaged yet. As my cousin, Hamza had a right to my hand, regardless of what Papa thought of him. Surely he knew I would have agreed. I looked at him carefully. He was different somehow, aside from the beard, but I couldn't pinpoint what disturbed me.

"Why did you attack me in the cab?"

He was taken aback. "I didn't attack you, Jaanan. I would never do a thing like that."

"You used chloroform! And what happened to Violet? You didn't hurt her, did you?"

Hamza jumped to his feet. "Jaanan, how could you even imagine such things? I had to keep you from crying out or trying to escape when you saw that there was someone else in the cab. I couldn't risk that you wouldn't recognize me and cause a scene that would attract attention. The punishment for treason is death, Jaanan. I can't afford to be noticed in even the smallest way. Violet is fine. She jumped from the cab and ran away. She's back in the Nishantashou house.

"She's very resourceful," he added with a smile. "She attacked me to save you."

It was the charming, self-deprecatory smile I remembered from Chamyeri. I couldn't help but return it. A warm current joined us again. What I had perceived before was its absence.

"You still haven't told me what you needed to rescue me from."

Hamza sat back on the divan, moving our tea glasses to the tray on the floor. He took my hands, palms together, and pressed them between his hands.

"Amin is plotting to—" He stopped uncertainly, then continued in a low voice, "To damage you. I heard that as soon as you returned to your father's house at Nishantashou, he planned to take you from there to his konak. Once you were seen to be living in Amin's house, willingly or not, you would have to marry him."

"Take me from my own house?" I scoffed. "How could he do that? No one would permit him entry. Has he bribed the servants?" I was so aghast I almost did not believe him.

"My sources tell me he has made an arrangement with your stepmother.

"I'm sorry," he added rapidly, seeing the look on my face.

"Who are your sources? Are they reliable?"

"Yes."

"Don't treat me like a china cup," I told him impatiently. "Tell me everything."

"He's in desperate circumstances. He already laid claim to you once. This would make it irrevocable. Not even Ismail Hodja or your father could avoid the shame if you didn't marry him then."

"He neither loves nor respects me. What does he want from me?"

"He gambles too much and has expensive taste in women. He's deeply in debt. He desperately needs your wealth and he needs it soon."

"But the wealth is Papa's and Ismail Dayi's. I have nothing of my own."

"You'll have a substantial dowry when you marry and later a sizable inheritance."

I could not read Hamza's face. His eyes were focused on a distant point beside my head. The current between us had become blocked, just as in the days when he was my tutor. He was reciting facts.

I was suddenly engulfed with rage at Amin for stealing both my childhood and my future, and at Hamza for not asking for me in marriage long before and sparing me this grief. He must have known I would agree and I'm sure Papa would have given his consent. I knew marriage now would be difficult, but surely that wouldn't matter to Hamza.

"So your friends have told you Aunt Hüsnü is helping that man"— I could not say his name—"that he intends to kidnap me from my own house and blackmail me into marrying him."

"Yes."

"And that is why you brought me here."

"Yes. I didn't know what else to do. I couldn't get a message to you at Chamyeri telling you to stay there. I wasn't certain you were safe there either, despite Violet's precautions. And I wasn't sure of Violet's motives."

Misinterpreting the look on my face, he added quickly, "I know you're close to Violet, but you should open your eyes. There's something odd about her, hungry. The way she watches you."

"Of course she watches me," I snapped, still defensive of my companion despite my growing doubts. "She sees to my needs. As for . . . that man, what possible advantage is it for him to do something like this? He must know by now that I would never marry him."

"Jaanan"—he squeezed the words from between his teeth—"you would have no choice. Believe me. It is his way of returning the harm you have done to him."

I thought for a few moments. Perhaps he was right. I was untutored in many of the ways of society, but I clearly remembered the warnings and stories that circulated in the summer harems.

"Now what do we do?" I was aware that I had put myself in Hamza's hands. He leaned forward and laid his hand on my shoulder. His fingers played with a lock of hair that had escaped from the scarf draped over my head.

"I don't know," he said softly. "You'll be safe here for a while, but you can't go out. The neighborhood women sit at the windows and watch who comes and goes."

"So I exchange one prison for another," I said softly, to myself.

"It's only for a short while, until we figure out what to do."

We . . . Was Hamza suggesting he would marry me himself? I waited for him to speak again, but he did not.

I wondered what my disappearance would mean. Did I still have a reputation that could be damaged? I had not had time to think about my future, to test which roads were still open to me. Had this closed another road? So far, the pens of others had drawn the features on the map that was my life.

I regarded Hamza, who was still silent.

"What do you think the consequences of this will be for me?" I asked him, hoping by his answer to decipher the calligraphy of his life on the thin pages of mine.

"Consequences? Of what?"

"Of my coming here."

"What do you mean?"

"The world will believe that I've been abducted."

"I had thought of it as a rescue," he responded defensively.

We sat for a while, busy with our own thoughts.

"May I speak plainly?" he asked.

"Please do," I said, perhaps more emphatically than I wished.

"I don't mean to hurt you, Jaanan." He paused, searching my face. "But since the attack by Amin, it has been difficult for you. Society doesn't forgive. I know." There was an undercurrent of bitterness in his voice that I had never noticed before. I was curious what his experience might have been. He had never spoken of it.

"I'm aware of that, Hamza. But I'm not alone. Papa won't forsake me, nor will Ismail Dayi." Nor would you, I added to myself, but with less certainty.

"You must tell Ismail Dayi that I'm safe," I insisted.

"I'll go myself and tell him." Hamza rose and signaled to the young man.

As her son embraced her, the old woman began to rock and keen quietly. Gently he pulled her hands from his vest and spoke to her again in Ladino, the vowels falling like rain onto her parched, beseeching face.

YOUNG ALMONDS, peeled and eaten raw, leave a raspy feeling on the tongue as if you have eaten something wild. The almond seller exhibited them like jewels: a pile of almonds in their thin brown skins resting on a layer of ice inside a glass box, lit by an oil lamp. Wheeling them about the streets on warm spring nights, the almond seller had no special call—his cart was a sacrament and people flocked to it.

The following evening, Hamza returned and brought me a plate of chilled almonds. We sat on the divan by the window, the plate between us, and talked. I pulled my thumb over the fragile skin. It slipped away suddenly, leaving a gleaming, ivory sliver between my fingertips. The Jewish woman had withdrawn to another room at the back of the apartment. We were alone. This no longer worried me.

Hamza threw the almond into his mouth without peeling it. In a swift movement he was next to me and had wrapped his arms around me. My face was crushed to his chest and my head scarf fluttered to the floor. He smelled of leather.

"Jaanan." His voice was thick and rough. I thought of the carnations embroidered on Mama's velvet cushions in stiff gold thread. They scratched my cheek when I laid it against the rich velvet.

I didn't struggle. This, then, is the path, I thought. Without hesitation, I opened the gate and stepped out.

33

Elias Usta's Workmanship

Kamil can go neither forward into the second courtyard nor back out the wrought-iron gates. He sits in the guardhouse and waits with increasing impatience for the soldiers to allow him entry. They stand implacably at each entrance to the squat stone building, clutching their rifles. The air smells faintly of flint and leather. Kamil stood waiting at the outer gate of Yildiz Palace for over an hour before he was allowed to advance to the guardhouse. He bided his time at the gate with pleasurable thoughts about Sybil, with whom he is invited to dine the evening after next.

At least, he thinks, here I am allowed to sit. On the opposite bench sits a clearly irritated sharp-nosed Frank in stately clothing.

When the shadows have fallen the length of the courtyard, a blue-turbaned clerk appears at the door. The guards snap into rigid poses and bow in unison, their leather armor creaking as they make the gesture of obeisance. The clerk barks at the ranking soldier and motions peremptorily to Kamil to follow him. The Frank also stands expectantly, but one of the guards steps in front of him, hand on the dagger at his belt. With a heartfelt comment in his own language, the Frank falls back onto the bench. Kamil bows but the clerk's back is already turned and he is hurrying away. Kamil lengthens his stride to keep up with him. The young man's lack of decorum and self-importance amuses him. At that moment, the clerk swings around and catches the expression on Kamil's face.

Cheeks flaming, he demands, "You. Show proper respect. You are not in the bazaar."

Kamil's clothing identifies him as a magistrate. He is surprised at the disrespectful tone. The clerk is very young. Probably a youth raised in the palace, Kamil decides, one of the many children of the sultan's concubines. They are educated and given responsibilities without ever having set foot beyond these yellow walls. Certainly never to the bazaar.

Kamil smiles at the clerk and bows slightly. "I am honored to be received by the palace."

Mollified, the clerk turns on his heels and hurries through an ornate gate. From behind, Kamil can see the young man's slight shoulders straighten as more guards snap their weapons into place and salute him. Kamil notes, with pleasure, that the wall is covered in white and yellow banksia roses, passionflowers, sweet verbena, and heliotrope. Silver-gray pigeons waddle complacently on the lawn. In the distance, behind a marble gateway, Kamil sees the square classical façade of the Great Mabeyn, where the everyday business of the empire is conducted by palace secretaries, where the sultan's correspondence is composed, and where his spies send their reports. His father must have reported to the sultan in that building, Kamil thinks.

They approach a two-story building so long that it stretches out of sight on one side. The clerk leads him through a door, along a narrow corridor, then out again into the blinding light of a large yard. Small workshops line the back of the building. Faint hammering and tapping, a strange creaking leak from their windows. The clerk stops by a room larger than others they had passed. Inside, a group of middle-aged men in brown robes and turbans sit drinking coffee from tiny china cups.

When the clerk appears, the men bow their heads in respectful greeting, but do not rise.

"I'm looking for the head usta." The clerk's voice is unnaturally high-pitched.

A man with a neatly trimmed white beard looks up.

"You've found him."

"Our padishah requires you to assist this man"—he looks disgust-edly at Kamil—"with his inquiries."

"And who is this man?" asks the head craftsman, looking benignly at Kamil.

"My name is Magistrate Kamil Pasha, usta bey." Kamil bows and makes the sign of obeisance.

The usta sweeps his hand toward the divan, ignoring the clerk standing by the door.

"Sit and have some coffee."

The clerk turns abruptly and leaves. Kamil hears laughter blow through the room, faint as leaves rustling.

A servant brews coffee in a long-handled pot over a charcoal fire in the corner and hands Kamil a steaming cup properly crowned with pale froth.

"So, you are one of those new magistrates."

"Yes, I'm the magistrate of Beyoglu," Kamil answers modestly.

"Ah." Knowing nods circle the room. "I'm sure you have your hands full with all those foreign troublemakers."

"Yes, I suppose so, though bad character knows no religion."

"Well said, well said." The usta glances at the door through which the young clerk had left.

After the required pleasantries and answers to the men's request for news from outside the palace, the head usta asks, "How can we help you?"

"I am looking for the workshop and the usta that produced this pendant." He passes the silver globe to the head usta, who looks at it with an experienced eye.

"This is Elias Usta's workmanship. It must have been made years ago, though. Elias Usta has long been retired. When his hands were no longer steady, he went to work as keeper at the Dolmabahche Palace aviary. We have heard nothing about him for many years. But this is definitely his work."

He signals an apprentice to bring a lamp and peers inside the silver ball.

"Yes, this is an old tughra. It belonged to Sultan Abdulaziz, may Allah rest his soul."

"Sultan Abdulaziz's reign ended ten years ago. Could it have been made after that time?"

The head usta ponders this. "It would not have been officially approved. But it is true that, with Allah's will, anything can be done at any time."

"Would Elias Usta have needed permission to engrave a tughra?"

"Permission must be obtained for each item to be inscribed with the seal."

"Who can give that permission?"

"The padishah himself, the grand vizier, and the harem manager. She would need instructions, however, from one of the senior women."

"I would like to speak with Elias Usta."

"I will send him a message. If he agrees to meet with you, I will let you know right away."

Kamil tries to hide his disappointment at yet another wait, but he needs permission to approach anyone inside the palace.

"Thank you." He bows.

Another man chimes in, "And we'll make sure they send an adult with a mustache to fetch you!"

To the sound of laughter, Kamil bows out of the room and follows an apprentice through the warren of corridors and courtyards to the front gate.

THE NEXT DAY, the apprentice appears at Kamil's office with a note:

It is with great regret that we inform you that Elias Usta was found dead this morning in the palace aviary. May Allah rest his soul.

Paper still in hand, Kamil stares unseeing out the window. It is the first sign that he is moving in the direction of the truth. Was it worth this man's life? He feels cold, but, as a sacrifice to the dead usta, does not move to close the window against the chill.

34

The Eunuch and the Driver

The Residence is in a wing at the back of the embassy building. Kamil pushes open the iron gate leading to the private gardens. The air is still crisp in the shade of the plane trees, but there is a delicate sheen of heat beyond its perimeter. Kamil looks up at the enamel-blue sky against which the silver leaves of the plane trees twist and flash. The sight cheers him momentarily, despite the new shadows that have entered his life.

His father has become more irritable and aggressive as Feride, with the collusion of her servants, slowly reduces the amount of opium in his pipe. He strides through the house, flailing at objects that fall to the floor and break; the noise seems to intensify his frenzy. Then suddenly he collapses onto a chair or bed and curls up like an infant. Feride and her daughters are terrified, her husband angry at the disruption. Kamil is unsure where this will lead. He has found nothing in books to guide him and worries that he is killing his father instead of helping him. He is too ashamed to ask the advice of Michel or Bernie. His only close friends, he realizes with a start. Perhaps today he can raise the subject of fathers with Sybil. He is reluctant to reveal himself about something so personal, but he is drawn to see Sybil. Even if the problem of his father is not broached, he thinks, he will find solace in her company.

Mary Dixon also has begun to shadow his life. At his last audience with the minister of justice, Nizam Pasha asked him pointedly what progress had been made in discovering her murderer. It has been almost a month since her body washed up behind Middle Village mosque. His impatient gestures implied that Kamil had failed not just the ministry, but the empire. And perhaps it is so. If he did not know the English ambassador, he might assume pressure was being placed on the minister from that direction. But Kamil thinks Sybil's father too distracted to muster a sustained attack. Did the British government take such an interest in a mere governess that it would pressure the sultan's closest aides or even the sultan himself? He wonders, could there be another reason for Nizam Pasha's intense interest? He remembers the old police superintendent's intimation of palace involvement in the murder of Hannah Simmons. Were they watching to make sure he found the killer this time, or that he didn't find him?

And now Elias Usta's untimely death. Kamil is worried about Sybil. Two Englishwomen were already dead.

Sybil opens the door herself almost as soon as he raises the knocker.

"Hello." She smiles a brilliant welcome.

"Good morning, Sybil Hanoum. I hope I haven't come too early." He finds it momentarily awkward to account for his presence. The reasons he gave himself for stopping by seem fanciful now. "I hope you forgive my intrusion. I know I wasn't expected until tomorrow evening."

"I received your message, Kamil Bey. It's always a pleasure to see you." She is blushing.

"I hope I find you well."

"Oh, very well. Very well, indeed. Isn't it a glorious day?" Sybil steps onto the path and looks about her with the serene enjoyment of a child. She is wearing a dress of pale lilac, trimmed in maroon. The colors reflect in her eyes and give them the same depth as the sky. She walks to the edge of the patio and gazes down at the red-tiled rooftops of houses clinging to the lower hillside, suspended above a sea of fog.

Kamil stands beside her. "Thick as lentil soup, I believe you say."

Sybil laughs. "That's your national dish, not ours. It's pea soup. Thick as pea soup." She turns to him and touches his arm. "Won't you come in? Have you breakfasted?"

"Yes, thank you. I have. But I wouldn't mind some of your delicious tea." For the British, drinking tea seems an end in itself, he thinks with relief, a ritual to which he can moor his visit.

She leads the way inside to the room off the garden and opens the French doors wide to let in the scented sunlight.

"How is your father?" he asks.

"He's well, thank you. Busy as always. He's been inquiring about some of the journalists we know. Apparently there's been a crackdown and many were sent into exile."

"These are dangerous days, Sybil Hanoum. Your father is a powerful man and protected by his office, but still he should be careful." What he means is that Sybil should be careful.

Sybil stares at him for a moment. "Do you really think Father is in danger? I can't imagine that anyone would harm the British ambassador. Think of the consequences for your regime. It would be an international incident. It could even lead to military intervention by Britain. Surely no one in their right mind would risk that."

"Unfortunately, these days one can't count on rational thinking. There are other forces too, not under our control. Even in the palace. This is strictly between us," he adds quickly.

"Of course. I wouldn't breathe a word."

Her pleasure at this confidence inspires him to continue. "The palace has destroyed other powerful people who became, shall we say, difficult. Besides, these things can be made to appear an accident. As you know, relations are strained between our governments. Some might wish them to deteriorate further. But I don't mean to worry you, Sybil Hanoum. It was, perhaps, impolitic of me to speak of this to you. But I know how much you care for your father. Perhaps a word or two from you about being careful and always taking a retinue with him, his clerks, a dragoman, a few extra guards. There are other means of protecting oneself that are less obtrusive. I'd be happy to speak with him about it, if he's so inclined."

Distressed, Sybil shakes her head. "Father has never been careful. I'm sure his safety doesn't concern him a bit. He has always lived just for his work," she says sadly. "It's as if he has put to bed all other parts of his mind, so that he has no distractions from his duties. But if you think it necessary, I'll try to get him to take some precautions."

Kamil understands from the flatness of her voice that her father, like his father, inhabits a land inaccessible to his family. He remembers a conversation he had with Bernie about Western and Eastern civilizations. Bernie argued that people in the West saw themselves as individuals, each with his own rights and responsibilities, in charge of a destiny of his own making. This could lead to sharing, if one had the same interests, or selfishness, if one did not. In the East, on the other hand, people were first and foremost members of their family, their tribe, their community. Their own desires were irrelevant; the solidarity and survival of the group paramount. Selfishness couldn't occur, because there were no selves, only fathers and sons, mothers and daughters, husbands and wives. Bernie's comparison seemed to make sense, at least in a general way, although Kamil could think of numerous exceptions, including himself. Yet he couldn't deny that there was in Ottoman society a widespread belief in kismet and in the evil eye that brought misfortune. And family feeling was very strong.

Still, he remembered thinking that his fellow classmates at Cambridge, young Englishmen away from home for the first time, were not so dissimilar from the young men he knew at school at Galata

Saray. One loved one's parents, certainly. But once out from under their supervision, there was plenty of personal ambition and mischief. If, as the English say, 'Boys will be boys,' then why couldn't 'fathers be fathers,' regardless of which society they belonged to? And here is Sybil, a representative of the individualistic West, tending to her father like any good Ottoman daughter.

"Perhaps you could simply be a fly in his ear. The important thing is to be aware of the risk."

Sybil giggles. "A flea in his ear."

"Ah, of course. Although I find that image, well, rather unappetizing. I think I'd prefer a fly in my ear." Kamil laughs. "English expressions. I've never gotten used to them. I think you have to be born English."

"It's the same with Turkish sayings. You have sayings for everything. But even when someone explains them to me, I don't understand them."

"Oriental inscrutability. It's what has kept us independent for so long. No one understands what we're saying, so they can't conquer us!"

The sun falling through the French doors has become hot and Sybil stands to draw the lace curtains. She sits again on the couch and, eyes lowered, adjusts and readjusts the folds of her dress. The room falls into a hush.

After a few moments, flustered, she raises her chin and says, "Oh, I promised you tea."

"That would be lovely. Thank you."

Sybil jumps up and runs to the velvet bellpull by the door. Her skirt catches Kamil's leg as she passes. They wait in companionable silence for the tea to be brought. Each spark of conversation is muffled by the still, amber air, then extinguished, as if the air in the room is too thin to support speech. The click of fine china, the sough of tea poured, and the thin rap of spoons against the porcelain cups embracing their warm liquid take the place of conversation.

Sybil slides her cup and saucer onto the side table. They seem too fragile suddenly in her hand. She is excited about what she thinks of as her investigation, but also nervous about Kamil's reaction.

"I saw Shukriye Hanoum, the woman who was engaged to Prince Ziya. She remembered Hannah."

"I see." He looks surprised. "Where did you find her?"

"She's here in Istanbul. Her father is dying. She came to pay her last respects."

She tells him about the death of Shukriye's children, her accusations against her mother-in-law, and the young kuma.

"That's barbaric. Did she tell you all this in front of the others? You said there were many visitors."

"No. I joined her and her sister in a private room afterwards."

"How did you manage that?" he asks, smiling and shaking his head at her audacity. "I thought you didn't know them."

"Asma Sultan and her daughter were there and, when they moved to another room, they took me along."

"What did you learn about Hannah?"

"Shukriye and her sister Leyla remembered Hannah from their visits to Asma Sultan's household where she was employed. I presume they were visiting Perihan, who seems to be a close friend. That surprised me, since Shukriye was engaged to the man Perihan loved. Perhaps Perihan is a more generous soul than she appears."

Kamil smiles at the innocence of Sybil's assessment. He knows better the unforgiving nature of royal intrigues that rage among the women as much as the men.

Sybil relates the conversation as she remembers it: Shukriye's belief that the secret police were responsible for Prince Ziya's death; Arif Agha's discovery that Hannah was meeting someone every week.

Interrupting the easy lope of her story, Sybil pauses and reaches for her tea.

"A carriage?" he prompts her impatiently.

She sets the tea down, clattering the cup. "Yes. The eunuch told Asma Sultan that the driver had light-colored hair like a European, but tightly curled like an Arab's. She thinks he might be a Kurd."

At this, Kamil is speechless. Ferhat Bey had claimed to know nothing of the driver. Perhaps the eunuch had told the superintendent a different story. Too many links in this chain, Kamil thinks irritably, and he doesn't know if one is connected to the next.

Sybil looks at him with a worried frown.

"Did they know where the carriage was going?" he asks brusquely.

"No." Puzzled, she adds, "Asma Sultan said her eunuch told all this to the police."

"The superintendent wasn't as forthcoming as I would have liked," he admits. "What else did you learn?"

"The women remembered Hannah wearing the silver pendant. They don't remember Mary wearing it. I told them the pendant was made in the palace, with the sultan's seal inside. They thought Hannah's pendant must have been a gift, maybe from the person she visited every week, perhaps a lover. Or from someone in the harem."

"You told them all this?" Kamil's back is suddenly tense.

"It just came up in conversation," Sybil equivocates uncomfortably. "Are you angry?"

"I'm not angry, Sybil Hanoum. I'm just very concerned." To calm himself, he reaches for his cup. The tea has developed oily streaks on the surface but he draws it down his throat. The room is stifling hot.

"You are not to repeat these things to anyone, do you understand? Shukriye accusing the palace, the necklace, or what is in it." He thinks of Elias Usta, dead among his birds. He had questioned the apprentice and learned that the usta died of a weak heart, but that none of his family had known the usta was ill. Kamil is certain Elias Usta's death was meant as a warning not to seek the door to which the pendant is the key.

Sybil is taken aback and a little offended by his stern tone.

"Why not? After all, that's how I got the information about the carriage. I tell the women something to get the conversation started in the right direction. It's like putting a grain of sand into a clam. It irritates the clam so it coats it a bit at a time and eventually you have a perfectly lovely, usable pearl." Sybil is proud of her skill in obtaining information and of her metaphor. She doesn't understand why, instead of thanking her, he has become so angry.

Kamil's face has drained of color. He rises to his feet. "You have no idea what you've just said, have you?"

Sybil stands also. They are face to face, only a few feet apart.

"What's the matter? I try to help you and now you're angry with me."

Sybil has backed against the door. She begins to cry.

"What have I done? What's wrong? What harm can any of this do?"

"What harm?" echoes Kamil hoarsely. "You have no idea, no idea. What else did you say to these women? Allah protect you, Sybil Hanoum. Did you think there were no spies in that room? Every word has been reported to the secret police, I can assure you of that."

He wipes the palms of his hands over his face.

"Don't you know that you've put yourself in great danger—and perhaps other parties to that conversation?"

"I didn't know." The pearl at the base of Sybil's neck rises and falls rapidly. Her cheeks are flushed and wet with tears.

"I'm sorry. My tone was unforgivable," he says in a low voice. "But, please, Sybil Hanoum, promise me you won't go to see these women again, at least not without my approval."

She nods, wiping at her eyes.

"And that you won't go anywhere without an escort."

"I won't be a prisoner in my own house." She stares at him, her hands in tight fists at her side. "I couldn't stand that."

"Of course not," he adds soothingly. "You are free to go out, Sybil Hanoum, but I beg you not to go alone, for your own safety."

She nods, but turns her face away.

Kamil stands by the door, his hand slick on the brass door handle, and watches her carefully for a moment.

"I'm only concerned for you. I'm not angry. You've given me some important information and I thank you for it."

He walks swiftly through the garden. The fog has burned away, replaced by a veil of dust thrown up by animals and carts. At the gate, he spits out the grit that has already accumulated between his teeth.

35

The Dust of Your Street

In the days that followed, the old woman no longer spoke with me except to announce that a meal was ready. I understood her completely and didn't blame her. She had thought she was harboring a decent young woman in danger of her life, but found that her home had become a place of fornication. I smiled at her, but brought the food into my room to eat alone. I knew she was more comfortable that way. Because of her son, she could not object to our presence.

Except for a narrow slot of light where the shutters met, the room was always dark, making it difficult to read the books and journals Hamza brought me. But I didn't feel imprisoned by the dark. On the contrary, it was there that I became free. I swam in it as I swam in the pond at Chamyeri, when I discovered my body for the first time. My only regret was that Mama, Papa, and Ismail Dayi were worried about me. But Hamza had promised to tell Ismail Dayi I was safe.

Was I safe? I wasn't sure what that meant anymore. At what point

has one sacrificed enough to be safe? Lines by Fuzuli came to me
unbidden in the dark:

> *I have no home, lost*
> *In the pleasure of wondering*
> *When at last I shall dwell*
> *Forever in the dust*
> *Of your street.*

THE OLD WOMAN knew something was wrong. Her face was tense
and the tendons in her neck protruded. She did not answer when I
asked her what was happening, but projected a silent fury. In
response she shoved a bowl of rice-stuffed peppers in my direction.
The languorous disconnection that had muffled my thoughts for the
previous week was dissolved. I left the food on the plate and withdrew to my room, closing the door. I sat on the chair by the bed. It
was completely dark. Without even a shadow, what was I, other than
a vessel forged in Hamza's hands? I couldn't weep. There was too
much danger.

FINALLY, HAMZA'S VOICE at the door, the woman in her hurry fum-
bling the lock. Hamza came into the room, disheveled, his turban
rimed with dirt. The woman spoke four words, hurling them at
Hamza.

"My son is missing." She stood with her back against the door, red
hands twisted into her apron. "He has stopped going to his place of
work." Her voice was reedy, wondering, already disbelieving. She was
shaping her memories to hold the future. "He never missed a day in
fifteen years. He has always been completely reliable, my son." The
room vibrated with her fear.

Hamza sat heavily on the divan. "Shimshek is dead, teyze," he said finally.

She didn't react at first.

"What happened?" I asked him. He shrugged wearily.

The old woman began to shake. No sound came from her mouth and no tears from her eyes. Instead, I wept for her. I went to embrace her, but at my touch, she began to struggle and a hoarse scream rose from her fragile, sagging throat.

Hamza rose and grasped her thin shoulders. "Madame Devora, you must be quiet. Please. Please."

Madame Devora. It was the first time I had heard her name. Over his shoulder, her red-rimmed eyes sought me out by the window. "Damn you."

My eyes slid away from hers. I was distressed to have caused her this much grief. I too was sick with feeling. I was sick with a surfeit of memories that deprived me of clarity. Should I act or wait? What could I do? What could I ever do now? It slowly dawned on me that not only was I living outside society and outside of time, but there was no way back. My shadow in the world was the effect my actions had on my family. That was all that could still be observed.

The old woman took Hamza's arm and spat, "Take her out of here," indicating me with her chin.

"I'll do what I need to do," he snapped. "Let go of me."

I went into my room and brought out my feradje and veil and laid them in readiness on the divan. I had nothing else. Hamza stood beside the open window, peering through the curtains.

"I spoke with your dayi," he told me, never taking his eyes from the street. "He said you should go back to Chamyeri."

He turned and looked at me directly for the first time. Dark shadows chased across his face. His sleeves were torn.

I reached for his arm. "You look tired, Hamza. You need to rest first."

I saw him hesitate.

WE BOTH HEARD the voice at the door, a man's voice with the same inflection as the old woman's.

"Madame, we would like to speak with you. It's urgent."

A neighbor? I could feel Hamza tense, an animal deciding which way to spring.

The voice at the door spoke quietly, but in my mind I already heard neighbors rustling behind the other doors on the landing. The old woman was backed into the farthest corner of the divan. I went to the door and put my ear to the wood. The man on the other side and I could hear each other breathing. I pulled at the latch, but Hamza sprang forward and caught me by the arm. As he pulled me away, there was a sharp crack; the wood splintered and the latch gave way. Two men pushed their way through. One was short and stocky, the other lean and quick, but it was the small one I distrusted instinctively, like one shies away from a snake even before recognizing what it is. Hiding behind me, Hamza held me by the waist and pulled me with him toward the window. Confused and angry, I struggled to loosen myself until, with a curse, he suddenly released me. I saw a flash of white at the window. The tall man leapt across the room and caught me as I stumbled forward.

"There." He pointed his chin at the window and the other man turned and ran down the stairs with an agility unexpected in one of his heft.

"Are you all right?" The tall man led me to the divan. "Please sit. There's nothing to worry about. You're safe now."

I nodded, shivering.

He crossed the room to the old woman and squatted before her.

"Are you here about my son?" she asked in a barely audible voice.

"Your son?"

When she didn't answer, he turned and looked at me curiously.

"Madame Devora's son has died," I explained.

His green eyes rested on me a moment, evaluating. "You are Ismail Hodja's niece?"

"Yes, how did you know?"

"We have been looking for you." He turned back to the old woman crouched on the divan. She was rocking back and forth, staring uncomprehendingly at the palms of her hands, clenched stiff as claws in a parody of prayer.

"Madame," he said softly, "Madame, we know nothing of your son's death. We are here for the girl. Can you tell us what happened? We'd like to help you."

She continued to rock, as if she had not heard.

"She only just learned of it," I explained.

"It often takes time for such a message, although heard by the ear, to be understood by the head," the man said to me quietly. "But never understood by the heart," he added, shaking his head sadly.

"Are you the police?" I asked anxiously.

"We didn't involve the police. I am Kamil, the magistrate of Beyoglu. The kadi of Galata asked me to find you. My associate"—he pointed with his chin toward the door—"works for the police, but as a surgeon. He'll be discreet. No one but your family will know you were gone."

I didn't respond. The experience of lying with Hamza that had so transformed me was to remain invisible, then, a footprint on wet sand to be erased by the next tide. While the other experience with Amin in the pleasure garden that had changed my body but left no other imprint was to be known to the world. I would need to formulate an explanation to my family that left out all that was important. I began to see that it was riskier to offer one's heart than one's body.

NEIGHBORS WERE CROWDING in at the door. The magistrate beckoned to a buxom woman in a pink-striped entari who bustled over importantly.

He identified his position to the somewhat disbelieving woman and told her to take charge of Madame Devora. He sent another neighbor for the rabbi. It occurred to me that Madame Devora had not asked Hamza how her son had died.

The magistrate surveyed the room, pushed the crowd out into the hallway and closed the door behind him. Madame Devora keened softly and rhythmically behind the broad striped back of her neighbor.

"Are you all right?" he asked me. "Are you hurt? Is there anything we can do for you before we bring you home?"

"Home?" I said the word as if I were looking it over for possible meanings. "I can't go home."

"Please come over here." He led me to the side of the divan farthest away from Madame Devora. I sat again and he squatted patiently before me. We were face to face. A handsome man, I thought, but hard.

"Tell me what you can, please, Jaanan Hanoum. Or, if you like, we can discuss this later after I've taken you to your father's house. I'm sure they'll be happy to see you are safe."

"No," I insisted, "I can't go there."

"Surely your father will have you back, Jaanan Hanoum. He was very concerned about your disappearance."

"You don't understand," I explained in a whispered rush. "I can't go back because I'm in danger there." I told him about my stepmother and Amin Efendi's plot. I didn't say where I had learned this.

He nodded but said nothing. There was a commotion outside the door. The magistrate's associate pushed his way through and shut the door decisively behind him. He was panting and the sides of his forehead were slick with sweat. It seemed improbable to me that this short, bulky man was a surgeon. I put on my feradje and yashmak, hiding my face, as was proper—although some might say I remembered this too late.

The magistrate motioned for him to stay where he was, then joined him. The room was small, however, and sound carried under the vaulted ceiling. Still breathing heavily, the surgeon told the magistrate, "He ran up the street and through the front entrance of an apartment building. I followed but just outside the back entrance is a big hamam. He must have entered the baths by one of the back doors. He could have hidden in any of the alcoves, or even run through it to the street in front of the hamam. I tried, but I couldn't find him."

"Did you see his face?"

"No, but his turban fell off. He had curly black hair and a beard. That's all I saw."

"I'm sorry. I'm so very sorry," I whispered to Madame Devora.

She didn't respond. The neighbor, however, scowled and I backed away.

"Will she be taken care of?" I asked the magistrate. "I'd like to help, if I can."

"I'll let you know if anything is needed, Jaanan Hanoum. But usually the community takes care of its own people."

He crossed the room to Madame Devora and asked the woman in pink stripes to leave them alone for a moment. She frowned again crossly, but moved away. The magistrate squatted before Madame Devora, so his eyes were level with hers. I could feel him willing her to look at him.

"Who was the man that ran from here?"

Madame Devora froze in place, only her eyes in motion, anxiously scanning the room. I looked hard at her, willing her not to answer. Her reddened hands were clenched in her lap.

"What happened to your son, Madame Devora?"

"That woman killed him." Her eyes locked onto mine.

"That's not true," I cried out.

"Was the man who ran from here involved too?"

"It's impossible," Madame Devora whispered.

"Impossible? Why do you say that?"

"They were friends."

"Who was?"

"It must have been . . ." She didn't continue. I let out my breath.

The magistrate signaled to his associate to bring Madame Devora tea from the kettle brewing in the kitchen.

When the surgeon arrived with a glass of tea balanced on his thick fingers, the magistrate stood aside. The man handed Madame Devora the tea, took the magistrate's place squatting before her, and addressed her in Ladino.

Madame Devora's eyes swept the room and stopped at my face with a look of hate. Then she responded in the rolling syllables of her dying language.

"No."

I understood that word. Madame Devora put her tea glass on the divan beside her and wrapped her white muslin head scarf around the bottom of her face, hiding her expression and refusing to say anything more. She began to cry.

The surgeon strode across the room and whispered to the magistrate. I positioned myself to hear what they were saying. I had spent long hours in this room and understood the qualities of sound projected by its thick walls and arched ceilings.

"She told me this woman caused everything. If it weren't for her, her son would still be alive."

"What does she mean by that? Was her son in an accident?" The magistrate bent his head toward his associate.

"I don't think so. I think he was killed. She told me a 'Turko,' a Muslim, brought the girl to this house. She claims not to know his name. Her son begged her to do this, although she herself thought it was wrong. She said she didn't know when she agreed what they planned to do here."

"What did they do?"

"She said they turned her house into a brothel."

My face burned.

"I see." The magistrate looked speculatively in my direction and moved farther away. It did him no good, as I could still hear.

"Why did her son agree to this?"

"From what we know of him, I doubt he would ever have dishonored his mother in such a way. Maybe he was coerced by this 'Turko' to put the girl up here. That might be a motive for a fight in which he himself was killed. Just speculation, of course."

"How long did her son know this man?"

"Eight or nine years. She doesn't know where they met. Her son told her very little—just said they worked together."

"At what, I wonder."

The rabbi of Galata hurried in. His velvet kaftan floated open behind him. A red turban wrapped around a felt hat framed his forehead. The rabbi's eyes surveyed the room, taking in the situation. Seeing Madame Devora, he slipped off his outer shoes and walked toward her. A young man who followed behind carried their Holy Book.

"We should go." The magistrate's associate was keeping a crowd of curious neighbors, mostly women, at bay at the end of the corridor.

"Take me to my uncle's house at Chamyeri, please."

A crowd of people had gathered on the street. The surgeon stood by an enclosed coach, his eyes darting in all directions. The magistrate spoke to him in a low voice. As soon as we were inside, the man vanished into the crowd.

When we had settled across from each other and the coach began to move, the magistrate said, "I've sent ahead to obtain your father's opinion on the matter of where you are to go." Seeing my anxious face, he reassured me, "I revealed nothing, but I urge you to tell him what you told me. He is your father." After a moment, he added, "It might not be as you think."

His attention was caught by a commotion on the street. When he turned back to me, his face slashed by light from the closing curtains, he offered, "If you wish, I will explain things to him."

"No, thank you, magistrate bey. I will do it."

A chain of amber beads slipped through his fingers in patterns as intricate as smoke. His long legs were tucked along the far side of the cab a discreet distance from my own. His eyes rested at a respectful remove, on the empty seat beside me.

"How did you find me?" I asked him as the carriage negotiated the steep, tight curves. Jeering children followed us all the way up Djamji Street.

"My associate's mother."

"His mother?"

"The women know everything that happens in the neighborhood. They watch from their windows and pass along gossip."

I said it sounded frightful.

"But wonderful for enforcing public safety. Although," he added, "they don't necessarily tell us what they've seen. Your maid fell out of the carriage as it rounded a corner and ran into a courtyard to get help. Apparently no one offered to help her, although she said she attracted a curious enough crowd."

"I suppose they wouldn't want to come to the notice of the police," I ventured, "since suspicion would fall on them before any-one else."

He gave me a brief, curious look. "Yes, I suppose that would be one reason."

We fell silent as the carriage passed through a market area, unwilling to compete with the hoarse cries of vendors, alternately aggressive and cajoling, and the quarrelsome voices of prospective buyers.

When we had rounded a corner onto the Grande Rue de Pera, he continued.

"Luckily, your maid remembered the direction of the carriage. South toward Galata. My associate happens to live in Galata. One day, his mother visited a relative on Djamji Street. Some other women there began to discuss the old woman who lives across the street, Madame Devora. For some time, the shutters to her bedroom had been closed in the daytime. The women worried that she was ill, since her son didn't seem to be around to take care of her and no one had seen her come or go. Yet just the other day a neighbor had seen her lowering a basket on a rope to the vegetable seller. She bought so much fruit she could barely pull the basket back up. They surmised from the quantity of food that she must be expecting guests, but then no one noticed any visitors."

"They probably knew just how much money was in the basket too," I exclaimed.

He laughed. "If these women were working for us, we'd solve many more crimes."

One front tooth was slightly awry. The hidden flaw introduced by its maker into every carpet that marks it as the work of humankind, not Allah who alone is perfect. The stern, efficient magistrate was just another man.

"Once the gossip started, I can imagine them bringing every detail to bear. Someone saw a strange man entering the building, a workman carrying tools, but no noise was heard from the building. The man apparently tried to keep out of sight, arriving in late afternoon, when the women's husbands weren't home yet and the women themselves were busy preparing dinner, but he was seen nevertheless. One hot night, the neighbors kept their carpets out on the sidewalk, sleeping in the open air. They said the mosquitoes kept them awake. A strange man came out of the building in the hour before the morning call to prayer. Unfortunately, they didn't see his face."

He looked pointedly at me before continuing.

"So they took action. They went to visit Madame Devora. Of course, they knew she was home. They know everything! When she didn't answer her door, they became convinced something was wrong, and they delegated my associate's mother to report it to her son, who came to me. We had already been looking in Galata, thanks to your maid's information. And that is how we came to find you."

Thus was I found and lost all at the same time, in both cases through the tongues of women, a force that shamed and secluded me for nothing more than losing a bit of flesh, and then rescued me from a shame and seclusion that I desired. We stopped at an official-looking building and the magistrate disappeared inside. When he reemerged he brought with him a taciturn widow in an all-enveloping black charshaf that covered even her lower face, who accompanied me for the rest of the trip home.

At Chamyeri, Ismail Dayi helped me from the carriage. The chaperone, who for the entire trip had stared silently through the gauze-curtained window, refused refreshment and ordered the carriage to return to the city. Ismail Dayi's shoulders looked stooped and thinner under his robes than I remembered. His face was pinched, his beard flecked with gray, and small spots of red glowed on his cheekbones. I bowed before him, took his hand and kissed it, then touched it to my forehead. He pulled me up.

"Jaanan, my lion."

"Where is Mama?" I asked, looking past him into the dim interior beyond the doors.

He took my hand. "Come inside, my dear."

Violet was waiting in the entryway. An egg-yolk-yellow kerchief tied around her head emphasized her black eyes screened by long lashes, eyebrows like an archer's bow laid across them. She moved toward me and we embraced. I inhaled the familiar smoky scent of her skin. Her cheeks under my lips tasted of salt and milk. But the tinder did not kindle into joy. The cook's boat had been cut adrift, then burned.

I pulled from her embrace and went to Ismail Dayi. He led me to his study, where we had spent so many happy winter evenings. Now the windows to the garden were open and the familiar scent of jasmine twined into the room.

Ismail Dayi lowered himself onto the divan. Violet adjusted the cushions behind his back. He waved his hand to indicate that she should leave. With obvious reluctance, she backed out of the room. For some moments we sat silently, our limbs wrapped in the scented warmth from the garden.

Finally, Ismail Dayi spoke.

"My daughter." His voice was husky—with illness? I did not know and I was suddenly ashamed of how much I had tested him.

"My dear dayi," I said, "you're the one who has worried and suffered for all of us. I'm so sorry to have been an added burden to you."

"My daughter, there was never a burden as sweet as you. I thank Allah for bringing you into my life."

He paused for a moment, then continued.

"Jaanan, I'm sorry, but I must tell you. Your mother has passed away."

I felt nothing. Or rather, only a rushing sound far away, as if a monumental wave were coming closer, but was still too far away for me to run for cover. How did I know about such waves? They were there in Violet's sea, in the lost fingers of Halil the gardener. They were the crushing, grinding behemoths that tortured Hamza's sea glass on their forges of sand until the stones glowed from within like blue eyes.

I was speechless. What opportunities had I missed? My hand remembered the feel of cold satin like a ghost limb.

Ismail Dayi tried to take my hand, but I pulled it away.

"What happened?" My voice sounded too steady, too matter-of-fact, and I felt ashamed of that too.

"She caught a draft and it went to her lungs. It was very rapid. May your life be spared, my dear."

He squeezed my arm. His touch opened a channel through which a current of sorrow began to flow. But I resisted it. Another vein of weakness when so much of me had run dry.

The waves were nearer. I bowed my head and let them rage through me, but said nothing.

Ismail Dayi stared sadly into the fire. "I never told her you were lost. I told her you had gone to your father's. I didn't want to worry her. She loved you greatly, my dear daughter."

36

Sea Glass

It was late spring that year when Mary finally came to visit me. I hadn't seen her since the fall. I took her hand and led her into the harem reception room. Now that Mama had cut the thread that bound her to the world, I was mistress of the cool blue and white tiles and splashing water. My body moved to a different music learned in Galata. I felt powerful. I wondered whether something in Mary would stir in response.

We sat on the divan. I signaled Violet to bring us tea. Mary was dressed in a loose white gown embroidered with red flowers that echoed the enamel blossoms in the gold cross she always wore at the base of her throat. It had been her mother's, she told me when I admired it. A lace bodice hid the mole on her shoulder.

Violet stood by the door, silver tray balanced in her hands.

"Put it here, Violet," I called, my eyes studying Mary. She seemed absorbed in the movement of the tray, following it to the low table, watching Violet's strong hands pour the coffee into tiny cups.

We waited for Violet to leave.

"I'm sorry about your mother's death. I thought, I must come to see you."

"Thank you, Mary. That is kind of you."

I said nothing to her about about my stay at Madame Devora's. It was a willing union that undid the other, unwilling one. I had found Hamza's sea glass necklace at the bottom of my jewelry casket and now kept it close to my breast.

Our cups chimed in the awkward silence.

"You know, I tried to come see you before, but your maid told me you weren't here. She wouldn't tell me anything more. Where did you go?"

"I was at my father's house in Nishantashou," I quickly improvised.

"Of course." She looked at me curiously and I was suddenly afraid she had also sought me there. "I wish I had known. It's much closer. Why didn't you send me a message? Didn't you know I was back?"

Seeing my look of confusion, she spat out, "Violet, again."

I glanced quickly at the door, then nodded. "I've received no letters since winter."

I could see Mary fighting down her anger. "Well, we're here now. I know you haven't gone out much since you speared that bastard Amin last year. I'm sure a stay in the city did you good."

I was surprised that the mention of his name no longer affected me.

"Well, I haven't been invited to many society events since then. I suppose people blame me, and perhaps they're right to. I was very stupid. I always thought I should be able to move about without a chaperone like any modern woman."

"In England, young women of quality"—she worked the word uneasily in her mouth, like a moldy fruit—"also are guarded by female watchdogs. It has nothing to do with being modern. We still hold the leashes of our own sex."

Women of quality. Mary did not seem to be quality in the English way, which I presumed to mean much the same as here—wealth and indolence. Was I still a woman of quality? I was wealthy, was I not? And inactive, again imprisoned in my golden cage at Chamyeri.

"You must have been bored out here," she continued. "That Violet can't be a very pleasant companion. She's so sour she'd curdle milk." I didn't tell her that the object of her scorn was probably listening on the other side of the door. Her description of Violet irritated me.

"She was my companion when we were younger, and she has been a good and loyal servant to my family. There is no cause to disparage her."

She reached over and took my hand. "I meant no offense. Forgive me."

My small hand nestled inside hers like a young bird.

"I've missed you, Jaanan. We haven't seen each other for a long time, but I haven't forgotten." She smiled at me uncertainly. "I wrote to you often. And I had to go back to England for a while. I hope you don't blame me for not coming to see you after I returned. It was impossible to get up here. The roads were impassable and none of the delivery boats would take me. Believe me, I tried. And then, when the roads were open, I thought you went away. I wish I had known you were in Stamboul," she added fiercely.

I looked into her light blue eyes, the color of beads used to ward off the evil eye. When I didn't respond, her hands parted the gauze panels of my veil and lifted them behind my shoulders. I felt suddenly naked, as I had never felt in the room in Galata.

To cover my confusion, I said in a polite voice, "Please have some more coffee." I rang the silver bell by my side.

We sat silently until Violet arrived with the coffeepot. She looked at us slyly from under her lashes.

Had I changed in some fundamental way? People project themselves onto the screen of society like shadow puppets. Perhaps the lamplight was too low and I was no longer recognizable. Had I forgotten my lines? Was there a plot at all? I no longer believed so.

Violet spilled some coffee on Mary's arm, then tried to wipe it away with her hand. Embarrassed, I pushed her away from Mary and asked her to leave. I dabbed gently at Mary's arm with an embroidered cloth. Violet had been a restless shadow to my every movement since my return. I asked her to sleep in her old room at the back of the house, but found her waiting for me wherever I came and went. I understood that she must feel guilty about leaving me in that coach, but explained to her that no harm had come of it. I had asked Ismail Dayi to find her a husband, as was his duty as her patron. I suppose she knew of this, since she listened at doors.

Violet still stood by the door, her black eyes intensely following every move of my hand as if she were devouring it. Mary too noticed and shifted uncomfortably.

"Make fresh coffee." I couldn't hide the annoyance in my voice. While I was away, she had slipped out of my control.

Mary's stockinged feet dangled uselessly from the divan, her slippers fallen to the carpet. I had hoped to please her with Mama's reception room, but she didn't seem to notice her surroundings. I straightened the gold bracelet on her wrist that Violet had knocked awry, my affection relearning its accustomed channels. I was reminded of her great kindness, and my body relaxed toward her.

"I came to tell you I was leaving."

"Leaving Istanbul?" I felt regret and relief. I pulled my veil across my breasts. "When?"

"In a few days."

It was too soon. "Has something happened?" I shivered with dread at losing my friend. The strength of my feeling surprised me.

"A good thing, Jaanan," she said with a grin. "I still can't believe it."

"Tell me," I demanded. "I am full of suspense."

"Well," she began, drawing it out, "I am now a woman of means."

"Means?"

"Rich, Jaanan. I'm rich!" She bounced on the divan.

"Why, that's wonderful." I laughed with relief. "I'm so happy for you, my dear friend. Congratulations."

"It means I can do as I please. When you have money, no one can tell you how to live."

"How did it happen?" I had assumed that since Mary worked, she belonged to a family without wealth, but I realized then that she had never told me anything about her family.

"My father died."

"Oh, I'm so sorry. Health to your head, my dearest." I reached out to comfort her, but she leaned back so she could see my face, grasped my arms, and beamed at me.

"I'm not sad, Jaanan. Not sad at all. My father threw me out when I was young. That's how I ended up in a boardinghouse, exchanging kitchen work for rent."

I gasped. "How is such a thing possible?"

"He said I had unnatural inclinations, as he put it. And he didn't like my friends."

"But had you no other family to turn to? Your mother? Your siblings?"

"My mother died when I was born," she explained, a flicker of sadness passing through her eyes, her finger caressing the gold cross at her neck. "I have no brothers or sisters. It's not like here where you can fall back on dozens of people you call family. In England, you're on your own."

"And your friends?"

"Well, I told you about my friends. They turned out less than worthless. On that account, my father was right."

"That's terribly sad, Mary, dear. You have a family and friends here, though. I am here for you, and all my family is yours."

Mary's eyes fell to one side. "I know," she whispered. "Thank you.

"Actually, Jaanan"—quickly, almost shiftily, the pink tip of her tongue moistened her lips—"I came here to ask you something."

There are moments when you understand that something is going to happen before you know what it is. There is an unpleasant weightlessness at the back of your neck. Time yawns as if to show its uncconcern, then rushes toward you at breakneck speed.

"Would you come with me to England?"

I was speechless.

"It would be great fun. We could live in a grand place, much nicer than here." She waved her hand around the reception hall.

She leaned closer and stroked back my veil again.

"We could be together, Jaanan. You and me. We wouldn't have to sneak off to that shack on the water." Her lips brushed my ear. "We could be together all the time."

I admit to confusion and knowledge chasing each other through my heart. Mary was my friend and I loved her. Now she was offering me a new life, a life of novelty and adventure, as had been foretold. I considered carefully. What life was left to me in Istanbul? Perhaps this was my kismet.

Mary mistook my silence for refusal. "If you're worried about missing your family, Jaanan, you could travel here whenever you like. The Wagons-Lits Company is building a direct rail line. Before long you'll be able to get on the Orient Express in London and get off in Stamboul." She clapped her hands. "Wouldn't it be wonderful? We could have such a life together."

Hamza, I thought. My hands toyed with the sea glass dangling from my neck. Hamza would never leave here. England would be exile.

"I don't know, Mary." I said slowly. "Let me think about it."

Mary leaned closer to read from my face what she could not read from my words, but I'm certain my confusion made me illegible.

She stroked my cheek, then pulled my veil back across it. "I'll wait patiently until you decide, Jaanan."

AFTER MARY LEFT, I found Violet in the kitchen wrestling a bucking fish from the pail at her feet onto the cutting board. She pierced its neck with the point of her knife and it stiffened.

"Where is the cook?" I asked her.

"Her mother is ill, so she went home early. I told her I'd prepare the meal."

The scales sprayed from beneath her knife as it scraped across the firm blue flesh. I watched as she held the fish down and, entering at the throat, slid the knife delicately down the chest and along the belly. Its ruby secrets spilled into her hand.

I FOUND THE letter under a pile of manuscripts on a shelf in Ismail Dayi's study. I had been looking for an illustrated copy of Fuzuli's romance, *Leyla and Mejnun,* that Ismail Dayi had found for me at the bookseller. It was to be a gift for Mary, in remembrance of our friendship, a celebration of her new life. The letter was on ordinary parchment of the kind used by clerks in government offices, but I immediately recognized Hamza's handwriting. It was dated two days after I had arrived in Djamji Street. The message began with a standard formula of greeting, then, in a kind of convoluted eloquence:

> The honorable Hodja is advised that certain necessary actions must be taken promptly in order to alter to everyone's advantage the unfortunate circumstances prevailing today. If you succeed in turning minds toward the good and only possible path toward a modern society, this will benefit many, but especially someone close to you.

ISMAIL HODJA SAT stiffly on the divan, the tea on the low table before him untouched. I sat beside him, holding the letter in my hand.

"Why did you never tell me about this, dayi?"

"It seemed an innocuous letter, on its face. It says nothing about kidnapping. I wasn't even sure the writer was asking me to do anything. I brought it to the kadi because it was an odd letter, dropped on my doorstep, while you were gone. Possibly it was an appeal to me to support the reformists. But whoever wrote it was too clever for his own good. He disguised his intention to such a degree that I couldn't make it out. Nevertheless, I believed there may have been an implied threat in the letter, that if I did not do this, harm might come to someone close to me. I didn't want to take any chances, my lion. You were missing and I had no idea where you had gone."

"But you knew who I was with."

Ismail Dayi looked at me curiously and took my chin in his hand.

"Of course not, Jaanan. If I had, we would have been able to find you sooner."

"No one came to you?"

"What do you mean?"

"I thought you knew," I whispered, half to myself.

"The man who kidnapped you was never identified, Jaananjim. We have no way of knowing his motivation."

Ismail Dayi looked at me oddly as he said this, as if he guessed that I was keeping something from him. Hamza had disappeared out of the window in Galata and out of my life. After my return home, it had seemed inappropriate to speak of Hamza to my dayi and, out of embarrassment, I avoided the subject other than to assure him that I was unharmed. So Hamza had lied about speaking with Ismail Dayi and he had never learned that I was safe. What else had he lied about? The thought infuriated me. He had lied and then he had disappeared again.

It was true that Madame Devora's son, the only other person who could have identified Hamza, was dead, but I was surprised that no one knew it had been Hamza fleeing through that window. I was certain, for instance, that the magistrate's crafty-looking associate had learned his name from Madame Devora. While they were speaking Ladino, I'm sure I heard Hamza's name among the unfamiliar words. I told my dayi that it had been Hamza who "rescued" me from Amin's plot and kept me in Galata. He looked shocked.

"It's hard to believe Hamza would do such a thing. I immediately thought of Amin Efendi—that he had abducted you and sent this letter," he said. "But it seemed an odd thing for him to do. I think he knows that a pinch of prosperity has more value than an okka of revenge. He's in exile in Crete now and has been very careful not to give any further offense. He wants to improve his chances to be called back to the capital. It would be foolish of him—and very unlike the man I know—to write a letter opposing the government. In his heart, Amin is a coward."

Ismail Dayi patted my hand. "He may not be entirely without blame, though. Hamza might well be right. Amin is certainly in debt. He could have had designs on you, even from Crete. Accomplices are cheap. Certainly your father believed what you told him about Amin's plan to take you from the house. Your father has banished Hüsnü Hanoum from his sight. Amin's sword struck wide. Such folly." Ismail Dayi clicked his tongue in disapproval, I could not tell whether of Amin, my father, Aunt Hüsnü, or of humankind.

Amin Efendi was a thousand years ago, I thought. I placed my hand on Ismail Dayi's arm, angry at the needless pain Hamza's silence and my own had imposed on this man, my chosen father. Hamza had written a letter in effect blackmailing my uncle. The language expressed perfectly his warring desire for approval and a blacker motivation that I had briefly glimpsed at the apartment on Djamji Street.

Ismail dayi looked thoughtfully at the letter in his lap. "So you think Hamza sent this."

"It's in his handwriting. What did the kadi say when you showed him the letter?"

"He sent me to Magistrate Kamil, who is more experienced in these matters. He thought we should take the implied meaning seriously—that if I didn't help the reformists, something might happen to you. He suggested I step up the tempo of my meetings with a variety of highly placed people here at home. It would look on the surface as if I were doing what the letter demanded. But we wouldn't necessarily discuss reform. He said we could debate the price of Smyrna dates, if we wished, as long as it seemed to a casual observer that something, possibly a political something, was happening."

"And what is the price of Smyrna dates, dayi dear?"

"I couldn't tell you, little one."

We both laughed, although my laughter was mixed with pain. I thought of Nedim's lines:

> *You and my mind treat each other as strangers*
> *As if you were a guest in my body, you, my heart.*

To save myself, I had bound my little craft to a mirage.

I SAT BY the edge of the water, cradling the sea glass in my hand, wondering what it had endured to earn its beauty, then let it slip slowly from my hand back into the elements.

37

Enduring Principles

ast autumn's leaves rustle underfoot behind the pavilion. A nightingale trills in the darkness, perhaps
dreaming. The moon that silvered Mary's blind face
has fattened in the sky, then faded again until the
world is dressed in shades of mourning. Ten miles to the south, Kamil
Pasha studies an engraving of *Gymnadenia*, before his finger falls
from the pages of the book in sleep. A shadow slips into Ismail
Hodja's kitchen door and moves swiftly through the corridors toward
his study. Light streams from beneath the door. The figure pauses,
presses his ear against the door, and, hearing nothing, pushes it open.

He sees two men kneeling side by side before a low table. Jemal is
all in white, a loose cotton shirt and wide shalwar. His hair flows
down his back like a river of ink. Ismail kneels beside him, dressed in
a quilted robe. Without his turban, Ismail Hodja looks fragile, a
fringe of thinning hair exposing a pale scalp. In his hand is a brush,
poised over a square piece of parchment across which extends an ele-

gant trail of calligraphic writing. A bottle of black ink and several more brushes rest on the table above the paper. Jemal holds a turquoise ceramic bowl in his right hand. Both are sunk in concentration; neither hears the door open. There is enough time for the intruder to note the muscular shoulders pushing against the shirt of Ismail Hodja's companion. He had expected Ismail Hodja to be alone. Suddenly Jemal turns and, before the man can escape, springs and winds himself about him like a snake, his angry, kohl-rimmed eyes close to the man's face. The bowl falls heavily to the carpet. A puddle of gray water seeps rapidly into the colorful wool.

Ismail Hodja lays down his brush and stands. "Why, Hamza, welcome. I wasn't expecting you at this hour." He gestures to Jemal to let Hamza go. Jemal does so with obvious reluctance, and squats nearby, within easy reach.

"I almost didn't recognize you," Ismail Hodja adds, gesturing toward Hamza's worn workman's clothing and his beard.

"I've come to ask for your assistance."

"Of course, Hamza, my son. I will do whatever is in my power. What is it that you need?"

"I'm sorry to intrude, my hodja," Hamza says softly, glancing nervously at the window. "I'm leaving for France tomorrow and I wanted to see Jaanan." His eyes take in the fallen bowl and wet carpet. "I'm sorry." He looks up anxiously. "Jaanan, is she here?"

Ismail Hodja looks at him carefully and suggests, "It's rather late to call on a young lady."

"Please. I need to speak with her."

"I'm sorry, my son. My niece has gone to France."

Hamza's face reflects his confusion. "France? Why on earth . . . When?"

"Last month. We'd been discussing it for some time," Ismail Hodja answers kindly. "You know how difficult life has been for her this past year."

"I wanted to protect her," Hamza says, half to himself. "She's in Paris?" he asks eagerly.

"Yes, your many stories of the city made an impression on her. She wants to study. She's safe there now, living with family."

"I thought"—Hamza begins, then stops.

Ismail Hodja regards him thoughtfully, waiting for him to continue.

"Why did she decide to go now?" Hamza asks.

"She has lost a friend and we thought it best that she recover far from anything that could remind her of it."

Hamza sits heavily on the divan by the door and puts his head in his hands. "I didn't mean to disappear for so long. I suppose she thought I was dead or—worse—that I didn't care about her. But when I get to Paris, I'll explain everything."

"It is not your absence she is mourning," Ismail Hodja explains. Hamza's head jerks up. "Although I know she is fond of you."

"Who, then?" Hamza demands.

"Her English friend, Mary Dixon."

Hamza looks puzzled. "What does Jaanan have to do with Mary Dixon? I don't understand."

"They met at an embassy function and became friends. My niece was much alone and it gave me great pleasure to see her bloom in this friendship. The poor woman drowned."

"Yes, I know."

"Then you probably also know that the police believe she was drugged before falling into the Bosphorus. Perhaps even pushed, Allah forbid. The world would be an unhappy abode indeed were it not for the strength of our faith. The following day, Jaanan's servant Violet had an accident and nearly drowned, but she survived, praise be to Allah. In any case, it is prudent that Jaanan be in a safe place, at least until the culprit is caught, lest his evil eye fall on other young women." He eyes Hamza's stunned face. "What is it that you wish to tell her, my son? I can pass a message on. Or, if you prefer to write, I can forward a letter to her."

"Nothing. I . . . it was nothing." Hamza stands. "If I could have her address, I will see her myself when I get to Paris. That is, if she's willing to see me."

Ismail Hodja studies Hamza's face for a long moment, then says, "She is staying with her father's brother near Arly."

"Yes, I know the place." Hamza bows his head. "Thank you, my hodja."

"I know you and my niece have been friends for a long time, but my advice is not to presume on that past tie." Ismail Hodja frowns. "Much has happened. You will have to regain her trust."

"I understand, my hodja." Hamza pauses, then stutters, "Actually, I came to ask something of you."

Ismail Hodja extends his hand toward the divan. "Let us sit together and talk."

Hamza doesn't move.

"We must have a parliament to rein in the sultan," he blurts out. "I beg you to ask the ulema, the religious scholars and judges, and your friends in the government to pressure the sultan."

"Why would I do something like that?"

"He's a tyrant, my hodja," Hamza begins earnestly, "arresting people, ruining them on a whim. His spending is bankrupting the country."

Ismail Hodja looks at Hamza curiously. "My dear son, as you are no doubt aware, I have tried to steer clear of politics. I have my own pursuits. These have endured"—he waves a hand at his library and the calligraphy on the table—"and outlived the minor lives and squabbles of ambitious men. Knowledge, beauty, and appreciation of Allah are the three enduring principles. Politics is just a fleeting shadow thrown against the wall by the sun."

Hamza's voice takes on a wheedling tone. "You have enormous influence, Ismail Hodja. How can you not use it for good? A word from you would move important men to reconsider their positions. If the ulema issued a fatwa in favor of reinstating the parliament, the sultan would have to listen."

Ismail Hodja wags his head from side to side. "You overestimate my influence. I am just a poet and a scholar. I am not a politician. I have a minor official post. I am a teacher, an observer, nothing more."

"You are a Nakshbendi sheikh. You have friends throughout the government. I know that people come here to seek your advice."

"How do you know that?"

"I've watched what goes on here. Princes and ministers arriving secretly at all hours. You can't tell me you're not involved in politics." Hamza's tone has become heated.

"I don't wish to argue politics with you, my son." Ismail Hodja puts out his hands and sighs deeply. "But you are overstating Sultan Abdulhamid's flaws. He has done much to modernize the empire. And despite his idiosyncrasies, he cares about his subjects."

"You're on the wrong side, my hodja. We will continue to work for a constitution and parliament from exile and we will succeed. The sultan himself may have to be eliminated. I came to warn you and ask you to join us before it's too late."

Ismail Hodja looks at Hamza with a puzzled frown. "There is something I've been meaning to ask you, my son. I know it was you that kidnapped Jaanan. Did you send me a letter threatening to harm her if I did not support your project?"

"What? I never threatened her."

"Yet the letter seems to be in your hand. Jaanan said she recognized your writing."

"Jaanan saw the letter?"

"Yes. I didn't show it to her. She found it among my papers."

Hamza is pale. "I didn't mean to threaten her."

"We have been like your family since you were a boy. My brother-in-law sponsored your career. You ate his bread. We are all fond of you, my niece more than anyone. How could you even think to hurt her?"

"I would never hurt Jaanan. It was only to get you to support the reforms. I would never have done anything to harm her. But she'll never believe that now. I only meant to help her."

"By kidnapping her and telling no one where she was? You let her believe we knew she was safe."

"I meant to come and speak with you, but . . . things happened that stopped me. My driver was killed, and I feared for my life. I didn't dare come here. Otherwise I would have explained the letter to you myself. It contained no threat to Jaanan, only a request for your help."

"Please sit," Ismail Hodja offers again. "We are your family. Everything can be discussed and, with the help of Allah, we will come to an understanding."

Hamza doesn't answer, his lips pressed in a grim line. "It's over now. She'll never . . ." He doesn't finish. Suddenly his fist punches through the wood of the door. Jemal moves to restrain him, but Ismail Hodja catches Jemal's eye and raises his chin slightly to indicate no. Hamza examines his bruised hand as if it belongs to someone else.

"You think you're my family?" he says finally, his voice bitter. "I had my own family. Thanks to you and people like you, they were destroyed. You're all hypocrites!" he bellows. "Look at you!" He eyes Jemal, who is poised to spring on him. "What would happen if everyone knew the truth about the respected hodja?"

Ismail Hodja lets himself down on the divan and shakes his head in disbelief. "Is that what you plan to do now, son?" he asks sadly. "You can no longer use my niece as leverage, so now you threaten my reputation?"

"It's people like you who are destroying the empire. You crush people like my family without a second thought. You and that buffoon, the sultan. You are all evil, dissolute autocrats, playing with life and death."

"It is your grief speaking, my son. Not the honorable young man I know. Your family lives in Aleppo, is that not so?"

"Leave my family out of this!"

"Your father was a kadi, was he not? What happened to him?"

"You know perfectly well what happened to him. It was your doing, you and the sultan. You poisoned his life," Hamza chokes out.

"The poison has entered your veins, my son. We must bleed it out. Your father embezzled funds from the royal treasury, if I remember correctly."

"That isn't true." Hamza lunges at Ismail Hodja, but Jemal is faster and catches his arms. Hamza twists in Jemal's grip.

"That may be, that may be." Ismail Hodja sighs. "It wouldn't be the first time that the palace has resorted to artifice to eliminate an opponent. But your father gave information to the Arabs, did he not? He tried to enlist French support for a revolt. A kadi acting against his own government."

Hamza stares at him. "How do you know this?"

"Those arrested gave information about your father's role."

"He always had the interests of the empire at heart. That didn't mean he had to follow what the sultan commanded, if it was against what he thought was right."

"The money was for the movement, then."

"What money? What are you talking about?"

"And that is what you're doing now, is it? Discarding the rules of law, morality, and human sentiment to do what you think is right. What is it you are trying to do?"

"Look who's talking about morality!" Hamza spits out, looking pointedly over his shoulder at Jemal. Jemal twists his arms until Hamza yelps with pain.

Ismail Hodja smiles calmly. "You do not know everything you think you know. And what you do know, others know as well." He shakes his head. "The hubris of the young. There is no profit in that direction, my son."

Hamza looks puzzled.

Ismail Hodja smoothes his beard thoughtfully, then fixes Hamza in a steady gaze.

"I will not help you in your political goal, my son. I do not support violence or, may Allah protect him, the overthrow of the sultan."

"It's the only way."

"I don't believe that. I will not support the reintroduction of parliament under such conditions. There are other, more civilized ways."

"You may change your mind," Hamza says viciously.

"If Allah wills it. Let him go, please, Jemal."

Jemal gives Hamza's arms one more twist before he lets them fall.

As Hamza reaches the door, Ismail Hodja calls to him, "Hamza, my son. How is your mother? You had a sister, did you not?"

Hamza pivots and leaps for Ismail Hodja's throat, Jemal right behind him. The two wrestle on the floor, upending the table and scattering sheets of paper. Unperturbed, Ismail Hodja gazes sadly at the blackness pressing in against the window. China cups and other small objects clatter to the floor. The glass narghile tips over, releasing water into the carpet.

"Don't you dare mention my sister," roars Hamza, struggling against Jemal's grip. "She will be your last victim. I'll make sure of that."

"Allah is merciful, my son. May the poison in your veins be cleansed now. Examine your true motives in this. I know you are a good man." He bows his head. "Selam aleikhum. Peace be upon you."

Jemal wrestles Hamza to his feet and pushes him out the door. As soon as they are out of sight of Ismail Hodja, Jemal kicks Hamza so that he falls to the ground. With one motion, Jemal lifts him and throws him over his shoulder. He carries him to the gate and drops him stomach first onto Hamza's horse tethered there, frees the reins, and slaps the animal's rump. When the horse has disappeared down the dark road, Jemal returns to the house, stopping in the kitchen to fetch a glass of water for Ismail Hodja before returning to the study. He was the one who had found Hamza's letter on the doorstep. He makes it his business to know about anything that might endanger his master. He does not believe in the peaceful draining of venom.

HAMZA CURSES AS he struggles to right himself in the saddle. The anesthetic of anger is rapidly giving way to pain as memories of his lost family mingle with the realization that Jaanan too is now lost to him. I will find her in Paris, he thinks, and explain everything. But he knows it will be difficult, if not impossible, to regain her trust. He

halts and remounts properly. With determination, he spurs his horse
onto the moonless road and turns south toward the city. What did
she have to do with Mary Dixon? he wonders, glancing anxiously
back at the screen of trees behind which Hannah too had abandoned him.

Suddenly the horse stops short. Someone is pulling on the bridle.
Hamza hears a lightly accented voice.

"I thought you a better rider than this, Hamza Efendi. You were
sitting on the horse backwards. Let me help you. Ah, I see you have
righted yourself. No matter."

Strong hands pull Hamza from the saddle. He lands off balance,
but with both feet on the ground. The dust he kicks up makes him
cough. Hamza can make out only the shape of the man, black against
black. He is short and stocky. Hamza twists and attempts to leap
away, but the man moves quickly. A blade glints briefly like a firefly. In
less than a heartbeat, it is at Hamza's throat.

"You'll come with me," says the figure.

"Who are you?" Hamza's eyes dart toward the forest, but he cannot run. The blade stings his throat and every breath causes it to
intrude farther. He tries to calm his breathing. When he dares, he
clears his throat.

"You have something to say?" The knife moves away infinitesi-
mally. Hamza can't feel the blade, but knows it is still there.

"Who are you? What do you want with me? I have little money,
but you can have it."

The shadow man laughs as if at a very good joke.

"You can take the horse too," adds Hamza nervously. There is
something very familiar about the man, but Hamza cannot place it.
He jerks away but the blade finds him again.

"What do you want?"

"I want to know why you're back."

The man whistles shrilly and a carriage approaches. The shadows
of three men wrestle Hamza inside.

38

A Shared Pipe

Kamil accepts the long chubuk pipe Ismail Hodja's servant has filled with fragrant tobacco, draws up his legs, and leans back against the divan cushions in the hodja's study. The morning ride was brisk and Kamil is glad of the warmth between his lips. The hodja is smoking a narghile, the long cord looped once around his arm, amber mouthpiece in his slender fingers. The servant checks the coal atop the rose-colored glass flask. As Ismail Hodja draws from the mouthpiece, the coal glows beneath the tobacco, its smoke bubbling down through the cooling liquid and along the tube to the hodja's mouth. His face beneath the turban is calm, but his eyes are troubled and red-rimmed with exhaustion.

"Have you learned anything, Magistrate Kamil?" he asks softly. "The police last night told me only that they arrested Hamza and wished me to make a complaint about his violent behavior." His eyes rest on the hole in the door. "I declined, of course." He adds angrily,

"I can't imagine how they could presume to know what goes on in my house."

"I visited Hamza in jail on my way here this morning," Kamil says. "The police are accusing him of murdering the two Englishwomen."

"What? That's preposterous."

"Hamza admits he betrayed your hospitality last night, but denies having anything to do with the murders. I must admit his arrest was a surprise to me. The police say they have evidence that Hamza met Hannah Simmons in your garden pavilion on the night she was killed." He looks at Ismail Hodja curiously from under his eyebrows, respectfully avoiding eye contact.

Ismail Hodja looks surprised. "When my niece was a child, Hamza used to come to Chamyeri to tutor her and then spent the night in the men's quarters. I banned him from my house after my groom Jemal saw him sneak out one night and bring a woman into the pavilion."

"You didn't tell the police this?"

"I never spoke of it to anyone."

"Did your groom identify the woman?"

"No. You may ask him if you like. It was in the months before that poor young woman was found dead. Jemal said he didn't see the woman up close, but thought she might be foreign by her dress. I remember because he was worried it might have been my niece's governess. But we had her room checked, and she was asleep." He puffs on the narghile. "I suppose it could have been Hannah Simmons."

Ismail Hodja's narghile has gone out. He gestures to the servant, who fetches a fresh piece of coal in his tongs and places it on the flask.

When the servant has withdrawn to the far side of the room, Ismail Hodja continues in an urgent voice. "There is no proof that Hamza did this crime. I know Hamza well, and I do not believe him to be capable of it."

"Did Jemal see a carriage?"

"Yes, and the driver. He was parked outside the gate by the road.

Jemal went to ask him who he was waiting for and apparently received an insolent answer." He smiles fondly. "Jemal does not suffer insults lightly."

Kamil's pulse races. "What color was his hair?"

"I don't believe Jemal said. We can ask him. A great deal of time has passed, but since we were so concerned about the matter at the time, it's possible he might remember."

"You said you had banned Hamza from Chamyeri some time before Hannah's death."

"Yes, but there is something I must tell you. I had a long talk with my niece before she left for Paris. She admitted to me that Hamza flouted my ban and continued to come here to see her. He had a secret call, like a nightingale, to tell her when he was in the pavilion. She was a child at the time and they were very close. She said when he came, they used to sit in the pavilion reading and playing games."

"So it's possible that he continued to use the pavilion at night for his trysts."

"Yes, I suppose so, but indiscretion does not make a young man a murderer. It was a long time ago, when he was a crazy-blooded youth"—he smiles at Kamil—"as I believe we all were at some point. I don't believe he had anything to do with the killing of those unfortunate women."

"Why did he come here last night?"

"He wanted to see my niece. And to ask me for some small service, which, unfortunately, I was unable to grant him."

Kamil waits, but the hodja does not elaborate.

The arrest report stated Hamza had threatened Ismail Hodja. Kamil asks, "Did your refusal make him angry?"

"Hamza's anger is directed at himself and against those who love him. We hate those who have seen us weak, magistrate bey. Our deepest rage is reserved for those who have seen us shamed and vulnerable and who responded with generosity. To be the object of a person's generosity is, in some basic way, to be humiliated. My brother-in-law treated his sister's son like his own, gave him a home, supported his education, helped him find a government position. What you might not know is that, without his uncle's help, Hamza would have had no life at all. His father had squandered his future before Hamza ever had a chance to claim it. Unfortunately, the fruit does not fall far from the tree."

"His father was kadi of Aleppo, I believe."

"Yes, a wealthy and powerful man, but a man with expensive habits and a pragmatic sense of loyalty. Hamza's father acted as liaison between a few of our Arab subjects and the French who hoped to wrest the province of Syria away from the empire. That was in the time of Sultan Abdulaziz, may his memory be blessed. When the plans were discovered, Hamza's father was ruined. He was accused of embezzling money from the treasury to finance a revolt, although it's possible he did it to pay his own debts. He was stripped of his position."

"Was he exiled?"

"In a sense. He was forbidden ever to return to the capital."

"Did Hamza know the reasons for his father's banishment?" Kamil beckons the servant to relight his pipe.

"He was studying in France at the time. When he returned to Aleppo, apparently he found his father sitting on a chair in the middle of an empty apartment. The creditors had taken their konak and even their furniture. His father refused to speak or eat, just sat staring at the wall. Hamza tried to rouse him, told him about Paris, his plans for a career. He promised to take care of the family's expenses, but his father never even looked at him." Ismail Hodja pauses to take another draught from his narghile. He exhales a thin stream of smoke.

"My brother-in-law learned all this in a letter from his sister," he continues. "After seeing the letter, I was inclined to view Hamza's behavior with more compassion. I am also certain that he meant Jaanan no harm. Quite the contrary." He frowns and shakes his head. "I tried to tell my niece this, but I'm not sure she is convinced. She has had more than her share of disappointments."

"I'm glad no greater harm has come to her."

"I was inclined to think badly of Hamza when I learned it was he who took her to Galata. She never spoke of it until recently. She thought I knew, since Hamza had promised her he would tell me where she was. He never did. Last night, he told me he had been in hiding since then, fearing for his life, and so was unable to keep his promise to tell me. He said his driver had been killed." He looks up at Kamil. "Is it the same man Jemal saw?"

"Yes. It must be. A man called Shimshek Devora. Jaanan Hanoum was held in his mother's house. Shimshek was killed that same week. Supposedly in an accident."

"May he rest in Allah's care."

They are silent for a few moments, their thoughts tangled in skeins of smoke. Birds squabble outside the window.

Finally, Ismail Hodja continues. "I've come to believe since then that Hamza was telling the truth. My brother-in-law—Jaanan's father—thinks it's possible that Amin Efendi was planning to abduct Jaanan from his home, with the connivance of . . . well, that is a matter for my brother-in-law. It would satisfy Amin Efendi's desire for revenge against the family and, if he could force the marriage, his need for money. So you see, Hamza, in his own misguided way, was trying to protect my niece. As for those unfortunate Englishwomen, my heart refuses to accept that he would harm them. Indeed, given what happened to his sister, I would have expected him to be kind toward women."

"What happened to his sister?"

"Ah, that poor girl. As the penniless daughter of a traitor, she was unable to contract a marriage. Who would bring her into their family and risk official displeasure? She was quite attractive, I understand, and many good families had inquired about a possible match when her father was still kadi. She had her heart set on one particular young man, so she refused the others. Her father doted on her and didn't insist, but he disapproved of the man she preferred because he was merely a merchant, although quite wealthy. After the disaster, even that family withdrew their suit. She threw herself into the moat of Aleppo's citadel when it was swollen with rainwater and drowned."

Ismail Hodja takes another long draw from his mouthpiece and lets the smoke dissipate before continuing. His shoulders slump with exhaustion.

"I can't tell you, my dear magistrate efendi, what any of this has to do with the deaths of these young Englishwomen. It is true that after his sister's passing, Hamza became harder. But that is a long way from a man capable of killing. For murder you need powerful meat—hatred, greed, jealousy, or ambition—not the thin gruel of self-hate.

39

The Gate of the Spoonmakers

amil waits on a stool under the giant plane tree in Beyazit Square that a poet once called the Tree of Idleness. Behind him stretch the outer wall of the War Ministry and the domes of Beyazit Mosque, its courtyard garden visible through the stone portal. The square hums with traffic, vendors of sherbet and baked simits crying out their wares, porters hissing their way through the crowd, trotting horses, carts, and children dodging one another.

Kamil spies Bernie's red hair approaching amid a sea of turbans and fezzes.

"Howdy. Been waiting long?"

"Not long. It's good to see you. Please sit. Would you like some refreshment?"

"Sorry. Afraid I have to decline. I can't stomach the tea here or the coffee. Both thick as tar. I don't know how you drink so much of it. No offense."

"None taken. They are quite strong."

"Maybe we could just walk around a bit. I don't know this area very well."

"Have you seen the booksellers' market? There's a good place to eat lunch nearby."

Kamil leads the way through the throng to a gate beside the mosque.

"This is the Gate of the Spoonmakers." To Bernie's questioning look, he shrugs. "I have no idea why."

They enter a quiet, sun-dappled courtyard. Each tiny shop around the yard is stacked to the ceiling with books and manuscripts. A few apprentices hurry past carrying packages to be delivered to customers at their homes. In the center is another plane tree, under it a bench next to a small fountain. Bernie lowers himself onto the bench and spreads his arms across the back, embracing the old vine-draped buildings. "Keyif," he mutters contentedly.

Kamil holds a tinned cup chained to the fountain under the stream of water and takes a draught.

"You should try this water. It's from a spring."

Bernie points to the ancient stone portal at the far end of the courtyard. "And what's that gate called?"

"What? Oh, the Gate of the Engravers."

"Of course."

Cup still in hand, Kamil frowns in the direction of the gate.

"You look like you've got a swarm of termites under your vest today, Kamil, ol' chum."

Despite himself, Kamil laughs. "That's disgusting."

"Well, it's true. Something isn't sitting well with you. Not well at all. Might help talkin' about it."

"There's too much happening, Bernie, and I'm not sure what to think about it all."

"Like what?" Bernie moves his arm to make room for Kamil on the bench.

"There's been an arrest."

"You mean for Mary's murder? That's great. Who's the scoundrel?"

"And Hannah's murder too."

"You're joking?" Bernie sits up and turns to look at Kamil.

"No, no, I'm not." He notices that blood has darkened Bernie's face so it looks burned by the sun. "Are you all right?"

"Yeah, sure. Dying of curiosity. Who did they arrest?"

"Hamza, the journalist. My associate, Michel Sevy, happened to be nearby when Hamza broke into the home of Ismail Hodja last night and threatened him. Apparently, Hamza confessed."

"Michel Sevy," Bernie repeats slowly, then asks, "What did Hamza confess to?"

"When I spoke with him this morning, he denied everything, but on my way back from Chamyeri, I stopped at my office and heard that he has admitted to killing both Hannah and Mary. I don't understand it. I'm going to visit him again this afternoon. I want to hear it from his own mouth. I suppose there's some logic to it," he muses. "At the end of almost every thread of inquiry there seems to be Chamyeri, but I suppose they could also lead to Hamza."

"What's the connection?"

"No proof other than the confession. That's the problem. Just coincidences. Hamza is a distant relation of Ismail Hodja. Some years ago, he appears to have used the hodja's garden pavilion at night to meet a foreign woman. This went on around the time Hannah Simmons's body was found."

"You think it was Hannah he was meeting?"

"The driver was the same man who picked her up every week."

"Admirable detective work."

"Thanks, but I owe some of that information to Sybil Hanoum."

"Wait a minute. Sybil? What does Sybil have to do with any of this?"

"She decided to investigate on her own. It's my fault. I suppose I encouraged her at the beginning. She was so eager to help, and I thought she might pick up some information from the women. I can't speak with them myself, of course. I didn't think there was any harm in it."

"Jesus, Mary, and Joseph. Sybil. I thought she was just paying social calls."

"From the descriptions, I think the driver was a young Jewish man named Shimshek Devora. He had distinctive hair, tightly coiled like Arab hair, but light in color. A chauffeur by profession."

"Have you talked to him?"

"No. He was killed. Fell under a carriage. Apparently an accident, but Hamza seems to think otherwise. There's one other link between Hamza and Chamyeri, but I don't know what to make of it. A few months ago, Hamza abducted Ismail Hodja's niece and held her in Shimshek Devora's mother's apartment. He told her a story about protecting her from . . . well, that's immaterial. I think he meant the girl no harm."

Bernie raises his eyebrows skeptically. "He abducted her for her own good?"

Kamil smiles indulgently. "As you know, Oriental motives are often inscrutable. In any case, Michel and I found her with some help from his mother who lives in the same neighborhood, but Hamza escaped. In fact, I didn't know it was Hamza until this morning when the hodja told me. When we found the girl, he ran off and we never saw his face."

"His mother?" Bernie mutters.

"Pardon?"

"Nothing. What else?"

"This Shimshek was involved—together with Hamza, as we now know—in some kind of business dealings, but we never discovered what. He died while the girl was being held."

Bernie gets up from the bench and stands by the fountain, staring at the trickle of water from the metal pipe. He reaches down to give the spigot another twist. The water continues to flow. He turns around to face Kamil. Arms folded protectively across his chest, he appears vulnerable, a boy in an elongated body.

"This Shimshek. Where did he live?"

"Galata, the Jewish quarter. Why?"

"Just curious."

Kamil looks closely at Bernie. "Did you know him?"

Bernie frowns and doesn't answer right away.

"I heard the name somewhere, but can't remember where. If it comes to me, I'll let you know. So this Shimshek used to pick Hannah up and took her to the pavilion in the hodja's garden to meet Hamza."

"The pavilion is only a short distance from the pond. Hamza could easily have strangled Hannah, thrown the body in, then driven off."

"But Hamza hasn't spilled any details about the murders yet?"

"Not that I know. Right after Hannah's death, Hamza went to Paris for several years. I suppose now we know why."

"You don't sound sure."

Kamil takes a deep breath. "I don't know. He had political reasons for leaving too. I'm sure the secret police had him in their sight. He was rumored to be a radical and he wrote inflammatory articles for a reformist journal."

"But why would he have killed Hannah?"

"That's what disturbs me. I can't think of a motive." He crosses his legs and takes out a cigarette, then looks up without lighting it. "Perhaps Hannah was pregnant. It's not in the police report, but it's possible."

"Sounds a bit far-fetched, if you ask me. Which you haven't." Bernie shakes his head no to Kamil's offered cigarette.

Kamil puts his own cigarette back, slips the silver cigarette case into his pocket, and takes out his beads. "It's not unheard-of. He doesn't seem the kind to want to settle down."

"I'd think it would make Hannah want to kill him, not the other way around."

They share a chuckle.

"Maybe she was angry enough to spill all his beans on him. After all, she was employed by the palace. If he was wanted as a radical, she could have turned him in with just a word to the right person."

"Spill *the* beans, pardner, *the* beans."

"Okay, spill *the* beans on Hamza. It's an odd image. What kind of beans? And why spill them? Why not throw them?"

Bernie mimics a sigh of exasperation. "I don't know. If Hannah was pregnant, it doesn't make sense that she would turn the father of her child in to the police. What about Mary? Why do you think he killed her?"

"I don't. But the police claim he confessed to it. Perhaps he was her lover, too. Why do people kill? Revenge? Maybe both women spurned him."

Bernie sits down on the bench beside Kamil. "I'll take one of those after all," gesturing toward Kamil's jacket pocket. Kamil fishes out his cigarette case and, snapping it open, offers it to Bernie. They sit for several minutes, Bernie quietly smoking and Kamil lost in thought, amber beads slipping like sand through his fingers.

"There's still the unexplained matter of the pendant." Kamil breaks the silence. "With the Chinese inscription." He looks curiously at Bernie. "It doesn't fit any of the motives. Both Hannah and Mary had it. I suppose Hamza might have given it first to one, then the other as a gift. Perhaps taken it from Hannah when he killed her."

"A gruesome thought."

"It's an odd gift, though. How did he get it? I'm sure it was made in the palace."

Bernie doesn't answer. He stares unseeing at the fountain.

"You don't look surprised."

"Well, I figured it was, what with the sultan's signature—unless it's a forgery."

"I don't think so. I showed it to the head craftsman, and he identified it as the work of a particular silversmith at Dolmabahche Palace."

Bernie stares at Kamil. "And did he tell you who he made it for?"

Kamil returns his look. "No. He was found dead the day after I asked to meet with him. They said his heart gave out."

Kamil gets up and walks over to the fountain. He stares at it, as if he has forgotten what it is for. "His family says he didn't suffer from a weak heart." He turns to Bernie. "But I suppose it's possible."

Bernie leans forward, elbows on knees, head propped in his hands. "Kamil, old buddy," he mumbles, "You'd better watch your back."

"What am I watching for?"

"You don't think it's too much of a coincidence that the old man dies just when you announce you want to meet him?"

"Of course I think it's suspicious. I don't believe in coincidence. Someone in the palace doesn't want me to know who had that pendant made," he adds thoughtfully. "It must be a powerful person to orchestrate these deaths and someone with a powerful motive to risk so much. The grand vizier? A minister? Perhaps the sultan himself?"

"Covering their tracks."

"Yes." He sighs and turns to Bernie. "The palace is out of my jurisdiction. You're right that anyone looking in that direction is in danger. If I were wiser, I would leave the question of Hannah alone." He thinks with greater sympathy of Ferhat Bey and his pauper's pension.

"Then why don't you?" Bernie suggests.

"Because I'm required to solve the case of Mary Dixon's death. The Minister of Justice Nizam Pasha seems to have taken a particular interest in my progress in this case. Perhaps he has come under pressure from the British. I don't know. Anyway, the evidence suggests that the key to Mary's death lies in deciphering Hannah's."

Bernie turns suddenly to Kamil and asks, "How did this Michel fellow happen to be at Ismail Hodja's place just in time to arrest Hamza? It's pretty far out of the way."

"I don't know," Kamil admits. "I imagine he had information through his informants."

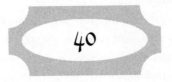

40

July 17, 1886

Dearest Maitlin,

I was so happy to receive a telegram from you this morning.
Please don't think me ungrateful for your advice, after having impor-
tuned you for it in so many of my own missives. I am aware of the
difficulties posed by becoming wife to a Mohammedan, as you put
it. In my letters, I've tried to paint a fuller picture of society here in
order to relieve your mind. Kamil is British trained and a thoroughly
modern gentleman. He is charming and commands such a high
standing in society—he is a pasha after all—that I'm sure he will
win over even old Lady Bartlethwaite, who is surely the hardest nut
to crack in Essex. Truly, there is no cause for distress, only the great-
est happiness for my future. Surely this is the future, and the adventure, dear sister, that you have always wished for me.

I have little to tell you, as I've stayed close to home recently.
Kamil has gotten it into his head that the palace women are dangerous and has asked me not to visit them anymore. He thinks this only

because he has never been inside the imperial harems. There is a great deal of intrigue, but they are all schemes by women trying to position themselves ahead of other women in the palace hierarchy. I don't see how that has anything to do with me. I am only another woman to tea, an entertainment that can be mined for information about the outside world. Really, they are more bored than dangerous, and, if dangerous, only to themselves.

Nevertheless, I was touched by Kamil's concern, which I take to be just another sign of his affection. In any case, I stay out of mischief by keeping busy with embassy affairs. Father has left more and more of the daily running of things in my hands, which is not always welcome, but does help to pass the time. A new embassy secretary has been appointed, but won't come out for another month. I'm worried about Father, Maitlin. I haven't been as honest with you as I should about the situation. Can you imagine—I have to coax him to bathe. He sleeps in his office now, rather than in the Residence, so his staff has set aside another room where he can receive visitors. I know you think I should ask the embassy staff to file a report suggesting he retire, but that isn't my place. They are beginning to talk, but the thing is that when he is at work, Father still cuts a good figure. He reads his reports, makes decisions, even gives speeches, although he doesn't travel much anymore. Some would simply say he works too hard, but I worry that there is more to it, and I am at a loss to think of a solution. If he were to return to England, Maitlin, I think he would die. There is also the selfish matter that I wish to remain here, and I can't see how that is possible if father is forced to leave. Kamil has not yet proposed the obvious solution. Until he does, I do what I can to make a go of things at the embassy.

I desperately need a diversion. Bernie has returned to his quarters at college to work on his book. A messenger came early this morning with an invitation—really more of a summons—from Asma Sultan to visit her at her summer place in Tarabya. That's the lovely, wooded area on the northern Bosphorus where Turkish society goes to escape the summer heat. The embassy has a summer villa nearby, but it's under repair, so I haven't had much opportunity to get away. Surely Kamil can't complain about my spending a pleasant afternoon with a starchy matron at her summer villa. It's to be very informal, the messenger said, and Asma Sultan will send a coach for me.

I'd better stop writing now and get ready. I remember it being quite a long way, although I haven't been there in years, so perhaps I exaggerate. It can't be that far if I am invited to come and go in one day. I must make sure to be back in time for dinner, as Kamil is dining with us tonight. I'll write more when I return. I'll pay special attention to everything so I can give you a full accounting.

41

Beautiful Machinery

eturning from Beyazit, Kamil encounters a crowd on the Karakoy end of the Galata Bridge. He calls to a group of young gendarmes and asks them what is going on.

"Bey, a criminal has been staked."

Kamil grimaces. He despises the old custom of impaling the head of a criminal in a public area, ostensibly as a lesson to the people that this is their fate if they stray from the path. These days, criminals are hung from lampposts, for the same effect. Under the present sultan, however, death sentences have usually been commuted. There have been no executions for some time. He worries what the foreign community will think when they see this, as of course they will. This time, the stake has been placed right at the base of the hill leading to Pera. The Karakoy side of the bridge is within the jurisdiction of his court, yet he knows nothing about anyone being sentenced to death. Perhaps it was a matter decided by the provincial Court of Inquiry.

But even that court must have its death sentences ratified by the grand vizier, acting for the sultan. Either way, he should have been informed. Kamil spurs his horse onto the bridge.

The gendarmes keep ahead of him, pushing people back. When he reaches the far end of the bridge, he is directly before the stake. A sign hangs at its base: *Traitor*. The head has not been cleanly separated from the body, a hasty and unprofessional execution. The man must have just been killed. The tissue still appears soft. The tip of the man's tongue protrudes from a beard stiff with dried blood. Soft black curls fall forward over the unnaturally inclined forehead. Kamil looks more closely at the blood-caked face. Hamza's eyes are wide open as if in surprise.

KAMIL THROWS THE bridle to a groom and runs into his office, startling the clerks who are cleaning their pens at the end of the workday.

"Who ordered this execution?" he bellows.

The head clerk comes forward, head bowed, and makes the sign of obeisance. "Magistrate Efendi, you did. The directive has your signature and seal."

"I never authorized such a thing."

"But it said you were carrying out the wishes of the court, that the decision had been ratified, and that the execution was to be carried out immediately."

"I did not write it. Who gave it to you?"

"Michel Efendi brought it himself, so we could register it. Then he took it to the warden."

"Michel? Where is he?"

"I don't know, bey."

The clerks make no pretense of returning to the files and papers on the desks before them, but whisper nervously to each other.

Kamil slams his door shut and falls heavily into the chair behind his desk. His chain of beads whips around his hand.

Michel has no authority to order an execution. And he, the magistrate, will be held liable for executing a man without a trial or the grand vizier's approval. What possible motivation could Michel have for doing such a thing, for killing Hamza and putting Kamil's career at risk? Did Hamza know something that threatened Michel?

What does he, Kamil, really know about the surgeon? It's true that they went to school together, but they only came to know one another much later. How did they meet? That's right. He ran into Michel on the street in Galata. That would make sense. Michel lived there with his mother. Didn't he? Kamil's beads fall silent.

Michel's mother, who had led them directly to Jaanan—and Hamza—at Madame Devora's house. Kamil had never met Michel's mother. It is improper to bring an unrelated man into one's home, so he had only Michel's account of where he lived.

Kamil thinks about this for a while. How could Michel have known Hamza would be at Ismail Hodja's house last night? He must have been lying in wait for him.

Kamil hates coincidences. But he can see no link between Michel and Hamza. Why was Michel interested in Hamza? How did he know to associate him with Chamyeri at all? How would Michel even know what Hamza looked like?

He opens the door and calls the head clerk.

Keeping his voice even, he tells him, "If Michel Efendi returns, please tell him that I have gone home, and that I would like to see him here as soon as possible, at the latest tomorrow morning before the second call to prayer."

"As you wish, bey." The clerk bows.

Kamil strides through the door and around the building into the stables. He chooses a fresh horse, waiting impatiently while the groom saddles it. He suddenly remembers the missing kitten. Had Michel lied about the tea they found at the sea hamam? If he knew the kettle had contained datura and that Mary had been killed there, Michel would have had a head start in finding the killer. And perhaps Michel had evidence that Hamza had killed Hannah as well. Why keep the information from him? Weren't they both after the same thing? Weren't they both working for the same people?

When the horse is ready, Kamil mounts and forces himself to ride away at an even pace. As soon as he is out of sight of the gate, he heads his horse north and spurs it to a gallop.

A SURPRISED YAKUP runs onto the front drive and takes the reins of the lathered horse as Kamil jumps down. Kamil wipes the sweat from his face with a dusty hand. Without a word, he charges into the villa and climbs the stairway to the study he made out of his mother's bedroom.

Going to his desk, he unlatches a side drawer and pulls out his father's revolver. He holds the weapon in his hand for a few moments, stroking the polished wood and tracing the grooves on the engraved barrel. The beautiful machinery of conquest and death. He lights a lamp so he can see better, loads the revolver, and fills a leather pouch with extra ammunition. He wraps a holster around his waist, then drops the gun into its sheath and the pouch into his pocket. He takes a deep breath, unsure of what to do next.

Lamp in hand, he walks into his bedroom and dips a cup into the clay jar on his dressing table. He takes a long draught of the cool water, then turns and descends the stairway at a more measured pace. His feet take him through the corridor leading to the back of the house, past the sitting room, to the stained-glass door, dark with moisture, leading to his most prized possessions. As he slips inside, the heavy, fragrant air thrills him, as it always does. A soft green light quickens the glassed-in room. He makes his way along a path between large-leafed palms and bromeliads. He has neglected to change to house slippers, so his boots click on the tiles. He places the lamp carefully atop a small table.

In the middle of the winter garden, shaded by the larger plants, stands a square bench filled with damp pebbles that hold thirty small earthenware pots, filled with slender green arches bursting along their stems or at their tips into a phantasm of colorful shapes. It reminds him of the fireworks celebrating the end of Ramadan. He stops at a large shadowy bloom and lowers his face to the velvety petals, inhaling its perfume, a mixture, he thinks, of vanilla and jasmine. It reminds him of a favorite milk pudding Fatma made for him as a child, and of the place between the Circassian girl's white thighs. The bright blue speculum seems to regard him warily. He resists the urge to draw the tip of his fingers over the black fur of the petals.

Loud voices recall him from his reverie. He turns to find a flustered Fatma at the door.

"Bey, there is a man at the door who insists you want to speak with him. He won't give his name. Yakup is still in the stable, so I answered the door."

"What does he look like?"

"Dressed like a tradesman, but very neat. He doesn't strike me as a tradesman at all. He acts as though he knows you, though. I'm sorry. Shall I ask him his name again?" She looks terrified that he might ask her to. "I told him to wait in the hall."

"Thank you, Fatma. Just leave him there. I'll come right away. Go back to the kitchen and send word to Yakup that he should return to the house."

He can still hear the *slapslap* of her slippers receding when the door opens and Michel steps through.

"Close the door," Kamil says quickly. "There's a draft."

Michel is the color of sand, from his mustache to his light brown shalwar. His hair is slick with sweat and a cloak is thrown over one arm. He is breathing heavily.

Michel stares directly at Kamil. "I understand you want to see me."

Kamil automatically slides into a new level of alertness.

"I wanted to ask you about Hamza Efendi's execution. Who signed the order?"

Truth and decorum.

"But you did, bey."

"I did no such thing. There was no trial."

"I wondered about that myself. But I was given the order and asked to bring it to the warden so that the sentence could be carried out immediately. It had all the correct seals, even the grand vizier's."

"Who gave it to you?"

Kamil notices the infinitesimal pause before Michel's answer. "It was brought to the police station, I presume by a messenger. My clerk gave it to me. I wasn't sure why you sent it to me first and not directly to the warden, but I thought you must have had your reasons." Michel's eyes have not wavered from Kamil's face.

Can a lying man keep such an expressionless face? Kamil wonders. Michel had brought the document himself to the Beyoglu Court, then to the police station. Perhaps immobility is a sign of the effort required to keep the muscles of his face under control, the ones that would otherwise betray him. Kamil would like to feel outraged by Michel's blatant lies, but against his better judgment wonders whether there is some truth in them. Perhaps someone else composed the execution order and forged the signatures. The grand vizier himself could have ordered it, bypassing lower administrators like himself. There is one way to find out.

"Where is the order now?" he asks Michel. "The signatures will tell us who authorized it. It will not be my handwriting or my seal on the paper."

Michel's expression does not waver. He is not surprised, Kamil thinks. "I gave it to the warden."

Kamil is suddenly certain that the document will never be found. The warden will put it into a file, and that file will disappear. He sighs, his legs and shoulders weary from standing.

"Come," he offers, walking behind the orchid box and indicating two chairs under the leaves of a small palm tree. "Let us sit and discuss this."

"I can't stay."

"You must make the time. I'm still curious about other aspects of the case." He walks over to one of the chairs and sits. Still holding his cloak, Michel moves closer until he is beside the other chair, but remains standing.

Kamil looks up at his associate's immobile face, wondering where is the man he had thought to call a friend. This is his outer shell, but the man scrutinizing him through those liquid brown eyes is a stranger. "How did you come to arrest Hamza?"

"All the indications pointed toward Chamyeri. You said that yourself."

"Yes, but others live at Chamyeri—Ismail Hodja, his niece, their staff. Only Hamza doesn't live there. Yet you chose to arrest him."

"What difference does it make? He confessed to the murders."

"When I spoke with him this morning, he denied it."

"You know the police have more efficient ways to gain the truth than simply asking for it." Michel shows a row of small teeth, half smile, half grimace.

Kamil ponders this. It is true that men's denial breaks readily under duress, but so does their will. He has never believed that a man's word forced from him is evidence. It is merely expedience.

"I'm still curious—how did you know to arrest him in the first place? What made you associate him with Chamyeri and Hannah Simmons, or with Mary Dixon?"

"Shimshek Devora, the driver." Michel shrugs. He has been so still that Kamil is startled by the sudden movement. "We know Shimshek picked up the woman Hannah," Michel continues in the droning voice of a schoolmaster, "and brought her to Chamyeri to meet Hamza. Hannah was found dead at Chamyeri. Who else could it have been? It was Hamza who abducted Ismail Hodja's niece and took her to Shimshek's mother." He shows Kamil his hand. "They're like fingers on the same hand."

"How did you know that was Hamza?"

"Madame Devora, of course."

"She didn't tell me that." Kamil pauses. "And neither did you. I only found out this morning. Ismail Hodja told me, and he himself only learned it recently from his niece. You are the only one who knew this, yet you said nothing."

He stares up at Michel, who has not moved. Kamil sees again the brown spider, absolutely still until startled.

"Is it ambition, Michel? Do you wish credit for solving the case yourself? It's all the same to me." Kamil gestures carelessly with his hand. "But you are a surgeon. Your promotion doesn't depend on solving cases."

"I don't know what you're talking about. I've kept nothing from you."

"How did you know Hamza was at Chamyeri the night you arrested him?"

"Ismail Hodja's house was being watched. Hamza was bound to show up sooner or later."

"Why were you looking for Hamza, when we at the court were singing an entirely different song?" Kamil could not help the bitterness and disappointment bleeding into his voice. "What about the pendant? Hamza has no link with the palace. How do we know there isn't more to this?"

Michel smiles mirthlessly. "It's not my business if the honorable magistrate is out of tune. I do my job."

Kamil feels hot, his heart galloping in his chest. He closes his eyes for a moment, inhales the fragrance of the room, and tries to calm himself.

Michel has come closer. "We're on the same side, Kamil," he says in an intimate voice. "We need stability and security, not this chauvinistic nationalist dream that could turn into a nightmare for the minorities. We're not Muslims and we're not Turks, we're Ottomans. It's a formula that has worked well for the Jews and for everyone else for a long time. People like Hamza want to destabilize the empire and sell it off piece by piece like scrap from a junk dealer's cart. Then, when all that's left are Turks, it'll be a Muslim Turkish empire, with no place for people like us. European nationalism—that crazy idea that every folk with its own language and its own religion deserves its own nation—it's infected the Young Ottomans. Mark my words, before long they'll drop their masks and call themselves what they really are, Young Turks. And where are *we* to go, I ask you? To a *Jewish* nation? There is no such thing on earth."

"I understand your concern, Michel, but I am on the side of impartial justice. No matter what Hamza did, he deserved a hearing. Execution without a trial is unjust, even if he was guilty. That betrays our country and its principles as much as the radicals. You of all people—a surgeon, a scientist—you should know that."

Michel shrugs. "Fate can be unjust."

"Fate." Kamil spits the word out. "Listen to you. You took this man's fate in your own hands and crushed it. It was your doing, not the hand of Allah. In any case, Nizam Pasha will not agree," he adds angrily. "He insists on the mechanism of the law, not telling a suspect's fortune."

"You'd be surprised at how open-minded Nizam Pasha can be," Michel responds.

Kamil looks up at him, startled. How far does this conspiracy of injustice extend? he wonders.

"I suppose it shouldn't surprise me that corruption is so resistant to change. I thought by taking part in this new judicial system, we could bring fresh straw into this stable of a city, but the same things go on, the same people"—he looks directly at Michel—"fouling the ground we walk on."

Kamil sees a flash of anger on Michel's face as he turns on his heel, cloak sweeping at the end of his arm. Then he is gone. A loud crash brings Kamil to his feet. The orchid box lies tipped on its side, spilling pebbles over the tiles. Atop the pebbles and shredded bark and soil, a rubble of color. Kamil falls to his knees and searches frantically, finds the black orchid, and lifts it tenderly. Its bloom is unblemished, but its neck is broken.

A harsh sob emerges from his throat as he grabs his revolver and slams through the door, brushing aside Yakup, who has come running at the noise.

"Did you see where he went?" he asks Yakup.

"No, bey. I saw no one. But this message just came from Feride Hanoum." Yakup takes a letter from his sash and hands it to him. "The messenger said to tell you she would like you to come right away."

Kamil breaks the seal and unfolds the letter.

Dear Brother,

Baba has fallen from the balcony. He is not aware of anything, but still lives. The surgeon says he cannot feel pain. That is a blessing, but he may not be with us long. Please come right away.

Your sister Feride

42

The Eunuch

A closed carriage pulls up at the embassy gate. The gate-keeper hurries up the path, followed by a black figure in a bright white robe and large turban.

"A royal coach has come for m'lady," the gatekeeper announces breathlessly.

The Residence guard asks Sybil whether she would like an escort.

"I think not. Thank you. I'm sure the palace has taken care of that." She relishes visiting Stamboul homes without fanfare and a trail of armed embassy guards—a precious relic of normalcy, simply a lady invited to tea.

The eunuch bows very low, touching his palm to his forehead and chest, then waits impassively to escort Sybil to the carriage. She has not veiled, but the eunuch seems not to notice. It is not the same self-confident, broad-shouldered eunuch that had accompanied Asma Sultan before. This man is tall and wiry, with a lined face the color of smoke and long, powerful hands. He does not speak or look at her, although Sybil has the feeling it is not out of respect, but aversion.

Servants and guards cluster at the doors and windows, whispering. Most have never seen a black eunuch except at a distance, when on horseback, escorting the carriages of royal ladies.

Sybil follows the eunuch to a carriage elaborately decorated with painted flowers. It is not the usual bulky conveyance that seats four or five harem ladies at once, but a sleek, smaller model designed for speed. The eunuch helps her up the steps, his hand black against her sleeve. When she has settled among the velvet cushions, he pulls a sheer curtain across the windows so she can look out without anyone seeing in and barks a command at the driver. He mounts a white stallion, its saddle embroidered with thread of gold and studded with rubies and emeralds. A long curved sword is cradled in his arm. She notes with surprise that there is no retinue, but supposes the armed eunuch is sufficient for an informal outing.

The carriage winds down the hill, then turns north on the shore road, picking up speed. Before long, they pass the entrance to Dolmabahche Palace. After that, the road winds inland through forested areas and then skirts villages built around inlets and coves. The closed carriage is hot and increasingly uncomfortable as the sun rises in the sky. The road has become a track and Sybil is jarred back and forth. She has forgotten the tedium of the trip to the summer villas. It has been many years since she last accompanied her mother to the British residence at Tarabya, although they had gone more comfortably by boat. She wishes she could fling back the curtain. The sheer cloth provides a narrow, blurred vantage on the landscape racing by and blocks the air. The velvet cushions stick to her sweat-drenched back.

She begins to worry that it was a mistake to accept this invitation. She will be able to stay only a short while in order to be back in time for tonight's dinner. Even if Kamil were not coming, she would still have to return in time to eat with her father. It has become their ritual to eat together. He becomes agitated when rituals are not carried out. Perhaps Kamil is right that I am too precipitous, she thinks, then chides herself for her lack of spirit. Maitlin, she concludes, would have done this without cudgeling herself with self-doubt.

Three long hours later, the carriage turns off the road. Sybil peeks out between the curtains and sees a white villa, a fairy-tale house of pitched roofs, lacelike trim, ornate turrets, balconies, and patios. The eunuch draws back the curtains and unlatches the door. She ignores his hand and climbs out of the carriage clumsily, her legs stiff from immobility. The eunuch moves to the end of the drive and waits. Sybil doesn't follow right away, but instead stands with eyes closed, breathing the scent of pine and sea and sun-warmed wood. She realizes that she feels happy and optimistic about life when she leaves the Residence grounds. She thinks how lovely it would be to live in such a house, a smaller one, of course, but overlooking the water, with Kamil. He had said his house was set in a garden by the Bosphorus, had he not?

Cheered by this thought, she looks around for a servant. She has brought a gift of realistic-looking wax flowers under glass, the latest fashion in England. The grounds appear deserted. Sybil points to the large box in the carriage. The eunuch picks it up and she follows him into the house. Behind her, the traces jangle as the driver turns the carriage.

43

The End of Dreams

amil strokes his father's motionless hand. He seems unhurt, the wound on his head hidden by the pillow, his broken limbs under the comforter. The comforter moves up and down slowly, irregularly, with the old man's breath. His face is puffy, eyes closed.

"He looks like he's sleeping," Feride says in a voice hoarse from weeping. "As if he'll wake up at any moment."

"You said the maid saw him climb over the railing?" Kamil is empty of all emotion, but he is aware that this is a temporary state, a putting off of the final reckoning.

"She said he was smiling and reaching out to someone. Maybe he thought he was going to Mama?"

"Yes, perhaps that's where he went."

"They'll be together soon. That's what he wanted more than anything else." Feride bows her head over her father's chest. "Baba." She stiffens. "Baba?"

The comforter is unnaturally still. The pasha's features have been sharpened by death, but the faint imprint of a smile remains, a footprint on the farthest shore of a man's life.

Feride begins to wail.

Kamil is silent, the storm still building in his chest. He puts his arm around Feride and holds her.

"Oh, what have we done?" she cries out. The question pierces Kamil and he begins to shake.

"Don't, my dear sister. There is no blame. We only wanted to help him live again."

"We've killed him," she wails. "We wanted him to be there for us, to be a normal family again. It was selfish of us. We should have allowed him his dreams."

"Yes," Kamil concedes sadly. "People should be allowed their dreams."

AN HOUR LATER, Kamil is galloping around the steep curves winding up the wooded hill to Robert College. Great oaks and sycamores obscure the sky and cast a green pall over the road as if it were underwater.

At the parade ground at the top of the hill, he flags down a young man and asks where the teachers live. He spurs his horse and, before long, is pounding on the door of a Victorian clapboard house set at the edge of the forest.

When Bernie answers the door, it takes Kamil a moment to recognize him. He is wearing glasses.

"Why, hello, there," he says, taking off his glasses. His hair is uncombed and he is wearing an old shirt and trousers with sagging knees. "You're not seeing me at my best, but do come in."

Kamil pushes past him. In the sparsely furnished living room, he turns and says, "What do you know about Michel Sevy? You know him, don't you? You recognized his name this afternoon."

"What's gotten into you?" Then, looking more closely at Kamil in the lamplight, Bernie sits on the sofa arm and asks, "What's happened?"

"They've executed Hamza." He doesn't mention his father. The memory is too raw to touch.

"What? But you haven't even held a trial yet."

"I know. It was done without my knowledge. By Michel Sevy."

"Damnation." Bernie looks up at Kamil, who is still standing in the middle of the room, hands on his waist. He takes a deep breath. "Kamil, my friend, sit down and let me get you something to drink."

"I don't want . . ." Kamil is still shaking with rage and with regret.

Bernie gets up and waves his hand. "Just sit. I'll tell you everything you need to know. But first you have to calm down."

When Bernie returns with two tumblers of scotch, Kamil seems calmer, but his nerves have simply welded into an iron resolve. He takes the glass from Bernie, but doesn't drink. He puts it on the table too hard, liquid spilling onto some papers lying there. Bernie rushes over and dabs at the papers with a handkerchief.

"My new book." He smiles sheepishly. Then, catching Kamil's intensely focused gaze, he turns a chair around and sits.

"Michel is a police surgeon?"

"Yes, you know that," Kamil snaps. He stands and moves toward Bernie. "Either you tell me who he is or I'll shake it out of you."

"Hey, hey, my friend. No need for violence. It's too late now, anyway, for poor Hamza."

"You knew *him* too?"

"Yes. Look, can I trust you not to pass this on to your superiors?"

"No." Kamil is still standing, one hand flipping his chain of beads back and forth in a steady rhythm. He is breathing heavily.

"Jesus, Mary, and Joseph. What on earth has happened to get you all in a lather like this?" He holds out a cigarette.

Kamil shakes his head impatiently.

Bernie sighs. "You'll need more than a cigarette to digest this news. Why don't you take a swig of your scotch?"

"Just talk."

"All right, then. But in the name of friendship—we *are* still friends, right?—I beg you to keep this just between us."

"I'd like to hear it first." He doesn't deny, nor does he acknowledge, the friendship. At this moment, it is irrelevant.

Bernie crosses his legs, then uncrosses them and leans forward, the scotch glass forgotten in his hand.

"All right. I do hope you have enough sense, after hearing this, to keep it to yourself. Eight years ago, Hamza was part of a group trying to engineer a coup against the sultan with British help. The sultan had just disbanded the parliament, so there were a lot of angry reformists, even in his own nest. Prince Ziya was one of them. He put the Brits in touch with someone in the palace. Hannah was the go-between, with Hamza receiving the information outside the palace and passing it on."

"How do you know all this?"

Bernie does not answer right away. He gets up and paces the room as if looking for a way out, drawing deeply on his cigarette. His other hand still holds the glass of scotch. Finally, he stops before Kamil and gives him a long look.

"You're my friend, Kamil. I don't want you any deeper in this shit. You're already up to your shirt collar in it."

"Are you involved in this?" Kamil asks sadly.

"Well, not precisely."

Bernie and Kamil stand tensely facing one another. Kamil's beads flip back and forth in a staccato.

"I need your assurance that this stays between us."

Kamil meets his eye. "I cannot give you such assurance."

Bernie sits suddenly on the chair. "Oh, what the hell," he mutters angrily. "I'm sick and tired of this skulking around. For what? So more people can get killed? I was shanghaied into this and I'm damned ready to get out."

"Into what?"

Bernie squints up at Kamil and says, "British Foreign Service."

"What? You? You're American."

"Good disguise, eh? Well, yes, I am American, but one of my relatives in England is in the Foreign Ministry—Sybil's brother-in-law, actually. They thought I would be less obvious. Who'd suspect an American of anything more than rudeness and bad taste?"

Kamil doesn't smile, but pulls over a chair and sits. "Go on." The puzzle of the case is calming him, as if each piece he puts together redeems a piece of his shattered life.

"Hamza was having an affair with Hannah. Our correspondent in the palace had the pendant made and Hamza gave it to Hannah as a gift. If someone inside wanted to communicate with him, they'd wait until she took it off, put a note in it, and she'd carry it out when she met Hamza. It was cleverly designed. You needed a key, but the lock was invisible unless you knew it was there. She probably didn't even know it could be opened. We used it to schedule our operation."

"And the Chinese—that was your contribution?"

"No. Our contact inside the palace came up with it. He has some kind of interest in China and copied out the characters, although not perfectly. It's why they called me in on this. I can read the characters. I puzzled over why that particular poem, but I can't figure it out, other than the possible connection to the revolutionary, Kung. It probably has a personal meaning to whoever sent it from the palace."

"Who is it?"

"We never found out. Even Hamza didn't know. The messages went in through the harem, but we don't know who sent them out. We've always assumed it was Ali Arslan Pasha, the current grand vizier. The top women in that part of the harem where Hannah worked were related to him.

"So you used Hannah."

"Yes, although we never thought any harm would come to her."

"What Hamza did was harmful."

"You mean, sleep with her or whatever they did in that pavilion? That was his business. Anyway, he was a free man. We had no say about what he did or didn't do."

"Did he kill her?"

"I don't see it," Bernie says thoughtfully. "There was no reason to. He seemed like a pretty good guy. I think he genuinely cared for Hannah. I'm not sure what motivated him, whether it was patriotism or something else. He did seem to honestly believe in modernizing the empire, but there was a real bitterness about it, like there was something personal in it for him, so I just don't know." Bernie throws up his hands. "Anyway, around that time everything went to the dogs."

"What do you mean?"

"Someone was on to us and spilled the beans. The secret police moved in. They got Prince Ziya. Killed him in Paris. I guess to warn off anyone else thinking of bucking the sultan. Then Hannah turned up dead. We never figured out how they found out about Hannah—who ratted. Anyway, I got out fast, so did Hamza. He had a driver, that Shimshek Devora, who must have known about all this too, but someone finally found him and shut him up for good. We always assumed the secret police were responsible for Hannah's death. I guess probably Mary's too—then framed Hamza for it. That would be typical. Two birds with one stone. Hamza comes back from exile years later and—boom—they use Mary to bait their trap. The secret police have long memories. They keep files on everything. Your government must have warehouses full of secret reports. Maybe that's why they have to keep building new palaces. They get pushed out by all that accumulated paper."

"What does any of this have to do with Michel?"

"Remember that night we went out on the town and that dog almost had me for dinner? That animal belonged to your associate Michel Sevy."

"How do you know that?"

"I saw him duck down an alley after I shot the dog. I recognized him. I have to admit, I was pretty surprised when you told me the name of your associate. I paid his office a little visit and, sure enough, it was the same guy on our tail eight years ago. Michel Sevy. The Chameleon, we called him. He didn't even bother to change his name.

He doesn't work for you or for the police. He's one of the sultan's own. I reckon he didn't like me snooping around."

"That's outlandish. Michel in the secret police?"

"Why not? Did you have anything to lead you to Hamza until Michel laid it all in your lap?"

"No. Most of the clues led in other directions."

"I remember you had a gut feeling that something wasn't right. Ask him yourself how he knew about Hamza."

"I did. He said he was having Hamza watched. He withheld evidence from me. But he didn't explain why."

"So now you know. Whether or not Hamza killed those women, he was going to hang for it because it let the secret police nail him as a traitor. I don't know why they didn't just shoot him on a dark night and get it over with the minute he stepped back in the country. Although that would have killed any chance they had of finding out who his contact in the palace was."

Kamil jumps up from his chair, fists clenched, knocking his glass to the floor. "We're a civilized country, Bernie," he shouts. "We have a judicial system. We don't just gun down people in the street like in America."

Bernie laughs. "That's what you'd like to believe, my friend. It's very unlike you to disregard all the evidence." He flings away the stub of his cigarette, which has burned out between his fingers. "Just listen to yourself. Like a preacher with a rod stuck up his ass."

Kamil takes a step in his direction. "How dare you!"

"Hey, hey, now. Whoah." Bernie stands up and backs away, hands held defensively before him. "What the hell is the matter with you today?"

Kamil's face twists grotesquely with the effort to contain his emotions. He is weeping, he knows—he can feel the wetness on his cheeks—but is powerless to stop.

Bernie seems stunned. "Kamil, old buddy. Calm down now. Obviously I don't have the whole story. Something's happened. Now, why don't you sit down over there?" He points at the sofa. Kamil doesn't move. "I'll be right back." He edges carefully toward the door.

Kamil can hear the creak of a cabinet opening, then the muffled clank and splash of a metal scoop descending into a clay jar of drinking water. Bernie returns a moment later, carrying a glass of water. Kamil is sitting on the edge of the sofa, head in his hands.

Bernie pushes the glass within reach on the side table and pulls a chair over to sit in front of Kamil. He waits quietly until Kamil raises his head, then hands him the water.

"Sybil told me you like a drink of water to calm the jitters," he admits bashfully.

Kamil takes a sip, then another. He sits back and closes his eyes for a few moments. When his breathing is back to normal, he asks Bernie for a cigarette. They sit for a while in silence, smoking. Bernie sips at his scotch.

Kamil is the first to speak. He wants to tell Bernie about his father, but doesn't.

"If Hamza didn't kill those women, who did?" His voice retains a small tremor, but he feels himself gaining strength. He will tell Bernie about his father later, when he has command over himself again.

"Michel is a foot soldier. It could have been him or someone like him. They found out about Hannah, so she was a target. Maybe they thought she could tell them who the traitor in the palace was. That's what they're really after. The shark in the sultan's pool. But she didn't know, so she had nothing to tell them. None of us knew." He looks away. "I hope she didn't suffer too much. She was a nice girl." A sip of scotch. "They probably would have killed her anyway."

"The silken cord. It was a warning to the plotters."

"What's that?"

"She was strangled with a silken cord, the traditional method of executing members of the royal family."

"I thought she drowned."

"She was strangled first."

Bernie wants to ask more, but decides he would rather live with a question than an answer. They sit together in silence, each weighing the burden of his own thoughts.

"What about Mary Dixon?" Kamil asks finally. "Why would the secret police want to kill her? Was she part of this?"

Bernie stands and walks to the window. His back to Kamil, he says thoughtfully, "That's the rub. There's something going on, but as far as I know Mary had nothing to do with any of it. I almost swallowed my tongue when you showed me the necklace she was wearing."

"What is going on?" Kamil asks carefully, bracing himself for an answer he is sure he doesn't want to hear.

Bernie turns to face Kamil. His expression is obscured by shadow but his hair, caught by the light, coils like hot wires around his head. He runs his hand through it, then goes to the sideboard, opens a fresh bottle, and pours himself another scotch. He holds the bottle out to Kamil, who shakes his head no.

"You remember that Chiraghan Affair a few years back—another attempt by the Young Ottomans to replace Abdulhamid with his brother Murad. The sultan's been walling himself up ever since. I understand he might be a bit sore after the Brits occupied Egypt, but that was four years ago, water under the bridge. No reason for him to turn his back on us and start hobnobbing with the Germans. That's never a good idea. And he's threatening to head up some kind of international Islamic movement. Those are dangerous games. We've got to stick together. What with Russia tearing up the countries around it like a hungry bear, we're just a little concerned that the Ottomans don't become their next meal. They've already taken a few good bites."

"I'm aware of the situation," Kamil says dryly. "What does this have to do with Mary Dixon?"

Bernie waves his scotch at him. "No offense meant. I'm just setting the stage, so to speak." He takes a long sip. "Well, as I said, we don't like the direction this sultan is taking. We need your empire stable to keep the Russians in check in Europe. That's better achieved under British protection, not by getting in bed with the Germans and with radical Islamic movements. The opposition, the Young Ottomans, were pretty well crushed after the Chiraghan Affair. But last year, we had a new communication from someone inside the palace, a letter posted in Paris and addressed to a safe house in London. It contained the same two characters for brush and bowstring. It proposed our assistance in a coup in exchange for British control over Syria. We provide a little money, a little muscle—and in return strengthen our own position in the region—well, that sounds like a mighty good bargain."

"The lion keeps the bear at bay so it can tear the haunches off its prey without being disturbed," Kamil comments sourly.

Bernie sips at his scotch and smiles indulgently at Kamil. "Kamil, my friend. This is politics, not philosophy. How do you think your empire got as fat as it is? By stealing food from the tables of other empires." He shrugs. "Besides, your grip on that province is pretty tenuous these days anyway. It's only a matter of time. Better to cut your losses now and let the Brits deal with it. They have plenty of experience wrangling territories that are trying to throw their riders."

Kamil glares at him. "Go on."

"Anyway, I came here to investigate—to make sure it was serious. This time we decided to cut out any middlemen, like Prince Ziya. Hamza was already back, but since the police knew about him, he kept his role in this quiet."

"What was his role?"

"To try to make a connection with the person in the palace. I had no idea he was using Mary, or the pendant again. We thought the pendant was lost until you found it on Mary's body.

Kamil is aghast. "An innocent young woman loses her life in this crazy scheme the last time and so you try it again, with the same degenerate accomplice? Mary had no idea, did she?"

"Probably not, assuming that's what happened. And I can't think of any other reason Mary would be wearing that pendant. I agree with you about Hamza. He plays his role too well. Played. The poor bastard." He looks for a long moment into his glass, then meets Kamil's eye. "This is not a pretty profession, magistrate bey. And to tell you the truth, I'm sick of it. This is my last assignment. I just want to go back to writing my book."

"So you really are a scholar."

Bernie looks offended. "Of course."

"Who else here knows about this?"

"No one, other than me, Hamza, and the person pulling strings in the palace. We kept the circle small." He takes a sip of scotch. "And now the secret police, God bless them. But for the life of me, I can't figure out how they would know about this latest communication. It's too early in the game. In fact, there *is* no game. We never received any messages after that first contact."

"What about Shimshek Devora?"

"Hamza's driver? I can see Hamza tying up loose ends. He's meticulous when it comes to self-preservation." He shakes his head slowly. "Still, he's known this Shimshek for years. Hard to fathom that he would kill a friend. He was pretty broken up about Hannah. Still, if the executioner's blade is aiming for your head, you'd probably shift whoever you had to, to get out of the way."

"And the pendant?"

"I'm still wondering how Mary got hold of it. Maybe Hamza took it back when Hannah was killed—I guess that makes him look pretty suspicious—and later gave it to Mary to wear into the harem, thinking someone would see it and put a message in it like before. Baiting the hook. But I still have a hard time believing he would murder the women."

He splashes scotch into a glass and hands it to Kamil, who takes it this time.

"I wonder who has such free access to the harem," Bernie continues. "Maybe one of the eunuchs. He could come and go, take the message to whoever it is outside the harem that's orchestrating this whole shebang. We just don't know."

Kamil tilts his glass and watches the golden liquid swirl, then takes a sip. "Whoever reported on Hannah could still be there, see the new pendant on Mary, and report it again."

"A snitch in the harem. Maybe," Bernie replies, rolling the word around his mouth. "But why? It would put that person in danger from the people behind the plot. I'd be surprised if whoever snitched the first time would still be hanging around the same harem, alive. I'd bet the snitch didn't know the whole story. You sell out a couple of people, but you don't realize they're just the small fry. There's a big hammer behind them just waiting to come down on you. Whoever knows about the plot—and the pendant—would be a target."

Kamil jumps to his feet. "May Allah protect her. Sybil Hanoum! She told the women about the pendant."

Bernie swings around and stares at Kamil. "What women?"

"She visited Prince Ziya's fiancée, Shukriye Hanoum."

"My God, I thought she was dead."

"She married someone in Erzurum. But she's back in the city, so Sybil Hanoum went to see her. Sybil Hanoum told the women there that both Hannah and Mary had the same pendant with a tughra inside. She probably also told them about the poem. Shukriye Hanoum apparently thinks she was punished because the sultan wrongly thought Prince Ziya was part of a plot to overthrow him." He looks at Bernie. "Maybe no one made the connection," he adds hopefully.

"Who else was there?"

"Shukriye's sister, Leyla, Ali Aslan Pasha's wife Asma Sultan, and her daughter Perihan."

Bernie closes his eyes. "Jesus, Mary, and Joseph."

44

The Past Is the Vessel of the Future

ybil and the eunuch pass noiselessly through enormous, high-ceilinged rooms, past vases taller than a man and table-tops of semiprecious stone balanced on elegant pedestals. Every surface is crammed with vases and statues. The room's contents are multiplied in enormous mirrors in gilded frames that line the walls. Sybil stops to admire a life-sized dog in translucent jade. She does not see the tiny figure, a statue come to life among the multitude, approaching her in the mirror.

Asma Sultan wears an unadorned brown gown with a simple veil of silk gauze draped over her head, a wren in a peacock house. She leads Sybil by the hand to a patio paved in intricately patterned colored tiles and overlooking the Bosphorus. There, behind a windbreak, waits a table laid with sweets and savories and a silver platter of fruit. The thin eunuch stands next to a brazier ready to brew coffee. Sybil wonders where the other servants are. She has seen no one else.

"Forgive my informality, Sybil Hanoum. As you see, this is more a picnic than a proper meal. I hope you don't mind. I am honored by your visit, but at my age, I prefer good company unadorned by the usual pomp and frippery."

Sybil is startled at Asma Sultan's command of English. They had spoken Turkish at previous meetings, so she had assumed Asma Sultan didn't know English.

"Thank you, Your Highness. I much prefer that myself."

"So I have heard."

Sybil straightens her skirt and tries to remember the correct manners. She remembers that it is rude to look someone directly in the eye. In the harem, women usually are seated next to one another, but here she is face to face with her hostess. She compromises by looking at a spot above Asma Sultan's left shoulder.

"Your English is flawless, Your Highness. Where did you learn it?"

"From my mother, a rare woman. She had a dazzling mind, a rage for life. She surrounded herself with the best art and literature from around the globe, in French, English, Persian, even Chinese. Particularly those designed or created by women. My mother herself was Russian, you know. She grew up in Paris and traveled a great deal before she was captured from a ship and sold to the harem. Once here, though, she made good use of the power and wealth that comes to a woman in the sultan's household, especially if she captures his eye."

"These artists were all women?" Sybil asks curiously.

"Some were wealthy women, like my mother, who commissioned art, and even played a role in designing it. But there are such creatures, you know, women artists and scholars. They are less well known because, sadly, only the men find patrons. My mother was a great patron. I profited from growing up surrounded by such a wealth of foreign culture and knowledge. In a sense, I was the ultimate project completed under her patronage. Few can appreciate that in a woman," she adds, with an undertone of bitterness. "Perhaps as an amusement when one is newly wed, but one that does not wear well. What use has one for such novelties in a harem, eh? Better to excel in needlework than foreign languages. That has been my daughter's approach, though I cannot say it has helped her."

Sybil does not know what to say and looks at her hands.

"As I said to you last week, my daughter had different expectations. She foolishly fell in love with her cousin Ziya. I was fond of my nephew and pushed for the match, but my husband gave her to a family with which he wanted an alliance. Where would politics be without brides, Sybil Hanoum? Empires would grind to a halt and begin to crumble. Perihan is unhappy, but uncomplaining. I point out to her that she escaped the fate of Shukriye, married off to the provinces." She smiles fondly. "And she spends as much time as possible with her dear mother."

"I think it shows a generous spirit that Perihan is so close to Leyla and Shukriye."

"Yes, she keeps an eye on them."

Sybil feels uncomfortable discussing Perihan's personal life in such detail when she isn't present. She is ashamed for Perihan.

To change the subject, she says, "You must have had a lovely childhood." She plucks a pastry filled with minced lamb from a serving plate and takes a bite.

"I suppose I did, but it was a childhood in a hundred rooms. I was never allowed to go out into the world and see it for myself. Still, I feel I have my hand on the pulse of the world, even here. My mother gave that to me." Asma Sultan silently regards the opposite shore as if seeking something there. "I remember the exact day she died, February 15, 1878, in the Old Palace. The Russian army was just outside the city. I could see the smoke of their campfires." She smiles. "I couldn't help but wonder if their generals were our relations. It's almost as if they were signaling to Mother, telling her to hold on, that they were almost there."

Sybil shifts uncomfortably in her seat. A breeze has begun to blow and she is feeling chilled.

"But they were too late." Asma Sultan turns back to Sybil. "She fell from the window of a small observation tower above the harem where she often went to get away from the other women. She told me once that from there she imagined she could see Paris and Saint Petersburg. They said it was an accident, but I never believed it." Her voice is bitter. "She would never have leaned out that window. She was afraid of heights."

"How awful," Sybil exclaims, shivering with cold and an unnamed anxiety. "Who would have done something like that?"

"She was Russian, Sybil Hanoum. The enemy was at the gates of the city. Perhaps they listened in on her silent communion with her uncles. I'm sure Sultan Abdulhamid feared her. He destroyed her like he destroyed my father."

Asma Sultan suddenly scrapes her chair back and stands. She leads the way to a plush divan on a sheltered portion of the terrace.

"Let us sit over here. It's more comfortable. Tell me about your life, Sybil Hanoum," she says lightly, as if nothing of consequence has been revealed.

Sybil sinks gratefully onto the soft pillows and wraps her shawl around her shoulders.

"I've hardly been anywhere. I came here when I was young. I have memories of the Essex countryside, a very brief stay in London, and then Stamboul. Which is lovely," she adds hastily.

"Ah, then you have traveled much farther than I, my dear. Tell me about Essex. You spoke of it the other day, but we were interrupted."

As they reminisce, the sun edges closer to the wooded hills. The eunuch serves coffee.

When Sybil has finished sipping from the tiny cobalt blue cup, Asma Sultan reaches for it and turns it upside down on its saucer. She smiles slyly.

"I can tell your fortune."

"Your Highness has unexpected talents," Sybil laughs. She feels reckless, but also lulled by the jewellike fruit on her plate, the flash-

ing expanse of water at her feet, the precious memory already fram-
ing itself in her mind of dining with royalty in the most beautiful spot
in the world.

Asma Sultan tests the bottom of the cup several times with her
slender finger. When she judges it to have sufficiently cooled, she
picks the cup up and peers into it intently. After a few moments, she
tilts it slightly to show Sybil.

"See? There is your past and here is your future." She points to
clots and filigrees of rich brown that coat the sides of the cup, coffee
ground as fine as powder.

"Can you read me my future, Your Highness?" Kamil must be there,
she thinks with the guilty hope that her desire be revealed as fact.

"Of course, my dear, of course." Asma Sultan scrutinizes the
inside of the cup, turning it this way and that until Sybil fears she can
no longer bear to wait.

Finally, Asma Sultan says, "The past is the vessel of the future. Let
me try to understand the shape of the vessel first."

"Yes, of course," Sybil responds, disappointed.

"A man, an old man who has known you all your life. Here he
is." She points to a long streak extending from the dregs to the rim
of the cup.

"That must be my father."

"There is also a woman here, a mother, your mother, I think. You
were very close to her."

"Yes. Yes."

"Here she disappears from your life." Pointing into the cup, she
looks up. "I'm sorry for your bereavement."

"Thank you, Your Highness." Gulls argue hoarsely high above.
"She's been gone some years now."

"And here are other women of the same age as you."

"One must be my sister, Maitlin. I don't know the others. Who
might they be?"

Asma Sultan twists the cup and holds it close to her eye. "They
are English. I see this by their dresses."

"Goodness," Sybil exclaims. "You can see that much detail?"

Fixing her black eyes on Sybil. "Oh, yes, my daughter, I can see."

"Two Englishwomen? In my past? My aunt, perhaps."

"Recent past. The cup is deep with time and I am moving up toward the future."

"Then perhaps someone at the embassy."

"Is there a woman important to you? A simple employee wouldn't appear in your cup."

Sybil thinks. "Really, I can think of no one who is English. I have a close acquaintance, but she is Italian."

"No." The slight tone of impatience in Asma Sultan's voice is immediately submerged by resignation.

"Ah, my foolish girl. You do not see your life as clearly as the eye of this cup does."

Stung, Sybil prompts, "Perhaps I'll have better success with my future."

"No, no, we cannot go on until the past has been fully explored. These women, look here, their signs end. Perhaps they returned to England?"

"Good heavens. It must be the two governesses. They have played quite a prominent role in my life of late."

"Governesses?"

"Hannah Simmons and Mary Dixon. The governesses who were killed. We spoke of them the other day at Shukriye Hanoum's."

"Of course. But why are they in the vessel of your past? You must have known them well, that they should play such a big role in your life?"

"No, I didn't know Hannah at all and I met Mary only a few times. We barely spoke. I suppose they appear in the cup because of their murders. I've been helping with the inquiry." Sybil couldn't quite hide the pride in her voice.

"I see." Asma Sultan's eyes slide closed for a moment. "Please continue."

"Well." She hesitates. "It seems the two deaths might be linked."

"Linked? How?"

"Of course, to start with, both were employed by the palace. And they were found in the same area."

"Where was that?"

"One at Chamyeri and one at Middle Village."

"Those are some distance apart."

"Mary's clothes were found at Chamyeri."

"I see. But all this might have been coincidence. Were there any other links?"

Sybil hesitates again, remembering Kamil's warning, but decides that the horse has bolted from the stable. She had already spoken of this at Leyla's. "They both had the same necklace."

"Why would that be of significance? Perhaps they frequented the same jeweler."

"But it had a tughra and a Chinese inscription."

"What did the inscription say?"

"Oh, I'm sorry, Your Highness. I can't remember." Sybil is flustered. "Something about a bowstring."

There is a pause before Asma Sultan asks, "That is unusual, but what would it have to do with their deaths?"

"It's not as trivial as it seems. It's possible that it's a secret code for some kind of plot against the sultan." She tries to be matter-of-fact, but excitement and pride color her voice.

Asma Sultan smiles thinly. "That is indeed important. So, these are the two women shaping your future."

"Oh, I wouldn't say that, Your Highness. I'm just helping, nothing more."

"Who else shares your theory of a plot centered on that necklace?"

"It's Kamil Pasha's idea, not mine."

"Who is this Kamil Pasha?"

"Magistrate of Beyoglu Lower Court, Your Highness."

"Ah, Alp Pasha's son."

"Do you know him?" Sybil asks, unable to keep the excitement from her voice.

Bemused, Asma Sultan responds, "I knew his mother. You are fond of the magistrate?"

"Why, no." Blushing. "I mean, I think he's a splendid investigator. If anyone can discover the truth of the matter, he can."

"I see. And who does he think is behind this plot—or is it plots? Has he had anyone arrested yet?"

"I don't think he knows yet. I suppose Hannah and Mary couldn't be involved in the same plot, since there are so many years between them. But it is odd that they both had that necklace, isn't it?"

"Forgive me. It all sounds rather fanciful."

"Yes, when I tell it to you like this, it does rather." Sybil smiles wanly.

Asma Sultan's intent questioning has made her uncomfortably aware that she has broken her promise to Kamil. She has lost any desire to hear her future foretold. The shadow of the villa has fallen over the patio, and her shawl is no longer sufficient to warm her. Sybil considers the long shadows and becomes concerned about the time. She is suddenly anxious to get away.

"Your Highness, it has been a great pleasure to speak with you and I treasure your hospitality, but I must beg leave to return home or I'll be late to dinner. Father doesn't like me to be late."

"Of course, of course. I'm glad to see you are a dutiful daughter. Fathers—they do expect so much of one. And you are expecting the magistrate to dinner tonight, aren't you?"

"How did you know?" Sybil is flustered.

"You mentioned it the other day at Leyla's."

"Oh, of course." Sybil beams and rises to her feet. "It was such a pleasant afternoon. Thank you very much."

"Oh, before you go, my dear, I'd like you to see something. Come, come over here."

Sybil follows Asma Sultan to an area of the patio screened by a stone lattice.

"I am going to show you something quite special. Not many people know about this. One of my mother's protégés was an architect.

She designed this especially for her. Arif Agha, go and steady Sybil Hanoum."

The eunuch appears beside Sybil, takes her arm in his long, steel fingers, and looks expectantly at Asma Sultan. Sybil is uncomfortable and wants to leave, but the eunuch holds her arm tightly. When she pulls at her arm, his grip tightens.

"Don't be alarmed," the old woman says gently. Her hand glides over the carved stone and stops over a protrusion. "You see this lever here. When you pull it, an extraordinary thing happens."

She pulls the lever and the part of the floor on which Sybil and the eunuch are standing begins to move downward with a low grinding noise. The eunuch lets go of Sybil's arm. She runs to the edge and tries to catch onto the receding tiles.

"Isn't this marvelous? This is a device that allows the women of the harem to fish and dabble in the sea without ever being seen by anyone outside."

Sybil claws at the tiles, but can't lift herself out. Soon the patio is far above her. She can see Asma Sultan's head silhouetted against the sky. She is still explaining.

"You can swim in complete privacy. My mother spent time here, fishing. Remarkable, isn't it? She said it reminded her of her girlhood, when she was free. After my father died, she was sent with his other women to live at the Old Palace. She never left there again. She told me she missed this spot most of all."

"Please let me up, Your Highness. I would love to hear more about your mother. She sounds like a fascinating woman. Your Highness?" Sybil's voice sounds hollow, reflecting from the cavernous walls.

"The seawater comes in through the grate behind you. You're perfectly safe. No one can see you."

"Please let me up now. My father will be worried. They'll call out the guard if I don't appear for dinner."

Asma Sultan steps closer to the edge of the patio high above. "Arif Agha," she calls down. "Another Frankish woman, Arif Agha. You're not deaf. You heard her. She has the ear—and perhaps something else—of the magistrate." She wheezes a laugh. "Haven't you had enough? Your fate is tied to mine. That's the way things are. You know what you have to do." She pauses, peering down into the shadows, then continues in a wheedling voice. "Some things can't be restored, Arif Agha, but others can." Her voice turns hard again. "And there is much to lose."

The eunuch listens spellbound, head tilted toward the sky, open-mouthed. Sybil thinks she hears him groaning. When she looks up again, the opening contains only sky.

Asma Sultan's disembodied voice floats down. "The past is the vessel of the future, Sybil Hanoum. Just as I said."

"I don't understand. Why are you doing this?" Sybil yells.

There is no answer except the seawater sloshing through the ornate ironwork grill set into one end of the room. Sybil looks around at the high arched ceiling of the underground space. It is painted to resemble the sky, one side light blue with clouds, the other fading to night, decorated with tiny stars and a sickle moon. She can dimly see that the platform on which she and the eunuch stand is an island about fifteen feet square and rests just above the water.

The eunuch is pacing back and forth, his eyes never leaving the square of sky high above them.

Sybil turns and asks him in Turkish, "What is happening here? Isn't she coming back?"

The eunuch stops; his gleaming eyes fix on Sybil. They hear the sound of oars splashing just beyond the iron grill, then receding.

"Do you know a way out of here? There must be a way up. I can't believe the sultanas would let themselves be trapped down here at someone else's mercy."

She speaks to the eunuch in Turkish to keep her spirits up, even though he hasn't said a word.

"I'm sure someone will come and get us. The embassy staff knows where I went." Even as she says it, she is unsure whether she told the staff her exact destination. They might think I've gone to the palace, she thinks. But surely they would find Asma Sultan and ask about me.

A sudden realization chills Sybil: Asma Sultan could say she hasn't seen me; that it was a mistake on my part; that I must have been invited by someone else. There's no proof that Asma Sultan invited me. It was a verbal message delivered by a servant. But I was picked up by Asma Sultan's eunuch. Everyone saw him. He will have identi-fied himself at the embassy gate.

The eunuch looks up at the sky, his body tense, listening. Sybil kneels and looks over the edge of the platform. The water isn't very deep. The underground walls are lined with marble reliefs of trees and flowers mottled with peeling paint. A small rowboat bumps against one far wall. She looks anxiously around for a way up or another lever, but sees only a marble stairway resting against the plat-form and leading down into the water. So that the women can swim, she thinks.

She paces about the platform, then sits at one end, trying to make conversation with the stubbornly silent eunuch. Above her, the square of sky slowly becomes streaked with pink, then blends more and more with the darker half of the ceiling.

Sybil is cold and her legs are stiff. Tired of inactivity, she bunches her skirts and folds them over her arm, stepping carefully onto the slick marble stair. When she has descended so that the water reaches her chest, her feet encounter the paved surface of the floor. Her skirts are drenched and heavy. She looks around at the eunuch, who hasn't moved, then climbs partway up again, removes her skirts, and heaves them onto the platform. This time, there is less resistance as she pushes her way through the water to the boat. She can't swim, so she is wary of a change in depth and pushes each foot forward care-fully, but the floor is even and she reaches the boat without difficulty. Inside are the remains of a velvet carpet, silk cushions, and two oars. A brass lamp hangs from the carved prow. She pulls the boat back to the platform to examine it. She is shaking with cold. The eunuch squats and stares at her wordlessly.

"Well, we've found a boat, although I can't imagine how we'll get it past that iron grate." Suddenly she looks down at the water. It is still at the same height. "We don't have to worry about high tide, do we?" she asks anxiously.

The eunuch doesn't respond.

"And we have a lamp. Let's see if we can light it."

She looks inside, then says excitedly, "Look, there's oil in here." In a small container in the base, she finds flint and lights the lamp. The eunuch turns away as if the light hurts his eyes. Sybil climbs into the boat and rows inexpertly to the wall. Holding the lamp high, she inspects every inch of it, fingers scrabbling among the flakes of paint, searching for a mechanism to make the platform ascend. Soon it is so dark she can no longer make out the eunuch on the platform, only the ghostly glow of his white robe.

45

A Thin Blade

"M iss Sybil was picked up by a eunuch in a carriage
early this morning. She said she was visiting a
member of the Ottoman royal family," the butler
says officiously.

Kamil tries to keep his voice patient. "Do you remember who she
was visiting?" Bernie paces the floor behind him.

"No, sir. I'm sorry, I don't." A note of anxiety has slipped into his
voice. "Has something happened?"

Bernie strides over and confronts the butler. "Freddie, aren't you
responsible for knowing what goes on here?"

"Yes, sir."

"Then how can you not know where Miss Sybil has gone?"

"She didn't tell me, sir. It wouldn't be proper for me to ask."

Bernie regards him with a look of disgust. "It's your business to
find out, Freddie, not just let anyone walk off with her."

Freddie barks at a servant to fetch the head English gatekeeper.
The young man hurries away.

Kamil asks the disheveled butler kindly, "When were you expecting her to return?"

The butler's eyes move to the dusk infiltrating the Residence windows. "She usually returns in time for dinner."

Kamil turns to Bernie. "I was expected for dinner about an hour ago."

"The ambassador has just finished dining, sir. I'm sorry." The butler looks abashed. "If Miss Sybil isn't here, he eats in his office," he explains.

Bernie's voice is menacing, "And you didn't think to be alarmed when Miss Sybil didn't return, even though she had invited a guest to dinner?"

"What could I do, sir? She's probably just delayed," he adds uncertainly.

Kamil takes Bernie aside and asks, "Should we tell the ambassador?"

Bernie shakes his head. "Do more harm than good. My uncle is a good man, but, between us, a bit of a loose cannon."

"I know what you mean." Kamil is relieved not to have to deal with Sybil's father now. He wants to find Sybil, and it is all he can do to stop himself from rushing out the door.

"Do the maids know anything?" he asks Bernie.

"No. I talked to the whole staff. The maid who helped Sybil dress said she told her she was going to visit someone in the palace. That's all. Let's go look in her room." He strides up the stairs two at a time, Kamil right behind him.

With some trepidation at this invasion of a woman's forbidden realm, Kamil follows Bernie into Sybil's bedroom. The room is spare but feminine, all white and beige, the room's outlines blurred by soft fabrics edged with delicate laces.

"Over here." Bernie gestures at a piece of paper lying on Sybil's writing desk.

They read Sybil's letter together. Kamil is startled by the revelation that she was waiting for him to ask for her in marriage.

"Damnation. Let's go find her." Bernie calls down to the butler,

"Get Sami. We need the phaeton." He turns to Kamil. "It'll be faster."

When they arrive downstairs, Freddie is gone, but the gatekeeper is there. They ask who picked Sybil up that morning.

"The, er, the eunitch"—the gatekeeper blushes scarlet as he pronounces the word—"the Negro, 'e gave me a paper." He holds out a piece of expensive parchment with a gold-embossed crest. On it are two lines of Ottoman in a practiced calligraphy, sealed in red. "I couldn't read it, sir."

Bernie snatches the paper out of his hand. "It never occurred to you to ask someone what it said? If anything's happened to Miss Sybil, it'll be on your head." The gatekeeper looks horrified.

"Miss Sybil?" he stutters. "What's 'appened to 'er?"

Ignoring him, Bernie shows the paper to Kamil. "What does it say? I have trouble with this kind of fancy writing."

"It's an invitation to lunch."

"From Asma Sultan."

"No. From Shukriye Hanoum." They look at each other speechlessly.

Kamil adds, "It's her family's seal."

"What in damnation . . . ?" He looks over Kamil's shoulder. "Where?"

"It doesn't say. It only specifies the date and time and that Shukriye Hanoum's servant will pick her up."

"But the eunuch brought it when he came to get her. It wasn't sent ahead of time."

"There must have been an earlier message. Clearly, this one is meant to deceive anyone looking for her."

"Mother of God. If Sybil hadn't left that letter, we'd be off on a wild goose chase. Come on in here. Be quick, man."

Bernie runs into a room off the main hall, pulls a volume from the bookshelf, and extracts a key. He unlocks a drawer and pulls out two pistols. He checks to see if they are loaded, then holds one out to Kamil. Kamil points at his feet. "I'm armed."

"You mean with that religious mumbo jumbo in your boots?" Bernie snorts. "That won't get you very far against a bullet!"

Kamil pulls a needle-thin blade from his boot. "Allah helps those who help themselves." He opens his coat to reveal the holster on his hip. "I need some paper."

Bernie points to a writing desk.

Kamil takes out a blank sheet and writes several lines in Ottoman, the script flowing smoothly right to left. He signs with a flourish, then rummages in the drawer and pulls out a cylinder of sealing wax. He removes a small brass seal from his pocket and imprints the insignia of his office on the bottom of the letter and again on the envelope.

Sami is waiting at the door with the phaeton. Kamil takes him aside and hands him the envelope.

"You are to mount the fastest horse in your stables and ride ahead of us to Middle Village. Do you know where that is?"

"Yes, efendi. I know the area well."

"Take this letter directly to the headman of Middle Village. It asks him to take his sons and go to the commander of gendarmes, not to the police. Sybil Hanoum's life may be in danger. Do you understand?"

"Yes, efendi. Not the police."

"Go with him. The headman is to show them this letter. It commands the gendarmes to issue them weapons and to accompany them to Asma Sultan's summer house in Tarabya immediately. Allah willing, their presence will be superfluous."

Kamil jumps into the phaeton. Bernie is already seated, hunched forward and restlessly twisting the reins.

"If we alerted the British guards, we'd have to tell the ambassador," Kamil shouts. "And I'm not sure of the loyalty of the police anymore. This is the best way."

The horses clatter down the drive toward the gate.

46

A Hundred Braids

I wanted a celebration, a proper setting for my response to Mary. Violet insisted on coming, saying she had prepared special foods for us. By the time we arrived at the sea hamam and the driver was dispatched with instructions to return in three hours' time, the lip of the sky bled magenta. But inside the walls of the sea hamam, we could see only the sky's unclouded blue eye following Violet as she spread the covers, set up the brazier, and unpacked the copper pans of dolma, cheese pastries, fruit, and savories. It was a feast. I slipped off my feradje, revealing a new gown of sheerest apricot silk under a striped satin tunic of apple and ginger. My breasts were wreathed in a transparent cloud of silk gauze. My hair was woven into a hundred braids wrapped in diamonds and pearls.

Mary had taken off her shoes. Her slim white feet dangled over the pool. In water, she was slippery as an eel. Like most women, she couldn't swim, but the water in the sea hamam wasn't very deep. I remember it made her anxious when I ducked below the surface. I used to slip along under the boards and burst up in a spray behind her so that she shrieked with fear. The hamam walls protected us from the wind, and the strait here was tamed, drawn continually like a fan across the sand. The water was so clear one could mistake it for a shadow.

I wondered whether anyone else had come here since we had abandoned it the previous year. The winter damp had warped some of the boards. I noticed that our mattress, the mattress Mary had hired someone to bring here in anticipation of our first visit, was stained where it had not been stained before. I supposed anyone could have come here while we were gone, perhaps young boys thrilled at being masters of a realm that soon would be off-limits, haram, dangerous. Once we had spread our new quilt, though, we were almost as before.

"Why did you bring your maid?" she whispered, looking at Violet sitting in a cubicle near the brazier.

"Violet? She can serve us. Don't you like being served?" I cocked my head at her, but I could see she hadn't decided whether I was joking.

"Well, I suppose."

"She insisted on coming and I couldn't say no. She's so unsettled by everything, even though my father has found her a good husband—so she won't be alone."

Mary looked at me expectantly, but I said nothing more.

I knew Mary didn't like to undress in front of strangers, so she wouldn't go into the water tonight. It was too cold, in any case.

"We'll just chat, then." I pulled the quilt out to the walkway circling the water and lay on it with my face to the sky. She came and sat next to me.

"Lie down, Mary. Come see the stars."

She let herself down, using her elbows, and arranged her skirts so that they covered her legs. She wore a simple white blouse. Her cap of hair shone gold in the dark.

The quilted satin smooth against our palms, we looked up into the square of night sky revealed by the geometry of the hamam walls.

"It looks like your hair, Jaanan. Braided with diamonds," she whispered.

I took her hand.

47

Villa at Tarabya

A gibbous moon floods the Bosphorus with light and throws into sharp relief the trees and bushes rushing by as the phaeton races north.

"If anything happens to Sybil Hanoum," Kamil points out, "the blame would fall on Shukriye Hanoum, since the invitation is written in her name. Clever. I wonder why Shukriye Hanoum, though. She's not a threat to anyone."

"Well, someone sure doesn't like her."

After a while, Kamil adds, "Sybil Hanoum said she thought Perihan Hanoum was angry because she had wanted to marry Prince Ziya but he became engaged to Shukriye instead. Apparently Perihan Hanoum's marriage is unhappy."

Bernie slaps the reins across the horses' backs. "Well, there's a motive to hate Shukriye enough to set her up. What do you know about her mother, this Asma Sultan?"

"A rather formidable but harmless lady, according to Sybil Hanoum."

Bernie grimaces. "All the perfumes of Arabia will not sweeten this little hand."

"Pardon?"

"Shakespeare. *Macbeth.*"

"It might be Perihan Hanoum at the villa, not her mother," Kamil cautions.

"Well, we'll see what we're up against. The woman or her daughter. Maybe the whole harem." He laughs nervously and turns his wind-reddened face to Kamil. "Think we can handle this?"

Kamil doesn't smile. "We don't know who else will be there. Perhaps the grand vizier himself." Grimly, "But I'm ready for a fight."

Bernie grins. "I'll bet you are." He pats his holster. "I'm glad you and this other friend of mine here are along for the ride."

By the time Kamil and Bernie reach the turnoff beyond the village of Tarabya, the moon has contracted to a mottled white disk.

"Asma Sultan's villa is farther north, I believe." Kamil uses his handkerchief to wipe the dust from his face as the phaeton slows at a crossroad.

"Git up," Bernie urges the horses.

The road ascends sharply again and the horses strain. A stand of pines and cypresses blocks the view before the vista opens onto an expanse of water milky in the moonlight. The phaeton picks up speed. After a while, they hurtle downhill again. Kamil can make out the enormous bulk of a house silhouetted against the reflected light.

"That must be it." Bernie points. "Strange. I don't see any lights."

"They might have their shutters closed."

The phaeton pulls up to the wrought-iron gate.

"There should be a night watchman," observes Kamil as he jumps to the ground. "He's probably asleep."

He peers around the gate, but the guardhouse is empty. Bernie has come up beside him.

He looks through the gate at the dark house. "Looks like no one's home. Do you think we got the wrong house?"

"It matches the description they gave us in the village."

"Does she have another one? She's a sultan's daughter. They have cartloads of money."

"It's possible. I suppose the invitation could have been to Perihan Hanoum's villa or even the vizier's villa. They all have their own konaks and summer houses."

"Do you know where they are? We'll have to check them all out, one at a time."

"I don't." Kamil tenses. "We'd have to go back to the village and ask the headman."

"Well, then, let's get on with it." Bernie looks closely at Kamil, staring at the dark villa. "What is it?"

Kamil shudders and turns. "I don't know. I think you have a saying, 'A crow walked across my grave.'"

"I never heard that one, buddy."

"You know, the old Greek name of this village, Tarabya, was Pharmakeus." He thinks of his father's body being washed in the mosque at this very moment, prepared for burial tomorrow morning.

"Pharmakeus. The medicine man?"

"The poisoner. Medea was said to have thrown away her poison here."

"Well, this place gives me the dithers. Let's get out of here." He climbs into the phaeton.

Holding the reins, he turns to Kamil. "You don't suppose she really did go to visit Shukriye Hanoum?"

"I suppose that's a possibility. But why would she write something different in her letter?"

Bernie shakes his head. "Maybe showing off for her sister. There's always been a kind of rivalry between them. Maitlin's the successful one." He flicks the reins. The phaeton strains after the horses. "Sybil's the one with fantasies. She's been stuck here too long looking after my uncle. No wonder she's invented herself a whole Orient of her own."

48

The Net

The moon appeared in our square of sky, bleaching us of color.

Mary turned her head to me. "Thank you for being a good friend to me. I wouldn't have lasted here without you." She moved her face forward and kissed me chastely on the lips.

I squeezed her hand. She lay with her head flung back, letting the moonlight seep into her eyes. I heard the chortling of the kettle boiling on the coals.

After a long while, she whispered, "Do you remember the sugared almonds?"

I didn't. "Yes, of course."

"And the time we caught a fish in here."

"You caught it with your hands."

"It was weak and tired. Who knows how long it had been trying to get out."

"It's cruel to have a net around the pool."

"Are they afraid the women will escape?" she asked, laughing at her own wit.

"I think rather it's to keep the men from looking in."

"Men will get in anyway," she said with a resigned certainty.

I leaned on my elbow and looked at her. Her hair was white. I let it flow through my hand.

"Together we're safe," I assured her.

She turned to me, surprised. The blue of her eyes came back into focus.

"Will you come?" she asked hesitantly.

I nodded yes and let my head rest beside hers, our eyes on the heavens. The moon had become a small, hard disk the color of alloyed gold. A wild dog barked nearby.

Violet put a glass of tea beside Mary and handed another to me, then withdrew into the shadows of her cubicle. I could see only the red eyes of the charcoal peering out of the brazier below the steaming pots.

49

The Floating Stage

Sybil sits shivering on the platform, holding the lamp. Her clothing is disheveled, hastily thrown over her wet body. Her throat is hoarse from shouting. Her eyes keep scanning the walls.

Sybil looks up at the eunuch. He is sitting just outside the circle of light, eyes closed. She wonders what kind of life eunuchs live. It is said they are powerful, but this man's shoulders are thin, his face a grim mask. His large hands are laced together in front of his knees.

"Arif Agha," she calls, thinking he might respond to his name.

He doesn't answer, but she sees a flicker of white under his lids.

"I do wish you'd say something. I think you can understand my Turkish. Can you speak English?" Exasperated, she adds, "Look, we have to get out of here. Parlez vous Français?"

Speaking in French reminds her of her visit to Shukriye Hanoum. She had found her story appalling but somehow fantastic, as though Shukriye were a character in an Oriental opera. She thinks wryly that she too is now an actor in a potentially tragic play, an Englishwoman and a eunuch trapped on a floating stage. She finds herself laughing. The eunuch's now-open eyes register surprise and, she fears, disapproval.

I'm being hysterical, she thinks, and forces herself to stop. Another look she has seen in the eunuch's eyes—malevolence—puts her on guard. She moves closer to the boat.

Suddenly she remembers where she has heard Arif Agha's name before.

"You're the one who told the police about the British woman Hannah, about the carriage that picked her up."

She isn't sure in the dim light, but thinks the eunuch grimaces.

When he doesn't answer, Sybil murmurs, "They never found who murdered her."

She peers at him suspiciously through the deepening gloom. It occurs to her that Mary worked for Perihan, and that Arif Agha had probably encountered her as well. Sybil wonders where retired eunuchs go. Arif Agha seems to have retired in plain sight.

"Another young woman was killed recently, Mary Dixon. Did you know her too?"

When the eunuch still doesn't answer, Sybil forces herself to stand and walk toward him, her hands held out before her in a conciliatory gesture.

"Look, Arif Agha, I don't care what happened. All I care about now is getting out of here. We have to help each other or we'll rot in here." She stumbles over the Turkish word for rot. "No one will find us here. We'll starve."

When she is an arm's length away from Arif Agha, she stops.

"If you're worried about getting in trouble, I can help you. When we get out of here, I'll take you to the magistrate of Beyoglu and you can talk to him, tell him what you saw. The police will be grateful if you help them. They won't hurt you. I promise." Sybil is aware of the duplicity of such a promise, which she has no way of keeping, but she needs Arif Agha's cooperation or, at least, his goodwill. She wonders anxiously whether the danger from the eunuch isn't as great as being trapped in this underground chamber.

She decides to make small talk, both to keep his attention and to keep her rising fear under control. "Have you been in Asma Sultan's service a long time?"

With a strangely distorted, high-pitched squeal, the eunuch scuttles backward like a crab and crouches at the far end of the platform.

"I can see why you'd be afraid of her." She looks upward at the now-dark sky. Suddenly animated, she moves closer to the eunuch and says, "I have an idea. I think I can protect you against Asma Sultan. I'm a friend of her daughter and other important people. I can make sure someone takes care of you." Smiling, Sybil spreads her hands. "I'll tell them you saved my life."

The eunuch uncoils himself in a sudden violent movement and leaps at Sybil. His mouth is stretched wide but emits only a strangled sound. With her arms, she wards off his hands groping for her neck. As they struggle, the lamp illuminates their faces. At the back of the pink cavern of his mouth is a lump of scar tissue. His tongue has been cut out.

The lamp rolls into the water. Sybil screams into the darkness.

50

Barely a Sound

hen Mary next looked at me, her eyes were like coals. She blinked and shifted her gaze around the platform.

"It's so dark. It's hard to see." She pushed herself laboriously up to a sitting position, then to her feet. "I'd like to go home. I don't feel well."

I got to my feet and took her elbow. "What's the matter?" I peered into her face.

"I don't know. I can't see." She shook my hand away.

"You're getting a chill. Have some more tea." I signaled to Violet that she should refill our glasses.

"I can't move my arm." Mary's speech had become slurred, with a hysterical undertone.

She staggered away from me, her foot knocking over her tea glass. The moonlight caught the edge of Violet's kaftan.

"Violet, come and help me. Mary Hanoum is ill." I realized suddenly that the carriage wasn't due to return for us for at least another hour and the village was half an hour's walk away.

I heard a splash behind me and swung around. Mary was gone. I raced to the pool, knelt on the boards, and looked over the edge. The obsidian water reflected rocking shards of moon.

"Bring the lamp," I shouted. I turned and climbed into the water. The light of the lamp made the surface more brilliant, but revealed nothing beneath it. I struggled through the pool, fighting my billowing clothing, my face against the water, feeling beneath the surface with both hands.

"I'll find her."

I looked up. Violet's lean brown body trailed a black shadow across the walls. She slid beneath the surface with barely a sound.

51

The Ming Vase

ernie pulls on the reins.

"Why are you slowing down?"

"I thought I heard something."

The night is alive with animal sounds, sudden trills, fish falling into the water just beyond the road. An owl hoots from the forest.

"There it is again," Bernie whispers. An odd cry, faint as if muffled.

"It must be coming from Asma Sultan's villa," cries Kamil. "There's no other house near here."

Bernie swings the phaeton around, whips the horses, and thundering back down the road, they halt at the gate and jump out.

"Let's get the lamps lit so we can see better."

"The gate is locked." Kamil clambers up the ilex that covers the wall like a green mantle. He reappears on the other side of the wrought-iron gate and unlatches it.

The iron creaks as they push the heavy doors open.

They move quickly down the carriageway toward the house. Kamil pushes open the unlocked front door. Washes of light dart across the walls as they move through the entry hall and down a corridor. They emerge in a room so vast that their lamps pick out only patches of parquet floor and the bases of man-width marble pillars.

"This must be the reception room," Kamil notes.

Bernie's lamp moves off and is soon lost in the gloom. Kamil hears a crash of crockery. Suddenly the air jumps with shadows as Bernie lights a gas lamp on the wall.

"Holy Mother of Jesus!" Bernie stares at the shattered object on the floor.

"What is it?"

"A Ming vase. I've never seen one that big before. It's priceless."

They look around. The room is hung with enormous gilded mirrors that multiply the illumination. Swags of colored glass chandeliers hang from the ceiling.

They pause, listening carefully.

"Nothing," Bernie says finally.

"She must be in this house somewhere. We should be quiet, in case the others are still here. We'll have the advantage of surprise."

"The hell with that," Bernie says, and shouts, "Sybil."

52

The Eye of the Pool

I was in waist-deep water tearing at my clothes when Violet's head emerged beneath my legs.

"Where is she?" I cried. "Why haven't you found her?"

Violet lifted herself onto the platform with her muscular arms, her body streaming with water. "She's stuck in the net."

"Allah save us! Can't you get her out?" I scrambled onto the platform to better take off the ballooning trousers that hindered me from submerging enough to join the search.

She moved rapidly to the pile of her clothing and returned with a short knife. Her body sliced into the black skin of water.

I removed the last of my clothing, held my breath, and flung myself in after her. My hands scrabbled about in the darkness like crabs. Handfuls of sand. Under the floorboards, even the moonlight disappeared. The slimy rope scraped my palm. I held fast and, tucking my foot into the net behind me, began to crawl sideways along it. When my breath gave out, I pushed off to the surface to get air. My foot twisted in the rope and I struggled to free it. Suddenly, powerful arms wrapped themselves around my chest and pulled me loose.

"Get out of the water and watch for her from up there," Violet demanded, thrusting me toward the steps. When I tried to return to the water, she warned, "If she dies, it'll be your fault. I can't take care of you both at once. You'll do more good up there. Hurry up."

Shaking, I climbed onto the platform. I hunched tensely by the side of the water, scanning the surface for signs of movement. Violet was gone a long time, and I began to worry that she too was caught in the net. I rocked back and forth, naked in the lamplight, uncertain what to do. I heard my voice, keening a prayer between chattering teeth. At last Violet's head appeared.

"She's gone. I don't think it's a good idea to bring her body up here."

I began to climb into the water again. "She must still be alive."

Violet blocked my way. "I've seen her. It's too late. She wrapped herself up in the net. I wasn't able to cut her loose."

"Allah protect us," I cried, struggling to get past her. I had seen the dead, but this was a death that I fully possessed. Violet's arm circled my waist and anchored my flesh to the wooden boards. When I had exhausted myself with struggling, she let me go.

"What should we do?" I knelt by the side of the pool, blinded by tears, by the lamplight. Violet's eyes were in darkness, but I could sense the intensity of her gaze.

"We can let the current take her," she said matter-of-factly, as if she were disposing of kitchen leavings. "No one will know where she died or how. By morning, she'll be frolicking with the dolphins in the Marmara. But we'll have to get her farther out where the current is stronger."

Frolicking. I couldn't decide whether to be appalled by Violet's levity or absurdly comforted by the image of Mary, golden hair streaming, riding a dolphin like a Greek deity.

"We have to call the police," I said numbly. "Ismail Dayi will know what to do."

"And tell them what? That three women were alone at night in an abandoned sea hamam and one died? How are we going to explain how she died? They'll blame you, you know."

I looked up at her. "Why me? It was an accident."

"They always blame the weakest person. The cracked vessel shatters first." Her face, lit from below, was distorted by the lamplight.

I rocked back and forth, eyes on the black window of water.

Violet submerged again. After a while, her hands pushed a shoe onto the platform, then another, Mary's skirt, shirt, and undergarments. I crouched by the pitifully small pile.

"The clothes would make the body float," she explained, gasping, climbing out of the water. "I couldn't get the jewelry. I'll try again." The bracelet of woven gold from the Bedestan where we first met. The silver pendant I unclasped in childish greed from Hannah Simmons's neck and gave many years later to Mary, who adored Ottoman jewelry. The necklace of a drowned woman was clinging to Mary, who had suffered her same fate.

Appalled, I stayed Violet with my hand on her thigh. "Leave it."

She explained in a calming voice, as if to a child, "I'm going outside now. There's a landing in the front. If I jump in there, I can pull her through from the outside. There's a strong current just a short way out. Stay here." She disappeared into the shadowy corridor. A dog barked, then was abruptly silent.

I sat on the wet quilt, its satin stained by seawater, regarding the garments of my friend whom I had meant tonight to join in living. They lay before me like the remnants of a lifeless sea creature. I pulled the lamp closer. The pool's black eye regarded me malevolently. The sound of a splash tore through the silence. A thin line moved across the water.

53

Chaos in
the Tapestry of Life

They move cautiously through the opulent rooms, listening for a reply to their calls.

Bernie looks around at the man-high china vases, the cabinets of china, gilded screens, statues, wall hangings.

"The person who collected all this is obsessed by China. These are all Chinese antiques, extraordinary antiques."

"Asma Sultan?"

"That's what it looks like."

Bernie stops at a shelf containing rows of scrolls. He unrolls one and holds it close to the lamp. He beckons Kamil over.

"Look at this—a Chinese manuscript. Someone here can read this stuff."

"Asma Sultan is your contact inside the palace?" Kamil asks incredulously.

"That's what it looks like." Bernie shakes his head in wonder.

"Why would she want to overthrow Abdulhamid? Her husband is his grand vizier."

"Perhaps she is unhappy with her husband."

"That would give half the women in the world a motive, but they don't go around scheming with foreign governments to overthrow their husband's employer just to get him fired. Besides, she'd be undermining her own welfare."

"Not really. As daughter of a sultan, Asma Sultan is wealthy in her own right."

"Well, her father was deposed and then killed himself, so I guess that could leave a chip on your shoulder about whoever replaced him."

They move from room to room, calling Sybil's name.

Kamil emerges from one of a series of bedrooms along a corridor. "It's an enormous house, but it looks abandoned. Perhaps it belonged to Asma Sultan's mother. She would have moved to the Old Palace after her husband's death."

"So maybe it's her mother who's out for revenge. Angry at being booted out of the palace after her husband is deposed. It fits the poem. Is her mother still alive?"

"I don't know."

Bernie swings the lamp around the room and calls out Sybil's name again. "We have to find her. I wonder if Asma Sultan killed Hannah. Once the secret police started sniffing around, she might have eliminated anyone who could lead them to her. She probably thinks Sybil knows something that could give her away."

He holds the lamp up to Kamil's face. "Can you have her arrested?"

"Arrest a member of the royal household?" He doesn't meet Bernie's eye. "No, my friend. My jurisdiction doesn't extend that far," Kamil answers slowly, shielding his eyes from the light.

He remembers Ferhat Bey's evasiveness that he had interpreted as incompetence. Perhaps the old superintendent had more courage than he, Kamil, the rational bureaucrat who cuts his morality to fit his jurisdiction. He reaches into his pocket for his beads, but they offer no comfort.

"In any case, I might no longer have a post. My superior, Nizam Efendi, will be delighted to hold me responsible for executing Hamza without a trial."

"Thanks to our friend Michel." He casts a sidelong glance at Kamil's grave face. "Anyway, I'd put my money on the secret police being behind all of these killings, not Asma Sultan. They probably wanted to find out from the girls who their contact inside the palace was. Problem is, they didn't know anything. I wish I knew who ratted on them."

There is a sound of glass grating under his boots.

"What's this?" Bernie brings his light closer to a broken object on the floor. "Well, this sure doesn't belong in here." He touches it with his toe.

"What is it?"

"Wax flowers under glass—the latest obsession in England. Looks like someone dropped it here. A bit incongruous in a house full of Chinese art, wouldn't you say?"

They look at each other's faces, grim in the lamplight.

"Sybil would have brought a gift."

Bernie calls out, "Sybil!" his voice lost in the cavernous room.

"We've checked the whole house. She's not here."

"Let's look outside." Bernie pulls open the glass doors and unlatches the shutters. They step out onto the patio.

Kamil gestures that they should stop and listen. There is the low boom of water echoing, but no other sound.

"What's that?" Bernie walks to the edge of the patio and looks over the balustrade. "Look. The water comes right under the house."

"That's so the residents can get into their boats directly from the house." Kamil peers into the darkness below the balustrade. "There might be some kind of boathouse down there."

Footsteps cause them to whirl around, hands on their weapons.

The embassy driver, Sami, emerges from the house with another lamp.

"Well met, Sami," Bernie greets him with a nod. "Glad you found us. Are the others coming?"

"Yes, efendi. They'll be here soon. I rode ahead."

They walk along the patio, shining their lamps in all directions.

"Over here." Kamil holds his lamp over a small table still set with food. "It's fresh." He reaches into his boot with his other hand and slides out the long, thin blade.

"Damnation. I'll bet the other guest was Sybil. Where the heck is she?" He calls out, "Sybil!"

"Help! Get me out! Help!" Sybil's voice is faint and curiously distorted. It is followed by splashing, then silence.

Kamil shouts, "Sybil, keep talking. Where are you?" He looks over at Bernie, whose mouth is set in a thin line. "It came from over there." He points toward the far end of the patio. "Be careful."

Bernie calls again, but there is no answer. He pulls out his revolver.

The men fan out and move slowly across the tiles toward the wall at the end of the patio. When they get closer, Kamil whispers, "Look. This isn't a wall; it's a carved screen. There must be something behind it."

He holds up his lamp and peers around the screen.

"Allah protect us. There's a hole in the floor. It's a good thing we have lamps."

"She's in there," Bernie says, and throws himself to the ground. "How deep is this? Jesus, if she fell down this . . ."

Kamil and Sami also lie on their stomachs peering into the dark square below them. Their lamps pick up the glint of water around what appears to be a central island. The island is empty.

"Look." The others move their lamps in the direction Kamil is pointing. Far below, a figure in a white turban is struggling through waist-deep water toward something lost in shadow. Sami hangs over the lip of the opening and dangles his lamp lower. The shadows flee, revealing Sybil, standing in a small boat bobbing against the wall, an oar in her hand. The figure is moving inexorably toward her, though gingerly, as if afraid of the water.

Sybil screams. They can see her face, the O of her open mouth.

"Put the light out," she shouts. "He can see me by your light. Get me out of here."

She had been hiding in the absolute darkness, afraid that any sound would reveal her position to the eunuch.

"Don't worry. We'll get you out." Bernie calls down. "But we need the light."

Bernie aims his gun at the eunuch, but hesitates. Sybil is too close.

Kamil pulls Bernie back. "The bullet might ricochet."

Bernie peers appraisingly at the water far below. "We can't jump in. It's too shallow." He turns to Sami. "Do you have a rope?"

"No, efendi. I'll go look for one."

"Sybil, how do we get down there?"

"The lever. There's a lever in the screen." The figure is close to her now and she stands, back against the wall, oar raised.

"Keep an eye on her," Bernie tells Sami. He and Kamil begin systematically to check the screen.

"Wait," they hear Sybil shout. "If you pull the lever the floor will go up and trap me down here. I think he doesn't understand English, so try this. Tell me when you've found the lever, but don't do anything until I say, 'Pull.' "

"Yes," Kamil shouts back. "We'll do that."

"I think I found it," Bernie grips the end of a stone protrusion, disguised as a tree in the stone carving. He pulls it slightly. They hear a grinding sound.

"Not yet," Sybil screams.

"We found it," Bernie calls to her. "Tell us when you're ready."

"Put your lights away," she calls.

"Are you sure?" Kamil asks anxiously.

"Do it!" Sybil shouts. Below them, they see her aim the oar at the white turban. Then all is dark. Sami has swung the lamps, still lit, out of range.

They listen intently, but hear only water splashing.

"Now." The word echoes. Bernie pulls the lever and the grinding noise begins again. They hear scuffling and a splash.

When the island comes into view, Sybil is lying face down on the tiles in wet bloomers and chemise, her hand still grasping the oar. As soon as the floor is flush with the platform, Bernie rushes to her and turns her over. Her eyes are open.

"Well, cousin," she gasps, smiling. "Wait until Maitlin hears about this."

Kamil keeps his face turned until Bernie has wrapped a cloak around Sybil, then takes her shoulders in his hands.

"Sybil Hanoum." It is all he can manage. His eyes linger on her plump neck bisected by two folds like a baby's wrist. He does not meet her eye. She is still smiling but has begun to shake violently. Under the pretext of adjusting the cloak, he wraps her in his arms for a moment, then hands her to Bernie. The English, he knows, consider their cousins too close for marriage, unlike the Ottomans. Still, he feels bereft when Bernie settles her in the phaeton inside the circumference of his arms.

Kamil climbs up front and takes up the reins. He is jealous, he realizes. He feels momentarily disloyal to his father, that a trivial emotion like jealousy could grow in the field of his grief.

On the road, they encounter the headman, his sons, and a group of armed gendarmes on their way to Asma Sultan's villa. Kamil stops to give them instructions for finding Sami, left to guard the hidden chamber, then snaps the reins.

"That was Arif Agha, Asma Sultan's eunuch," Sybil explains between chattering teeth. "The one who reported Hannah's trips to the police."

Kamil and Bernie exchange looks.

"He probably snitched to the secret police back then too."

"The police superintendent hinted that Arif Agha took bribes. I assumed it was just from the municipal police. It didn't occur to me that he also sold information to the Sultan's spies. A eunuch who knows too much and talks too much," Kamil muses.

"A rat by any other name."

To Kamil's puzzled look, he replies, "Shakespeare. *Romeo and Juliet.*"

"A fool."

"Why did he attack you like that?" Bernie asks Sybil, rubbing her shoulders.

She shrugs. "It doesn't make any sense. After all, we were both in the same predicament down there. I told him if he helped get me out, I'd protect him against Asma Sultan by telling everyone he had saved my life. He'd be a hero. That's when he jumped at me. The poor man," she whispers. "He's had his tongue cut out. He's probably terrified."

Sybil's eyes wander toward the shimmering sheet of water appearing and disappearing below them as they move through the wooded hills.

After a while, she continues, "Asma Sultan called something down to him just before she left. She told him his fate was tied to hers, and that he knew what he had to do. Maybe she was telling him to attack me."

"Could be." Bernie rubs Sybil's hands to warm them. "Did you see all that Chinese stuff?"

"Yes, I did. It belonged to Asma Sultan's mother. I meant to tell you about it."

Surprised, Kamil turns and asks, "You knew about it?"

"I heard about it at Leyla's the other day. I had planned to tell you over dinner tonight. Yesterday, you were too worried about me to listen." She smiles happily.

"As you can see, I had good cause to worry." But Kamil is smiling too. Bernie looks from one to the other, amused.

"The Chinese collection was the missing piece," he says.

"Of what?"

"Asma Sultan had that pendant made. She is our correspondent inside the palace."

"Your correspondent?" Sybil is confused.

"It's a long story, cousin. I'll tell you when we're warm and cozy in front of a fire."

Kamil turns to Bernie. "I wonder if her daughter is involved."

"Is this a plot?" Sybil asks excitedly. "There really was a plot?" She claps her hands with pleasure. "Oh, wait until Maitlin hears about this."

"Sybil Hanoum," Bernie says with mock seriousness, "may I remind you that you were almost killed?"

"Yes, isn't it marvelous?" They all burst out laughing. Kamil turns away to hide the tears of relief, mixed with sorrow, blurring his sight.

"Perihan and her mother are very close," Sybil explains. "I can't imagine one would do something without the other knowing." She thinks a moment. "Asma Sultan said an odd thing this afternoon. We were talking about Perihan and Leyla being friends, and she said Perihan was keeping an eye on her. Do you think she was spying on Leyla?"

"They watch Leyla," Kamil muses aloud. "They try to incriminate her sister Shukriye in Sybil Hanoum's disappearance." He realizes with a shock that he almost said death. "Why?"

"Leyla reports to the secret police?" Bernie ventures.

"That would make her very dangerous to Asma Sultan."

They ride for a while in silence. Bernie keeps his arm around Sybil's shoulder. A filigree of moonlight illuminates the road's dark tunnel through the trees. The horses' backs shudder with light. Kamil counts his accomplishments like a child warding off the darkness. Sybil is safe. He allows himself a glance over his shoulder. Her hair has tumbled out of its pins. Her eyes meet his and he looks quickly away, but not before she has seen his smile. Hamza, a traitor, responsible for seducing and possibly killing young women, has been stopped. If instead the secret police killed Hannah and Mary, these, like Asma Sultan, are beyond his reach and he must defer to Allah for their judgment.

But Baba, Baba, whose dream he had stolen.

Perhaps it is true that only Allah is perfect and human endeavors intrinsically flawed. In an otherwise orderly and rational universe, Allah has woven chaos into the corner of every man's life as a reminder.

After a while, the carriage emerges on a hillside overlooking vineyards and the vast sparkling waters of the strait. The upper side of the road is tangled with raspberry bushes. Fireflies throb in the vineyards below, exhaling light. Far in the distance, night fishermen row across the silver water.

54

Death Is Too Easy

The river Seine is frozen. I cannot see it from my window, but I have walked on its back. The snow reminds me of Istanbul, the long cypress shadows, the brilliant glint of icicles hanging from all the eaves, a gerdanlouk for our house at Chamyeri. White chunks like common sea glass melting. I hadn't expected Hamza to die, not in that way, not in any. It is true what philosophers say, that words have the heft of a sword and must be wielded as carefully. In my anger, I hurled words into the world, spoke Hamza's name, and impaled him on it. How was I to know that my words would put him together in that pond with Hannah, he embracing from above, she from below? Never can I believe that he read fairy tales to me in the afternoon and killed her in the evening. But it doesn't matter now. I have killed him. And Mary has given me life. Mary. My friend, my love, yellow-haired queen of the dolphins. It is because of her that I am now here in the world.

Vengeance. Another word. Perhaps you say I have wielded enough words and should now be silent, that I can't be trusted with words. But come now, haven't I pleased you with my array of sentences, my whispers—let's be clear—my honesty? I am not a killer.

What about Violet? you ask. The pond in the forest behind Chamyeri is clear-eyed. Violet owned the water, or so she thought. But I had learned that one could drown in knee-deep water, especially with the senses obscured and limbs made dumb by a special tea. I served her the same tea she had given Mary. When Violet slipped on the rocks in the pond, I held her head, stroking her black hair streaming in the water. At the last moment, I took Violet's hand and turned her to face the sky. I saved her so the regret would be hers, not mine. So that she remembers. Death is too easy—I have learned how dreadfully easy.

I had found the second teapot when I went back to the sea hamam the following day. I wanted to make sure I wasn't dreaming, to rest my hand in her grave. There was no tea in that pot, but long, thick strands. Dried tube flowers, like the ones Violet had prepared as an infusion for Mama to breathe into her lungs to ease her cough. I hurled the pot, like a snake, into the water, but the poison had long done its work. When I confronted her, Violet admitted she had kept Mary below the water until she exhausted herself. It was to save me, Violet insisted. I have been saved from myself so thoroughly that I am left with a stranger, I replied before leading her to the pond. There our bond was forged, and now it is cut.

Mary, though—she is not dead, but one of those princesses of my youth pinned to the sand, waiting. My words will make her live again. Her feet like fresh milk cupped by my hands.

A fire is burning low in the grate, but the room is warm with the colors of home. My dayi has sent me carpets and books and even a samovar so that I may feel his proximity. I spend my days in study and learn to wield many kinds of words, gauging their power. The secret is in how you hold the sword, in the flick of the wrist.

Acknowledgments

I am deeply grateful to my agent, Al Zuckerman, and to Amy Cherry, my editor, for their faith in this book and for their expert guidance. I also wish to thank Stephen Kimmel, Edite Kroll, Elizabeth Warnock Fernea, Roger Owen, Donald Quataert, Kevin Reinhart, and Corky White for reading and commenting on the manuscript; Feride Çiçekoğlu for her gift of a pomegranate; and Carl Leiden for getting the ball rolling. Thanks to Linda Barlow, friend and mentor. A special debt of gratitude is owed to Michael Freeman, tireless editor, muse, and hand holder, who believed it would happen.

THE SULTAN'S
SEAL

Jenny White

THE SULTAN'S SEAL

Jenny White

JENNY WHITE ON THE SETTING FOR
THE SULTAN'S SEAL

By the late 1800s, the Ottoman Empire had been thriving for almost five hundred years. Founded on even older civilizations—the Byzantines, Greeks, Romans, and, before that, other civilizations not as well known today—it was a truly multi-ethnic, multi-denominational empire. Jews, Armenians, Greek Orthodox Christians, Muslim Turks, Arabs, people of all faiths from the Balkans, European "Franks," and many others mingled in the streets and in households. They were craftsmen, traders, and servants, but they also held important positions as doctors, merchants, bankers, and advisors to the sultan.

It was a period of profound social and political change, when educated and wealthy urbanites were acquiring European customs and technology. Some were interested in European political models, like the parliament. Despite European support for the independence movements that were breaking the empire apart, including the Balkans, Greece, and parts of the Arab world, many young Ottomans admired European political values, science, and ideas about society. Some Ottoman leaders felt they could only fight European attacks by emulating their enemy.

Another European idea, nationalism—the idea that a nation should be organized around the identity of "a people"—began to take root. By contrast, an empire could contain many kinds of people, all keeping their separate identities, since they were united only by virtue of being subjects of the same ruler. Nationalist aspirations led to movements for independence from the Ottoman Empire, but also to backlashes and intolerance.

Ottomans worried, with some justification, that nationalism would lead to the purging of minorities. (Minorities were mostly defined in religious terms in those days. Only in the age of nation-states organized around the principles of nationality and nationalism did the term "ethnicity" come into use, often to refer to a people defined by a shared language.) The spread of nationalism led to population exchanges and expulsions across the region by newly independent states and, eventually, by the Ottoman Empire and its successor in the twentieth century, the Turkish nation-state.

In the 1880s, one could see the shape of the future, but it hadn't yet taken on a concrete form. People were trying out new roles. They were debating things like the place of religion in society, the challenge posed to faith by science and reason, the abolition of slavery, and the role of women in the home and in society. How should minorities be incorporated into the political scheme of the empire? Should they act first and foremost as Ottoman citizens or should their loyalty be to their own sect? What does it mean to be modern? What are the costs of progress? What are the rights and obligations of the individual and those of the family and society as a whole? Should one be given preference over the other?

The Ottomans were worried about the consequences of change, the decline of the family, and losing the moral fiber of society. In many ways, these are questions with which people in Europe, the United States, and elsewhere are still struggling today.

DISCUSSION QUESTIONS

1. What questions raised by characters in the book are still debated today?

2. How do the discussions about the place of women within *The Sultan's Seal* resonate with today's issues? Is there power within the harem or does being separate from men keep women from being powerful? In what ways do the characters try to exert power for themselves and over others?

3. What are some of the differences between Europe and the Ottoman Empire at the time, as seen from the European point of view, represented by Sybil and Bernie, and from the Ottoman point of view, represented by Kamil? Was there more than one Ottoman point of view about the ideal form of society and political organization? What is the difference between the views of Kamil and Michel? Between Jaanan's father and her uncle, Ismail Hodja?

4. What does being modern mean to Kamil? How does Kamil differ from Jaanan's father, who takes a second wife in order to be modern? Do they fit your definition of modern?

5. What role does religion play in people's lives? Is Jaanan's understanding of Islam the same as that of her mother and her uncle? Does Michel's Judaism play any role in his actions?

6. Kamil wrestles with the seeming incompatibility of faith and reason. Does he find a solution with which he can live? Can faith and reason ever be reconciled?

7. What does Kamil mean when he worries that the introduction of rational thinking, order, logic, and control will bring about the loss of nuance, sensuality, chaos, and emotion? What concrete things is he worried will disappear?

8. What attracts Sybil to Ottoman life and why? Do you think a Western woman could give up her culture and truly become "Eastern"?

9. How does Mary understand her relationship with Jaanan? How does Jaanan understand it? Compare Mary's relationship with Jaanan to Violet's.

10. What roles do love and sex play in Kamil's life? In Jaanan's life? Is there a difference in the effect that love and sex have on their lives? If so, why?

11. How does Hamza's past affect his relationship with Jaanan and her family? Can Hamza be trusted?

12. What role does the family play in the lives of Kamil, Sybil, and Jaanan? Is there a difference between Ottoman and British society in the makeup of the family and in the role of the family in the lives of individuals? What is your ideal family?

13. Kamil has very few friends: only Bernie and Michel. Why is he so closed off from other men?

MORE NORTON BOOKS WITH READING GROUP GUIDES AVAILABLE

Diana Abu-Jaber — *Arabian Jazz*
Crescent
Rabih Alameddine — *I, the Divine*
Robert Alter — *Genesis**
Rupa Bajwa — *The Sari Shop*
Christine Balint — *The Salt Letters**
*Ophelia's Fan**
Brad Barkley — *Money, Love*
Andrea Barrett — *Servants of the Map*
Ship Fever
The Voyage of the Narwhal
Rachel Basch — *The Passion of Reverend Nash*
Charles Baxter — *Shadow Play*
Frederick Busch — *Harry and Catherine*
Lan Samantha Chang — *Inheritance*
Abigail De Witt — *Lili*
Jared Diamond — *Guns, Germs, and Steel*
Jack Driscoll — *Lucky Man, Lucky Woman*
John Dufresne — *Deep in the Shade of Paradise*
Love Warps the Mind a Little
Ellen Feldman — *Lucy*
Paula Fox — *The Widow's Children*
Judith Freeman — *The Chinchilla Farm*
Betty Friedan — *The Feminine Mystique*
Helon Habila — *Waiting for an Angel*
Sara Hall — *Drawn to the Rhythm*
Patricia Highsmith — *Stranger on a Train*
Suspension of Mercy
Selected Stories
Hannah Hinchman — *A Trail Through Leaves**
Linda Hogan — *Power*
Dara Horn — *In the Image*
The World to Come
Janette Turner Hospital — *The Last Magician*
Due Preparations for the Plague

Kathleen Hughes *Dear Mrs. Lindbergh*
Helen Humphreys *The Lost Garden*
Erica Jong *Fanny*
Shylock's Daughters [not on the website]
Sappho's Leap
Beth Kephart *Seeing Past Z:*
Starting a Neighborhood Workshop
Binnie Kirshenbaum *Hester Among the Ruins*
Barbara Klein Moss *Little Edens*
James Lasdun *The Horned Man*
Karen Latuchie *The Honey Wall*
Don Lee *Yellow*
Joan Leegant *An Hour in Paradise*
Vyvyane Loh *Breaking the Tongue*
Lisa Michaels *Grand Ambition*
Lydia Minatoya *The Strangeness of Beauty*
Tova Mirvis *The Ladies Auxiliary*
Walter Mosley *Always Outnumbered, Always Outgunned*
Patrick O'Brian *The Yellow Admiral**
Jean Rhys *Wide Sargasso Sea*
Josh Russell *Yellow Jack*
Kerri Sakamoto *The Electrical Field*
Gay Salisbury and
Laney Salisbury *The Cruelest Miles*
May Sarton *Journal of a Solitude**
Susan Fromberg Schaeffer *Anya*
Buffalo Afternoon
The Snow Fox
Jessica Shattuck *The Hazards of Good Breeding*
Frances Sherwood *The Book of Splendor*
Vindication
Joan Silber *Ideas of Heaven*
Gustaf Sobin *The Fly-Truffler*
In Pursuit of a Vanishing Star
Dorothy Allred Solomon *Daughter of the Saints*

Ted Solotaroff	*Truth Comes in Blows*
Jean Christopher Spaugh	*Something Blue*
Mark Strand and	
Eavan Boland	*The Making of a Poem*
Manil Suri	*The Death of Vishnu*
Barry Unsworth	*Losing Nelson*
	Morality Play
	Sacred Hunger
	Songs of the Kings
Brad Watson	*The Heaven of Mercury*

*Available only on the Norton Web site:
www.wwnorton.com/guides